Brooklyn

Also by Tracy Brown

Hold You Down

Single Black Female

Criminal Minded

White Lines

Twisted

Snapped

Aftermath

White Lines II: Sunny

White Lines III: All Falls Down

Boss

ANTHOLOGIES

Flirt

Brooklyn

Tracy Brown

ST. MARTIN'S GRIFFIN
NEW YORK

This is a work of fiction. All of the characters, organizations, and events portrayed in this novel are either products of the author's imagination or are used fictitiously.

First published in the United States by St. Martin's Griffin, an imprint of St. Martin's Publishing Group

www.stmartins.com

Design by Meryl Sussman Levavi

Library of Congress Cataloging-in-Publication Data

Names: Brown, Tracy, 1974– author.
Title: Brooklyn / Tracy Brown.
Description: First edition. | New York : St. Martin's Griffin, 2024.
Identifiers: LCCN 2023036049 | ISBN 9781250834959 (trade paperback) |
ISBN 9781250834966 (ebook)
Subjects: LCGFT: Urban fiction. | Novels.
Classification: LCC PS3602.R723 B76 2024 | DDC 813/.6—dc23/eng/20230814
LC record available at https://lccn.loc.gov/2023036049

First Edition: 2024

1 3 5 7 9 10 8 6 4 2

In Loving Memory

Tracy was a writer's writer. She had a vivid imagination and was filled with enough ideas to write a hundred more books. She was always trying to improve her craft and took to heart every suggestion she received about her writing. She was working on three books simultaneously at the time of her death. But this book, *Brooklyn,* is one Tracy would probably gladly have chosen as her final opus. She was so excited to get to write a mystery and even more excited when her longtime editor, Monique Patterson, said she loved it. Tracy felt Monique brought out the best in her, and was proud to call her a friend, as well as an editor.

Tracy's writings are a legacy that anyone would be more than pleased to leave behind. But Tracy was so much more than an author, and all her other life experiences contributed to the rich pictures she was able to paint on each page. She listened to ever-changing playlists as she wrote and was often inspired by performances she had seen at New York's Joyce Theater, where she was a member of the board of trustees.

In addition to her novels and ghostwriting projects she worked on with celebrities, she wrote and directed two stage plays titled *Brand New* (2016) and *Redeemed* (2017). Tracy was the 2017 recipient of a proclamation from the New York City Council in honor of her outstanding service and enduring contributions to the community. She was the recipient of a citation for exemplary service from the New York State Senate's 20th District; the 2017 awardee of a certificate of honor from the New York City Public

Advocate's office; and the 2013 recipient of the Humanitarian Award from the National Council of Negro Women.

She always reached back to help others. She was the director of the nonprofit organization We Are Ladies First LTD (d/b/a "Ladies First"), an organization that is on a mission to inform, inspire, and empower young women in urban communities. Ladies First provides an undergraduate scholarship and mentorship, sponsors young women to tour historically Black colleges and universities, and hosts financial planning and career readiness workshops.

And she didn't forget the futures of those in prison. Tracy volunteered as the instructor of a creative writing course for young ladies in a correctional environment of the New York State foster care system. It is a course that she had also taught to scholars at the Staten Island charter school Eagle Academy.

Above all else, Tracy Brown was a proud mother and grandmother. Her family came first no matter the myriad other obligations, which were legion. In addition to creating all her amazing books, she had a full-time job with a group of lawyers.

Tracy Brown always believed in dreaming big and she left her indelible mark on this world. Think of this amazing woman as you enjoy her final offering. She will be missed.

THE END

CLOVE LAKE PARK
Sunday, February 9, 2003

I'm dying.

The hands around my throat press tighter with each second that passes.

My fingernails dig into those hands desperately as I battle to breathe. I fight for my life, kicking violently at my tormentor, some of them landing, none of them causing the suffocating pressure on my throat to relent. I try to scream but no sound escapes me. The silence makes the horror even worse.

I can't believe this is how it ends. I've been slick and slippery my whole life. One step ahead of everyone else. I pride myself on that.

But I fucked up this time. And I'm about to pay for it with my life.

It sinks in as I stare up into the pitiless eyes of my grim reaper. I feel life slowly exiting my body. The pain becomes unbearable, and I feel my limbs start to relax. But I know the relief I'm experiencing isn't a good thing. This isn't a peaceful feeling. This is final.

If I thought God would listen, I'd pray. I know it's pointless, though. God knows I deserve this.

But I'm not ready to die.

I strike hard, scratching, slapping, bucking my body with all my might to free myself. For a cruel and fleeting moment, it seems to work. I gasp for air as the pressure on my throat decreases. I struggle to scream, but my voice is hoarse. Dazed, my ears ringing, I feel the pressure intensifying again. I try fighting, but I'm easily overpowered now. My hands are pinned beneath heavy knees, and I can't breathe. I look pleadingly into my killer's eyes. The hate in those eyes is palpable, and I know that there will be no mercy for me.

Monday, February 10, 2003

The vine-choked woods were quiet that morning. Eerily so. A gray squirrel scampered swiftly up a large oak tree. The branches swayed against the force of the relentless winter wind. A bird flew overhead, gliding in elegant contrast to the ugly scene on the ground.

"This was such a beautiful place until now."

Detective Ivan Ramos spoke solemnly to his partner Detective Charles Lee as they stood feet away from the gruesome crime scene in Clove Lake Park.

"I wonder what the fuck happened to this girl."

Chapter One

Church Girl

December 1995

The church was rocking like a rap concert. People were on their feet finishing the pastor's sentences like lyrics to a song they all knew.

Reverend Elias James stood tall in the pulpit with the Bible gripped firmly in his hand. His deep, melodic voice boomed across the sanctuary, eliciting shouts of "Hallelujah!" and "Amen!" from the crowd.

Brooklyn Melody James was a seventeen-year-old beauty. Named after the borough where she was born, she seemed to embody the spirit of the place. Tough, trendy, edgy, and popular. Although she was born there and bore its name, she had few memories of the place. Her parents had moved to Staten Island, the city's forgotten borough, when she was just a child. In a place with such an interwoven community, her golden skin, bright eyes, and dimpled smile made her a magnet for just about every type of attention. Boys wanted to date her, girls wanted to be her friend, and *everyone* seemed eager to be liked by her. As the middle child in her family, she felt like the black sheep at times.

Amir was the firstborn, a son, the heir to Daddy's throne. His name meant "ruler" in Arabic, a sign that the bar had been set high for him from birth. He had graduated high school the year prior and was taking some time off from school while he decided what to do next.

Hope was the sweet baby girl of the family. The gentle and sheltered one. She was respectful, always following the rules of the family and of the church. She had a pure and gentle heart that made her popular with children. It also made her a favorite of the church elders, who often held her up as an example of what God wanted the youth to strive for.

Of the James siblings, Brooklyn was the most outgoing, the most outspoken, and by far the most challenging of them all. She questioned everything, never failed to speak her mind, and had no problem challenging authority. Without realizing it, she managed to do everything her mother didn't have the courage to.

The church her father was preaching at today was a Baptist congregation in the Bronx, celebrating their elderly pastor's thirtieth anniversary. It was clear to Brooklyn as she watched the reaction from the packed house that they hadn't heard such a rousing sermon in a long time. Half the sanctuary was on their feet, hooting and hollering so heartily that the sound shook the room.

Brooklyn watched her father work. She had heard him preach this sermon before. It was an old favorite that he often reverted to when he was invited to churches as a guest preacher. This was one such Sunday.

She sat on the cushioned front pew next to her mother Sabrina. Her brother Amir and her sister Hope sat to the right of her. To the world, they looked like a picture-perfect family. A postcard for Black excellence. But Brooklyn knew the truth. Behind their carefully crafted public image of stellar Christian living were many twisted secrets.

Elias reached the grand finale of his sermon as sweat seemed to drip from every pore of his body. Brooklyn's gaze roamed to the choir stand, aware that it was now the moment they had all been waiting for. Scanning the soprano section, she found her best friend Erica and watched as she calmly stood up, stepped to the microphone, and unleashed her anointing—a voice so angelic and clear that people began to weep.

As Erica sang her song, Elias summoned the congregation to the altar for prayer. Brooklyn watched as the flood of people rushed forward, many of them falling to their knees. Her mother Sabrina stood and joined the host church's aging first lady at the altar. Together they stood with their hands interlocked and their heads bowed, ad-libbing as the prayer went on.

Brooklyn watched it all, thinking that this was one big well-orchestrated production. Her father was the main attraction, but the choir was always the crowd-pleaser. No matter how stale the sermon or how recycled the scripture, even the worst Sunday service could be salvaged by some good old-fashioned singing. Once the altos and sopranos came together with the musicians, and the rhythm of the drums and tambourines hit the sanctuary, it was time for church.

She glanced at the drummer Jordan as he looked at Erica and nodded, signaling that it was time to hit the song's crescendo. His tempo sped up a notch, the beat of his drumsticks intensified, and Erica hit the high notes effortlessly.

Elias shouted "Amen!" and the spirit moved freely through the church. Brooklyn had seen it all before. The fainting, shouting, hands raised to the sky, mouths parted wide with praise. All while the ushers rushed forth with the offering baskets, urging everyone present to empty their pockets in Jesus' name.

"Will a man rob God?" Elias quoted scripture as the ushers moved slowly down the aisles.

Brooklyn watched as her mother demonstratively dropped a hefty envelope into the basket, setting a fine example for everyone else to follow suit. Brooklyn had to resist the urge to laugh, aware that her mother knew full well that that money was going to find its way right back into her household in one way or another. The trustees of both churches were already waiting in the back to split up the loot the moment the shakedown was over.

As the ushers conducted their business, the choir joined Erica for the chorus of "At the Cross." The whole room was on their feet now, and Brooklyn clapped her hands to the beat of Jordan's drum. She made a mental note to compliment him on a job well done during the ride back to Staten Island. Today's service had been a well-executed performance on everyone's part, which meant the envelope her father would be taking home would be a hefty one.

By now, Brooklyn understood that money was the name of the game. Sure, the goal was to save souls and spread the Gospel. But growing up as a preacher's kid had taught her that behind all that was a desire to increase membership, thereby increasing the tax-free tithes and offerings they could rely on each week. The goal was to book popular guest preachers and to go "on tour" and do preaching engagements at other churches where the offerings were often higher than the ones they got at home. In Brooklyn's eyes, it was all a hustle. One big game with everyone fighting for status, power, and prestige, which all equaled cash. And her father was the greatest hustler she had ever seen.

Not unlike the ones she encountered outside the church's doors.

Crime had ravaged New York City over the past decade or more. The mayor had empowered the police to conduct themselves like a gang in order to regain control of the city. Poverty, despair, and hopelessness had driven multitudes of people to the altars at houses of worship across the nation. And Promised Land Church in Staten Island, New York, was no different. That was where Reverend Elias "Eli" James and his lovely wife Sabrina were the pastor and first lady. Along with their three children, the couple greeted their faithful congregants each week, always perfectly coifed and perfectly groomed. Every detail tended to by Sabrina James's critical and unflinching eye.

Brooklyn looked at her mother now and grinned. To anyone watching, it might have appeared that she was a loving daughter staring fondly at her beautiful mother. But Brooklyn's smirk was a cynical one. She knew the truth about her mother and hated her for it. Behind the image of purity and perfection was an unsavory truth. Their family was a fraud, and her mother was the ringleader.

To the church, the first lady was a loving wife and mother who served the Lord with no ulterior motives. At home, she was a hawk, watching over the family's movements and maneuvering them all like a chess master. In Brooklyn's eyes, Sabrina was a cold and heartless woman, too eager to overlook her husband's womanizing, whoremongering, and philandering. Too willing to believe lies that were easier to accept than the truth.

But the insiders knew the real deal. Among the inner circle was an unspoken truth that Eli was a handsome man who took full advantage of his role as pastor. Brooklyn watched him laying hands on breathless women at the altar. He kept a weekly appointment at the barbershop, sported a neat mustache and goatee, maintained a sepia skin tone, and was always dressed to impress. He even smelled good, the scent of him often lingering pleasantly in his wake like a sweet savor.

His wife was a vision of loveliness herself. Sabrina was a fair-skinned woman with long hair, doe-shaped eyes, and a shy smile. She spoke softly, dressed appropriately, and quietly supported her husband as the walking personification of a virtuous woman.

At least in public, she did. At home, it was another story altogether. There, she tossed sarcastic, biting remarks at her children. She cut silent glances in their direction dripping with threats and warnings. They were never allowed to step out of line, and she carefully analyzed and criticized their speech, posture, manners, and most of all their friends. It was their mother who chose the guests invited to their birthday parties, who they spoke to on the phone, and where they spent their rare moments of free time.

Brooklyn's thoughts wandered involuntarily to the root of her distrust and disdain for her mother. It began the year she turned thirteen. She had blossomed that year from a young and naive tomboy into a curvy and carefree teenager. The shift had happened overnight and was obvious to everyone except Brooklyn herself. She had felt like the same little girl, just with blooming breasts and hips that swayed when she walked. Unaware that her sweet dimples and sparkling eyes were suddenly garnering smiles of a different kind from the men around her. Sabrina became more protective of her, and Elias agreed with his wife's approach. They limited her sleepovers at the homes of her friends, much to Brooklyn's dismay. But she was permitted to spend the night with her cousin Nicole and her "Uncle" Morris.

Morris was Sabrina's stepbrother. They had been raised as siblings and were only ten months apart in age. Morris's father had married Sabrina's mother when the children were ten years old. Sabrina had grown up extremely poor in Brownsville, Brooklyn. She was the only child of a single mother who had struggled desperately to keep them afloat. When Sabrina's mother Gloria had met and married George McDonald, everything changed. Sabrina and her mother moved out of their rundown, rat-infested tenement building into a home with a backyard in Clinton Hill. Sabrina adored her stepfather, George. Whenever she spoke about him, it was evident that she respected and revered the man. Even after Sabrina's mother died, she continued to enjoy a beautiful father/daughter relationship with the man who had raised her and elevated her out of poverty. She cared for him so much that she let him come and live with the family when he got too old to care for himself. Brooklyn remembered those days fondly. "Papa George" had always been willing to listen to her ramblings about school, her friends, and the TV shows she liked. He colored with her, both of them going outside the lines, and she listened to his stories about the old days. Before George died, Sabrina promised him that she would always look out for her stepbrother Morris. And she had kept true to her word.

As Brooklyn grew up, she spent a lot of time with "Uncle Morris" and his family. He and his wife—a heavyset woman by the name of Audrey—had two children: a son they called "Junior," who was away at college, and a daughter named Nicole, who was the same age as Brooklyn. The two girls spent a lot of time hanging out together. With Sabrina's approval, the girls took turns over the years enjoying fun and giggle-filled sleepovers at each other's homes.

That fateful summer had been no different. The girls hung out together enjoying ice cream cones and chattering on for hours. One particular weekend, Nicole had invited Brooklyn for a sleepover at her house, and Brooklyn's parents had agreed. Uncle Morris and his wife took the kids to the pool that Saturday afternoon, and it was one of the happiest memories Brooklyn had of her time with her "play cousin." She and Nicole were about to start eighth grade and both of them were excited about it. They chattered endlessly that day about boys, music, and all the things teenage girls are obsessed with. Morris's wife splashed around in the water with the girls while he sat poolside and watched them all. The girls had such a great time that neither complained when it was time to leave.

They had McDonald's afterward—a rarity for Brooklyn, because her mother always cooked meals from scratch at home. She enjoyed the treat and thanked her aunt and uncle repeatedly as they devoured their meals. When they got back to Nicole's house, they showered and watched TV for a while and were both knocked out before 10 P.M.

Brooklyn awoke in the middle of the night with a start. Instinctively, she sensed danger. She was laying on her back and could hear her cousin snoring on the top bunk above her. So, she knew that the presence she felt hovering over her was not Nicole's.

With her heart beating fast, she focused her gaze in the darkness. The T-shirt she wore was pulled up, exposing her new breasts. Instinctively, she tugged at it, but a strong hand gripped hers and prevented her from covering herself. Her vision finally clearing, she looked fearfully into the eyes of her so-called "Uncle" Morris.

With his free hand, he held a finger over his lips signaling her to be silent.

Brooklyn stared back at him in the darkness as he took the same hand, the same finger, and slipped it beneath the flimsy fabric of the pajama shorts she wore. She felt his touch against her private parts and clenched her knees together.

Morris stared back at her. "Open up."

She shook her head.

"Your mother told me she's worried about you. Bouncing around here getting everybody excited. She thinks you're moving too fast. I been watching you, too." His eyes lingered on her breasts. "I see why she's worried. Just relax. I'm not gonna hurt you. I just want to check to see if you're still a virgin. Open your legs."

She stared at him, pondering what he said. Her mother had been keeping a closer eye on her lately. But she would certainly not approve of this situation. And even if she did, her father would never allow this. Brooklyn shook her head again. Uncle Morris was full of shit.

With her free hand, she tugged her T-shirt down and pulled herself upright in the bed. She shoved his hand away and pulled her legs against her chest. With her back pressed against the headboard and the wall, she grabbed a pillow and positioned it in front of her as a shield against her predator.

"NICOLE! AUNT AUDREY!" She yelled at the top of her lungs.

Morris jumped back, stood up, and began flapping his arms up and down urging her to quiet down.

"What you yelling for? I told you—"

"GET AWAY FROM ME!" Brooklyn yelled. "DON'T TOUCH ME!"

"I'm not touching you!" Morris protested, his hands raised now in surrender.

"I'm telling my father!"

"Brooklyn!" Nicole climbed swiftly down the ladder, her gaze shifting from her father to Brooklyn and back again. "What happened?"

"Your father was touching me."

"I was not!" Morris shouted as his wife rushed into the room.

"What's going on in here?" Audrey wore a head scarf and an oversized nightgown as she stood frowning. She looked at Brooklyn. "What's wrong with you?"

"He touched me! He was feeling on me while I was sleeping."

"I was NOT!" Morris shouted, defiantly. "I came in here to check on them. I pulled the covers up over her and she woke up and started talking crazy."

"You're LYING!" Brooklyn was on her feet now, shouting with all her might. "I WANT TO GO HOME! CALL MY FATHER!"

"Brooklyn, calm down," Audrey urged her. "I'll call him. But you gotta stop screaming."

"I want to go home," Brooklyn reasserted. She looked at Nicole and saw her staring at her father, questioningly. Nicole looked torn, as if contemplating the possibility that he was a monster. "He did it," she said to Nicole. "He had my shirt up to my neck. When I woke up, he grabbed me and told me to be quiet. Then he told me a lie about my mother wanting him to check if I'm still a virgin. He tried to—"

"Brooklyn, get your stuff," Audrey said, avoiding her husband's stare. "Come on, baby. I'll call your parents to come and get you."

"You ain't calling them in the middle of the night with this bullshit," Morris said.

"Come on," Audrey repeated, gesturing at Brooklyn.

"I'm talking to you!" Morris shouted, stepping toward his wife.

Brooklyn rushed to pack her belongings into her overnight bag.

Audrey didn't back down. Finally locking eyes with Morris, she glared at him. "I'll bring her home myself then."

Morris seemed prepared to respond. But there was something in the way Audrey looked at him that made him pause. His breath caught audibly in his throat, and he stood speechlessly.

Audrey turned to her daughter. "Get dressed and ride with us."

Morris found his voice then. "What the fuck, Audrey. Don't tell me you believe this bullshit!" He shook his head in exasperation. "I didn't touch that girl."

Brooklyn slid her feet into her sandals and stood near the bedroom door, waiting.

"What'd you come in here for in the first place?" Audrey demanded.

"I told you. I came in to check on them."

"It's summertime, and you thought she needed covers over her? Did you check and see if Nicole was covered up, too, or just Brooklyn?"

"I didn't—"

"Where did she get that shit about checking for her virginity? She's a kid. She didn't make that up!" Audrey stood with her shoulders so tense that it was clear that she was ready to fight.

Morris took a step back as he replied. "She's twisting my words around."

"She's a little girl, you sick muthafucka!"

"She's a fuckin' lying-ass brat! You know I ain't like *that*. It's HER! Walking around here like a little slut all weekend, talking about boys, and dancing all the time. You've been seeing her!" He shook his head and pleaded with his wife. "She's bugging! I covered her up. She woke up. I told her I'm keeping an eye on her. I was just looking out for my sister. That's all that was. Trying to make sure she ain't out here letting these boys take advantage of her. Making sure she ain't being a bad influence on Nicole."

Brooklyn knew he was crazy then. Not only was his excuse for touching her body absurd, but Nicole was far more sexually experienced than she was. Nicole bragged all the time about not being a virgin. Brooklyn wondered now if having Morris for a father was the reason for that.

Audrey stared at him, and Brooklyn knew she wanted to believe him. She shook her head, turned to the girls, and herded them toward the door. "Let's go."

Audrey didn't even bother to get dressed. She snatched a pair of shorts and slid them beneath her gown, grabbed her car keys, and ignored her husband's protests as she loaded the girls into the car and drove away.

Brooklyn sat in the back seat while Nicole rode shotgun. The car was dead silent as they drove for the first few minutes. Then Audrey looked through the rearview mirror at Brooklyn.

"Are you telling the truth?"

Brooklyn stared back at her. "Yes." She wasn't sure why she felt the urge to apologize. But she pressed her lips closed and looked out the car window and wished it all away instead.

Audrey glanced at her daughter. "Did you hear anything?"

Nicole shook her head, her eyes focused on the road ahead. "Just Brooklyn screaming like crazy."

The way she said it let Brooklyn know that their friendship was over. Nicole's tone was flat and somehow still dripping with blame and contempt. For Brooklyn and not her father.

Audrey rode in silence after that. Brooklyn sat in the back seat with her arms clutched around herself for comfort. She breathed a little easier as they pulled into the empty parking spot in front of her house where her father usually parked the church van. She remembered then that her father and some members of the congregation were down at a leadership conference in Virginia that weekend. As they climbed out of the car, she noticed that the lights downstairs were on. They approached the door, and Audrey reached to ring the doorbell. She paused when the door opened and Sabrina stood before them.

Sabrina ushered them in, wordlessly, and looked at Audrey. Her expression was hard to read. Somewhere between dread and horror.

"Sorry to come by so late," Audrey said. "We had a situation tonight."

Sabrina nodded. "Morris called and told me what happened." She looked at her daughter and smiled.

Brooklyn felt reassured by that. She had always thought her mother was beautiful. That night, Sabrina looked especially lovely as she sat in her silk bathrobe, void of any makeup. Brooklyn had rushed toward her mother and hugged her. Sabrina cradled her in her arms and rocked her, lovingly.

"Hey," she cooed in Brooklyn's ear. "You okay?"

Brooklyn shrugged. She wasn't.

Sabrina turned back to Audrey.

"Come in the living room," she said, leading the way.

Sabrina let go of her daughter and walked beside her. Audrey and Nicole trailed behind.

Sabrina sat down on the sofa and watched as everyone else took seats.

"What did Morris tell you?" Audrey asked.

Sabrina sighed, appearing weary. "That he went in to check on the girls. Brooklyn woke up and panicked. She thought he was touching her, but he was just covering her up."

Brooklyn felt her heart sinking fast. Her mother spoke as if what she was saying was a proven fact instead of Morris's poor attempt at damage control.

"That's not what happened," Brooklyn said, adamantly.

"So, what did happen?" Sabrina asked.

Brooklyn sat forward. "I was asleep. I woke up and he was over me."

"What do you mean *over you*? Was he on top of you?" Sabrina was frowning.

"No . . . he was . . . like . . . just standing over me."

"Mm-hmm." Sabrina stared back at her.

Brooklyn started sweating, unsure if it was from the heat or the fury inside of her. "My shirt was pulled up. I tried to fix it, but he stopped me. He told me to be quiet and he put his hand up my shorts."

Sabrina was shaking her head from side to side as Brooklyn spoke.

"He told me to open my legs and said that he wanted to check and see if I'm still a virgin. I sat up and pulled away from him. I yelled out for help."

"No!" Sabrina said it so firmly that it stunned all of them. "No. That didn't happen. Morris wouldn't do that."

Brooklyn's heart began to sink. "He did. He called me a slut. Ask Aunt Audrey."

Sabrina looked at Audrey.

Audrey seemed shocked by what she was witnessing.

"Sabrina, I know this is hard. The whole way over here, I felt like a zombie. Like I'm having a bad dream. But Morris had no business being in there. It was after midnight. If he wanted to check on the girls, all he had to do was peek inside and see them sleeping and walk back out. When I ran in there, Brooklyn was upset. She was scared to death. I don't want to believe this either. But let's not pretend that Morris is some kind of saint."

Sabrina laughed. She shook her head in disbelief. "He might not be a saint, but Morris would never do *that*. He knows the difference between grown women and a little girl." Frowning, she looked at her daughter. "What is wrong with you, Brooklyn? Do you know what you're saying?"

Brooklyn nodded. "I'm telling you what happened."

"And I'm telling you that you're lying. You have no idea what you're talking about. You were asleep. Your shirt rode up on you and he was probably fixing it."

"He touched m—"

"He did NOT, Brooklyn!" Sabrina's face was so tight with rage that her veins were visible. "Morris is my family. He would never do that to me. To you! This was a misunderstanding. That's all it is. Don't tell that story again. You got it wrong. That's the end of it."

Brooklyn stared at her mother in horror. Her ears were ringing and for a moment she felt like she might faint. She suddenly felt afraid despite the fact that she was back in the safety of her family home. She wanted to cry but fought back the tears.

She sat in stone silence as Sabrina and Audrey continued talking about the incident. Sabrina kept repeating that Morris was innocent, and Audrey was insistent that something wasn't right. In the midst of it all, Brooklyn looked at Nicole. She saw her staring down at the floor silently with her hands folded in her lap. No matter how long and hard Brooklyn stared at her, Nicole never looked up. Not even once.

Finally, Audrey rose to leave in frustration. She cast one last sympathetic glance in Brooklyn's direction as she followed Sabrina to the door. In Audrey's gaze, Brooklyn saw all the things she had sought from her mother. She could see that the woman believed her. She saw compassion and understanding, sympathy and affirmation.

Nicole didn't bother looking at Brooklyn as they left. Sabrina walked them to the door and thanked Audrey for bringing her daughter home.

By the time she came back, Brooklyn was upstairs in her bedroom.

Hope was asleep. Brooklyn gathered up her clothes, rushed into the bathroom, and took a long shower. She cried then, her tears mingling with the water cascading from the showerhead. She did her best to scrub away the icky feeling she had after having a grown man's hands on her body, and the even more repulsive feeling of her mother's denial. She put on a pair of Snoopy pajamas and went back to her room.

Sabrina was waiting for her there.

Brooklyn froze in the doorway and stared back at her in the darkness. It felt eerily similar to the scene in Nicole's bedroom an hour ago with her "Uncle" Morris. Staring back at a figure in the darkness who she suddenly knew she couldn't trust.

Sabrina whispered as Hope slept nearby. "We won't speak of this again. Not to your father or anyone else. You understand me?"

Brooklyn nodded.

Sabrina walked toward her. "Morris would never hurt you. This was all just a big mistake."

Brooklyn didn't respond and tried not to recoil when her mother touched her cheek.

"I understand you don't feel comfortable around him," Sabrina said. "I'll keep him away from you from now on. You don't have to worry." She stood inches away from Brooklyn and stared into her eyes. "Now just let this go."

She walked out, and all the admiration Brooklyn once had for her mother disappeared, too. Brooklyn climbed into her bed, gripped her pillow, and cried until the sun rose.

Everyone noticed the shift in Brooklyn's demeanor in the days that followed. Her usual smile was gone. She barely spoke or even made eye contact with anyone. Hope and Amir did their best to strike up conversations with her, but Brooklyn avoided anything more than small talk. Sabrina pretended nothing was wrong while she handled her duties as first lady in her husband's absence. Brooklyn suffered in silence for three days until her father came home.

Brooklyn waited patiently for her chance. It was a long wait. She noticed that her mother was extra affectionate toward her husband when he got back from Virginia. She barely gave him time alone, doting on him nonstop from his first moment home. She hung on his every word as he told her about the conference. Brooklyn watched, aware even in her young mind, that her mother was being strategic. She was occupying Elias's time and attention to ensure that Brooklyn didn't have an opportunity to speak to her father alone.

That suspicion enraged Brooklyn. She sat quietly all day, watching her parents and accompanying them to church that evening. When they returned home for dinner, Sabrina darted back and forth from the kitchen to the dining room, talking to Elias as he sat at the table going over the schedule for the rest of the week.

"The women's ministry is going to host a tea. Deaconess Curry wants to teach a workshop on health and hygiene for the young women of the church."

Elias nodded. "Sounds like a plan. When is it happening?"

"The first Saturday of next month. We're going to use the sermon you preached on the second chapter of Esther as inspiration." Sabrina set the food on the table and called the kids down to eat.

Brooklyn got to the table first and made sure she took the seat next to her father. He smiled at her and pinched her cheek, playfully, as she sat down.

"Hey, baby girl. You've been awfully quiet today."

Brooklyn smiled back at him. But before she could respond, Sabrina interrupted as she took her seat at the table.

"Brooklyn, since you're part of the junior women's ministry, I'm hoping you'll volunteer to help out with the tea." Sabrina looked at her daughter. "We can definitely use your help."

Brooklyn nodded, refusing to respond to her mother verbally.

Amir and Hope arrived at the table, and they all bowed their heads as Elias said grace. After the prayer, they all began piling their plates with food.

"Daddy, did you bring us anything back from your trip?" eleven-year-old Hope asked, her eyes twinkling in anticipation.

Elias laughed. "Uh-oh. I think somebody's getting spoiled."

Hope giggled.

Elias winked at her. "Don't I always bring you something?"

Hope nodded, excitedly. "So, what is it?"

Amir laughed at his baby sister's impatience.

"Calm down," he teased.

Elias shook his head. "I brought you a seashell necklace."

Hope dropped her fork and clapped her hands excitedly. "Thank you!"

"I got one for your sister, too," Elias said, winking at Brooklyn. He nodded at Amir. "Got you a wallet from the leather outlet down there. I'll give it to you after dinner."

Amir and Brooklyn thanked their father for his generosity. Amir piled his plate high with mashed potatoes and smothered them in gravy.

Brooklyn watched the whole family behaving like normal. And she couldn't blame them. None of them knew the torment she was dealing with over what happened to her. Except her mother. Sabrina knew everything and was actively ignoring it. Brooklyn seethed.

"Daddy, while you were gone, I thought about what you told me." Brooklyn saw the questioning expression on the faces of both her parents and reveled in it. She knew this would be a game changer. "You said that it's important to love the Word of God. Not just study it. But love it. Learn it. Commit some scriptures to memory to help keep me focused."

Elias smiled, proudly, and nodded. "That's right. I'm glad you listened to what I told you."

Brooklyn smiled back at him and watched her mother visibly relax and go back to eating dinner.

"'Exodus 20:16. Thou shall not bear false witness against thy neighbor.' That's what I studied last night."

Sabrina's head snapped in Brooklyn's direction. Elias looked at his daughter with admiration. Amir and Hope continued to eat their food, cluelessly.

"So, I have to tell you the truth," Brooklyn said. "Even though Mommy said that I should lie."

Elias looked at his wife.

"*Brooklyn*," Sabrina said, warningly.

"What's going on, Sabrina?" Elias asked, his brow furrowed.

Brooklyn set her fork down. She was far from hungry. With her heart beating in her chest, she spoke up for herself. "Uncle Morris touched me in the middle of the night while I was sleeping over in Nicole's room, and Aunt Audrey brought me home early."

"Eli, that's not what happened." Sabrina's voice was low and shaky.

"It did," Brooklyn insisted. "I keep trying to tell you, but you won't listen." She felt tears welling up in her eyes and didn't try to stop them. She looked at her father. "I'm telling the truth."

Elias looked like all the blood vessels in his face might pop. "Touched you how?" he asked Brooklyn.

"He touched my private parts while I was sleeping. And when I woke up, he told me to be quiet. But I screamed until Nicole and Aunt Audrey woke up."

Hope frowned, confused. Amir's mouth fell open in shock. Elias stared at Brooklyn in horror.

Sabrina stood up and pounded hard on the table. "I'm not gonna sit here and let you lie like that."

Elias jumped to his feet then, too. "You must have lost your mind!" His voice boomed so loudly that everyone stared back at him in fear.

"What she's saying is not the truth, Eli," Sabrina said. "Brooklyn's not telling the whole story."

"You're calling her a liar?"

He charged toward his wife.

Sabrina backed up.

Hope began to cry. Amir jumped up and stood between his parents.

"Dad, wait!"

Elias stared into his son's fearful eyes as he shielded his mother, and it stopped him. He looked past his wife and locked eyes with Brooklyn.

"Come with me," he said.

Brooklyn got up and walked toward her father. But Sabrina pushed past Amir and stood blocking Elias's exit.

"Eli, please!"

"Move out of my way," Elias said, sternly.

"What are you going to do?" she asked, desperately.

He grabbed his wife roughly by the face. "Back UP!" He shoved her aside, grabbed Brooklyn by the hand, and they headed out the door together.

He opened the passenger door of his Cadillac, and Brooklyn climbed inside. He rushed around and climbed behind the wheel, then quickly sped off in the direction of Morris's house.

"Tell me what happened, baby girl. Don't be afraid. Daddy won't let anybody hurt you. Just tell me the truth."

Brooklyn let out a deep breath. She opened her mouth and the words rushed forth like rain. When she was done, Elias was visibly emotional. He shook his head from side to side several times, muttering under his breath. Finally, he looked over at his daughter.

"I'm gonna handle this."

Brooklyn nodded. They pulled up in front of Morris's house, and they both got out of the car. Elias held her hand tightly as they rushed toward the front door. Ignoring the doorbell, Elias banged loudly on the door with his fist.

"OPEN THE DOOR! MORRIS! OPEN THE DOOR, DAMMIT!"

Brooklyn could sense her father's rage building with each bang. The door rattled and swung open. Audrey stood before them looking fearful and weary.

"He left," she said. "Your wife called. Warned him you were on your way. He's gone."

"Shit!" Elias shouted.

It was the first time Brooklyn had ever heard her father use a swear word. She watched him trying to decide what his next move would be. She felt so proud of him, even as he paced the front porch in frustration. Despite his helplessness in the moment, he was *trying* to do something. She stared admiringly at her father attempting to do what he could to confront her attacker. He was willing to put his reputation and his freedom on the line for his daughter. And that was far more than she could say for her mother.

"He packed a bag?" Elias asked Audrey. He was sweating hard as he stared at her, expectantly.

Audrey shook her head. "He left too fast to take anything with him." She closed her eyes and sighed. She opened them again and looked at Elias. "I won't be here when he gets back, Eli. This is the last straw for me. I've been putting up with too much for too long. The women were one thing. But this . . ." Audrey looked at Brooklyn, sadly. "This is too much."

"I'm gonna kill him, Audrey. You know that, right?"

Brooklyn's eyes widened and her heart began pounding loudly in her chest. Her mind raced with thoughts of her father going to prison, of Nicole's father being murdered, of everyone blaming her. Panic registered on her face.

Audrey exhaled loudly. "You're a pastor, Eli. You know you can't hurt him. Even if he deserves it."

Elias punched his hand angrily and began pacing the porch. Brooklyn watched him, now doubtful that she had done the right thing.

She looked at Audrey. "Is Nicole home?" Brooklyn asked.

Audrey didn't respond right away. "She's here. But she's upset, Brooklyn. Despite what he did, she loves her father. She's mad right now—with me, with you. With everyone except Morris."

Brooklyn looked down at the ground, wrestling with doubt. She was second-guessing all of it. Yelling that night in Nicole's room, demanding to be brought home early, telling her father despite her mother's protests. None of it seemed worth all of this.

Elias looked at Audrey, helplessly. "You said Sabrina called him? She told him I was on my way?" His expression was incredulous. "Why would she do that?"

Audrey shook her head. "When she called, me and Morris were fighting. We've been fighting ever since I brought Brooklyn home the other night. I told him that I'm leaving, taking Nicole with me. He's been threatening me and blocking me from leaving. It almost got physical."

Brooklyn tried to imagine that and pictured big-boned Audrey whooping her husband's ass.

"Then Sabrina called all upset. Morris grabbed his wallet and left. Now I'm in here rushing around, packing bags so we can get out of here before he gets back."

"Where are you gonna go?" Elias asked, his pastoral instincts kicking in.

"To my sister's place in Park Hill. I'll stay with her for a while until I get on my feet."

Elias shook his head. "You can do that for now," he said. "But the church takes up an offering each week for people in need. You're in need, Audrey. So, we'll help you. Come down to the church tomorrow and I'll make sure you get on your feet."

"Thank you, Eli. I appreciate that." Audrey stared at him for a while. "I don't think I want your help, though."

Elias looked confused.

"Sabrina is not a woman I can respect. I took Brooklyn home the other night, and what I witnessed made me sick to my stomach. I brought that woman's daughter home to her, told her that my husband was in that bedroom when he had no business being there. I told her what Brooklyn said, how scared she was when I saw her pressed up against the wall calling out for help. I even went so far as to tell Sabrina that I believed Brooklyn even though I didn't want to. If I can find it in my heart to believe your daughter, I don't understand how your wife can't do the same thing." Audrey shook her head in amazement. "Morris is family to her. I get it. But he's not her blood. Brooklyn is. I can't accept help from a church where a woman like that is held up as an example of godliness. You can keep your money."

Elias stood speechless staring back at her.

"If Morris comes back before me and Nicole get out of here, I'll call you," Audrey said. "Otherwise, I suggest you give it a few days. See if he comes back. Then you can do what you have to do. I completely understand that as a father you want to protect your daughter. I admire that. But, Eli, don't let Morris be your downfall. You have way more to lose than he does. You have your church, your kids, the respect of your community. Don't throw all of that away because of him."

Elias stood motionless as Audrey shut the door in his face.

Brooklyn stared at him, aware that he wasn't sure what to do next. She had never seen her father look so lost.

"Daddy?" Her voice was low and sweet.

Elias turned to face her. She saw him fighting back tears, saw the tension in his shoulders, and her heart broke for him.

"Thank you for believing me. For coming over here. I know you love me. But I don't want you to hurt anybody and go to jail. Can we just go home?"

Elias didn't respond, battling with his emotions. He wanted to yell, to hit something, to cry from helplessness and frustration.

"It's my job to protect you," he said in a low but firm voice. "I will always do that. I promise you that man will never touch you again."

Brooklyn believed him. She nodded, walked over to him, and hugged him tightly.

Elias hugged her back, planted a kiss on top of her head, and led her back to the car.

As they drove home, he looked at Brooklyn. "Has anything like this ever happened before?" His voice was low as he asked. He was afraid to hear the answer. "Anybody ever do or even say anything to you that made you feel uncomfortable?"

Brooklyn shook her head. "No. I would have told you. Nothing like that ever happened to me. That's what I told Mommy. But she just kept saying I was misunderstanding the situation."

Elias gripped the wheel tighter. "You didn't misunderstand a thing, baby girl. Your mother done lost her mind."

He drove the rest of the way in silence. When they got home, he burst into the house loudly and made a beeline for Sabrina.

"What kind of woman are you? What kind of mother?"

"Let me explain, Eli."

"EXPLAIN WHAT? That you believed that piece of shit Morris over our own daughter?"

"That's not what happened," Sabrina insisted.

"You warned him that I was coming over there."

"What was I supposed to do? Let you go over there and get yourself arrested? You're not thinking straight."

"I'M not thinking straight?" Elias shook his head in disgust. "What kind of mother doesn't believe their own child? Audrey told me that nigga had no business being in there. She said Brooklyn was scared to death. When Brooklyn said he touched her, you told her she was wrong. How the hell can you side with a pedophile over our baby?"

"Eli, I told her—"

"YOU TOLD HER TO LIE TO ME!"

Sabrina shook her head. "I never told her to lie. I just said there's no need to blow this thing out of proportion." She stepped closer to her husband with her hands held up in a prayer position. "If I thought for one minute that anybody would hurt my child, I would be the first to defend her. But I'm telling you that Morris would never cross that line."

"So, why was he standing over her in the middle of the night? Why were her breasts out and his hand up her shorts?" Elias pointed to his daughter, outraged. "You calling her a liar?"

"No." Sabrina shook her head. "I'm just saying that it was late, she was just waking up out of a deep sleep, and we shouldn't jump to conclusions. She was screaming so he told her to keep her voice down."

"Come on now!" Eli waved his hand, dramatically. "You sound crazy, Sabrina. We're talking about a grown-ass man and a little girl!"

"I wasn't there. I'm not defending him."

"It sounds like it!"

Sabrina was crying now. "I know. But I keep going over it in my head. I keep asking myself . . . is it my fault? Did I miss something? I've known Morris my whole life. If I thought he was like that, you know I *never* would have sent Brooklyn over there in the first place." She looked at Brooklyn, still crying, and spoke to her between sobs. "I'm so sorry, Brooklyn. It's not that I didn't believe you." Sabrina squeezed her eyes closed dramatically and tilted her head toward the ceiling. "Everything I do is out of devotion to this family." She opened her eyes again and looked at her husband. "When Audrey came in here and told me what happened, I was shocked. I felt sick to my stomach. Before she got here, I had already cried my eyes out. Thinking about Brooklyn and how confused she must be. And thinking about you and the church, and how this could ruin everything you've built."

Elias sucked his teeth. Sabrina stepped toward him, desperately.

"I told her not to tell you. Not because I want to cover for Morris. But because I knew how you would react. I knew you would go over there, and things would get violent. That you would act off impulse and forget who you are. You're not just some man, Eli. You're a pastor, a pillar of this community. You're a man of God. When your rage subsides, and the smoke clears, you'll come back to yourself. And you'll see that there's a godly response to this. And that's what you're called to do."

Elias stood with his chest heaving, staring silently back at his wife. Brooklyn watched and waited.

"I told Brooklyn to keep quiet because I wanted to protect her, to protect *you*. I'm sorry. I am. And you're right. What Morris did is sick. He needs help. Not from us. He's out of our lives for good. But you can't put your hands on him."

"He put his filthy hands on my child." Eli spoke through clenched teeth.

"And God will make sure he pays for that." Sabrina picked the Bible up from the shelf nearby and held it up. "'Vengeance is mine, sayeth the Lord.' Isn't that what you preach all the time?"

"You using the Bible to defend a pedophile?" Eli scoffed.

"I'm reminding you to practice what you preach. You stood up there last week and talked about distractions. You said that every time we get close to our destiny, the devil sends a diversion to make us lose focus. You warned the church to keep their eyes on God, no matter how hard the enemy comes against us—"

"I know what I said, Sabrina."

"Then you know that this is the biggest distraction the devil has ever thrown in your path! If you fail this test, you'll lose every blessing that's been laid up for you. Think about it. If this got out, the *church* would pay the price. You hurt Morris and you'll lose the pastorship. Promised Land just got approved for funding from the borough president's office, and you know how hard we worked for that. A scandal like this could put your plans for the recreation center in jeopardy. Not to mention the shadow it casts over Brooklyn. She's just a child, Eli. The last thing she needs is a bunch of people whispering, gossiping about her when she's so young."

Eli glanced at Brooklyn. She stared back at him, aware that her mother's words were getting through to him.

Sabrina continued. "The devil is busy. He's a liar and the truth is not in him. Don't let him tear this family apart." She stepped closer to her husband. "You married a God-fearing woman who believes in divine justice. I believe in *you* and what we've worked all these years to build together. And I know we can get through this. We have to."

Brooklyn watched her father sit slowly down on the couch. He closed his eyes, hung his head, and held it in the palms of his hands as if to steady his thoughts. Brooklyn knew it was over then. Her mother had managed to talk him off the ledge.

Sabrina looked at her daughter while Elias wrestled with himself. She locked eyes with Brooklyn and, with a subtle nod of her head toward the stairs, directed her to go to her room.

Brooklyn still remembered the sinking feeling in the pit of

her stomach at that moment. She walked to her room in a daze, barely aware of the low drone of her mother's pleading voice as she kneeled down in front of Elias and prayed to God for strength to weather this storm. Brooklyn knew that was the end of it. Somehow, Sabrina had convinced Elias that her motives had been noble. Brooklyn learned the toughest lesson of her young life. That her mother was a cunning and crafty woman whose goal was to keep the scam going at all costs. As long as Eli remained the pastor and the money kept rolling in, Sabrina pretended not to notice a thing. Even her children's pain.

Brooklyn and her siblings never saw "Uncle" Morris again. But he never faced justice either. His name was never spoken within their family, and the whole situation seemed to have been swept out of everyone's memory. Except Brooklyn's.

Since then, the funds had continued rolling in and Eli had been able to build the recreation center he had dreamed of. Promised Land was so much a part of her upbringing that it felt like an extension of their family. All the elders did their best to guard the secrets and indiscretions. But the youth knew what was up. They heard the whispered conversations their parents had after service about the pastor's wandering eye, the first lady's designer wardrobe, and the constant infighting for power and status. And they saw the way each part of the ministry fueled the machine. The ushers smiling sweetly as they handed programs to the congregants each Sunday morning. The deacons and their wives dressed to impress and perched in the front rows of the sanctuary adding perfectly timed "Amens" to the sermon. The musicians and the choir alternately tugging at the parishioners' heartstrings and rousing them into joyous frenzies. Prominent guest speakers and popular mass choirs making guest appearances. All of it added up to large offerings, consistent tithes, and saved souls.

Snapping out of her reverie, Brooklyn turned her attention to the altar. She and her brother Amir exchanged knowing glances as their mother joined in the prayer circle for Janine Mills—one of her father's rumored side pieces. Amir laughed discreetly and looked away.

Brooklyn and her siblings had heard their parents' many heated arguments about the time Elias spent with Janine at all hours of the night. Her calls for "prayer" had been a thorn in Sabrina's side for years. But you would never know it now, watching them all praying fervently with their eyes closed and the most earnest expressions on their faces.

Brooklyn looked at her younger sister Hope and saw her praying with equal fervor. Brooklyn admired that about Hope. She was so sweet and obedient, and she gladly went along with the scam. She seemed so unfazed by the phony life they were living and the hypocrisy that surrounded them. Sometimes Brooklyn wished she could be that way, too. Immune to it all. But for her it was tough to ignore the hard lessons life in the church had already taught her.

In Brooklyn's eyes, her mother was a laughingstock. A woman who allowed her husband to make a fool out of her with women she held hands and prayed with in her role as first lady. Brooklyn often wondered if her mother was a great actress, playing a part so well that it looked real. But if it was an act, Sabrina was nailing it with dangerous precision. It seemed that all she truly cared about was being Elias's wife, the first lady of Promised Land, and the envy of people whose opinions shouldn't matter.

Brooklyn didn't want to be anything like her mother. She admired her father, though. In him, she saw someone who was unapologetic about pursuing his desires. When he stepped into a room, every man held his lady's hand a little tighter, and every woman swooned. His car was one of the fanciest, his home was one of the biggest, and his closet looked like an atelier's dream. He had a fine family, a thriving church, and everything he ever wanted. Brooklyn wanted to be just like him.

As church let out and the people began to drift back out into the real world, their real lives, and their very real problems,

Brooklyn sat in a pew with her friend Erica and shook her head as they watched the all too familiar scene.

"How long you think it's gonna take for them to wrap all this up so I can get back home?" Brooklyn pointed her chin in the direction of her parents standing across the room. They were deep in conversation with the pastor of the host church.

Erica chuckled. "That depends on how long it takes Mrs. Hutchinson and the rest of the gang to finish counting. Once they total up the offering and everybody gets their cut, the deacons will have our church bus loaded up in no time."

Mrs. Hutchinson was Erica's aunt. It always made Brooklyn laugh hearing her best friend refer to her own aunt in such a proper way. But Mrs. Hutchinson insisted that *everyone* besides her children address her that way. Her son and two daughters were allowed to call her "Mama." But everyone else was instructed to refer to Erica's aunt Mary as "Mrs. Hutchinson." She was proud of her late husband's last name. Like her son, he had been a hustler and a risk-taker. But he was well regarded and commanded respect. And she had loved him deeply. So, even in death, she honored him.

Brooklyn nodded and stared impatiently at the closed door to the count room—the section near the pastor's office where the tally took place. Mrs. Hutchinson was the president of the trustee board and had proven herself loyal and trustworthy to Pastor Elias and Promised Land. In fact, Mrs. Hutchinson paraded around like she *was* Promised Land. Aside from the trustee board, she served on the scholarship committee and the missionary board. She had keys to the church's doors and access to Pastor James 24-7. It wasn't unusual for her to be the determining factor in whether a wedding or funeral service would be held at Promised Land. She was the church's wealthiest member and its most consistent tither. For that reason, she was able to call the shots. And she knew it.

Mrs. Hutchinson wore the biggest, fanciest hats for Sunday

service. She dressed in expensive clothes, designer shoes, and jewelry that would get her robbed if it weren't for the fact that her son Alonzo was one of the biggest drug dealers in the borough.

Alonzo never graced the church with his presence. But his wealth helped fund the church's endeavors, because his lifestyle afforded Mrs. Hutchinson a lot of disposable income. The privilege she enjoyed as a result was hard to ignore. It made some people jealous. It made her one of Brooklyn's favorite church members.

She looked forward to seeing what Mrs. Hutchinson would wear for each occasion, how she would style her hair, and which of her hats she would wear. Watching her, Brooklyn learned that money equals power. And that it didn't matter how she got that money. If she surrounded herself with the right kind of people, they would all look the other way.

Erica rolled her eyes.

"You know she likes to take her time and make sure she don't leave a penny behind."

Brooklyn laughed. She loved Erica like family. The two had practically grown up side by side in the hallowed halls of Promised Land. While Erica sang her heart out at choir practice, Brooklyn was always somewhere seated nearby, enraptured. They went to Sunday school together, vacation Bible study, and came of age confiding in one another. Erica was one of the few people Brooklyn truly trusted.

Brooklyn looked at her friend. "I need you to cover for me again tomorrow."

Erica uncrossed her legs, shook her head, and sat upright in her seat.

"Nope. You're trying to get me in trouble."

"I'm not. I promise this will be the last time."

Erica looked at her sideways. "You gonna sit here and lie in church?"

Brooklyn laughed. "I'm serious. I just need you to cover for me one more time. I'm telling my parents that I have study group tomorrow after school. I'll be home by eight. I just need you to vouch for me until then."

"Why? Are you sneaking off to Manhattan again?"

Brooklyn didn't deny it. "Maybe."

"You better not get caught," Erica warned. "If your parents find out I've been lying for you, they'll be pissed."

Brooklyn smiled and rolled her eyes. "Don't worry. I won't get caught. They have enough to worry about."

She watched her father now standing just a little too close to Miss Nancy, the widowed deaconess who wore all her dresses just a little too tight and her hemlines just an inch too short. Everyone had heard the whispers about Miss Nancy and Pastor James. That the two of them had been messing around long before Miss Nancy's husband died of a heart attack at his construction job.

Brooklyn's gaze settled on her mother, condescendingly. First Lady James, always so docile, so blind, deaf, and dumb. For Brooklyn, she was a constant reminder that fairy tales do not exist. Her mother demonstrated how dangerous it was to foolishly love and remain loyal to a man and his vision. Sabrina had gotten lost long ago and, in her place, stood a shadow of her former self. A woman whose only goal was to keep perpetuating an unrealistic image of perfection. Just once, Brooklyn wished her mother would march over to Miss Nancy, snatch her weave out, and tell her to stay the fuck away from her husband.

Erica opened her mouth to speak, but they were interrupted by Brooklyn's younger sister, Hope. She was fifteen years old and small for her age. To Erica, she resembled a sweet little fairy with a gentle quietness to match.

"Mom said to get ready to board the bus. Mrs. Hutchinson and the trustees just finished up."

"Cool," Brooklyn said. "Now scram. Grown folks are talking."

Hope didn't protest before walking off. Erica looked at her friend and shook her head.

"Why are you so mean to her? Hope is so sweet and harmless. You treat her like a gnat."

Brooklyn chuckled. "I do not. Believe it or not, she's my favorite in the family. Everybody else sweats me too hard."

Erica scoffed. "I don't really think Amir cares what you do."

Brooklyn scanned the sanctuary until she spotted her brother standing near the exit talking to Jordan, the drummer.

"He might not," Brooklyn admitted.

"Did he decide whether he wants to work or go to college?"

"He hasn't mentioned it," Brooklyn said, shrugging. "Knowing Amir, he hasn't decided yet." She smiled at Erica. "All I know is I'm getting out of here the first chance I get."

Erica knew it was true. Brooklyn had always been too big for their tiny world. As they gathered their belongings and made their way out to the church van for the trek back to Staten Island, they got their story straight for the next day. Brooklyn went home and played her role in the supporting cast of her family. And behind her sweet, dimpled smile, she held her secrets. Just like all the others.

Chapter Two

Drifting

In addition to attending the same church, Brooklyn and Erica attended Curtis High School, and recently they had perfected the art of cutting classes together. They shared a mutual love of mischief, fashion, and boys. Every now and then, they ditched their later classes and their after-school activities and took the ferry to Manhattan. As mature and well versed about the city as they pretended to be, they hadn't veered very far outside of their small Staten Island community without the supervision of their family or their church. So, when they cut class and took the ferry to Manhattan, they didn't go very far. They hung out in Battery Park or walked to the mall at the World Trade Center. Because they didn't have much money, they mostly window-shopped, trying on things they knew they couldn't afford. Then they would catch the ferry back home, boy-watching along the way. Most of the time, their escapades were largely uneventful.

But there was one particular day when Brooklyn cut class alone. Erica had been taking an important trigonometry test that factored heavily in her final grade. Brooklyn had decided to venture into Manhattan without her friend. She took the ferry to Manhattan and walked around the Financial District, people-watching and looking at all the holiday decorations. It was December, and the streets had been lined with fake Santas ringing bells and collecting donations. Brooklyn walked around smiling from ear to ear. There was something about the Wall Street area that excited her. It felt alive, pulsing with the energy of people making moves and getting money. Everyone and everything seemed expensive. Drivers sat behind the wheels of luxury cars waiting for their wealthy passengers to finish conducting business inside one of the many banks and brokerage firms nearby. Women strutted in high heels and men wore custom-made suits. Brooklyn wanted to be part of this crowd someday. The high rollers, the movers, and the shakers. She imagined herself wealthy, calling the shots in some powerful role. She just had to figure out how to get there.

After her excursion through lower Manhattan, she stood in the ferry terminal on Whitehall Street waiting to catch the 6 P.M. ferry back to Staten Island. It was rush hour, and the terminal was packed with commuters. Brooklyn had her headphones on, listening to Ol' Dirty Bastard's "Return to the 36 Chambers" album in her Sony Walkman portable CD player. It was a CD that her parents would never let her have, one of many that she kept hidden in her secret stash. As far as Elias and Sabrina knew, their daughter was listening to Hezekiah Walker & the Love Fellowship Crusade Choir on repeat.

She mouthed the lyrics to "Shimmy Shimmy Ya" and bopped her head to the beat as she stood waiting for the doors to open and boarding to begin. She didn't notice the tall, stocky guy standing close to her, didn't hear him when he spoke. She did feel it when he tapped her on the shoulder. She turned her head in his direction and slid her headphones off.

"Yes?" She stared up into the eyes of a familiar-looking man.

"Pardon me," he said. "I feel like I know you from somewhere."

Brooklyn squinted her eyes, trying to recall where she had seen him before. She shrugged, unsure.

"I've been standing here looking at you for a minute now, trying to figure it out. My friends call me Zo." He extended his hand.

Brooklyn looked at him. He was about six feet tall, handsome, and muscular. He wore a Chicago Bulls starter jacket, dark jeans, and a pair of Timberlands. She noticed the thick gold chain peeking out around his neck and it clicked. "Zo? Is your name Alonzo?"

He nodded, a smirk forming at the corner of his lips.

Brooklyn smiled and shook his hand. "I'm Brooklyn. Me and your cousin Erica are friends."

His eyes widened then. Erica was in high school. Surely, this curvy beauty was older than that.

"Oh," he managed. He glanced over her again. Brooklyn had on a bomber jacket, a pair of jeans that hugged her in all the right places, and a pair of Reebok boots. She looked so good that he licked his lips absentmindedly.

"And I know your mother," Brooklyn said. "She goes to my church. Mrs. Hutchinson."

The dots connected for Alonzo then. "*Ohhh*! You're the pastor's daughter!"

Suddenly he recalled seeing her standing outside the church one Sunday afternoon when he had picked his mother up from church. He had asked about her then, assuming she was at least eighteen. His mother had simply said, "*That's the pastor's daughter. She ain't your type.*"

Brooklyn hated being known by that moniker. "The pastor's daughter" felt like a role she was forced to play. It made her cringe.

Alonzo noticed. "You don't like that title?"

She shrugged again. "Not really. You can just call me Brooklyn."

The doors opened and the passengers moved forward slowly as they boarded the ferry. Brooklyn and Alonzo walked side by side in the sea of people and made their way to seats near a window. They sat across from each other and Brooklyn got a good look at him. He was ruggedly handsome with a laid-back demeanor that she found appealing. He seemed sure of himself. She was flattered that he had chosen to sit with her. After all the things she had heard about him, he was respected and even revered by those who knew him. He was a popular guy, evidenced by the greetings he received from several other passengers who recognized him as they walked by.

"So, Brooklyn," he said. "How old are you?"

She thought about lying. There was something endearing about him that made her want his attention. She wanted him to stick around and knew that the chances of that were slim if she told him the truth. She rolled the dice anyway.

"Seventeen."

He sighed. "When you turning eighteen?"

She chuckled. "Few months from now."

He smiled. "Okay. That's what's up."

Brooklyn crossed her legs.

"You go to school in Manhattan?" he asked.

She shook her head. "No. I'm not coming from school right now. I was window-shopping."

He seemed surprised by that. "See anything you like?"

"Yeah. Success." She chuckled as she said it, but she wasn't joking. "I walked around Wall Street and saw all the . . ." She looked around, choosing her words carefully. ". . . rich people with their fancy cars, expensive clothes, and jewelry. I like all of that."

Alonzo nodded. "I thought you church folk don't believe in those things. Money is the root of all evil or some shit."

"That's what they *say*. But what they do is something different. The church parking lot is full of fancy cars, and the sanctuary is full of people in their finest clothes. So, what does that tell you?" Brooklyn stared out the window at the Statue of Liberty as they floated past it.

"Money makes the world go 'round," he said.

Brooklyn looked at him and nodded. "Exactly."

Their attraction had been instantaneous. Their conversation flowed easily. She made it clear that she knew what he did for a living. Erica had spoken of him extensively throughout their friendship. So, Brooklyn was already aware that "Zo" was the family savior. The Robin Hood who hustled by night and gave generously to the community by day. He paid the rent for relatives who were facing eviction, settled tuition accounts when unpaid balances threatened expulsion. He gave out turkeys on Thanksgiving, toys at Christmastime, and was a quiet and consistent contributor to Promised Land Church.

One of the lessons Brooklyn had learned growing up in her family was that morality was flexible. She reasoned that if the church could profit from Mrs. Hutchinson and others like her who filtered drug money through their coffers, there was nothing wrong with what Alonzo was involved in. They were flip sides of the same coin. Alonzo was selling crack. And Promised Land was selling hope.

Their romance began building slowly after that. Whispered phone calls late at night and secret meetups at the mall. He took her shopping, showering her with jewelry, clothes, and trinkets that she hid from her parents. She walked out of her house each day wearing carefully scrutinized outfits her parents had bought her. But once she got to school, she made a beeline for the girls' bathroom, where she changed into the designer duds and flashy accessories that Zo had given her. She had the best of both worlds. Popular and revered in two dimensions. At school, she was the smart and capable young lady with a bright future ahead of her. She was one of the cool kids. She learned how to intercept the cut cards her school sent home and made deals with her teachers to do makeup assignments for the classes she missed. At church, she was the pastor's daughter, part of the "first family." And she enjoyed all the perks that came along with that, too. Brooklyn was living a double life and loving it.

She wasn't bothered at all by their age difference. He was twenty-four years old, and she was seventeen. He reminded her constantly that if their relationship was revealed too soon, he could be in a lot of trouble.

"Your father would have my ass locked up in a heartbeat," he often said.

"For what?" she asked one late spring afternoon. "We're not having sex."

Alonzo looked at her. He saw the sparkle in her eye and the curl at the edge of her lip as she grinned at him. He smiled despite himself.

"I keep saying we should wait until your birthday," he said.

He wished he could make it sound convincing. But they both knew he wanted her in the worst way. They had been messing around for months, kissing, touching, coming so very close to going all the way. Each time, Alonzo tore himself away, convinced that no pussy was worth going to jail for.

She moved closer to him on the couch in his apartment. "I don't want to wait anymore." She brushed her lips against his ear and whispered softly. "I want you."

She grabbed at the bulge in his pants, squeezed it, and pressed her body against him.

He kissed her intensely. She held on to him tightly. She could feel the rigidness between his legs and knew that he wanted her, too.

He pulled back a little.

"You sure?" There was a desperation in his tone as he asked the question.

She nodded, and that was all the assurance he needed. He peeled her out of her clothes, removed his, too, and slowly, tenderly ushered her across the threshold from girlhood to womanhood.

Brooklyn hadn't told anyone about her secret romance. She certainly hadn't told a soul that she had lost her virginity. The pastor's daughter having underage sex with a grown man. A scandal like that would rock the church. Although she trusted Erica, she didn't even tell her the news. Somehow, keeping it from her family and from her best friend made the secret sweeter. Their relationship was unknown to anyone but them. But she had felt more connected to Alonzo than ever now that he had been inside her. In her daydreams she started to imagine a future by his side.

She knew it would cost her dearly. Her parents would certainly never approve. Taking the proceeds of his drug sales disguised as "offerings" from his mother was one thing. But having him as a son-in-law would be too much. According to her father, a drug dealer was someone who brought harm to their community. He had preached countless funeral sermons for young men whose lives had been cut short due to street violence. He warned Amir not to get caught up in anything illegal. And he did his best to shelter his daughters from boys who were up to no good. Brooklyn knew that she was playing with fire. She just couldn't help herself.

She wasn't from the streets and knew very little about that life. But she was wise enough to know that what Alonzo did for a living was dangerous. She worried about him when they weren't together. He risked death and incarceration every time he stepped outside. But it was the only life he knew. He began to share his story with Brooklyn during their increasingly rare time together. Unraveling slowly for her the tale of his parents' romance, his father's untimely death, and the expectation all of his peers and even his uncles placed on him to fill his father's shoes. It only made Brooklyn admire him more, hearing how brave he had been stepping into his role as the leader of a growing circle.

As much as she longed to spend more time with Alonzo, Brooklyn struggled to find the time. She couldn't escape the watchful eyes of her parents—her mother especially—very often. Erica was getting sick of covering for her all the time. She was worried that Brooklyn was cutting school too often and that her entanglement with the mystery guy in her life would land Erica in hot water, too.

Whenever his name came up, Brooklyn did her best to ask questions about Alonzo without giving herself away. She feigned disinterest at first, then followed up with a seemingly harmless question. She was able to glean information that way.

"My aunt is throwing a barbecue for Memorial Day," Erica said one afternoon. "Zo is driving us to New Jersey to get a bunch of alcohol from the discount store today."

"Mrs. Hutchinson drinks?" Brooklyn asked, surprised.

"No!" Erica shook her head. "But all her brothers do. Zo and all the rest of our cousins, too. So, she stocks up on everything just to make sure she doesn't run out. My aunt has two sides to her. The churchgoing, sanctified side. And the side that likes to let her hair down and have a good time. That's why the church folk don't get invited to her *real* parties." Erica laughed. "The deaconesses would be appalled."

Brooklyn laughed, too. Erica had no clue that Brooklyn had been imagining the fabulous Mrs. Hutchinson as her future mother-in-law.

"Zo's an only child?" Brooklyn asked, pretending not to know the answer.

"Yeah. Well, he's his *mother's* only child. His father had a couple of kids with different women. But he *married* my aunt. That had special meaning to her. That's why she still insists on everyone calling her '*Mrs. Hutchinson*' to this day."

"I think she's fly," Brooklyn said. "Always dressed to impress, never a hair out of place."

"Just like your mother," Erica said. "Mrs. James gives my aunt a run for her money with the wardrobe!"

"I guess." Brooklyn shrugged, always reluctant to give her mother a compliment.

"Why are you so hard on your mother?" Erica asked.

Brooklyn sighed. "She's too judgmental. Imagine growing up with a perfectionist scrutinizing every move you make, rewriting history to suit their needs. She's exhausting."

Erica thought about it and had to admit to herself that Mrs. James was the image of perfection—always saying and doing the right thing at exactly the right time. Whenever she came around, everyone straightened their posture and subconsciously watched their words. Erica had always viewed it as regality. But now she imagined that it had to be tough living with that energy 24-7.

"She just wants what's best for you. Parents go about it the wrong way sometimes. But at least you have a nice roof over your head and all that."

"You do, too. Don't act like your family is struggling just because your apartment is in the projects." Brooklyn chuckled. "I wish I could trade places with you sometimes."

Erica could tell that Brooklyn longed to break free from her family. "Soon you'll be eighteen and no one can stop you from living the life you want. In the meantime, just try to stay out of trouble. And remember that all that glitters isn't gold. I have more freedom than you. My mother isn't standing over me watching my every move. But that's because she's working two jobs so she can save enough money to move us out of the projects. We have a nice place because Zo gives us things, stocks the fridge with groceries, hits us off with money. And I'm not gonna act like I don't love it. I appreciate my cousin for what he does for our family. But I hate the risks he has to take out there doing what he does. I wish my aunt practiced what she preached a little more. Like your mother does."

Brooklyn had to work hard not to laugh at that one. Erica had no idea that the first lady was a fraud. If Sabrina was practicing what she preached, Brooklyn wanted no parts of a religion like that.

"I'm sure Mrs. Hutchinson did the best she could," Brooklyn said. "Her husband died, and she raised a son who was bold enough to do whatever it took to make her life easier. I'm sure she knows what he's up to. But she loves him still. Unconditional love sounds amazing to me. It's the only kind of love I want."

Erica noted the faraway look in Brooklyn's eye. "You're thinking about your secret boo, ain't you? When are you gonna tell me who it is?"

Brooklyn laughed. "I was gonna ask if you would cover for me—"

"NOPE!" Erica cut her off. "I told you. I don't want no beef with your parents. You figure out a way to do your sneaking around without me from now on. Especially if you're not gonna tell me who it is!"

Brooklyn groaned, but she knew that Erica wasn't budging.

With no alibi and her parents hovering over her, she was finding it harder to steal away. As spring faded into summer, Brooklyn began to devise a plan. She would convince her parents that she had landed a summer job. She just needed to iron out the fine details.

She started with Amir.

Her brother had recently landed a job in Midtown Manhattan working in the mailroom at a law firm. He was two years older than Brooklyn and had somehow resisted their parents' efforts to persuade him to go away to college. Pastor and First Lady James wanted desperately to brag to their friends that their only son was studying law or medicine at Morehouse or Howard. Instead, Amir had elected to take a break from school while he tried to figure out his next moves. He wasn't sure what he wanted to be, wavering between culinary arts and drama as majors. Neither career path earned the approval of his parents. So, in an effort to appease them, he had taken a job at a firm where the church drummer Jordan Sharp worked as a paralegal. With Jordan's assistance, Amir had gotten the entry-level position and had been working there for three months now. The family had gone to dinner to celebrate him passing his probationary period. Now, Brooklyn intended to use her brother's good fortune to her benefit.

She would tell Amir the truth—or at least a version of the

truth that he would be able to digest. That she was in a relationship with a guy their parents wouldn't approve of, and she wanted a bit of freedom. She hoped to convince Amir to go along with the lie she had concocted. That she, too, had obtained a job—off the books of course—as a messenger in Manhattan. She just needed Amir to go along with the whole thing. And for Alonzo to agree to "pay" her enough to avoid her parents' suspicions.

She had a substitute teacher for her last class of the day and came home from school early on a Friday afternoon in June. She wanted to get home before Hope and Amir got back so that she could page Alonzo and speak in private while she made plans to see him that evening. He always stressed to her that she should never show up at his apartment unannounced—for her own safety. So, she needed to speak with him ahead of time to make sure it was cool for her to come over. Her parents had traveled to Philadelphia for the funeral of one of Elias's fellow pastors. They were expected home on Saturday night. Brooklyn was hoping to seize the opportunity to make up for lost time with her secret lover.

The second she opened the front door, it was clear that someone was home. At first, she feared that her parents were still there. But she hadn't seen the family car outside. She heard music playing faintly upstairs, and she stood hesitantly at the foot of the stairs listening. For a while, all she could hear was music playing. Then it got weird. Between the notes of the music, she could hear the guttural groans of a man having sex. Her heart sank, assuming at first that it was her father, that she had walked in on one of his rumored trysts with the many women in his congregation. She climbed the stairs slowly, the moans clearer now. As she stepped onto the upstairs landing, she realized that the sounds weren't coming from the direction of her parents' room after all. Instead, she found herself drifting toward Amir's door. The sounds got louder as she cracked the door slowly open. Amir was lying across his bed with his legs spread wide and Jordan, the church drummer, was crouched between them. Amir was gripping Jordan's head, guiding the rhythm of his mouth as he pleased him.

Brooklyn gasped loudly and stifled a scream, snapping her brother out of his trance, and he spotted her standing in the doorway. Jordan turned in her direction, too. For a moment, Brooklyn felt faint.

"Brooklyn!"

Amir called her name as she ran down the hallway, down the stairs, and bolted from the house.

She walked to the park in the nearby projects in a daze, still not fully processing what she'd seen. Amir was *gay*. She wondered how she had missed that all these years. Until today, she would have sworn they were as close as siblings could be. They shared their secrets with each other—didn't they?

She reminded herself that she was living an entire life that no one in her family—including Amir—knew anything about. It suddenly became clear to her that she wasn't the only one with an alter ego.

She sat down on a bench under a cluster of trees and cried. She wasn't sure why she was crying but she knew that she felt overcome with a flood of emotions. She was shocked, embarrassed, and most of all afraid. She knew that if her parents ever found out, Amir would be disowned.

She went back through the years in her mind searching for signs she had possibly missed. Amir had always been quiet and withdrawn. But she had never suspected for one second that her brother was gay.

And Jordan.

Brooklyn had always known him to be a man of few words. As the church drummer, she had interacted with Jordan on countless occasions. She knew him for his diligent work, his skill on the drums, and knew that her father considered him an integral part of the team. Jordan had a calm and easy demeanor with a soothing voice to match. He was handsome, slim, and brown-skinned with welcoming eyes. He was so unassuming that she barely gave him a second thought until the moment she had found him taking her brother to paradise with his mouth.

The thought made her shudder. She wondered how long it had been going on. She got up and started walking, directionless. There was no way she could go back home. Not right now. She reasoned that everyone needed space to process the day's events.

She didn't realize she was in front of Erica's building until she found herself opening the heavy lobby door. She took the elevator to her friend's apartment and knocked on her door.

Erica could tell immediately that something was wrong. Brooklyn looked like she had seen a ghost.

"What's wrong?" Erica asked, as Brooklyn stepped inside.

Brooklyn shook her head, aware now that she couldn't even tell her best friend. Telling Erica what she had seen would mean outing both Amir and Jordan without their consent. She trusted Erica, but she wasn't sure that she could keep a secret like that.

"You home alone?" she asked.

"Yeah. I just got in. What's the matter?"

Brooklyn slunk down on the couch. "I have to tell you something."

She wanted to tell her that she felt lost, confused, overwhelmed by the unexpected truth she had walked in on. But she told a different truth instead.

"I want to tell you a secret I've been keeping. But I don't want you to get all upset and start overreacting."

Erica frowned, immediately aware that this was going to be a big revelation. She prayed that it wasn't one of the deacons or ministers at church.

"What is is?"

Brooklyn cleared her throat. "I've been messing around with your cousin. Zo."

Erica's face registered all of the shock she felt inside. "BROOKLYN, NO!" She shook her head. "Zo is a grown-ass man!"

"We're only seven years apart. When I'm twenty-three and he's thirty, that won't even be an issue."

Erica looked at her like she was crazy. "Come on! You can't be serious. Girl, that's not a good idea. Trust me." Erica shook her head again. Brooklyn was her best friend. She hated to see her being made a fool of. But Alonzo was her cousin. She couldn't betray him, either. She felt stuck between a rock and a hard place. "Alonzo is cute, and he has money. But he's not the kind of guy you need."

Brooklyn sighed. "I knew you would act like this."

"I'm just trying to look out for you. I don't want to see you get your feelings hurt."

"You saying that he has a girlfriend or something?"

Erica rolled her eyes. That was an understatement. "I'm saying that he's too old for you. We're not even out of high school yet. And the life he's living is dangerous. You deserve better than that. And you know it."

Brooklyn laughed. "Okay, Saint Erica. So, I guess you're the only one without sin since you're casting all these stones."

Erica laughed, too. It was true that she wasn't innocent. She sang like an angel on Sundays. But she had her own secrets, too. She had been falling hard for one of the seniors at their school. His name was Shawn, and she hadn't told her overprotective family about their romance yet.

"Me and Shawn are not the same as you and Zo. Shawn is heading to college. Zo is headed for trouble."

Brooklyn frowned. "Don't say that. He's smart about what he does."

"So, why'd you walk in here looking like a lost little puppy a few minutes ago? Seems like he's got you worried about something."

Brooklyn came up with a quick lie. "I was thinking about telling

Amir. I thought I'd tell you first and see what your reaction would be. Judging by this conversation, I'll keep it to myself."

Hours later, Brooklyn clung to Alonzo as he slid out of her, the slickness between her thighs audible in the quiet of his apartment. He kissed her on the forehead, then her nose, and finally her lips before he rolled over onto his back and let out a heavy sigh.

Brooklyn had paged him while she was at Erica's house. He had called her back within minutes and was happy to hear that she was enjoying a rare night without parental supervision. He picked her up in front of Erica's building and took her back to his place.

She lay beside him now, dazed and spent. She hadn't shared the revelation with Erica and now she considered telling Alonzo about it. But she wasn't sure how he would react. Homosexuality was a tender subject for most men. She wasn't ready to hear any negative remarks or slurs about her brother. So, she opted to keep it to herself.

"What's on your mind?" Alonzo asked, noticing her silence.

"I want to figure out a way to see you more often. Once I get out of my parents' house, I'll be able to do what I want. Until then, I need to make them think I'm working or something, so they let me have more freedom." She sat up and began outlining her plan. "I'm gonna tell them I found a job in Manhattan. Something that pays off the books. Like a messenger or something."

Alonzo nodded. "That's what's up."

"Then I can spend more time with you. I just need you to hit me off with like two or three hundred dollars a week so it looks legit."

Alonzo laughed so loudly that it startled Brooklyn. He stared back at her, wide-eyed.

"Wait . . . let me get this straight. You want me to pay you to hang around with me?"

Brooklyn chuckled. "Not like that. I'm saying you could give me an allowance or something like that. I could front like I'm working, and my parents won't think nothing of it."

He shook his head. "Nah, that won't work for me. I like you and all that. But I'm a businessman. If I'm paying you, you gotta put in work."

"So, put me to work. What can I do?"

He laughed again. Then he laid back and thought about it. He seemed to contemplate a few things before shaking his head again. "You're a church girl. The pastor's daughter. What kind of work can you do, Brooklyn? What you out here looking for?"

She sighed, still reeling from what she had witnessed earlier, still hearing Erica's warnings about Alonzo. "I don't know what I'm looking for," she admitted. "But whatever it is, I'm not finding it in church or in school. I definitely ain't finding it at home. I just want to get out of here, Zo. I want to do my own thing. Until I figure out what that is, I just need to get out from under the microscope of my parents."

He looked at her, so young, beautiful, and innocent—so determined to grow up too soon.

"You can't hang your hopes on me, shorty. I'm not gonna sit here and lie to you. I'm probably gonna break your heart."

Brooklyn wasn't expecting that, and her body language showed it. Her facial expression changed, and her shoulders slumped.

"Not on purpose," he assured her. "But you're young. I'm older than you—not just in years, but in life. I could sit here and sell you a dream. Tell you, yeah, I'll give you three hundred dollars a week and you can ride around with me on some Bonnie and Clyde shit. But I would be lying to you. The life I live is grimy, it gets ugly. I'm on the go a lot. I need a girl who understands that."

She understood what he was saying, but his words still hurt. She nodded and stood to leave.

"Don't get mad at me for keeping it real with you. A corny nigga would've strung you along. But I'm not like that."

"I don't need your pep talk," she assured him. "I just need a way out."

He took her hand and held it tightly in his. "Come here."

She straddled him and tried hard not to cry. It wasn't his rejection of her plan that stung the most. It was the sense of hopelessness she felt, mainly because her home life was a wreck.

"I want to keep seeing you," he said, his tone softer now. "So, I'll give you five hundred dollars a week."

She visibly brightened then, a slow smile forming on her lips.

"But you gotta do something for it."

She frowned then. "What?"

"Once a week . . . maybe twice . . . I'll send you uptown. You pick something up for me and bring it back here safely. And I'll give you enough money to keep your parents off your back."

"Thank you," she said, beaming now. She grinded her hips on his lap. "Does the job come with benefits?"

He smiled and nodded quickly. "Yes!" He scooped her up, laid her down, and spread her legs apart.

Brooklyn moaned, feeling his tongue go to work against her clit expertly. She closed her eyes, spread her legs wider, and melted in his mouth.

Later that night, she climbed out of Alonzo's car at the end of her block. Even though her parents weren't home, she knew that Amir and Hope would be. She didn't need them asking questions, so she kissed Alonzo goodbye curbside and tucked the pager he had given her into her pocket. Then she walked the rest of the way home.

She wasn't sure what to expect as she entered the house. It was eerily silent as she climbed the stairs. The door to Amir's bedroom was closed. Brooklyn stared at it, tempted to go and knock on it. Might as well get the awkwardness out of the way. But she wasn't sure what to say or where to start.

She found Hope in the bedroom they shared. The two of them had a complex relationship. Though they were only two years apart, the gulf between them couldn't have been wider. Hope was calm, docile, and proper. She was petite with a shy smile. More than anything else, Hope wanted to please God, her parents, and live a holy life devoted to serving the community and the world at large. She was wide-eyed and pure, an animal lover and responsible babysitter. She often helped out at the church's after-school center. All of it annoyed Brooklyn to no end. Hope's eagerness to be obedient and helpful only highlighted Brooklyn's reluctance to do the same.

Brooklyn watched her sister now, doing her homework with a bunch of papers laid out on her bed. Among the textbooks, she spotted Hope's pink Bible. It was never far from her, and Brooklyn often teased her about it. She thought about what Erica had said earlier about Brooklyn being mean to her sister. She didn't mean to be. She just hated seeing another Goody Two-Shoes in the making.

"What subject are you studying now?" Brooklyn asked, trying to start a conversation.

Hope seemed surprised by it. She hesitated a moment before answering softly.

"Math."

Brooklyn groaned. "Ugh. I can't help you with that. I barely get Cs in it."

Hope laughed. "It's cool. I don't need help."

Brooklyn nodded. Silence hung for a few moments between them. Hope cleared her throat.

"You don't have any homework?" she asked.

Brooklyn nodded. "Yeah. But I'll do it later."

Hope turned back to her work. She knew all about her family's duality. Hope was quietly observant. She saw everything, though she spoke about nothing. Her obedience to the rules was her way of doing her part to ease the tension in the home. If she could live up to her parents' expectations, that was one less thing everyone needed to worry about.

She knew the unspoken truth within the family. That her brother Amir was struggling in his father's shadow. As the preacher's son, he was expected to be his father's apprentice, preparing to ascend to the throne someday. Instead, Amir had made it known that he did not feel compelled to enter the ministry. In fact, he wasn't sure *what* he wanted to do with his life. College was pointless until he figured out a career path. In the meantime, he drifted around chasing his tail. With Hope, he was always attentive, loving, and willing to listen. And Hope listened in return. She was her brother's counselor and confidante. Because Amir was full of secrets, too.

Since she attended the same school as her older sister, Hope also saw the side of Brooklyn that her parents knew nothing about. She knew that there was a version of Brooklyn that she hid from their family. Brooklyn was one of the cool girls at school. But Hope moved in a different crowd. She felt more comfortable among the nerds, the comic book geeks, and the misfits. The sisters were as opposite as could be.

Hope glanced at Brooklyn now, and pensively broke the silence.

"I like math because everything about it makes sense. It all checks out."

"Numbers don't lie." Brooklyn agreed.

"If everything in life was that simple, things would be a lot easier." Hope shrugged. "That's why I pray all the time. I know it gets on your nerves because I see you rolling your eyes whenever I'm doing it. But I trust that God has a plan for us. Praying helps me make sense out of the things I don't understand."

Brooklyn's face was expressionless as she listened. "Okay, Hope. If that's true, help me understand it, too. How is it okay for us to stand up there day after day smiling and acting phony? Meanwhile, Mrs. Hutchinson funnels her son's drug money through her tithes and offerings, and we act like we don't know. God is real, but this church thing is all a scam."

Hope looked crushed by the impact of her sister's words. "Nobody's perfect."

"I never said anything about being perfect." Brooklyn sucked her teeth. "I don't blame you for not understanding. When we lived in Brownsville, you were little. So, you don't remember it like Amir and I do. When I was about ten years old, Daddy was working at the post office, and he hustled on the side. Nothing major. But every now and then, he would come home with a bunch of clothes, money, jewelry for Mommy. We never knew how he did it, but we knew we had more than most of our friends. Daddy had a friend who invited him to church for a christening. After he came home, it was all he could talk about. How captivated the "audience" was by the minister. And how all the money they made at that church was tax-free. The next thing we knew, he was in theology school. He started traveling from church to church preaching and getting paid. Then we moved to Staten Island and became the Huxtables. So, there was no burning bush talking to him and urging him to preach. No parting of the clouds and a voice from heaven like he preaches about in that pulpit. It's all about money. Like you said, numbers don't lie."

Hope stared at Brooklyn when she was done talking. Finally, she picked her notebook up again, and nodded.

"I'm not that much younger than you. I remember more than you give me credit for. Things got better when we moved out here. Better neighborhood, better schools. More time together as a family." She shrugged. "I choose to focus on the good."

She turned her attention back to her homework, reminded why the divide between them was so wide.

Brooklyn thought Hope sounded just like their mother. Disgusted, she walked out of the room and shut the door behind her. She walked to Amir's bedroom door and stood there for several moments. She could hear the TV playing low in the background as he talked to someone on the phone.

Tentatively, Brooklyn knocked on his door.

At first no response came. After a long silence, she turned to walk away but was halted by his voice.

"Yeah?" Amir called out.

Brooklyn opened his door, stepped inside, and found him lying on his back against the mountain of pillows on his bed. He spoke into the phone in his hand as she entered.

"Let me call you back," he said. He hung up and looked at her. "Hey. What's up?"

She sat on the edge of his bed and tucked her feet beneath her.

"Nothing. Just sick of sitting in my room listening to Little Miss Perfect. I need to be around somebody normal for once."

"You think I'm normal?" he asked, his voice unsure.

She pulled herself closer to him and hugged him tightly.

"Yes," she said in his ear. "I know you are."

They held each other for a while, silently. She took a deep breath and sat back and looked at her brother.

"There's nothing abnormal, unusual, or unholy about you, Amir. There is nothing wrong with you."

Amir wiped his eyes with the back of his hand and nodded at that. He couldn't look at her for several moments as her words sank in.

He looked at her.

"If I tell them, it'll break their hearts. And you know it."

His voice was low, careful not to let Hope overhear.

"Why didn't you tell *me*?" Brooklyn asked.

"How?" Amir asked. "I didn't know how. And I've been keeping it a secret for so long that I just got used to it." He dabbed at his eyes roughly. "I didn't know how to tell anybody." He looked at her and she could see the pain and torment in his eyes. "I love Jordan. But I don't know if it's the real thing. He's the first . . ." Amir struggled to find the right words. "I didn't want to admit the truth for years. You know why. I don't have to explain it to you. The way I feel goes against everything we've been taught."

"When did you know?" she asked, gently.

He shrugged. "Ten or eleven maybe. I had crushes on boys, but I never acted on it. I would never approach anybody at school. Never had much time to make friends outside of that. Mom and Dad made sure that every second of our day was full of stuff to do. But one day after church, I was helping Jordan pack up to go home. And . . . the way he looked at me . . ." Amir shook his head, seeing the expression in his mind now as vividly as a photograph. "I could tell that he knew. And in his eyes, I could sense that it was okay with him. That he wasn't scared of it or repulsed by it. He touched my hand." Amir smiled at the memory. "I wasn't sure what to say. So, we just held hands for a minute. Then, Ms. Mills came in to get her Sunday school booklet, and we let go."

Brooklyn pulled her knees in close to her chest and kept listening.

"I waited a few days before I made my move. I couldn't stop thinking about it. I was scared that I had imagined it. Maybe he wasn't looking at me the way I thought he was. I second-guessed myself. But I finally got the courage to go and talk to him. I went to church that Wednesday night when I knew they were having choir rehearsal. I hung out downstairs helping Deacon Stillman clean up while they rehearsed upstairs in the sanctuary. When they were finished, I went up there and made sure that he saw me. I could tell he was stalling, waiting for everyone to leave. So, I hung around. Finally, when the coast was clear, I walked over to him. I said, '*I don't know how to do this.*' All awkward and shit. But he didn't seem like this was new to him. He said, '*Just speak, Amir.*' It sounded so simple."

Brooklyn watched tears pooling in her brother's eyes and she reached for him. Gripping his arm, she gave it a reassuring squeeze.

"So, I asked him if I could call him. I knew people could be listening. It's like the walls have ears sometimes. We were standing in the church sanctuary. It felt like it wasn't the right place for me to say what was on my mind. And he gave me his phone number. I called him that night. We talked for hours. He told me he had been struggling with who he is inside and who he's supposed to be as a man. And I knew exactly what he was talking about. Because I've been feeling that way my whole life.

I told him that I feel trapped in this family. He listened. We started hooking up when we could. Sneaking away after he got off from work. Meeting in places nobody would spot us. We were in the park one day chilling, listening to music, and I kissed him. I was so relieved when it happened. It made me feel free even though nobody knew about it but us."

Brooklyn smiled, knowing exactly how that felt. She felt the same way during her stolen moments with Alonzo. Their relationship felt thrilling, forbidden, and she liked it.

"I'm sorry about what you saw," Amir said.

"*I'm* sorry," she said. "I was just shocked. I needed some time to digest it and figure out what to say. But I shouldn't have reacted like that."

Amir shrugged. "I don't blame you. It's my fault. Jordan is embarrassed, too. He's scared you'll tell. If anybody finds out, we'll both be in a lot of trouble."

Brooklyn studied her brother's face. He was so handsome, the perfect combination of their parents. He had always been quiet and withdrawn, and Brooklyn was only beginning to understand the reasons for that.

"You can trust me. Always. What I saw today, what you told me today—none of it changes the fact that you're my brother. And I love you." She squeezed his hand. "I can tell that you care about Jordan. Don't be ashamed of it. You can't help who you love."

He squeezed her hand back. "I do love him. I never thought it could happen. That I could feel normal and accepted by someone. That I could be one hundred percent myself. Not just in a relationship but in life. I've been stifling a major part of who I am for years. With Jordan, I don't have to hide."

Brooklyn's eyes searched his for some clarity. "We always talked about getting out of here. Now's the time. Why don't you just leave here and start a new life out in Hollywood? You said you wanted to be an actor. Growing up in this family gave you a crash course in that."

Amir laughed. "Hollywood! You make it sound so easy."

"Because it *is* that easy. You don't need their money, Amir. You're smart enough to make it on your own. Little Hope is brainwashed into this life. But me and you are different. We're not supposed to get stuck here."

Amir nodded. "You're right, Brooklyn. But everybody's not as brave as you. Whatever trouble you get yourself into isn't as big a deal as being gay."

She took a deep breath and decided to open up to him.

"What if I told you that I lost my virginity to a grown-ass man and I think I'm in love?"

She watched shock waves roll across his face as he stuttered and stammered for a response that evaded him. She touched his arm to steady him.

"It's okay. See? You're not the only one with secrets. The pastor and first lady would kill me if they knew. The church would be appalled. And they would have every right to be."

"What grown man? And what do you mean you're in love?"

"He's not somebody you know. He's not from around here," she lied.

"Where did you meet?" Amir asked.

"That doesn't matter." Brooklyn brushed a strand of hair out of her face, stalling. She wasn't ready to reveal all the details of her double life just yet. "He's a good guy, treats me nice and all that. I really like him."

"How old is he?"

"Twenty-something."

"Brooklyn . . ."

"Don't start lecturing me. I didn't do that to you."

Amir had no comeback for that. He exhaled. "I just don't want you to get in trouble. If you get caught, you know what's gonna happen."

She huffed. "I'm worried about what happens if they find out about you, too. That's why we have to get out of here. Neither one of us can be ourselves. We have to play these roles and follow these rules that only apply to us. There's nothing keeping us here. Especially you. You're grown and you can call your own shots. Just get out of here." She stared at him. "Are you staying here for Jordan?"

Amir shrugged, unsure. "Maybe part of the reason I stayed here *is* because of Jordan. For the first time, I have somebody I can be myself around. We got our own thing that nobody else can touch. If I leave, what will I have then?"

Brooklyn felt sorry for her brother in that moment. She was younger than him, but could tell that she was already far wiser than he. She considered telling him that he would always have himself, and that should be more than enough for him. That Jordan wasn't the key to his happiness. That he should stick to the plans they whispered together over the years in huddled corners at church functions. Plans to escape the restricted world they were raised in.

She smiled at him. "I get it. Just know that I still love you. And there's nothing you can do to change that."

Amir yanked her into a strong hug, and she kissed his cheek.

"Now, I need a favor. We both have our secrets," she said. "If you help me keep mine, I promise to keep yours."

His eyes narrowed. "What do you mean?"

"You taking that job is a great big FUCK YOU to them. You're working with your boo, getting money, and hopefully plotting your way out of here."

Amir nodded. "We talked about getting a place together. Not out here. Maybe in Manhattan somewhere."

Brooklyn's eyes widened. "Good!"

"But I want to do this the right way. If that makes sense. I'm not gonna tell everybody I'm gay and embarrass the family—the church. I'm just gonna move away quietly. Let them tell the story their way. '*Amir moved to Manhattan to study film*' or whatever. Mom will make up something that sounds impressive. And Dad won't have to know. At least not right now."

Brooklyn stared at him. She understood. Daddy's approval had been something they all sought like sustenance.

"I'm glad you're doing this. I'm glad you and Jordan are happy."

"Thank you," Amir said. "But what does all that have to do with me keeping your secrets?"

"I need you and Jordan to help me convince Mom and Dad that I have a part-time job, too. I want to spend the summer having fun instead of going revival hopping with them."

Amir scoffed. "How are we gonna do that?"

Brooklyn smiled wide and scooted closer to him on the bed. "Here's my plan!"

Chapter Three

Money-Making Manhattan

Brooklyn was scared to death.

So far, everything had been going as planned. With Amir's help, she had convinced her parents that she had a job working as a part-time messenger delivering important documents by hand to executives in lower Manhattan. It hadn't taken them much convincing. Once Jordan and Amir vouched for the fictitious agency that Brooklyn supposedly worked for, the rest was easy.

In fact, Sabrina had been proudly bragging to all the church ladies about her children's employment and prospects for the future. Everything was going as planned.

For the past two weeks, Alonzo had paid Brooklyn to listen and learn. She knew the drill, had gone over it a thousand times. Still, her heart thundered in her chest as she stood on the train clutching a JanSport backpack stuffed with cash.

Alonzo had given her clear instructions. He had even sent her on trial runs uptown to make sure that she knew the way and was familiar with the area. First, he had her take the 1/9 train to Harlem nonstop from South Ferry. He instructed her to get off at 125th Street and walk three blocks to a bakery with a red awning on 128th Street. He had a specific pastry order prepared and waiting for her. She picked it up and brought it back. The next time she made the trip, he had her transfer to the 2/3 train at Chambers Street and take it to 110th Street. There, he had her stop in a laundromat on St. Nicholas Avenue and pick up a pager from a girl named Anna. After meeting with her, she walked across town and took the 4/5 train back downtown to Bowling Green, walked the few short blocks to the ferry terminal, and took the trip back to Staten Island.

Brooklyn had started to feel like a test dummy.

"What's all this transferring trains and walking crosstown for? I feel like you're just sending me on silly missions to get me out of your face for a few hours a week."

Alonzo had laughed. "You're in training. What happens if the train you're used to taking is out of service? Or if the cops got the drug-sniffing dogs on the Seventh Avenue line and you need to walk across town to the Lexington line? What if you get in trouble uptown by yourself? You know two safe spots now—the bakery and the laundromat—that you can duck into and get low. Everything I'm telling you is for a reason."

She was an eager student. And today would be her biggest test yet. She stood outside of the building on West 134th Street and whispered a silent prayer. She chided herself, aware that what she was doing was ungodly. She was nervous and tried her best to calm herself as she boarded the elevator and pressed the button for the fourth floor. She glanced at the slip of paper in her hand again. Apartment 4M. She noticed her hand trembling as she held it in front of her and quickly tucked it away.

She stuck it in her pocket and stepped off the elevator when it stopped with a jolt on the fourth floor. She began walking slowly down the hallway, peering at each apartment to check the label. She arrived at 4M and stopped. She pulled the straps on the backpack a little tighter and took a deep breath. Gently, she knocked on the door.

She could hear loud voices and music coming from inside the apartment, but she couldn't make out much of what they were saying. She worried about the number of people she could hear inside. Alonzo had told that that she was there to meet "Stacey." But the voices on the other side of the door sounded aggressive and male.

She knocked again, a bit harder this time. She saw the peephole cover slide to the side and held her breath as she heard the locks being unlatched. A man stood before her staring at her like she was an oasis in desert.

"Damn, you're beautiful. How you doing? What's your name?" His eyes danced over her as he spoke. He was tall, light-skinned, and handsome. But there was a discernable edginess about him.

"Zo sent me," she said, sticking to the script. "Stacey's expecting me."

"What's your name though, shorty?"

She tried to think of an alias on her feet but found herself stammering. "Brooklyn," she muttered at last.

"Nice to meet you, Brooklyn. My name is Hassan. Everybody calls me '*Hass*.'" He ushered her inside where two men stood towering over her. "These are my boys Wally and Roscoe."

She nodded at them. She looked at Hassan, expectantly. "Is Stacey here?"

He grinned. "I'm sorry, beautiful. I was so caught up in your sex appeal that I lost my train of thought for a minute."

She was too nervous to be flattered. She looked at the other two guys who stared back at her unsmiling. One was tall and stocky like a bodyguard. The other was slim and mischievous-looking. Both of them looked menacing.

"You're in the wrong part of town, Brooklyn. You don't look like you belong here," Wally said.

Brooklyn knew he was right but struggled to keep her poker face on. "I just want to see Stacey and handle my business."

Roscoe nodded. "Okay, shorty. How old are you?"

"Grown."

"You sure?" he asked. "You got a little baby face."

A woman emerged from the kitchen area and frowned at the three men crowding around Brooklyn.

"Back up off her. Damn!" She looked at Brooklyn apologetically. "You would think these niggas ain't never seen pussy before."

Brooklyn laughed.

"I'm Stacey," the woman said. She was a tall, curvy girl with a short haircut, doorknocker earrings, and a gold nameplate around her neck. She wore a pair of baggy jeans, a black T-shirt, and a cropped denim jacket. "Roscoe's my brother and these are his little friends."

Hassan laughed. "Oh, we're his little friends now? I see how it is."

Stacey smiled. "Come in, Brooklyn. Zo told me you were coming. He didn't tell me he was sending a little kid, though."

Brooklyn looked down at her wardrobe, suddenly self-conscious. She thought she looked mature, but apparently she was wrong.

"It's cool," Stacey assured her. "That's good for what he got you doing. You look like you're coming from school. Harmless and shit."

Brooklyn nodded. She handed over the backpack like Alonzo had told her to do.

Stacey looked through it quickly, nodded, and handed it to Roscoe. He walked over to the counter and began counting out the money inside.

Stacey looked at her. "So, Brooklyn, is this your first time coming uptown for Zo?"

She shook her head, nervously, her eyes darting around the apartment. "No. I did it before."

"You strapped?" Wally asked, grinning.

Brooklyn wasn't and now she wondered why Alonzo hadn't thought of that. She stared at Wally, deadpanned. "You trying to find out?"

Stacey's mouth dropped and she applauded Brooklyn's response. "OKAY! I like her!"

Hassan stared her up and down like a snack. "Me too."

"She's good," Roscoe called out from the kitchen, done counting.

Stacey nodded and handed her an identical backpack that was already full. "It's heavy," she warned Brooklyn as she handed it over. "Can you handle it?"

Brooklyn hoisted it on her back and nodded. "Yeah. I got it."

"You came here all by yourself?" Stacey asked.

Brooklyn didn't respond, assuming the question was rhetorical since there was clearly no one with her.

Stacey nodded, seemingly impressed. "That means that either Zo trusts me, or he doesn't give a fuck about you."

Brooklyn's heart sank. Sadly, she wasn't sure which scenario was true.

Stacey walked her to the door past the probing eyes of the three guys.

"You go straight home now, Brooklyn. No talking to strangers," Wally teased.

Hassan rushed and held the door open for her. As she drew closer to him, he leaned in and spoke to her in a seductive tone. "If you were my girl, I would never have you out here doing this."

She smiled.

"And you got dimples, too?" Hassan's eyes danced. "Just gorgeous."

Brooklyn walked out and Stacey followed her.

"Don't mind them," Stacey said. "They're harmless. But you be careful out here for real. Zo should be ashamed of himself."

Brooklyn turned and faced her. "I know I look young. But Zo's not making me do anything I don't want to do."

"Did he tell you how much time you're facing if you get caught with what you have in that bag?" Stacey let the question linger. She pulled a piece of gum from her pocket and stuck it in her mouth. "Some niggas are tricky. Have you thinking you're making your own decisions, all while they're manipulating you like a pawn on a chessboard. Like I said, be careful."

Stacey walked back into the apartment and Brooklyn took the long journey back to Staten Island.

The trip seemed longer than usual, mostly due to her nervousness. Stacey had given her a lot to think about. She sat on the subway asking herself why she was doing this. She was a pastor's daughter, a high school student, and she was risking it all for a thrill. For the excitement of having sex with a grown man, of being part of some "in" crowd that she clearly didn't fit into. She thought about what Erica said. That Alonzo wasn't the right guy for her. Alonzo had admitted it himself. She knew that she was playing with fire. And she wasn't sure why she liked it.

She got to the ferry terminal on Whitehall Street and walked over to the pay phones. She paged Alonzo with the code he had given her, alerting him that she would be catching the next boat. She stood in the terminal waiting for boarding to begin and recalled meeting Alonzo for the first time in that very place. She had caught his eye and he had sparked a conversation with her. Now, they were embroiled in a taboo love affair, and she was carrying a backpack full of cocaine for him. She imagined what her mother would say if she knew. Sabrina James would surely self-destruct. The thought of it made Brooklyn smile.

She realized then that it was part of the thrill. Knowing that if her mother ever found out, she would disapprove. It fueled Brooklyn's rebellion and made her feel powerful somehow. She knew that to Erica, and clearly to people like Stacey and her crew, a dalliance between a young girl and a man like Alonzo was questionable. But he made Brooklyn feel like a woman. When she was with him, she wasn't the sweet little church girl with the dimpled smile. She was a young lady with ambition. A young lady capable of making shit happen.

Alonzo was waiting for her on the other side, just as they

planned. She got into his car, and they drove back to his apartment. He took the backpack into his bedroom and sorted through the contents in private. Brooklyn went to the kitchen and opened the refrigerator looking for some juice. She found a carton of Minute Maid and a half-empty bottle of white wine. She frowned, wondering when he had started drinking that. She grabbed the juice, shut the refrigerator, and grabbed a glass from the cabinet. He emerged from his bedroom, grabbed her by the waist, and hoisted her into the air, spilling some of the juice in the process.

Brooklyn squealed.

"Stop, Zo! You're making a mess!"

He set her down and planted a long kiss on her lips. "Good job today. I knew you could do it."

She smiled. "We make a good team."

Their partnership lasted the whole summer. Four days a week—since Brooklyn insisted on taking Mondays off—she pretended to head to Manhattan for her messenger job. Instead, she vacillated between two routines. Some days she went to midtown Manhattan and downtown Brooklyn and shopped for clothes, shoes, and jewelry that she stashed in the deepest corners of her closet. Other days, she met up with Alonzo, spent the morning having passionate sex in his king-sized bed, and then headed uptown to meet with Stacey and her crew.

Brooklyn had formed some sort of bond with the Harlem crew over the course of the summer months. Typically, Stacey was alone and the two of them chatted about simple things. Money, music, current events. And men. Stacey seemed to sense that Brooklyn was lost and that she had found some type of sanctuary in Alonzo.

"Don't get too swept up in his world," Stacey warned her. "I was like you once. Then my man got locked up, and I had to start at the bottom again. Thankfully, I had my brother to help me. You gotta make sure you have a safety net. Don't expect that nigga to catch you every time."

Brooklyn enjoyed her conversations with Stacey. After a few interactions with them, she came to find some joy in the banter she shared with Hassan, Wally, and Roscoe, too. Wally was a big guy with a powerful presence and a dry sense of humor. Roscoe was quieter, less imposing, but he was all about business. He seldom smiled.

Hassan was different. Brooklyn wasn't sure what it was that set him apart from the very beginning. Maybe it was the way he flirted with her, openly and brazenly. Or the way he shifted his voice to its lower register when he spoke to her. Whatever it was had her full attention. She found herself putting on her cutest outfits to go uptown, styling her hair differently each time to garner more of his compliments.

He walked her to the train one afternoon in late August.

"You've been coming up here for a few months now," he said. "You're a quick learner."

"Thank you."

They descended the stairs leading underground, mingling with other passengers of various backgrounds. Brooklyn loved that about the city, that it was always bustling with activity and crawling with people of all ethnicities and income levels. Staten Island—while technically part of the city—seemed much less diverse by comparison.

"Stacey even likes you," Hassan said, snapping her out of her thoughts. "And she don't like too many people."

"I like her, too. She gives good advice."

Brooklyn paid her fare and passed through the turnstile. Hassan stood on the other side of the gate talking to her through the gaps.

"Yeah," he said. "She's like that with all of us. I talk to her all the time about the shit I'm dealing with. She's like a hood therapist."

Brooklyn agreed. She looked at him, quizzically.

"What kind of shit do you need advice about?"

He shrugged. "Money. How to make it and what to do with

it. I talk to her about women sometimes. Y'all are hard to figure out."

Brooklyn scoffed. "Whatever!"

Hassan laughed. "Y'all are like puzzles. A thousand fragile pieces."

"Wow. *Fragile*. Good word. Was that on your vocabulary test this week?"

He laughed harder. "Oh! Vocabulary test? I should be asking *you* that question, little girl. How old are you really?"

She smiled. "Old enough to know that I don't have to answer that."

"You're full of secrets, huh?"

"Not really. Why? What do you want to know?"

"Are you and Zo a couple or are you single?" he cut right to the chase.

Brooklyn shrugged. "I'm not sure, honestly."

"But you like him?" Hassan pressed.

She nodded. "Yeah. I like him."

They both watched the train roll into the station. Through the gate, he handed Brooklyn a piece of paper with his phone number on it. "If that ever changes, hit me up."

She took it and smiled. He waved at her and walked away as she boarded the train and headed downtown.

She didn't tell Alonzo about her flirtation with Hassan or about her budding friendship with Stacey. As far as he knew, Brooklyn was heading straight to the spot and coming straight back without getting too involved in what was happening. He had no idea that Brooklyn was learning the game bit by bit.

Brooklyn was doing what her parents had taught her through the years. What she had learned from Mrs. Hutchinson and the church elders. That people believe what they want to believe. Her job was to keep the illusion going. At home and at church, she was the obedient pastor's daughter. With Alonzo, she was the eager student and naive young girl. But she told herself that she was fooling all of them. She wasn't docile or compliant like she led the world to believe. She was plotting, planning for the day when she would make her move. All she had to do was keep performing and she would have what she wanted. To be at the top of the pyramid. Just like her daddy.

Elias was preoccupied lately with the expansion of the church's recreational center. Sabrina was busy soliciting additional funds from local politicians, community leaders, and business owners. Amir and Jordan were continuing their romance while Brooklyn spent her days in Alonzo's arms.

They didn't always meet at his apartment. Sometimes they met at the park and drove around in his car. He'd take her to eat, to do a little shopping, and then they'd go to a motel and have sex for hours before he dropped her off close to home. Their sex was always passionate, always intense, always unprotected.

Brooklyn thought she had everything under control until September came and her period did not.

She was already emotional about the summer coming to an end. Labor Day meant the end of her "part-time summer job," therefore the end of her adventures uptown. She felt cut off from a world she was just beginning to explore. Alonzo told her that it was okay, that he would see her whenever she found the time to slip away, just like they had done before. But Brooklyn wasn't satisfied. As she returned to high school and began her senior year, she fell into a deep depression.

It took her a while to realize what was happening. She was in denial at first, certain that her cycle was just late. But by the third week of September, she was ready to face the truth. She knew that she was about to make the biggest decision of her life.

She talked to Amir about it one Sunday after church. They had fulfilled their duties of the day by looking and acting the part to the pleasure of their parents. Hope was holed up in her room talking on the phone with one of her study buddies. Brooklyn slipped into Amir's room and sat on his bed while he organized his closet.

"How's everything going?" she asked.

Amir laughed. "I should be asking you that. I feel like you've been ducking me for the last few weeks."

Brooklyn looked down at the floor, guiltily. She had been strategically avoiding being alone with her brother for too long since she started making trips uptown. She knew that he already had questions about the guy she was involved with. She was worried that he knew her too well for her to lie to him convincingly. If he probed her too hard or pressed her for details, she wasn't sure that she could keep up the facade.

"I think I got myself in some trouble," she said.

He stopped with the hanger in midair and looked at her. "What happened?"

"The boy I told you about . . . I've been spending a lot of time with him."

"Brooklyn, don't tell me . . ."

"I think I'm pregnant."

Amir dropped the hanger on the floor and leaned against the wall for support. He let out a deep sigh.

"Don't worry," Brooklyn said. "It's okay. I have it all under control."

He huffed.

"Trust me. I'm not that far along. Few weeks maybe. I thought about what my options are."

"What options?" Amir seemed genuinely confused.

Brooklyn understood. In their world, her options were few. But she was determined to go her own way.

"For most girls, this is how it starts. Teen mother, deadbeat baby daddy, downward spiral. I could spend years stuck here chasing dreams that never come true. But that's not me. That's not gonna be my story. I'm handling this on my own."

"What does that mean?" Amir looked as scared as Brooklyn had felt during the first few days after her missed period. But she had done her research and come to terms with her choice.

"I'm gonna get rid of it. And then I'll be more careful from now on. Lesson learned."

Amir frowned at her. She sounded so cavalier about it.

"Wait a minute, hold up. Brooklyn, who is the father? Why have you been so secretive about him? Do I know him? Does he know about this? And what do you mean you're gonna handle it on your own?"

"He's not somebody you know. He's not from around here."

"Where's he from?" Amir asked.

"That doesn't matter." Brooklyn wasn't ready to reveal all the details of her double life just yet. "He's a good guy, treats me nice and all that. I really like him. But not enough to get stuck having a baby at my age. I haven't even told him yet."

"Why not?"

Brooklyn sighed, suddenly weary of Amir's line of questioning.

"I'm just saying, he has a right to know about it," Amir said.

She nodded. "I'm gonna tell him. But my mind is made up, Amir. I know it's a sin to have an abortion. I'll spend the rest of my life praying for forgiveness. But that doesn't change my decision. Daddy preaches that no sin is greater than another. So, what I'm doing—what you and Jordan are doing—is no worse than the shit he's doing."

Amir thought about that. He shrugged. "I don't know if that's true. Maybe you're right. I'm just worried about you. That's all."

"Don't be," she advised him. "Just don't judge me."

"Never," he vowed.

She went to bed that night and imagined what a child would look like with Alonzo's eyes and her smile. She imagined the fit that her parents would throw. She imagined Alonzo's reaction to the news and felt dread wash over her.

Even though her mind was already made up, she wanted to believe that Alonzo cared for her. That their dalliance over the past few months had meant more to him than just sex.

She told him the news one afternoon at his apartment after school.

"You're too young to be a mother," Alonzo said. "And I'm not ready either."

"The system is designed to kill Black babies."

Brooklyn said it bluntly, then tossed the positive EPT pregnancy test kit on the bed. It was a phrase she had read in the "right to life" pamphlet a lady at the Planned Parenthood center had given her.

Alonzo stared at the pregnancy test laying among the crumpled sheets. He shifted his gaze to Brooklyn as he stood at his dresser, pulling cash out of the top drawer.

"We should have used protection. We made a mistake. But you're too young to be a mother. You're too good to be just another statistic. We both know what you have to do."

Brooklyn stared back at him. She wasn't shocked by his reaction, just disappointed. It was clear that he wasn't remotely happy about the news. She had expected just a little smile, a slight glimmer of hope. But instead, he seemed bothered. Now she wished she never told him in the first place. She picked up the pregnancy test.

"I just wanted to see what your reaction would be. I thought you might be happy. Even a little bit."

"I'm happy," Alonzo lied.

"No, you're not." She shook her head. "But it's cool. I planned on having an abortion anyway. It's not even a baby yet," she said. "I looked it up. It's just a few cells in there, so if I do it now, while it's still early, it's not that deep. My mind was already made up before I told you."

He looked at her, his brow furrowed. Brooklyn was an enigma to him. "You don't have to pretend that you don't care. I know you grew up in the church. I'm sure this is hard for you."

"I'll pray about it," she said. "God forgives us for a lot of different things." She gestured at the gun on his dresser to illustrate her point.

Alonzo looked at it and smirked.

Brooklyn continued. "I'm not ready to be a mother. And the last thing you need is a kid to slow you down. My parents would lose their minds. The church would make a federal case out of it. Everything would be chaotic." She sighed. "I went to the Planned Parenthood center and found out how to do it without anybody finding out. All I need is for you to pay for it. And come with me so I don't have to go through it by myself."

He leaned against the dresser and met her gaze. "You know I got you."

She strolled over to him, tossing the pregnancy test into the trash can as she walked. She slid her arms around his waist and kissed him softly on his lips.

"My appointment is Friday morning. I'll meet you here at nine."

His eyes widened. "Damn! You don't waste no time, do you?"

She shook her head. "Time is money." She smoothly slid one of the hundred dollar bills out of his hand.

He laughed and mushed her in the head playfully. "You're crazy."

She smiled, showing those dimples he loved so much. "You are, too. That's why we're good together."

He was there as planned on that rainy Friday morning in early October, leaning against his car wearing a white T-shirt, a Yankees fitted, baggy jeans, and a pair of Filas. To Brooklyn, he looked as handsome as ever. She looked far less glamorous than she usually did when they got together. Instead of her usual skintight jeans, she wore a set of baggy black sweats from the Gap. She wore her hair in a ponytail and no jewelry. She hugged him tightly and he rocked her warmly in his arms.

"You change your mind?" he asked.

Brooklyn pretended not to hear the apprehension in his voice. "No. But I won't lie. I'm kinda nervous."

It was an understatement. She was scared to death, unsure what to expect. Much like the first time they had sex, she wondered if it would hurt, whether anyone would find out, and how she would feel when it was all over.

"We don't have to do this today. We have time. We can get out of here and go get something to eat."

Brooklyn shook her head. "We gotta handle this today. I'll be okay."

He pulled her close. "Stop trying to act so tough all the time. It's okay to let your guard down with me, hard rock."

She smiled, hugged him back, and exhaled. She was glad he was so supportive. Being with him made her feel a little more at ease. He held the car door open for her as she got inside.

On the short ride to the clinic, neither one of them spoke much, both lost in their thoughts. They listened to the radio and made small talk. As they parked a short distance from the facility and prepared to get out of the car, Brooklyn stopped him.

"Am I your only girl?"

He laughed. "What kind of question is that?"

"Just answer it."

"Yeah. You never see me with anybody else."

"But I'm not around all the time. When I'm not, do you mess around with other girls? Maybe older chicks who have their own apartment?"

He laughed again, shaking his head. "Nah. I'm too busy on my grind. It's just me and you."

Her eyes bore into his. "You don't have to lie to me."

"I know. Why are you asking me this now?"

"Because I'm starting to really like you. When I realized I could be pregnant, for a second I imagined a life with you. I don't know if that's how it's gonna go with us. But if it does, I need you to know that you don't have to lie to me. I watched my father lie to my mother, watched her lie to herself my whole life. I want to be with somebody who tells me the truth. Somebody I can trust."

Alonzo nodded. "I hear you loud and clear."

She gathered her things and got ready for the grim task ahead of her.

He stopped with his hand on the door handle and smirked at her. "And, just so you know, ain't no other girls. I got my hands full enough already with you."

She laughed, leaned over to kiss his cheek, and decided to believe him.

Brooklyn woke up in a room all by herself. She felt stickiness between her legs and knew that it was over. She stared up at the bright light above her, closed her eyes, and cried.

A nurse walked in and saw her.

"Oh," she cooed. "What's wrong? Are you in pain?"

Brooklyn shook her head. She wasn't sure how to describe what she was feeling. So many things all at once. Sadness, guilt, and shame all swirled together. She lifted her hands to her face but was impeded on one side by the IV in her arm. Flustered, she used her one free hand to wipe her tears away.

"Don't cry," the nurse said. "You're okay."

Brooklyn nodded, comforted by her words and her soothing voice. As the young nurse took her vital signs, Brooklyn admired the finger waves in her hair. She appreciated the nurse's calm energy at a time like this.

"Your vitals are good. Can you move your legs for me?"

Brooklyn did as she was told.

"Okay. Any numbness, tingling, or pain anywhere?"

Brooklyn shook her head.

"Great." The nurse picked up a clipboard and appeared to be rattling off a checklist. "So, is this your first abortion procedure?"

Brooklyn nodded and guilt washed over her again.

"Have you considered which birth control measures you'll use going forward?"

Brooklyn groaned. These questions seemed ill-timed. Suddenly all she wanted was to be alone.

"It's important to make sure that you don't end up back here," the nurse said. "Abortion is not a suitable method of birth control to use on a routine basis."

Brooklyn stared at the wall in silence while the nurse carefully removed her IV.

"There are several options. You can have the doctor insert an IUD. That's a device placed inside your uterus to prevent pregnancy."

Brooklyn winced at the thought of another invasive procedure.

"Or we can prescribe you an oral contraceptive."

"What's that?" Brooklyn asked, desperate to get this over with.

"Birth control pills. If you choose that option, you'll have to make sure that you take them every day, preferably at the same time. If you miss doses, it lowers the effectiveness." She removed her gloves and disposed of them before looking at Brooklyn again. "Have you thought about it?"

"The pills," Brooklyn said. "I'll take those."

The nurse nodded. "Regardless of which method of birth control you choose, you need to start using condoms. Don't rely on your partner to have them. Ladies carry them around now because we figured out it's up to us to protect ourselves. Other contraceptives might prevent pregnancy, but the only way to protect against HIV and other sexually translated diseases is to use condoms."

Brooklyn stared at the nurse blankly, wishing she would go away. She was annoyed by her presence now and her facial expression showed it.

"We'll bring you something light to eat, and then you'll be released. Is someone here to take you home?"

Brooklyn nodded.

"Good," the nurse said. "You'll be out of here in no time."

To Brooklyn's relief, the nurse set two small packs of crackers and some water on the tray table and left. Brooklyn was glad to see her go. She thought about what she had just been through, wondered whether the baby would have been a boy or a girl. Shuddering at the thought, she sat up in the bed, grimacing a little at the ache in the hollows of her gut. She hadn't eaten a thing since dinner the night before, so she hungrily devoured the crackers and washed them down with a long gulp of water.

She thought about her parents and what they would think of her now. She sneered at the thought, deciding that it didn't matter. They were so caught up in their make-believe world—pretending that the James family was the picture of godliness—that they didn't notice how imperfect things truly were. That Amir was gay, and that Brooklyn had just terminated an unwanted teen pregnancy. For all she knew, Hope might have been living a double life of her own. Meanwhile, their parents were busy counting money and practicing hypocrisy in various forms.

The nurse returned with her clothes and some instructions on how to care for herself post-procedure.

"Follow up with your GYN in six weeks. No sex until then. Be gentle with yourself. Don't forget that your body needs time to heal from what you've been through. Make sure you take it easy."

Brooklyn thanked her and decided that maybe the nurse wasn't so bad after all. She was given a starter pack of birth control pills and a prescription for more. When the nurse was gone, she got dressed and quietly exited the room.

She found Alonzo slouched in a chair in the back corner of the waiting room. He stood and walked toward her when she entered.

"How you feel?"

Brooklyn could see the concern on his face and could hear it in his tone of voice. She shrugged.

"I'm okay. I just want to get out of here."

He nodded. "Let's go."

He took her by the hand, and they left together and walked to his car in silence. He could sense that she was deep in thought, and he wasn't sure how to break the ice. When they got into his car, he put the key in the ignition, sat back, and looked at her.

"You wanna talk about it?"

She stared straight ahead at the dashboard as she spoke.

"I feel okay. Physically. But deep inside I feel really sad. I know I did the right thing for right now. I wasn't ready for a baby." She wiped a tear away. "But I still feel guilty. I want to take a shower and wash this whole day off of me. I want to start over, Zo." She turned and stared absently out the window on the passenger side. "I gotta get the fuck out of here. This place feels like it has me in a chokehold."

"You mean the church and your parents and all that?" he asked.

"Yeah. Them, my teachers, *everybody's* always watching me. But it's not just the people. It's this place in general. I want to leave Staten Island and just escape from all this . . ." The words escaped her, and she flopped her hands in her lap helplessly. "I wake up every day here and I know exactly what to expect. I know I don't belong here. I want to leave all this behind and be in charge of my own thing."

"What's that thing?" he asked. "What you wanna do?"

She thought about the things that interested her. She liked to pamper herself and imagined herself in the beauty business. Maybe she could start doing hair and run a salon of her own someday. She liked expensive clothes even though her parents wouldn't let her buy them. She often looked at the designer labels people on the subway wore with envy, imagining better ways they could have styled their pieces. She imagined herself owning a boutique.

She shrugged. "I'm not sure."

Alonzo smirked. "When you figure it out, let me know. And we'll make it happen." He took her hand and linked his fingers with hers. "You went through a lot today. It's got you thinking a lot and worrying too much. Just take it easy right now. Try to take your mind off everything." He grinned. "You hungry?"

"Starving!" Her stomach growled for emphasis.

He started the car. "Let's eat." He glanced at her once more. "Shit ain't gonna be like this forever. We're gonna get up out of here. Both of us. I won't be hustling forever. Just long enough to get established. When I get to the level I'm striving for, I'm gonna look out for everybody I rock with. Including you. Once I get this money flowing how I want it to, it's on. Whatever you want to do. I mean that. I got you, Brooklyn."

She felt her icy heart melt a little. And for the first time in weeks, she felt hopeful.

Chapter Four

Revelations

"Do you feel guilty?" Amir asked.

They sat together on the back pew of the church near the exit, waiting for their parents to wrap up their business so that they all could go home. Sunday service had ended hours ago, but for the pastor and first lady the duties didn't end there. Their sister Hope was downstairs in the lower hall helping the Sunday school teachers clean up. Amir seized the opportunity to ask the question. Moments alone with Brooklyn were increasingly rare these days.

"I prayed for forgiveness," she said.

Her eyes swept across the room, taking it all in. She admitted silently to herself that it really was a beautiful church. The stained glass windows reflected the autumn sunshine beautifully. The cushioned pews had neatly stacked Bibles and hymnals placed perfectly for each congregant's use. The pulpit loomed over it all with three throne-like chairs for the pastor and his associate ministers to perch upon.

"It's weird sitting back here, right?" she asked, changing the subject. "We're usually up front. All eyes on us. Being back here is the real bird's-eye view." She grinned. "Who's passing the offering plate without tipping, who's sneaking out early. This is the best seat in the house."

Amir searched her face for signs of remorse. He found none, and that worried him.

"I need you to talk to me, little sister. I know you think you have everything under control. But it's hard for me to keep your secrets and help you cover your tracks if I don't know what's going on."

"I understand."

"I'm worried about you."

She sighed. "It's all good, Amir. I promise." She raised her eyebrows and tilted her head to the side. "But I'm worried about you, too. We had a conversation months ago about you getting out of here, living your life for real. And you're still here."

"You don't know what my plans are."

"So, tell me. What's this big master plan? Because it seems to me like all you're doing is getting up every morning and repeating the same routine. Living the same lie."

He recoiled a bit at her choice of words but recovered quickly. "I remember the way the family almost fell apart when that situation happened with Uncle Morris. I never saw Dad that upset or saw Mom that scared. What he did to you was wrong. And how they handled it was worse. But I learned something important when that happened. Our family, this church, the whole thing—it's fragile. One scandal can bring it all tumbling down. Even if it's something that wasn't our fault. You weren't to blame for what Uncle Morris did to you. And it's not my choice to be the way that I am. But it doesn't matter. Because if the world knew the truth about any of it, the whole thing crumbles." He sighed, staring down at his hands in his lap. "I'm not gonna be the reason that happens. I plan to live my life. Someday. Away from here where it doesn't affect this." He gestured around the sanctuary. "I'm still trying to figure out how to do that. Maybe I'm moving too slowly for you. But I'm moving at my pace."

Brooklyn decided to let it go. Even though she wanted to press further, she realized that her brother wasn't budging.

"You just worry about yourself," he advised. "Make sure you're not risking your heart."

Brooklyn sighed. "I'm not. I really like him. We're just counting the days until graduation so I can bounce."

"That's not until next year. In the meantime, you and your mystery guy better take your time. Don't make the same mistake twice."

She sighed. "Okay, big brother. I won't."

Erica and Jordan approached. Amir and Brooklyn were both grateful for the distraction. They greeted their friends as they sat down nearby.

"Wassup, y'all? Your mother said to tell you they're almost done." Erica delivered the message as promised.

Brooklyn rolled her eyes. "Thanks."

"I'm about to get out of here, too," Jordan said. "Gotta work in the morning."

Erica didn't notice the eye contact between Jordan and Amir when he said it.

Brooklyn might not have either if she wasn't aware of the secret love affair between them. She watched their exchange and stared at Jordan as he spoke about the high-profile case he was working on as a paralegal at his firm. She had never given much thought to Jordan over the years. Like Amir, he was humble and unassuming. Brooklyn hadn't noticed how handsome he was, how well-groomed and confident. His voice was deep and melodic, and she found herself hanging on his every word as he spoke. She was seeing him with fresh eyes, suddenly understanding a little better the reasons why Amir was reluctant to leave. Jordan was on the rise in his career, maneuvering at the firm and in the world at large as a heterosexual man. He had tons of reasons to hide the truth. Like Amir, he was allowing the world to perceive him in a way that made them feel comfortable.

But unlike Jordan, Amir wasn't establishing himself in some big corporate career and solidifying his future. Brooklyn understood that Amir was shrinking himself to fit inside of a world he didn't belong in. She only wished he could see that for himself.

She groaned seeing her parents approaching. Erica cleared her throat and Jordan straightened up.

"Good evening, young people!" Elias's voice was as exuberant as the expression on his face.

"Hey, Pastor and First Lady!" Erica said.

Jordan greeted them as well, while Brooklyn looked her parents up and down. As usual, her mother wore a pencil skirt and neat blouse with a sensible pair of heels. Her hair hung loosely at her shoulders, and she had her perpetual smile plastered on her face.

"Great service today," Sabrina said. "Let's get home so I can put these pies in the oven before it gets too late to eat a slice." She rubbed her tiny waistline, hoping someone would point out how fit she was and that she had nothing to worry about.

Brooklyn ignored her and stood up. She hugged Erica goodbye. "See you tomorrow."

"I have to talk to you," Erica whispered. "Call me tonight."

Brooklyn pulled back and searched her friend's face for clues of what she wanted to discuss. Erica smiled back at her, aware that the adults were watching.

Brooklyn nodded.

She couldn't stop thinking about it the whole way home. She wondered what her friend wanted to tell her, and she waited anxiously for a chance to use the phone when her parents were occupied with other things.

Finally, while her parents were engrossed in an episode of the TV show *60 Minutes*, Brooklyn called Erica while she knew she had at least an hour to speak freely.

"Hey," she said when Erica answered. "What's going on?"

"Not much. Just finished eating dinner. Getting ready for school tomorrow."

Brooklyn rolled her eyes, annoyed that Erica was droning on about mundane things when she had been sitting on the edge of her seat for hours.

"What did you want to talk to me about? You sounded so mysterious when you whispered in my ear at church."

Erica sat on her bed with the cordless phone and closed her eyes. She knew that what she was about to tell her best friend would break her heart.

"It's about Alonzo."

"What? What about him?" Brooklyn hadn't spoken to him since Friday. She had paged him after school, hoping to see him for an hour or so before she had to be home for her father's birthday celebration. But Alonzo said that he was busy, and the rest of the weekend had been packed with family activities that prevented her from contacting him again.

"What happened?"

"I'm in a tough position," Erica said. "He's my cousin. He looks out for my family, and I love him. I just want you to know that telling you this feels a little like I'm betraying him."

A shiver of dread ran down Brooklyn's spine. She could already tell where this was heading.

"I understand," she said.

"Zo is older than us. I tried to warn you from the start that you might not be ready for a guy like him. He has a lot of money, access, and power. He has a lot of girls, too."

Brooklyn wished it stung less than it did. "I'm not dumb. I assumed I wasn't the only one."

"Did he tell you about Janine?"

Brooklyn sucked her teeth. "I'm not worried about other girls. I know what Zo is like when he's with me. And that's all that matters."

Erica groaned. "Brooklyn, he's getting ready to get married."

"Married?" Brooklyn froze.

"It's this girl named Janine. She's older than us. Like twenty-two, I think. She's in college and he pays for it. Got her in an apartment on the other side of the island in this nice building. He bought her a car. I didn't know it was that serious until he brought her to my aunt's house for a dinner party yesterday. She was flashing the ring around, showing everybody. And I pulled

Zo to the side and asked him if he told you. He shrugged it off, said that you know what time it is. So, I figured it's the right thing to do as a friend just to tell you. In case you didn't know."

Brooklyn wasn't sure what to say. She thought about the child she had aborted weeks earlier, the promises he made to look out for her. She felt dumb.

"Married?"

"I'm sorry to be the one to tell you. Zo should have been man enough to tell you himself. But my aunt always tells me that men like to have their cake and eat it, too. I know you care about him. I know this hurts. Just know that he's my family, but I'm on your side. You deserve better than this."

"I'm not even sure what to say," Brooklyn admitted. "Thank you for telling me, though. I'll see you in school tomorrow."

She hung up the phone and cried quietly to herself. With tears blurring her vision, she picked the phone back up and dialed Alonzo's pager number. She put in her special code—111—and her home phone number. Alonzo had never called her at home before. Brooklyn had been too afraid of the questions her parents would ask about who he was and what the nature of their relationship was. She knew that she was taking a chance. But she needed to talk to Alonzo immediately. Her heart wouldn't let her wait.

She felt powerless, waiting by the phone for him to call back. She paged him again and again, but he never called. She thought back to their last conversation and recalled how evasive he'd been about what he was doing and where he was going. All he would tell her was that he was busy, too busy to see her.

She tried to recall whether the mood between them had been any different the last time they were together. The doctor had advised her to avoid sexual activity for at least six weeks. In that time, she hadn't seen much of Alonzo. He was hustling, she was back in school, and she assumed their prolonged absence from each other was just a consequence of their lives. Now she knew the truth. That he was likely done with her, and the feeling of freedom and the thrill of the life she had been living for the past several months was a temporary high. Suddenly she felt her life was in a freefall.

All night she thought about the child she had aborted, the trips she had made uptown, and the bond she thought she had been building with Alonzo in the months since their relationship started. She felt betrayed, abandoned, discarded. Those feelings kept her awake all night, lying in the darkness of her bedroom eager for sunrise.

She left the house early the next morning pretending that she was headed to school. Instead, she made a beeline for the projects, stormed into Alonzo's building, and charged up the stairs. She didn't bother waiting for the elevator, too high on adrenaline to be patient.

She rushed down the hall to his apartment and banged on the door several times. She paused a moment, then banged again in quick succession. She heard movement, the locks being undone, the chain sliding from its latch, and Alonzo stepped out into the hallway.

"What the fuck are you doing here?" he demanded, his chest heaving. "Knocking on my door like the fuckin' police!"

"Who's in there? Why can't I come inside?"

"You don't ever come over here without telling me first!"

"I tried paging you, but you won't call me back!"

"Then you wait until I do!"

Brooklyn's heart broke a little more. Alonzo had never talked to her in this tone of voice before. His tone and body language were aggressive. It was clear that her presence was unwelcome there.

Her instincts told her there was a reason for that.

"Who's in there? Janine?"

His face registered surprise. For a moment, it seemed like he was prepared to deny it. But he smirked, stepped back, and nodded.

"Yeah. Erica told you, huh?" He shrugged. "So, now you know.

I wasn't trying to hurt your feelings, Brooklyn. I kept telling you that—"

"You told me that you had my back. Remember that?"

The door opened behind him, and a woman stood behind him wearing nothing but a T-shirt and a pair of black panties. She was pretty, brown-skinned, and voluptuous. She stared at Brooklyn with a disgusted expression on her face.

"Who's this?" she asked Alonzo.

"Who are *you*?" Brooklyn asked, her face twisted up as well.

"Janine," the woman said. "Can we help you?"

Alonzo stood between them looking like he'd rather be anyplace else.

"She's leaving," he said.

"No, I'm not." Brooklyn started taking off her earrings like she had seen girls do countless times in the school cafeteria and in movies.

Fueled by heartbreak and embarrassment, she charged past Alonzo and rushed Janine, catching her off guard. The force sent both of them tumbling into the apartment, where they fought viciously in the doorway.

"Stop!" Alonzo yelled repeatedly to no avail.

Brooklyn grabbed Janine by the hair and swung at her, landing blow after blow. But she was no match for her opponent. While Brooklyn landed several hard slaps and a few scratches, Janine easily overpowered her. She straddled Brooklyn, raining down punches to her face and head mercilessly until Alonzo finally managed to drag her away.

"BITCH!" Janine yelled, towering over Brooklyn as she lay in a defeated heap on the apartment floor. "Get the fuck out of here!"

"Chill!" Alonzo yelled at her, nudging her gently toward the living room. "Go in there. Let me get her up."

"I'm not going nowhere. This ho done lost her mind. Who is this little fucking girl, Zo? You got these silly bitches coming in here trying to fight me?"

"RELAX!" he yelled, helping Brooklyn off the floor.

She could feel that her lip was swollen, and her left eye was throbbing. Her body ached as she stood. She had never felt more embarrassed in her life. But the defiant spirit within her longed to have the last word.

"You're the silly bitch, thinking he's gonna marry you."

Janine stormed into the living room and grabbed a bottle off the coffee table. Brooklyn watched her, staring at the bottle in her hand, recognizing it as the same type of wine bottle she had seen in Alonzo's refrigerator the last time she was there. As Janine rushed toward her with the bottle in her hand, Brooklyn ducked, Alonzo stepped between them and began wrestling the bottle from Janine's hand.

Brooklyn forced a laugh as Janine riddled her with insults and vowed to kick her ass again the next time she saw her.

"Whatever, bitch!" Brooklyn yelled back.

A couple of Alonzo's neighbors opened their apartment doors to see what all the fuss was about. Embarrassed and afraid that someone would recognize her as the pastor's daughter, she rushed down the hallway and ran down the stairs as fast as she could.

When she got outside, she didn't fight the tears that poured forth. She knew she looked terrible. She could taste blood in her mouth and the pain in her inner cheek where her teeth had cut the flesh. She could feel her left eye swelling and wondered how she would explain this to her parents.

She walked aimlessly down the block, considering what would happen if she just never went home. If she just got on the ferry to Manhattan, and blended into the sea of people there. There, no one would look twice at her torn jacket, black eye, and swollen mouth. She wanted desperately to get away, to run for her life and escape the fishbowl she was living in. She felt like everyone was watching and controlling her, manipulating her, and lying to her. It made her sick to her stomach.

She heard a car horn as she walked down Richmond Terrace. At first she ignored it. But when it honked twice more, she turned in the direction of the car and saw Zo behind the wheel.

"Let me take you home," he said. "Stop acting like that."

She stopped walking. "You know what? FUCK YOU!"

"It's like that, huh?" He drove slowly beside her as she kept walking. Ignoring the drivers behind him blaring their horns at him to speed up, he talked to her through his open window. "I don't want to end off like this. I apologize, Brooklyn."

She stopped again and watched as he pulled over to the curb. Against her better judgment, she walked over and climbed into the passenger seat.

"I'm not going home," she said. "So, don't drive me there. Just say what you gotta say and let me go."

"Where you going looking like that?" he asked. He flipped down the visor over the passenger seat and angled the mirror so she could see herself.

Brooklyn saw herself and wanted to cry. The left side of her face looked like she had been in a battle with Mike Tyson. Her lip was swollen and crusted with dried blood. Her eye was discolored and red inside.

"I'm getting the fuck out of here," she answered. "That's where I'm going." She shook her head. "I must be a fucking idiot thinking I could trust you."

"I never lied to you, Brooklyn."

"You damn sure didn't tell me that you were getting married. You never mentioned her at all."

"I was gonna tell you. I just needed time."

"Cool. Well, now I know. You can leave me alone from now on."

She ignored his protests as she climbed out of the car. She slammed the door for good measure and stormed off toward the nearest bus stop a block ahead.

Then she heard the screeching of tires and the sound of Alonzo's car horn blaring. She turned around and saw that an unmarked police car with its blue light flashing on the dashboard had cut Alonzo off as he prepared to weave into traffic.

"GET OUT OF THE CAR WITH YOUR HANDS UP!"

Brooklyn gasped, dropped her backpack, and ran in the direction of Alonzo's car. She saw him climb out of the car with his arms raised above his head. The police were out of their vehicle now, and the two officers approached him slowly with their guns drawn.

"What did he do?" Brooklyn demanded as she continued running toward the scene. "Why are you bothering him?"

"Step back!" one of the cops demanded, glaring in her direction.

"No!" she shouted. She was only a few feet away from them now. She watched as they cuffed Alonzo and began rifling through his pockets. "What the fuck is happening? What did he do?"

"Do you know him?" one of the cops asked Brooklyn. "Did he beat you up like this?"

"No! He didn't do anything."

"What's he, your boyfriend?" The cop huffed. "Real winner you got here."

The other officer searched Alonzo's car for something. Brooklyn continued to shout.

"What's the reason you pulled him over? Did y'all even read him his rights? I don't think you're supposed to search the car without a warrant!"

Brooklyn heard footsteps nearing. She groaned, realizing it was Miss Nancy, the deaconess from Promised Land Church who lived for gossip.

"BROOKLYN! What are you doing out here? What happened to you? Who is this?" Miss Nancy stared in Alonzo's direction.

"He's my friend. The cops are bothering him for no reason."

"Your friend?" Miss Nancy frowned. "Is that Mrs. Hutchinson's son?"

Brooklyn didn't respond. She stormed over to one of the cops and got in his face.

"He didn't do anything. What's the problem?"

The cop loomed over Brooklyn. "I'm not gonna tell you again. BACK UP!"

Brooklyn felt Miss Nancy pulling her backward.

"Brooklyn, come with me," Miss Nancy demanded.

Brooklyn was frantic. "They only pulled him over because he's a Black guy driving a nice car."

"Then they'll have to let him go," Miss Nancy reasoned. "He have anything in the car that might get him in trouble?"

Brooklyn shrugged, then shook her head no. Miss Nancy seemed to understand what that meant. She nodded, knowingly, and looked at the cops again.

"Let me talk to the officers. I'll be right back."

Brooklyn watched as Miss Nancy greeted the officers politely and explained who she was.

"I'm Deaconess Nancy Allen from Promised Land Church. These young people are the children of our pastor and one of the church's trustees. I'm sure this is just a misunderstanding."

The officer seemed unimpressed. "I appreciate your concern, ma'am. But I have to ask you to let us do our job. The young lady is free to go. The driver is under arrest."

"For what?" Miss Nancy asked.

"Drug possession with intent to sell." He looked at Brooklyn. "You mind if we search your backpack?"

Brooklyn watched Alonzo being ushered into the back of the police car and felt her heart sink.

Miss Nancy answered for her. "You can search it. This is the pastor's daughter. She has nothing to hide."

Brooklyn watched the officers go through every crevice of her bag and thought back to her trips to Harlem over the summer. Each time she had transported backpacks stuffed with cash and drugs. A search like this would have meant doom for her. Even now, knowing that there was nothing incriminating in her bag, her heart pounded in her chest as she watched the officer conducting his search. Finally, he handed the bag back to her and nodded.

"You're free to go."

Miss Nancy thanked the officer and ushered Brooklyn to her car nearby. "Let me take you home."

Brooklyn protested, but Miss Nancy made it clear that she wasn't asking. The moment they were in the car, she started it up, and lit into her with questions.

"Did he hit you, Brooklyn?"

"No!" she said for the umpteenth time. "I got in a fight with a girl. He was just trying to take me home."

Miss Nancy nodded. "It's okay. We've all been in fights before."

They rode in silence and Brooklyn was grateful for it. Her mind was reeling. Alonzo was marrying someone else, that woman had kicked Brooklyn's ass, and then he had been arrested right before her eyes. She felt like her whole world was crashing down around her.

It took her too long to realize that Miss Nancy wasn't driving her home. By the time she realized that they were pulling up in front of Promised Land, it was too late to protest. To Brooklyn's chagrin, her mother was standing at the gate talking to Mrs. Hutchinson.

"Stay here," Miss Nancy said. "We don't need the whole church seeing you like this. Just let me go and get your mama."

Brooklyn wanted to ask her not to, but she knew it was futile. Miss Nancy dreamed of moments like this. Brooklyn watched as Nancy walked over and delivered the news to both women that their children were in crisis. Mrs. Hutchinson ran off in the direction of her car and drove away quickly.

Sabrina stared in the direction of Miss Nancy's car for what felt like forever before she strolled toward it. Brooklyn felt a lump in her throat and knew that she was in major trouble.

Sabrina walked over to the passenger door and opened it. "Get out of the car, Brooklyn."

She did as she was told, avoiding eye contact with her mother.

Miss Nancy inserted herself again. "It was just a fight," she said. "Brooklyn said Alonzo didn't lay a hand on her."

Sabrina nodded without taking her eyes off her daughter. "You're supposed to be in school," she said, evenly.

Brooklyn didn't answer.

Sabrina turned to Miss Nancy and forced a smile. "Thank you for bringing her here."

Miss Nancy smiled back, brightly. "Of course, First Lady! If there's anything you need, I'm just a phone call away."

Sabrina grabbed Brooklyn by the arm and marched her toward her car. The second they were inside, she turned to her daughter, glaring.

"Do you know how embarrassing this is? You're supposed to be in school. Instead, you're out here running around with a grown man! Did he beat you up?"

Brooklyn didn't answer. Sabrina was trembling with rage, her eyes full of contempt as she stared at her daughter. She shook her head and looked away, disgusted. Seeing several of the church personnel outside, knowing that this would be a topic of discussion thanks to Miss Nancy was all mortifying to her. She spotted her husband approaching, walking swiftly in their direction and she climbed out of the car to meet him halfway.

Elias was out of breath when he got to her. "What happened? I was in a meeting with the city councilman and Miss Nancy said you were down here." He glanced toward the car and saw his daughter slumped in the passenger seat. "What's Brooklyn doing here? Is she okay?"

"No, she's not okay. She's supposed to be in school. Instead, Miss Nancy found her in a confrontation with the police."

"What?" He glanced at Brooklyn again. "The police?"

"I was outside talking to Mrs. Hutchinson. Miss Nancy came

over and told us that she was driving down Richmond Terrace and she saw a commotion between Mrs. Hutchinson's son and the cops. She said that Brooklyn was there yelling and screaming, and she was all beaten up—"

Elias didn't need to hear any more. He was already half running toward the car.

Brooklyn saw him coming and braced herself. He pulled the car door open and looked at her bloody and bruised face, her torn jacket, and he visibly fumed.

"What happened to you? Get out of the car!"

Sabrina was suddenly at his side.

"Let's handle this at home, Eli. There's a lot of people around." She imagined that Miss Nancy was already inside spreading the gossip to anyone who would listen. "I'll take her home. You meet us there."

Brooklyn got nervous. The short ride home would surely feel like an eternity alone in a car with her mother.

Elias wanted answers now.

"What happened to you?" he asked his daughter again.

"I got in a fight with a girl who's been bothering me. I was on my way home, and Zo saw me walking."

"*ZO*?" Elias's voice was loud, causing Sabrina to look around nervously, always concerned about public perception. "*Alonzo Hutchinson*? Since when did you get involved with him enough to call him '*Zo*'?"

"Eli, let's do this at home," Sabrina urged again. "We don't need anybody to see her like this."

Without another word, Elias turned and faced his wife, breathing deeply. Then he walked off toward his car. "Meet me there now!"

Sabrina got behind the wheel, started the car, and followed her husband home.

"Brooklyn, you've been lying to us. I know you have. And I'm sick of it. This is the last straw."

Brooklyn frowned but didn't respond. She wondered what the hell her mother was talking about. Sabrina knew nothing about the depth of Brooklyn's relationship with Alonzo, her absences from school, her activities as a drug mule. All she knew was that she'd had a fight and a minor run-in with the cops. If that was the last straw, Brooklyn believed it was because Sabrina had been waiting for an excuse to pounce on her.

There was no further conversation, not even the gospel music her mother typically played in the car. The ride felt like doomsday to Brooklyn. She knew the face-off she was about to have with her parents wouldn't be easy.

The moment they got inside, Sabrina ordered Brooklyn to go and clean herself up and change clothes. Brooklyn did as she was told, gently washing the dried-up blood off her face. She was sore and appalled by her own reflection staring back at her in the mirror. She put some cocoa butter on her face and changed into a FUBU sweat suit before she joined her parents downstairs.

While Brooklyn got herself together, Sabrina continued giving her husband the story.

"Like I told you, Nancy was driving and found Brooklyn out there with that boy—that *hoodlum* Alonzo! The cops had pulled him over and she was making a scene, screaming, and cursing at them. Nancy said they searched Brooklyn's backpack, asked her a few questions, and let her go." Sabrina exhaled deeply. "As for the way she looks, she insists that Alonzo didn't lay a hand on her. Told Nancy the same thing. So, not only is she cutting school, running around with thugs, and having encounters with the police, but she's fighting in the street, too." She threw up her hands, frustrated by her inability to understand her own child.

Brooklyn stepped into the kitchen where they sat huddled together at the table. She glanced sheepishly at her parents.

Elias's face was contorted as he began walking toward his daughter while trying to process the information his wife had just given him.

"Brooklyn, tell me what happened."

She looked at him with tears in her eyes. "Daddy, a girl at school has been bothering me. Picking on me for being a church girl and all of that. I got sick of ducking and dodging her all the time. So, today I went and confronted her, and we fought. I was walking home, and Alonzo saw me. He offered to give me a ride. He's Erica's cousin, so we met through her. But we weren't doing anything wrong. He's just my friend. He offered to give me a ride home, and that's when the cops just pulled him over for no reason."

She began to cry softly.

Elias pulled her into his arms. "It's okay. Calm down."

Sabrina sucked her teeth. "You can't be serious!" she hissed. "Stop babying her, Eli! She's been lying to us and running around with some idiot who almost got her arrested."

Elias side-eyed his wife. Sabrina angrily stormed upstairs.

He looked down at his daughter. "You know you're in trouble, right?"

She nodded.

"What's going on with you? And don't lie to me." Elias could sense that his daughter was in turmoil. It was written all over her. He led her to the couch, and they sat down together.

"It's nothing serious."

He huffed. "Looks serious to me."

"It was just a fight. She's bigger than me, and I've never been in a fight before. So, I lost." She shook her head, embarrassed to admit that. "I didn't tell you about it because I was trying to handle it myself. Trying to avoid her if I could. But I got tired of running from her and I fought back."

"What's this girl's name?" Elias asked.

"I don't want to tell you. I don't need you coming to my school making a big deal out of it. Everybody already thinks I'm a goody-goody. If you get involved, it's only gonna make things worse."

Elias thought about it. "What about this '*Zo*'? Are you telling me the truth about him?"

Brooklyn nodded. "He was just being nice. He saw how I looked and wanted to help. The cops stopped him, and I tried to defend him. But I wasn't doing everything Miss Nancy said I was doing. She's being dramatic."

Elias shook his head. Nancy was known for exaggerating. But something in his gut still worried him about Brooklyn.

"You know that you can talk to me, right? About anything, anytime."

She nodded.

"You can trust me. Your mother, too."

She stared back at him, tempted to remind him of her history with her mother. But she knew that she was already treading on thin ice. So, she kept her mouth shut.

"She's upset. Just give her some space. In a little while, when she calms down, we'll talk about this." Elias rubbed his head. As a pastor, he often felt the weight of other people's problems. They paled in comparison to the pressure he was feeling now seeing his own child in distress.

"Come take a ride with me," he said. "I have some sick and shut-in members to visit. You can sit in the car while I visit with them. Give your mother some time to calm down."

Brooklyn didn't protest.

Chapter Five

Forgive Them, Father

She spent the afternoon with her father going to visit his sick and elderly congregants at nursing facilities and in their homes. While he went inside and spent ten to fifteen minutes at each location, Brooklyn sat in the car listening to music on the radio and wondering what was going on with Alonzo. She knew he had been arrested and couldn't help worrying about his well-being. Even though he had broken her heart, she still hated the idea of him being caged.

She kept peeking at her reflection in the mirror even though she knew it wouldn't improve magically. She looked terrible and dreaded the inevitable questions that would surely come when she faced her family and peers.

After he completed all of his visits, Elias drove back to the church. He needed to grab some paperwork from his office, he explained, then they would go and get something to eat.

Brooklyn remained seated in the car as her father climbed out. Elias stood waiting for her to get out and frowned when he realized she wasn't budging.

"I'm not ashamed of you," he said. "Your mother is worried about image and all that. I'm not. You're my daughter. Beat up or not." He grinned at her, reassuringly.

She sighed. "What if somebody sees me and asks what happened?"

"Church is empty tonight except for a missionary meeting.

Half of them have cataracts, so they won't know what they're looking at."

She laughed, got out of the car, and followed him inside.

She breathed a sigh of relief as she realized that the missionaries were conducting their meeting downstairs in the lower hall. She followed her father into his office without being seen and took a seat in the corner.

"It's very peaceful in here," she said. "I bet people come in here and tell you everything."

He chuckled. "Sometimes." He grabbed the paperwork from his desk, tucked it into the inner pocket of his trench coat, and walked over to Brooklyn. "Other times, we do a lot of praying in here. I want to pray with you now."

Looking up at him, she nodded. They closed their eyes, and Elias held his daughter's hands as he prayed for courage, and wisdom to deal with the bullies in their lives—and for the healing of her body, mind, and spirit.

"Finally, God, we ask that you heal our family. Strengthen us. In Jesus' name. Amen."

"Amen." Brooklyn rose from her seat and followed her father out.

As they paused outside Elias's office while he locked it up for the night, the door of the church swung open, and Mrs. Hutchinson rushed in.

She seemed relieved to see the pastor and began speaking almost immediately.

"Thank God you're here. I need to talk to you in private."

It was clear to Brooklyn that Mrs. Hutchinson was in a rush. She held a large Timberland shoebox in her hand and had a Gucci handbag draped across her shoulder. Brooklyn recognized the size 11 shoebox from Zo's apartment.

Elias unlocked his office door and ushered Mrs. Hutchinson inside. He looked at Brooklyn.

"Wait here."

Brooklyn nodded and watched him step into his office and shut the door.

The moment it closed, Brooklyn pressed her ear against it and listened as hard as she could.

"I need you to hold this for me. The cops are searching everywhere and seizing everything."

Brooklyn could hear Mrs. Hutchinson's anxious voice clearly. But her father's muffled response was unclear. She pressed her ear closer but could only make out the sound of Mrs. Hutchinson's voice as she spoke between sobs.

"They said they pulled him over because of the tints on his windows. They're charging him with drug possession with intent to sell. I got lawyers and all that, but even they say he's facing some time."

Brooklyn made out some of Elias's response.

"Don't worry, Mrs. Hutchinson. God is in control. My family and I will be praying for you. You know we'll do everything we can to help you get through this."

"Take this as an offering," Mrs. Hutchinson said.

"Thank you so much." This time Brooklyn heard her father's voice loud and clear.

She heard their footsteps approaching and rushed over to a nearby chair. By the time her father and Mrs. Hutchinson emerged, Brooklyn was sitting cross-legged pretending to read through a Sunday school booklet.

"Thank you," Mrs. Hutchinson said. She smiled at Brooklyn as she stepped out. "Y'all have a good night."

She exited the same way she came.

Brooklyn looked at her father. "Everything okay?"

He nodded. "Yup. Come on."

She followed him out, thinking about what she'd overheard. It sounded like Alonzo was in big trouble. Despite the fact that he had broken her heart, she still felt bad for him. She prayed that he was safe and things worked out in his favor. She wondered what was in the shoebox his mother had rushed into the pastor's office carrying, and what the police had already found in their case against Alonzo. She wondered how much of an "offering" Mrs. Hutchinson had given.

They stopped at McDonald's on the way home. As they pulled into the parking lot, Brooklyn groaned.

"I know you're not ashamed of me. But I'm too ashamed of myself to walk in there looking like this. It's bad enough I have to face my friends at school."

He nodded. "Okay. I understand."

They used the drive-through and ordered their food. Then they parked in the lot and sat eating together in his car. Brooklyn marveled at how much her father clearly loved her. He seldom let the family eat in his car unless they were on long road trips. But Elias made an exception for Brooklyn that day. They spread their paper wrappings in their laps and dug into their cheeseburgers together.

She felt guilty for lying to him and wished she could tell him the truth. That she had suffered her first heartbreak and gotten beaten up as the icing on a very unsavory cake. The thought of her father's disappointment kept her from telling him what was really going on. Her goal now was to keep the illusion going. To make him believe that she really was the daughter he wanted her to be.

"I'm sorry for embarrassing us," she said as she finished her Quarter Pounder. "I know Miss Nancy is gonna spread the news all around the church. I know it makes us look bad. I'm sorry, Daddy."

"People are gonna talk. There's no stopping that. Let them talk." He finished his own burger and looked over at her. He took her hand in his. "You're my daughter and I love you. I want to protect you. But as much as I love you, God loves you more. And when I can't be there to protect you, He's always there watching over you. So, I don't worry about you too much. I know that you're protected by your father in the physical and by your Father in heaven."

She loved him so much at that moment and knew it would be seared into her memory for life. Without realizing it, Elias had said exactly what she needed to hear to comfort her weary soul. There was so much about her life that her father wasn't aware of. The drugs she had transported, the child she had aborted. Reminded that God had been watching over her through all of it, she became emotional. Tears poured forth from her eyes and Brooklyn cried. Elias reached over and held her until her quaking shoulders stilled and her breathing steadied. Then he started the car and drove them home.

It was just after 6 P.M. when they got home. They walked in and found Hope and Amir sitting in the living room watching TV. The second they saw Brooklyn's battered face, they both reacted.

"Brooklyn!" Hope exclaimed, her hands covering her mouth.

"Who did this to you?" Amir demanded, standing to his feet.

Brooklyn gave them the rundown.

"It's okay. I got into a fight with a girl from school."

"What girl?" Hope asked, frowning. As far as she knew, Brooklyn was popular and loved at school.

Amir frowned, too. He thought about the side of Brooklyn the rest of the family knew nothing about. He wanted to believe her story about a fight with a girl from school. But something in his gut told him there was much more to the story than that.

"It's okay," Brooklyn said again. "I promise it's not a big deal."

Amir was still skeptical. He didn't respond, looking from Brooklyn to their father and back again. He had arrived home from work that evening and found his mother storming around the house frantically, mumbling to herself, clearly agitated. Seeing his father and sister coming through the door with Brooklyn looking like she'd been to hell and back again was further proof that something wasn't right.

As if reading her son's thoughts, Sabrina charged into the room ready for war.

"You think you're so smart, Brooklyn! Lying to us and running around like a slut. I ought to wring your neck!"

Brooklyn froze and stared back at her mother.

"WHOA!" Elias protested. "Sabrina, what's wrong with you? She already told us—"

"LIES!" Sabrina yelled. "Everything she's been saying is a lie."

Brooklyn's mouth fell open as her mother tossed her coveted belongings onto the coffee table. The gold earrings and necklace Alonzo had bought for her, the ticket stubs from their trip to the movies, her birth control pills, the aftercare instructions from the abortion clinic, and an open pack of condoms with a couple missing. It sunk in that she was busted. She looked at her mother with guilt written all over her face.

"Start talking!" Sabrina yelled.

"Ma . . ." Brooklyn shook her head, helplessly. "You went through my stuff?"

Sabrina scoffed. "You can't be serious! Are you *questioning* me right now?" She looked at Elias with amazement. "You hear her?"

"Brooklyn, what's all this?" Elias asked.

Brooklyn held her hands up in surrender. "I met Alonzo a few months ago. We hang out at the library sometimes, in the park. It's no big deal."

"Did Alonzo get you pregnant?" Sabrina snatched up the carbon paper from Planned Parenthood and waved it in Brooklyn's face like a fan. "You had an abortion?"

"What's she talking about?" Elias's voice was much louder now.

Sabrina's gaze remained fixed on Brooklyn. "I asked you a question," she said. "Have you been out there messing around like a common whore?"

Brooklyn's fists clenched. She felt her temperature rising. "Don't call me that."

"BROOKLYN! What the hell is she talking about?" He stared at her, threateningly.

Sabrina didn't wait for her to respond. "Your daughter's been out there disrespecting this family and the church we built. That's what's going on!" Sabrina shouted.

Brooklyn stared back at her wordlessly. She could feel her adrenaline rushing. Some sort of fight-or-flight response. She considered running back out the door.

"Did you get an abortion, Brooklyn?"

Elias asked the question even though he knew the answer already. The evidence was right there in his wife's hands. She stood with her chest heaving, feeling like a failure as a parent. Over the past few minutes, she had discovered that there was a side of her daughter that she knew nothing about.

"Daddy," Hope said, stepping into the room. "Calm down."

Brooklyn looked at her sister, grateful for the interruption. Amir was close behind. He locked eyes with Brooklyn, sympathetically.

Brooklyn turned to face her father. She had always been daddy's little girl. She knew that what he was about to learn would disappoint him and that reality filled her with dread.

He stared at Brooklyn. "Answer me."

Sabrina didn't wait for Brooklyn to respond. She handed her husband the paper in her hand and watched him read it. She picked up the earrings, the necklace, the condoms, and all the trinkets of young love that Brooklyn had kept tucked away in a shoebox at the top of her closet. Sabrina stuffed them all into her husband's hands, one by one, disgust written all over her face.

"She's a lying, dirty TRAMP, Eli! And I want her out of this house!" She snatched the paper out of his hand and waved it in Brooklyn's face. "You're going to a group home because I'm not going to stand here and watch you destroy this family!"

Brooklyn took a step back. She had never seen her mother

so out of control. For the first time in her life, she worried that Sabrina might get violent.

"She's cutting school, lying to us, having sex with a grown man. Some drug dealer driving her home in a car that cost more than the project apartment he lives in. She had an abortion, Eli! And it's probably not the first time. She lies about everything."

As she watched her mother lay it all out like evidence in the case against her, Brooklyn fumed. She felt violated and exposed. She felt that her mother was the least qualified to judge her. She avoided her father's gaze as her mother continued ranting.

"Brooklyn, speak up!"

Her father's voice startled her, and she looked at him, shocked. She couldn't recall the last time he had yelled at her. She fought back tears.

"Daddy, give her a minute." Hope stepped closer to the fray and spoke soothingly, doing her best to coax peace within her family, even at such a turbulent moment.

Amir stood quietly in the corner. Brooklyn looked to him for reassurance but found him staring down at his feet. Fury bubbled up inside of her like a kettle on high. Each of them looking like hypocrites to her. All but Hope.

"Let her explain," Hope urged. She looked at Brooklyn and nodded, urging her to plead her case.

Brooklyn cleared her throat. "I met Alonzo at the ferry terminal after school one day," she said softly. "I was sneaking around to see him, and I'm sorry."

"Sneaking off and doing what?" her father demanded.

Brooklyn forced herself to look at him, her eyes pleading, but she didn't respond.

"So, you've been sneaking out of school, dishonoring yourself and your body with a grown man." His heart broke with every word he uttered.

"I'll be eighteen in a few days," Brooklyn protested softly. "I'm not a kid anymore."

A look crossed her father's face unlike anything she had seen before. Disdain and repulsion dripped from his downturned mouth and cold gaze.

"I'm ashamed of you," he said.

The words hit Brooklyn like a punch in the face.

Her father wasn't done.

"We trusted you," he said. "Gave you everything you ever wanted. All we asked in return was for you to carry yourself with some respect and dignity."

"Like you do?" Brooklyn asked, facetiously.

As the words flew out of her mouth, her father's hand slapped her hard across it. She recoiled from the blow, sobbing.

Hope rushed forward, putting herself between her father and sister, defensively. "Don't do this," she pleaded. "Please, Daddy." She blocked Brooklyn with her body, hoping he would back off.

Through tears, Brooklyn watched her father looming furiously over them, her mother standing idly by, and Amir cowering silently across the room. Brooklyn had never been more disappointed in her brother in her whole life.

"You DISGUST me!" Elias shouted.

"*I* disgust you?" she asked, her voice cracking with emotion.

Her father had always seemed to understand her, always protected, and defended her. He stood glaring at her now like an outcast, his love and adoration withdrawn from her for the same offenses he was guilty of. Lusts of the flesh. She couldn't stomach his hypocrisy. His rebuke of her stung so deeply that it brought her to tears.

He nodded. "Yes!"

Brooklyn laughed. Now she was prepared to abandon what little respect remained for this so-called family. She backed up, aware that what she was about to say would cause her father to get violent.

"You sleep around with every woman you can get your hands on."

Hope spun around and faced her, shock etched across her face.

"BROOKLYN!" she shouted.

Brooklyn backed up further as her father tried to push past Hope.

"Mom acts like she don't know, but *she knows*." Brooklyn turned her attention to Sabrina now. "Just like you knew about what Morris did and you tried to make me lie and cover it up."

She saw her mother wince a little hearing that. Brooklyn turned her anger back in her father's direction for good measure.

"And you went right along with her the second she reminded you to focus on the money. You got your handouts and built your rec center. And I got silenced."

"Brooklyn!"

Everyone seemed shocked by the voice echoing across the room. Amir stepped closer to the melee with his hands pressed together, pleadingly.

"What are you doing?" He shook his head. "Stop. You're going too far."

Brooklyn's eyes widened. "*Really*, Amir? You want to take *their* side?"

He heard the underlying threat in her tone and shook his head again. "Don't do this. This ain't right."

"Wow," she said, painfully. "I never thought you would turn against me, too."

"I'm not against you," he pleaded.

"You know me," she said with tears in her eyes. "So, defend me! You're gonna let them kick me out of here and talk to me like I'm garbage and all you can do is tell *me* to stop?" Her voice cracked with emotion.

"You made a mistake, Brooklyn. They have a right to be upset. I'm not taking sides. I'm just telling you to chill. Let everybody calm down."

"Nobody's calming down," Sabrina insisted. "She's getting out of here. The whole neighborhood is gonna be talking about this. The church! She's an embarrassment."

She lifted up the clinic discharge paperwork again and faced her daughter. "I know all about you now. Lying, sleeping around with some grown man, skipping school, living a double life."

Brooklyn shook her head at Amir and wiped her tears. She turned to face her mother. With Sabrina in her crosshairs now, she spoke with calmness and clarity. "Congratulations, Ma. Seems like you know everything. All the sins of your children. So, you must know that Amir's gay. Right? That he's been messing around with Jordan the drummer."

A thick silence filled the room.

"What did you say?" Elias's neck snapped in Amir's direction.

Amir stood looking like a deer caught in headlights.

But Brooklyn wasn't done. She glared at Amir, seeing him as a weakling trying to disappear into the corner of the room. He looked mortified, which only fueled her rage even more.

"So, you tell me, Amir," she taunted. "Do they have a right to be upset about that, too? Or is it just the things *I* do? Let's talk about your mistakes!"

Sabrina held her hands to her face and stared at Amir, horrified. Elias looked at his son, seething.

"What the fuck is she talking about?" he yelled.

Brooklyn saw the terror in her brother's eyes, but she didn't back down. The corners of her lips turned up in the slightest smirk.

"Tell them what I walked in on. Right here in this house." She looked at her parents. "Ask *him* if *he's* been having sex and who he's been having it with. Then let me know if you're disgusted."

Sabrina lunged in Brooklyn's direction and hit her so hard that it sent her spinning to the floor. Hope rushed in and gripped her mother's arms.

"No!" she yelled. "Please!"

Brooklyn scrambled to her feet, clutching her face as it throbbed with pain.

Elias felt all the blood rush to his head. The sensation rocked him, and for a moment he felt like he might lose consciousness. His daughter had terminated a pregnancy. His only son was gay. He wasn't sure who to pounce on first. He quickly stripped out of his suit jacket and charged in Amir's direction. A guttural roar came out of him, causing all of the women to recoil in fear.

Brooklyn watched in silence as her mother and sister did their best to hold Elias back. She drowned out the sound of the raised voices in the room, the coffee table getting turned over in the melee. Deafened momentarily, she watched her father barreling wildly toward Amir, while Amir pressed himself against the wall with his hands out in front of him. She saw the fear on her brother's face and hated him for it. She wanted him to fight back, to join her in the mutiny they had talked about in secret. Instead, he stood there crying like a bitch.

She wouldn't remember the profane words her father called Amir that night. Or her mother's pleas as she begged for mercy for her son, mercy she had not extended to Brooklyn. She didn't hear her sister's desperate prayers or her brother's protests. But she would never forget the feeling she felt in the pit of her stomach as her father swung at Amir, landing blow after blow. She felt sickened by it and wanted desperately to get out of there.

Brooklyn thought about running out the door, but she had no money, none of her clothes, nowhere to go. She looked down at the floor, scanning it frantically for her prized possessions. Finally spotting them, she scooped up her earrings and her necklace. The ringing in her ears stopped and the ruckus in the room commanded her attention again.

"You satisfied now?" Her mother stood yelling in her face. "You happy?"

Brooklyn saw her brother doubled over in the corner and her father standing over him with his clothes in disarray. Hope was crying, pleading with her father to stop.

Brooklyn didn't answer her mother. She rushed past her, ran up the stairs to her room, and shut the door. She could hear the arguing going on downstairs. Her father was demanding that Amir get out of his house. Objects were being tossed around, and Brooklyn could hear her mother weeping as she pleaded with her husband to calm down.

"Elias, please. Let's pray, baby." Sabrina begged. "Come on. Just stop for a minute."

Brooklyn sucked her teeth as she folded her favorite clothes and packed them neatly into her backpack. She noted that her mother seemed so eager to protect Amir but had been unapologetic in her condemnation of Brooklyn. She turned as the door opened abruptly behind her.

Hope barged in, clearly upset. Tear stains streaked her face.

"Why would you do that to him, Brooklyn? What did Amir have to do with the trouble you got yourself into?"

"He stood there with his mouth shut while they attacked me. You don't understand. I confided in him. I trusted him. At least you tried to help, and I appreciate that. But that nigga didn't say a word. Meanwhile I've been covering for him for months."

"You think you're the only one who knew?" Hope looked at her sister with the same contempt Brooklyn had seen in the eyes of her parents. "I knew. Maybe all of us did in some way. We might not have seen it with our own eyes, but we knew it. For YEARS! And you would have known it, too, if you cared about anybody else but yourself. You were too selfish to notice how depressed he's been for so long, or how hard he was struggling to fit in. Not just because he's shy or antisocial. But because he's gay, and we all knew Daddy would react like that. He's kicking him out in the street."

"A few minutes ago, he was ready to kick me out, too. And where was the cavalry coming to my defense?" Brooklyn asked.

"I defended you!" Hope yelled.

"Thank you," Brooklyn said, half-heartedly. "But tonight showed me how it really is around here. I'm the one who's the problem. Just me, apparently. So, fuck it. From now on, let's play dirty."

Hope closed her eyes and prayed silently for the strength to deal with the madness within her family. She opened them again, shook her head at Brooklyn, and rushed back downstairs to help her brother.

She heard the front door slam and her father's voice booming.

Sabrina slammed open the door to Brooklyn's room, grabbed her by the shirt and pushed her back against the wall. Her voice trembled as she spoke.

"You have single-handedly destroyed this family. Nothing will ever be the same and I'm not sure if you even care." Sabrina's body shook uncontrollably. "Your brother is gone and it's your fault. God knows what might happen to him out there on the street. All of it is your fault. You're getting out of this house. If Amir has to go, so do you. I'm putting you in a group home, Mt. Loretto, some type of military school—something! You're on the road to hell, Brooklyn. If you don't seek God, one day life is going to chew you up and spit you out. I'm not going to sit around and watch it happen. You're getting out of here. And I can't wait to see you go."

She stormed out of the room, and Brooklyn stood there staring at the shut door. Her mother's words replayed on a loop inside her mind.

Her heart sank at the thought of being sent to Mt. Loretto. It was a place her mother had threatened to send her before. The Catholic charity–run facility was on a sprawling, gated campus on a tree-lined street that seemed harmless on the outside. But it was a school for wayward girls. An institution that Sabrina had studied extensively and had often threatened to enroll Brooklyn in over the years whenever she stepped outside the lines Sabrina had drawn around her precious family dynamic. The rules were strict, and being sent there would mean total isolation from her friends. And from her freedom. Dread washed over Brooklyn.

She heard the sound of her father raging downstairs and her mother's pleading voice. Brooklyn snatched a tank top and some leggings from her dresser drawer. She rushed into the bathroom to take a shower to drown out the noise. She took her backpack with her, scared now that her mother would seize every opportunity to search through her stuff. She washed and tried her best to calm her nerves before she reluctantly returned to her room. Her parents were in their bedroom now. The door was open, and she overheard their conversation.

"Where's he gonna go, Eli? We can't just throw him out like that. You wouldn't even let him take anything." Between each sentence, Sabrina sniffled.

"He's dead to me. That shit is an abomination. How can I get up there and preach the gospel when my son is messing around with men?"

There was a pause before Sabrina responded, her tone unemotional and matter-of-fact.

"Brooklyn is no better. We gotta get her out of here immediately."

Brooklyn slipped quietly into her bedroom. Hope was lying in the fetal position crying softly in her bed. Brooklyn could hear her sobs as she dabbed at her eyes with a wad of tissues balled up in her hand. Brooklyn climbed into bed, still sore from the beating she had endured that day. She closed her eyes and wished she could change all the decisions she'd made when she woke up that morning. Going to Alonzo's apartment, fighting Janine, arguing with the police, and drawing the unwanted attention of Miss Nancy. She wished she could undo all of it.

Most of all, she regretted leaving her mother alone at home for those hours. Taking the ride with her father had given Sabrina plenty of time to go through Brooklyn's things and uncover the truth. She chided herself for keeping the paperwork from the clinic. That had been a dumb move.

She thought about the look on her father's face when he learned the truth. She realized that had been the thing that sent her over the edge. Her mother was someone whose approval didn't matter one bit to Brooklyn. But her father was different. She thought about the time they spent together that afternoon, how he had held her as she cried. She wondered how things would be between them from now on.

She was certain that there was nothing she could ever do to repair the rift she had created within her family. Amir was gone, and her parents were in crisis mode. Hope was an emotional wreck, and none of them would probably ever forgive her for exposing the truth about their family's sins. She felt no remorse, even for Amir. She reasoned that he had his chance to pick a side. It wasn't her fault he had been rejected by the side he chose.

She turned over and thought about Alonzo. Until Erica revealed the truth about him, Brooklyn thought he was going to be her ticket out of the life she felt trapped in. Now, she realized that she would have to figure her own path of escape. She decided that she would run the first chance she could. And once she got out, she was never coming back.

She didn't sleep. Couldn't really. Thoughts of her brother haunted her every time she closed her eyes. She assumed that now he hated her, and she felt sad about that. Each time she tried to doze off, the events of the past several hours replayed in her mind. Finally, she gave up and lay awake staring up at the ceiling. As Hope slept softly and the house fell into that dead-of-night silence, a switch in her mind was triggered. She realized that her path to freedom had been laid out perfectly for her. It was a new day and her time was now.

She climbed out of bed at 3:30 A.M. while Hope was still asleep. She slipped a T-shirt and hoodie on, pulled on a pair of thick socks, and put some jeans on over the leggings she was already wearing. It was November and cold outside. She had to prepare for the chill. She looked around her room and tried to etch each detail into her mind. She packed her diary, her toothbrush, some extra socks, and some underwear. She made her bed up, neatly fluffing all the pillows and ran a sweeping hand across the comforter. Just like her mother taught her. Then she walked out of the room and shut the door slowly behind her.

The door to her parents' room was closed. She walked silently past it. She paused as she neared the door to Amir's room. It was slightly ajar, and the room was dark. She wondered where he was and if he was safe. Guilt flooded her like a tidal wave, knowing deep down inside that she had betrayed him. She reminded herself that Amir hadn't had the decency to throw her a lifeline when she needed it. She picked up her chin and pushed forward with her plan.

Quietly she crept downstairs and into her father's study. She slid open the desk drawer on the upper right and retrieved the keys to the kingdom. Shutting it again, she tiptoed out of there. She stopped in the living room and looked around, searing the image into her memory. Then she retrieved her thick winter parka from the hallway closet, crept to the front door, and slipped out into the night.

It was dark and quiet outside. Brooklyn realized that she had never been outside this late. The realization filled her with a mixture of thrill and trepidation. She rushed down the street with her heart pounding hard in her chest. For the first few blocks, she glanced around anxiously, looking behind her to make sure that no one was following her. There weren't many people outside. Each time a car drove past, she pulled her hood down farther to cover her face. She chided herself for being paranoid. Then, as one dark car drove slowly past, the driver honked his horn at her. Her heart leapt in her chest, and she panicked. Gripping the straps of her backpack, she took off and ran the rest of the way to the church.

Breathless, she arrived at the gate trembling with fear. She looked around at the quiet block and assured herself that no one was watching her.

"You're okay," she told herself. "Just keep going."

She pulled the keys out of her pocket and flipped through them in search of the right one. She knew that the largest one was the key for the padlock on the gate. After fiddling with it for a few tense moments, she finally unlocked it and shut it behind her.

She rushed to the doors of the church and told herself that she was almost there. Just a few more steps and she would be on her way. She searched the ring for the key she had seen her parents use countless times over the years and slid it smoothly into the lock. She turned the knob, walked inside, and was immediately struck by the eerie silence inside. It was pitch-dark, but she could make out the familiar silhouettes of the pews and the altar. She strode quickly through the sanctuary, assuring herself that God would forgive her for what she was about to do.

She went to her father's office and unlocked it. She stepped into the room and paused. As a kid, she had sat in the corner doing her homework while her father met with the deacons, trustees, and local politicians. Just a few hours earlier, he had prayed with her there.

She recalled the look on his face when he learned the truth about her. Repulsion and shame. It was an image she would never forget.

Walking over to his desk, she sat down in the chair and began rifling through the adjoining file cabinet. She knew that her father kept a stash of cash there. "The building fund" as he called it. She found the slim envelope in the back of the drawer, just as it always was. She slid it out and began counting the cash inside. She counted it again and confirmed the total of $1,300. She had been hanging around Alonzo enough to know that it wasn't much. But it would be enough to get her out of Staten Island by morning. She tucked it into the front pocket of her backpack and zipped it.

As she rose to leave, her foot hit an object underneath the desk. She glanced down at it and her heart skipped a beat. Mrs.

Hutchinson's box. She stared at it for a moment, hesitantly. Then she bent down and picked it up. Placing it on the desk, she opened it and gasped.

The box was full of cash. Lots of it. She froze, thinking instantly of Alonzo and what he would do if this money came up missing. She thought about Erica and the fact that Alonzo and Mrs. Hutchinson were her family. She knew that it was wrong. But she also knew that she needed that money. She reminded herself that Alonzo had lied to her, rejected her.

She started counting the money, then quickly realized that she didn't have enough time. There was far too much cash and she had to get going before she got caught. At any moment, her parents could wake up and discover her missing. Looking at the money spread out in front of her, she did her best to estimate the total. It was easily several thousand dollars in all denominations. She shoved it all back into the box, shut the lid, and picked up the phone on the desk.

It took several rings. It was, after all, the middle of the night. Brooklyn hung up and dialed again. This time, the call was picked up on the fourth ring.

"Hello?" the gravelly voice answered.

"Hey," Brooklyn said hurriedly when Stacey answered. "It's Brooklyn. I'm in trouble and you're the only person I can call. Can you help me?"

Stacey groaned, still half asleep. "Brooklyn . . . what the fuck? You alright?"

"Yes and no. I just need your help. Can I come to you? I have nowhere else to go."

Stacey hesitated. "You got beef?"

"No," Brooklyn lied. "I just got beat up. Alonzo got arrested. I need somewhere to go. Just until I figure out my next move."

Stacey thought about it. She assumed that Alonzo had gotten violent with Brooklyn. She sounded so scared. "Okay," she said. "Come uptown. I'm here."

"Thank you," Brooklyn said. "Please don't tell anybody I'm coming."

"Okay, okay," Stacey said. "I got you."

Brooklyn hung up and looked at the clock on the wall. It was 4:20 A.M. She knew a ferry would be leaving at 5:00 and tried to figure out how to get there. Unlike the other boroughs, Staten Island had no yellow cabs. She decided she would hop on the next bus heading in that direction. Grabbing her backpack, she slid it on and clutched the shoebox against her chest. She stopped, set the keys to the church down on her father's desk, and left. She shut the door to his office, strode smoothly through the sanctuary, and glanced at the altar.

Brooklyn paused, kneeling down in front of it with the box of money held tightly to her chest.

"God, forgive me for what I'm doing. Forgive my family, too. Please watch over Amir . . ." She opened her mouth to say more, but the words escaped her.

She stood up, walked quickly to the door, and rushed out into the night.

As she hurried down Richmond Terrace toward the bus stop, she considered going back. Just putting everything back the way it was and facing the wrath of her parents. Guilt tugged at her, mercilessly. She stopped walking, convinced that going home was the right thing to do. Then she could hear the rumbling of a bus approaching in the distance. She took it as a sign to keep going. She rushed to the bus stop a few feet ahead and flagged the driver down as he approached.

"I don't have any change," she said as she climbed onboard without paying and sat in the back. To her relief, the driver didn't protest.

Brooklyn sat near a window and watched the scenery as the bus barreled toward the ferry. She sat back in her seat and got lost in her thoughts.

So, this is what freedom feels like. Kinda scary, not knowing what's about to happen. But at least I know I can take care of myself. I can go wherever I want and start a new life.

She sighed as the realization sank in. Staring out the window, she promised herself that she was never coming back here. She was leaving Staten Island for good.

Chapter Six

Runaway

Brooklyn sailed across the Hudson on the John F. Kennedy vessel of the Staten Island Ferry fleet. She was one of few passengers that morning, most of them heading to work. She sat in a seat near the window and watched as the island she had called home for years faded from sight for what she hoped would be the last time. She was glad to see it go.

All she could think about was the money.

She sat back and looked around at the people seated nearby. She wondered what they would think if they knew that the shoebox on her lap was stuffed full of cash. She smirked, betting that she had more money in her possession than most of them had in their bank accounts. She waited until the ferry approached the Statue of Liberty. Then she made a beeline for the bathroom.

She locked herself inside a stall and opened the shoebox. She began counting, stacking the cash into stacks of $500 inside the lid of the box. She kept going, focused, with her feet planted firmly to steady herself against the ferry's rocking. She counted ten stacks of $500 and set it aside. She stuck them inside of a sock she retrieved from her backpack, then stuck the sock way down at the bottom of the bag. A voice came over the loudspeaker announcing that the ferry was preparing to dock. There was still a great deal of cash inside the box. She closed it, emerged from the stall, and joined the rest of the passengers as they disembarked.

She caught the train uptown like she had done countless times before. Her trips to Harlem for Alonzo had always taken place in the daytime. On those occasions, she had the benefit of the city's bustling population, allowing her to easily blend in with the students and commuters. This time it was different. There were fewer people on the train and a heavier police presence than she was used to. She avoided the cops on patrol, careful to keep her head down so they wouldn't notice the bruises on her face and her swollen lip and eye. The last thing she needed was for them to start asking questions, requesting her name and ID, asking where she was going. She had no answers for those things. She hadn't thought that part of her plan out well enough. All she had determined was that she didn't want to wake up that morning in her family home having to face the wrath and disappointment of her parents.

She thought about Amir, imagining that he had likely sought refuge at Jordan's place. She pushed past the guilt she felt about exposing his secret, assuring herself that it had been for the best. Now they were both free from the tyranny of their parents, and Brooklyn had enough cash to give them both a fresh start.

Emerging from the subway, Brooklyn squirmed as rats scampered past and homeless people dug through trash cans nearby. She walked swiftly, dodging the rodents, and keeping an eye out for stickup kids and rapists. She clutched the box tightly as she walked to Stacey's building on 134th Street. She walked inside, took the elevator upstairs, and walked down the familiar hallway. She stopped at apartment 4M and knocked.

Stacey unlatched the many locks on the door and opened it. She stepped aside and let Brooklyn in.

Brooklyn slid her hood off and looked at Stacey.

Her eyes widened. "Damn. Alonzo did that to you?" Stacey asked.

"In a way," Brooklyn said. "But not really."

Stacey led her into the living room and gestured toward a chair. Brooklyn sat down while Stacey walked into the kitchen.

"You're lucky I was home," she called out. "Just came back

from out of town this morning. Been gone for three weeks." She came back into the room with a block of ice wrapped in a towel. She handed it to Brooklyn.

"Thank you." Brooklyn held it to the left side of her face, which hurt the worst. "I appreciate you letting me come here." She glanced down the hall toward the rooms she had never been invited to enter. She assumed they were bedrooms and had no idea who or what might be in them. "Are we alone? Can I talk freely?"

Stacey nodded. "Nobody's here." She lit a blunt she plucked out of an ashtray on the end table. She held it up, offering it to Brooklyn.

"No thanks."

Stacey lit it and exhaled. "You can talk freely."

"Alonzo was cheating on me."

Stacey laughed, to Brooklyn's surprise. Brooklyn frowned and stopped talking.

"My bad," Stacey said, shaking her head. "Baby girl, what did you expect?"

Brooklyn felt foolish.

"How old are you? For real?"

"Seventeen."

Stacey groaned.

"But I wasn't lying when I said that I was turning eighteen this year. My birthday is next week."

"You're still too young to be fucking with a nigga Zo's age. Guys like him do the shit they do with young girls like you because they know you'll let them. You'll let them fuck you for little to no benefits, let them put you to work risking your freedom." Stacey shook her head. "They know a real woman won't go for that shit." She puffed her blunt again. "Zo's dead wrong for stringing you along at your age. Got you all caught up in your feelings. So, what happened? You confronted him and he hit you?"

Brooklyn shook her head. "I tried to fight the girl," she admitted. "Didn't go like I planned."

"Hm!"

"After the fight, I broke out. Zo came after me and the cops pulled him over for tints on his windows."

"Damn!"

"He got arrested. A lady from my church saw me—"

"Your church?" Stacey tilted her head sideways, intrigued. "You're a church girl? Man, Zo really ain't shit!"

Brooklyn sighed. She forgot how little Stacey knew about her outside of being Alonzo's "girl." She searched Stacey's face, nervously. Finally, she decided to come clean.

"I'm in trouble, Stacey. I need to lay low for a while. Zo and my family can't find out where I am, or I'll be in major shit."

Stacey set the blunt down.

"Can I trust you?" Brooklyn asked with tears in her eyes.

Stacey wasn't sure what it was about Brooklyn that endeared her to Brooklyn. Maybe it was some sisterly instinct. But there was something in her eyes, an innocence, that made Stacey feel protective of her. Brooklyn seemed like a scared little girl trying to act brave. Stacey sat forward.

"I don't fuck with Zo like that," she said. "He comes uptown to get money. Just like everybody else. So, yeah. You can trust me."

Brooklyn relaxed a little.

"Having said that, I don't want to invite unnecessary beef to my door either. So, I'll hear you out. Depending on what you tell me, I'll let you know if I can help you. But I won't make any promises other than the fact that I won't tell anybody that you came here tonight."

Brooklyn thought about it. She nodded.

"My father runs a church. He's the pastor. So, I grew up in a strict family. I met Zo and we started kicking it. I thought we were sneaking around because of my family and my age. But I found out that he was keeping me a secret for other reasons. I know it sounds dumb and you think I'm naive. But I cared about him. When I started making trips to Harlem for him, it was my idea. At least . . . he made it seem like it was my idea. I was just looking for a way to spend more time with him. But he saw an opportunity to put me to work. And I was down with that. Then I got pregnant."

"Jesus," Stacey muttered. She picked up the blunt again and relit it.

"I had an abortion. My parents didn't know and I wanted to keep it like that. I couldn't make the trips uptown for him anymore. He stopped seeing me as often. Then I found out he was cheating, got in the fight, he got arrested, and the lady from my church saw me at the scene. She brought me to my parents. My mother went through my room and found all the stuff I had hidden. They found out about the pregnancy, my relationship with Zo, everything."

She left out the part about her outing of Amir.

"The whole family got into a fight," she summarized. "They were gonna send me to a group home. So, I ran away."

Stacey looked like she had been sucker-punched.

"And you came here, Little Orphan Annie?" She scoffed. "I'm not trying to get in the middle of some family court bullshit—"

Brooklyn opened up the shoebox at her feet and showed Stacey its contents.

Stacey stared at it with her mouth agape. "Where did you get that?"

"I don't think you want to know," Brooklyn said. "But I need to make sure that Zo and my parents have no idea where I am."

Stacey tried to compute everything. She wondered what she should make of Brooklyn. This girl seemed full of surprises.

"How much money is in there?"

Brooklyn shrugged. "I didn't have time to count it. But I know it's a lot." She left out the part about the $1,300 in the front pocket of her backpack and the $5,000 tucked in a sock among her clothes.

"You robbed Zo?"

Brooklyn didn't respond.

"Or is this the church's money?"

Brooklyn didn't blink.

"Hm." Stacey finished her blunt in silence, pondering everything.

"You have guts. I'll give you that. Seventeen-year-old girl out here moving work, robbing hustlers, disobeying her righteous parents."

"I'm sick of being locked down, everybody controlling me, manipulating me. I'm ready to be on my own."

"What do you need from me?" Stacey frowned. "You have a Timberland box full of cash. Why'd you come here?"

"I don't know where to start," Brooklyn admitted. "I need ID, a place to sleep. I'm not planning on staying in New York for long. If it wasn't for my brother, I would have jumped on a Greyhound bus and went anywhere. But I can't leave without making sure he's okay. I need to give him some money, make sure we're on good terms." She choked back tears at the thought of Amir. "I just need somewhere I can lay low for a few days until I connect with him. Then I'll get out of your way."

Stacey's eyes were low as she sat studying Brooklyn. "You got Alonzo *and* your family looking for you." Her lips spread slowly into a wide smile. "Brooklyn, girl, you wild!" She laughed, marveling at the box of money Brooklyn had set on the coffee table. She was used to seeing large sums of money. But she wasn't used to seeing it coming from an underage runaway who had just robbed a church. She counted it mentally, estimating it to be about $8,000.

"I'm not looking for Daddy Warbucks," Brooklyn said, still not appreciating the Little Orphan Annie reference. "I have my own money. I'm happy to pay you for your trouble, too, if you'll help me. Please."

Stacey wasn't sure whether to be impressed or wary.

"You should go back home, Brooklyn. What if your parents call the cops on you? You got me out here harboring a fugitive."

Stacey's smirk let Brooklyn know she wasn't too concerned about that.

"You don't have to let me stay with you," Brooklyn said. "I understand that I'm laying a lot in your lap right now. I just need somewhere to sleep. I need a day or two to get my hands on some kind of fake ID. But I made up my mind. I'm not going back to Staten Island. Period."

Stacey could tell she wasn't playing. "Okay," she said. "Relax. I got you."

"Thank you, Stacey." Brooklyn let out a deep breath and shook her head. "I should have listened to you when you were giving me all that advice about men. I thought Zo was different."

"That's okay. Don't be too hard on yourself. You're young. But I listened to your story. And what I've learned about you so far is that you don't stay down too long. You bounce back. You *hit* back. That lets me know you ain't one to fuck with. So, you'll survive."

Brooklyn smiled.

"You can sleep on the couch for now," Stacey said. "You look exhausted. I'll bring you some pillows and blankets and shit like that. I got a spare room in the back. The crew stays here sometimes, and they sleep in there. Later on, I'll clean it up for you and you can chill there until we find you something long term."

Brooklyn rested her head back against the sofa and closed her eyes. She willed herself to take Stacey's advice and relax. It had been a very long day, perhaps the toughest one she had experienced in her life so far.

"Your life is gonna be a lot different now," Stacey warned her. "Being alone in the world ain't as easy as it seems. I hope you're ready."

"I'm ready."

Stacey stood up and went to get Brooklyn some bedding.

Brooklyn stifled a yawn. She glanced at the cable clock and saw that it was 6:34 A.M. By now, her parents had discovered that she had run away. She imagined her father frantically searching for his keys and realizing they were missing, pictured her mother desperately dialing Erica's house to see if Brooklyn had sought refuge there. She wondered if they were searching for Amir with equal fervor, and how long it would take them to discover that she had stolen the Timberland box full of Mrs. Hutchinson's cash and disappeared for good.

As much as she tried to push thoughts of Amir to the back of her mind, he remained at the forefront. She was thrilled that she had finally escaped the clutches of her old life. But she was saddened that Amir had been an unexpected casualty. She hadn't expected it to play out that way. She had been desperate for him to speak up, to stand up for her and for himself. She reminded herself that he was an adult and that he had what it took to make it on his own. Just like she did.

By the time Stacey returned, Brooklyn had already fallen asleep. Stacey covered her with a blanket, laid a pillow down beside her, and shut the lid on the shoebox. She looked at Brooklyn, shook her head in bewilderment, and let her sleep.

Brooklyn woke up just before noon. Typically, she'd be in school at this time of day. Or she'd be plotting to cut class to sneak off and see Alonzo. Just a day ago, she had been living a double life. Today she felt free as a bird.

Stacey let her know that she had left a towel and washcloth in the bathroom in case she wanted to take a shower. Brooklyn brought her backpack in the bathroom with her to make sure Stacey didn't look through it. She wanted to keep the money she had tucked away a secret. At least for now. An insurance policy to ensure that she would land on her feet if things ever got rocky between them.

She thought about her little sister, alone now in the house with their parents. It was the way it should have been all along, Brooklyn decided. Hope was the only one who seemed truly willing to play the role assigned to her from birth. She would be fine. In fact, she would probably thrive in the absence of all the tension.

When she was done showering, Brooklyn dried off and got dressed in a pair of jeans and a midriff shirt she had folded inside her backpack. She stood in the bathroom mirror and brushed her hair into a neat bun. She pulled out her pouch with her name in graffiti letters emblazoned across it—a gift from her father. He had given it to her on no particular occasion, simply because he had seen it during his travels and it reminded him of her. She had filled it with her favorite things, usually resting it on top of her dresser each night. Now she retrieved her gold jewelry from it and adorned herself with it. She zipped the pouch again and tossed it aside, just as she felt her father had done to her.

She wondered if the police had been alerted or if her parents had announced her disappearance to the church. She wondered if her mother and sister had shed tears for her the way they had so openly done for Amir. The thought of him brought tears to her eyes. She briskly brushed them away and stepped out of the bathroom.

She came out of the bathroom and found that Stacey had company. She scanned the room, smiling. Wally and Roscoe waved at her.

Hassan looked at her and frowned.

"What happened to your face?" he asked, concerned.

Stacey sucked her teeth. "I just told you not to go asking her a million questions, and what's the first thing you do?"

Brooklyn chuckled. "It's okay." She looked at Hassan. "I got in a fight. No big deal."

"You're too pretty to be fighting. Don't let it happen again." He winked at her.

Brooklyn smiled. Her eyes settled on the Timberland box on the coffee table, and she wondered if Stacey had told them what was inside. She clenched the backpack in her hand a little tighter.

"I set the room up for you like I said," Stacey told her. "Grab your stuff and come check it out." She nodded at the box for emphasis.

Brooklyn walked over and retrieved the Timberland box from the table. She followed Stacey down the hall and walked into a small bedroom with a twin-sized bed and a brown wooden dresser in the corner. On the bed sat a lockbox with two keys.

"Put your money in there. Keep the keys on you. That way you don't have to worry about somebody stealing it."

Brooklyn nodded. "Thank you."

"Wally's gonna get you an ID and Hassan said he'll help you find a place. Depending on how long you plan on staying."

Brooklyn thought about calling Erica. Her best friend would be the first person her parents would reach out to. She imagined a frenzy of activity as her family looked for her—not necessarily because they were concerned for her safety. But certainly, once they discovered the missing money in her father's office. Erica would be able to provide an update on the status of things. But Brooklyn decided that it was too soon to call her. Erica's parents were probably watching her like a hawk now that the truth about Brooklyn had been exposed.

"I'll make some calls later on," she said.

Stacey nodded and left the room. Brooklyn transferred her cash from the shoebox to the lockbox, counting it as she went. As she counted the last stack, she heard a knock at the door. She paused, making a mental note that the total so far was $7,849, shoved the rest of the cash in the box, and locked it.

"Come in."

Hassan walked in and apologized for interrupting her.

"Just wanted to come and ask you if you want to go get something to eat."

"Where?"

"Wherever you want to go," he said. "Your pick."

She thought about it. She tucked the keys to the lockbox in her backpack, slung it across her shoulder, and nodded. "Let's go."

They stopped at a diner for lunch and sat at a table near the door. Brooklyn ordered pancakes, eggs, and bacon. Hassan ordered a steak and potatoes.

As they sat eating together, he turned on the charm.

"Even all bruised up, you still look cute."

She rolled her eyes.

"Maybe it's because you're not like these girls uptown. You seem a little classier. You know what I'm saying? Like you're above the bullshit, even with the black eye and all that. It's the way you carry yourself."

She grinned "Thanks. I think."

"Oh, it's definitely a compliment. I'm talking about the girls in our circle in particular. Stacey's special. She's the queen bee. Untouchable. We all respect her. But Carla and Missy—those are Roscoe and Wally's girls—they're cool and everything. Just typical Harlem girls. Flashy, fly, upscale. You're real regular. And I like that."

Brooklyn frowned a little. "Regular? No. There's nothing regular about me," she assured him. "Trust me." She chewed her food aggressively as she spoke.

He laughed. "My bad, beautiful. You're absolutely right. I just like your style. That's all I'm saying."

She shrugged it off. "Speaking of style, where can I find some clothes? I didn't bring much with me, and I need a few things."

He wiped his mouth with his napkin and sat back. "You want me to take you shopping already? Damn. Maybe you are like these Harlem girls after all."

Brooklyn laughed. "Nigga, I have my own money. Just show me where I can get some fly shit."

He tossed a tip on the table and nodded. "Okay. I'll show you where it's at."

Two hours later, Hassan stood watching Brooklyn bouncing toward the entrance of yet another clothing store. They had eaten lunch already and had been heading back to Stacey's apartment when Brooklyn begged him to make "one stop" at a shoe store on 125th. That was four stores ago.

Brooklyn felt euphoric. Harlem was crawling with stores and street vendors. Normally, she had to have tunnel vision when she came here. She never had the chance to browse the stores, and even if she did, there was no way her parents would have let her wear any of the things she was buying.

"You like shopping, huh?"

"Yes! Especially because this time I'll get to buy the stuff I really want. Not the long-sleeved, below the knee, crewneck shit I'm usually forced to wear."

"Who forced you to dress like that? Zo?" Hassan asked.

"My parents," she said. "The enforcers." She browsed through a rack of dresses. "My parents were strict, kinda hypocritical at times. And I couldn't take it."

Hassan nodded. "You're a free spirit then?"

"Yes." She wouldn't allow herself to think of home for too long. She didn't want to imagine the storm she had stirred up and how frantic things might be in her absence. Shopping was a very welcome distraction from thoughts like those.

She led him through all the formerly forbidden stores—Mandee, Guess, Wild Pair, and Benneton. By the time she was done, she had bought two pairs of Air Max, a bunch of Tommy Hilfiger shirts with bare midriffs and baggy jeans to match, and a few curve-hugging dresses for good measure. For once, there was no one to tell her that anything was too short, too tight, or too revealing. She bought a new coat and some winter clothes, too. When she was done, both of them were juggling bagloads of items.

As they headed back to Stacey's, Hassan tried to ask questions without being too invasive. "Been a while since I saw you. I figured Zo had you somewhere spoiling you rotten."

"Nah. I wish!" She looked at him. "I know Stacey told you not to ask me too much. That's because my story is kinda complicated. But in a nutshell, Zo broke my heart. Now, I'm out here doing my own thing."

Hassan nodded. "Good for you. Live your life."

She noticed again how cute he was when he smiled. "What's your story?" she asked. "No girlfriend?"

He laughed. "Not anymore. I fucked things up with the last one. Now I'm married to these streets."

She nodded. "How's that working out for you?"

"Not bad," he said. "It's a lot less complicated."

"I bet."

"I'm not giving up on love though. If at first, you don't succeed or whatever the saying is."

Brooklyn agreed.

"You want kids someday?" she asked.

"No time soon!" he laughed. "My family is wild enough on its own. Throwing a kid in the mix would make it ten times worse. Moms thinks she's still a teenager. My little sister Laray is fifteen and thinks she's grown. My brother Dawan is locked up. So, I'm taking care of everybody."

He followed Brooklyn out of the store when she failed to find anything she wanted.

"That's a lot of weight on your shoulders," she said. "How old are you?"

"Nineteen."

Brooklyn's eyes widened. He seemed so mature for his age. "You're so young and you have to make sure everybody's okay. That's a lot of responsibility."

"I can handle it. Just gotta be smart about it."

"How long has your brother been away?"

"Three years so far. With good behavior, he could be home in five."

Brooklyn tried to imagine what it would be like to spend that many years of her life in prison. In many ways, she felt like she had been in one all her life.

"Stacey said you don't plan on staying long."

"I'm not sure what I plan on doing right now," Brooklyn said, honestly. "The only thing I know for sure is that I'm doing what makes me happy from now on. And shopping makes me happy."

"I can see that!"

As they walked the few blocks back to Stacey's building, Brooklyn peppered him with questions about Stacey. She wanted to know more about the woman.

"I don't know what it is about her," she said. "But there's something comforting in her presence."

"That's how we all feel about Stacey. She's four years older than Roscoe. She got in the game through her man. His name was Buster. Big hustler out here back in the day. He had her by his side the whole way. Then he got killed. She was right there and watched it happen. That's why she's so hard on the outside. So tough. Stacey's been through a lot."

"Damn." Brooklyn said.

"Underneath all that tough shit, though, she's a sweetheart. Stacey will give you the shirt off her back if she fucks with you. If she don't, she won't even answer her phone. So, the fact that she answered her phone when you called and opened her door when you came tells me a lot. If Stacey fucks with you, you must be alright."

They arrived back at Stacey's apartment, and she seemed surprised by Brooklyn's impromptu shopping spree.

"New wardrobe?"

"New life."

"Okay." Stacey looked at Hassan. "That was a long lunch break, nigga."

"My bad. I didn't know I took a shopaholic with me."

Brooklyn laughed. "Sorry. I got a little carried away."

Wally looked at the bags in her hands and shook his head. "A little?"

Roscoe stood up from the couch and waved his hand. "Come on, muthafuckas. We got moves to make."

Wally and Hassan followed him out.

Hassan looked at Brooklyn as he left. "See you soon I hope."

"See you soon."

Stacey locked the door behind them and sat down on the couch. On the coffee table in front of her—in the very spot where the Timberland box had once been—sat four kilos of cocaine. Next to it were three large Ziploc baggies full of little vials with orange tops.

Brooklyn sat down and reached in her backpack. She pulled out a stack of cash and handed it to Stacey.

"That's a thousand dollars. Take it for letting me stay here and for the ID and all that. How long do you think it will take to get it?" She was eager to make her next move. She was nervous that if she stayed in one place for too long, she would get sloppy.

"Wally will have it in a few days." Stacey reclined. "I called Zo's house today. Just a test to see if he answered."

Brooklyn waited expectantly for the outcome.

"Some girl picked up the phone. Said her name was Janine."

Brooklyn was annoyed by the mention of her nemesis.

Stacey noticed Brooklyn's reaction and assumed the girl had been the one to blacken her eye. "She said Zo is in a lot of trouble. For some reason, he was dumb enough to be driving around with one of these in the trunk." She held up one of the Ziploc bags packed to capacity with orange vials. "So, I don't think you have to worry about him for a while. Not unless you know his friends and all that. Because they'll still be coming uptown to do business."

"I'll be gone by then. Once I get in touch with my brother and get what I need from Wally, I'm out of here."

"You sound so sure of yourself." Stacey thought she sounded dumb, but she was trying to spare the young girl's feelings. "You don't have enough money to survive on for too long. Especially if you plan to keep shopping like that." Stacey nodded toward the litany of bags at her feet. "You're handing me a thousand dollars, talking about hitting your brother off with money, too. You should be saving, not spending." Stacey shook her head. "You're making grown-up decisions, and at the same time you're acting like a kid. First chance you get to spend the day without Mommy and Daddy and you're running around like you hit the jackpot."

Brooklyn felt ashamed of herself. Her fun afternoon suddenly seemed like a very poor move.

"I'm not trying to be hard on you," Stacey said, though her tone didn't soften one bit. "I'm just saying you gotta be smart. You want to be on your own. But you gotta figure out how you're gonna survive. If you get an apartment, how are you gonna pay the rent?" She pointed at her head. "Think!"

Brooklyn straightened her posture, nodded quickly, then got up and walked out.

Stacey watched as Brooklyn walked into the bedroom with her bags in tow.

She shut the door behind her and tried her best to block out Stacey's words. She pulled out each of the clothing items she had bought, admiring them and imagining how she'd look in each piece. She laid all the clothes and accessories across the bed, stood back, and stared at everything.

For reasons too many to name, Brooklyn began to cry. She felt an overwhelming sadness and a weight in her chest that was unfamiliar. After a few moments, she could finally admit that she was consumed by guilt, doubt, and fear. She wasn't sure that she had done the right thing.

She pressed *67 on the cordless phone from the bedside table. Then she dialed Erica's phone number.

After a few moments, she heard the familiar sound of her best friend's voice.

"Hello?"

"Erica, it's me. Brooklyn."

She heard her friend gasp.

"Brooklyn! Where the fuck are you?"

"I'm okay," Brooklyn said, quickly. "Calm down."

"You have to come home," Erica said. Her voice was barely above a whisper. "Everybody's looking for you."

"I know they are."

"No!" Erica's voice was more forceful now. "You *don't* know, Brooklyn. It's about Amir."

Brooklyn's heart dropped. The pressure she had been feeling in her chest intensified and she felt the heat of thick tears pooling in her eyes. "What happened?"

Erica was crying audibly. "He's dead."

"NO!" Brooklyn's free hand flew up to her face in horror.

"He killed himself."

"OH MY GOD!" Brooklyn shouted. "NO, Erica. Tell me you're just saying that to get me to come home."

"I would never do that," Erica said between sobs. "This ain't a game, Brooklyn. It happened today. He jumped from the roof of Jordan's building. Your family needs you. You have to come back."

Brooklyn set the phone down on the bed and wept. She shook her head in denial, picked up the phone again, and gripped it tightly.

"Erica, I'll call you back."

She hung up and looked at Stacey as she knocked and entered the room. Having heard Brooklyn's sobs from the bathroom, concern was etched all over Stacey's face.

"What's wrong?" she asked, seeing the phone in her hand. "What happened?"

"My brother is dead."

Stacey froze. "What?"

"He killed . . . himself. He jumped . . . off the roof of a building!" She cried so hard that her body quaked.

Stacey rushed forward and held Brooklyn close to her as she cried. She had no idea what to say to her at a time like this.

"You gotta call home," Stacey said after a few minutes. "Call and talk to your family."

Brooklyn shook her head. "And say what? This is my fault."

Stacey wasn't sure what Brooklyn meant by that. But it didn't matter. She picked up the phone and handed it to her. "Call your family."

Brooklyn's hands shook as she took the phone. She blocked the number as she had done before dialing Erica. Then she pressed the numbers shakily and waited as the phone rang like a death knell in her ear.

Someone picked up on the third ring.

"James residence."

Brooklyn's heart pounded hard in her chest at the sound of her father's deep voice.

"Daddy?"

Elias paused. "Brooklyn, where are you?"

"I'm—"

She heard a commotion and a flurry of voices on the other end of the phone and paused.

"Hang it up!" Sabrina yelled in the background. "Hang up the phone, Eli!"

"STOP!" Elias yelled. He turned his attention back to the phone in his hand. "Brooklyn?"

"Yes. I'm here."

"Your brother is gone. You need to come home." Her father's voice was low and solemn.

"I don't want her here," Sabrina yelled in the background. "SHE DID THIS!"

Brooklyn could hear her mother crying, speaking incoherently between sobs. She tried to focus on her father's voice as he spoke into the receiver.

Elias walked into his office with the phone and spoke wearily.

"Brooklyn, I lost my only son. I don't want to lose you, too. I know you made mistakes. I made some, too. I forgive you. Your mother will, too, eventually. I need you back here."

Brooklyn didn't bother wiping the tears that fell from her eyes. "What happened to him?"

"He committed suicide."

Brooklyn heard the pain in her father's voice as he said it. She thought she could hear the faint sound of him crying.

"Because of what I did? What I told you?"

"Brooklyn, come home and we'll talk about it," Elias said. "There's too much going on right now. Your mother is distraught. Hope is all by herself. She needs you. We all do."

Sabrina rushed into Elias's office and knocked the phone from his hand. It landed on the desk with a loud thud.

Brooklyn heard the commotion on her father's end of the phone. "Daddy?" She listened as her parents argued with the phone inches away.

"You're begging that demon to come back into this house? For WHAT, Eli? Hasn't she done enough?"

"Sabrina, I'm not gonna tell you again—"

"NO! If she comes back here, I'm leaving. I'm taking Hope and I'm leaving you, that church, and all this shit behind!"

"You're not going nowhere!"

"She's the reason Amir took his life."

There was a long pause. Then Brooklyn heard the brokenness in her father's voice.

"What about me?" Elias asked. "Huh? I threw him out of here. What was he supposed to do?"

Sabrina grabbed the phone and spoke venomously into it.

"Don't you come back here. Stay gone. You got what you wanted. You destroyed this family because YOU were in trouble. You betrayed your brother and shamed yourself. You took that money from your father's office, and you chose the streets over the life we tried to give you." Sabrina was weeping as she spoke, her words pouring forth from the depth of her soul. "I release you. Vengeance is mine sayeth the Lord! God is going to punish you for this. He's going to make sure you never have peace. Because Amir is gone. You can never undo that. Now stay the FUCK away from here."

The phone went dead, and Brooklyn sat frozen for several long moments. She wiped the tears from her eyes and looked at Stacey.

"I have to go home."

Chapter Seven

The Family

She was dressed in all black the day she returned. It wasn't intentional. Brooklyn looked down at the clothes she had on as they drove down the Henry Hudson Parkway that afternoon in late November. She had been in a fog ever since Erica told her the news. It felt like she was having an out-of-body experience as she dressed after that phone call. It hadn't occurred to her until that moment that she needed to dress respectably to face her father. None of the midriffs, plunging necklines, or tight jeans she had just purchased on 125th Street would do. She looked down at the black T-shirt and baggy black Girbaud jeans she wore and decided they were fittingly understated and somber. She felt empty inside. Amir was dead. And she could practically feel the stickiness of his blood on her hands.

Stacey drove silently for a while, aware that Brooklyn was in a very fragile mental state. It had taken her some time to get the strength to even stand up from the bed, to get dressed. Stacey had finally coaxed Brooklyn's address out of her. Once she got it, Stacey called her brother Roscoe and told him she needed to borrow his car. Stacey didn't own one, didn't have to since Harlem was home base for her, and she seldom ventured far outside of it. But now she was behind the wheel of Roscoe's green Lexus steering it down the road to Staten Island.

She looked over at Brooklyn and felt sorry for her. She saw her own reflection in the young brokenhearted girl. Stacey had grieved for her man for so long that she wasn't sure the mourning ever ended. It just got so familiar that it became part of her personality, as imbedded in her as her DNA. She didn't want that for Brooklyn, a grief so wide that it swallowed you whole. She was so young and already life had literally whooped her ass.

Stacey spoke softly. "You want to tell me the whole story?"

Brooklyn felt empty inside. Since hanging up the phone, she hadn't said very much. There was just too much for her to process, too much pain. She was dazed by the sheer magnitude of the past twenty-four hours. Everything hurt inside and out. She worried that it might hurt to talk.

But she needed to verbalize what happened to tell the truth, even if it was only to herself. She heard Stacey ask the question that prompted her to speak. But as she began to talk, Brooklyn was reciting the story out loud for her own hearing. Reliving the trauma for her own clarity. Stacey just happened to be an innocent bystander.

"I should have never gone to Zo's house yesterday. After the fight, after Miss Nancy brought me to my parents, it was all downhill from there. Daddy took me with him to handle his business. While we were gone, my mother went through my things. My personal, private things."

Brooklyn's tone was flat, even. She stared straight through the windshield at the traffic ahead as if entranced.

"We don't get a lot of personal things in a family like mine. Everything is scrutinized, analyzed. So, having secrets was my way of having something that was mine. My mother spilled all my secrets out in front of my father. She showed him everything. About Zo and the abortion. My father was angry."

Brooklyn cracked then. She wiped tears away as she spoke.

"The things he said . . . He told me I disgust him. The whole time, my brother was standing there with his mouth shut, avoiding eye contact. And I thought he was a coward."

She paused to cry, and Stacey took the chance to process what she had already heard.

"My parents were pissed. *At me*. That seemed unfair because all of us have our secrets. Including them."

Stacey nodded.

"I stood up for myself, but I went too far. My father slapped me. My sister tried to get in the middle of it."

Stacey didn't react, though this was the first time she had ever heard Brooklyn mention having a sister.

"I got really mad. Called them all hypocrites." She thought about Amir yelling her name, recalled the look of shock and fear on his face. "My brother . . . Amir . . . He told me I was going too far. He was like, 'Don't do this. They have a right to be upset . . .'" Brooklyn was crying openly now. "And he knew my secrets. He was the one person that I told the truth to. I expected him to be on my side. It felt like he was betraying me, ganging up on me. So, I decided—fuck it! I aired it out. I told them Amir's secret and all hell broke loose."

"His secret?"

Stacey waited. Brooklyn seemed to be having a hard time with this part.

"He's gay." Brooklyn saw Stacey's eyes widen. "I came home a few months ago and found him having sex with the church drummer."

Stacey gripped the wheel.

"I was upset, ran out, and all of that. But then we talked about it, and I told him my secrets, too. He helped me cover my tracks when I was hanging out with Zo. I told him about being pregnant and the abortion. He talked to me about his feelings for Jordan—the drummer. I tried to encourage him to leave. He's grown. There was no reason for him to stay there and keep lying to everybody. But he was afraid to rock the boat. We agreed to keep each other's secrets. We had an understanding. But when the shit hit the fan, he left me hanging.

"My father beat my brother up and kicked him out. Then my mother told me I fucked up the family. She was gonna put me in a home for 'children in crisis.'" Brooklyn quoted the brochure her mother had given her the last time she had gotten in trouble. "I made up my mind to leave. But first I took my father's keys, snuck into the church, and grabbed a stack of money out of his drawer. You know the rest."

Stacey's mind was reeling. She connected all the dots. Brooklyn had appeared on her doorstep looking like she had been in the battle of her life. Apparently, that wasn't far from the truth. Stacey glanced sidelong at her. Brooklyn was like an onion with countless layers to peel back. So far, Stacey had discovered that Brooklyn would lie, cheat, steal—and fight dirty if she had to—in order to survive. Stacey learned that Brooklyn had a ruthless side, which wasn't necessarily a bad thing in the world Stacey operated in. Something in her gut told her that Brooklyn wasn't all bad.

"I thought he would just go to Jordan's house for the night. I was gonna call my friend Erica so she could tell Amir to meet me somewhere. I planned to split the money with him. We could have left town together. Or, if he stayed, at least he would have enough money for a while. All he had to do was make it through the day. I was gonna call . . ."

Brooklyn closed her eyes. Anger, sadness, rage, and regret battled for dominance inside of her. She wanted to scream at Amir, ask him why he did this to himself, why he gave up so easily. Then she hated herself for blaming him when she had been the one to push him over the ledge. It was her fault, she decided. Whatever may lie ahead for her, she deserved it.

They drove in silence. Brooklyn's mind was loud enough for both of them. Her thoughts raced with unanswered questions. She dabbed at her eyes intermittently as they traveled across the Goethals Bridge into Staten Island.

Brooklyn spoke softly, directing Stacey through the familiar streets. Brooklyn hadn't decided how she might handle the situation. Or what she might say. She just knew that she was sorry. So very sorry for everything.

When they turned onto her block, Stacey slowed down. She looked at Brooklyn.

"You okay?"

Brooklyn shrugged. "I don't know. But I need to see my father. I owe him an apology. I know my mother doesn't want to see me. I don't care. I owe it to my father and my sister . . . and to Amir."

They arrived at her house and Brooklyn stared at it from inside the car. The place looked so peaceful considering the tumult she knew existed inside. She took a deep breath, looked at Stacey and exhaled.

"I'll be right here waiting for you."

Brooklyn slowly climbed out of the car. She crossed the street, her eyes scanning the windows for signs of her mother. She saw both family cars parked outside and assumed that both of her parents were home. She nervously unlatched the gate, walked through it, and approached the front door. With her hands trembling and her knees weak, she rang the doorbell.

The moments that elapsed felt like an eternity. At last, Brooklyn heard the locks being undone and the door slowly cracking open. Her sister Hope stood before her, red-eyed and crestfallen.

Hope looked at Brooklyn warily for a moment. She whispered to her sister. "I'm glad you're okay."

Brooklyn began to cry and rushed forward to hug her.

Hope held on to Brooklyn tightly and closed her eyes as she hugged her back. So much had happened, so much trauma and grief had taken up residence in their home that it made her break down.

Hope sighed deeply and pulled away. She began explaining what she knew.

"After Daddy threw him out, Amir went to Jordan's apartment in the projects. He stayed there overnight, and he came back here first thing this morning. He tried to sneak into his room to get some of his clothes and stuff like that. But Daddy caught him. They got into a big argument. Daddy wouldn't let Amir pack his things, wouldn't talk to him. Mom tried to pack some of Amir's clothes and give him some money, but Daddy wouldn't let her."

Hope felt weak as she recounted the events. "I talked to Amir outside for a few minutes, and I could tell that he was really upset. He wanted a chance to explain it in his own words. He wanted to see if there was some way to fix everything. He seemed like he was falling apart emotionally. We talked for a while and then Amir left. I begged him not to. I asked if I could go with him. But he said he just wanted to take a walk. I told him I would walk with him all day if he wanted. I could tell he didn't need to be by himself. But he told me he was going back to Jordan's apartment, that he would be alright. I believed him. But he wasn't alright. He never went to Jordan's apartment."

Brooklyn's knees buckled a little.

Hope continued. "By then, we had realized you were gone. Daddy went out, trying to find you. The police came and told us what happened to Amir. I was here with Mom when they told her. She fell apart. The cops said that he jumped off the roof around noon. So, all of this is . . ." Hope shook her head, lost for words, and choked back tears. "Mommy's talking crazy right now. She doesn't want you here. She's threatening to leave Daddy if he lets you back in here, threatening to hurt you. She blames you. And Daddy, too, probably."

Hope seemed so much older than she had just days ago. Staring back at each other now, the sisters spoke like equals.

"Daddy told me to come home," Brooklyn said. "Where is he? I want to see him, and then I'll go."

"He went to—"

"Who is that?" Sabrina interrupted them. She craned her neck around the doorframe and locked eyes with Brooklyn. "You had the nerve to come back here?"

"I'm not here to stay," Brooklyn said.

"You're damned right you're not! You're not welcome here."

"I just want to see Daddy."

Hope rubbed her mother's back and looked at Brooklyn, helplessly.

"There's a meeting at the church," Hope said to Brooklyn. "Daddy's there now addressing the deacons and elders."

"You're going to hell." There was no love in Sabrina's eyes as she looked at her daughter. Only disdain. "You killed your brother. You ripped your father's heart out. You killed your unborn baby. Then you told him that your brother is gay. You robbed him of any hope he had for Amir to be the man he wanted him to be. You changed the way Elias saw his only son. All these years, he's been planning on a future that you snatched right out of his grasp with no regard for what it might do to him. Or what it might do to your brother! You turned your back on Amir and it killed him. Might as well have killed your father, too. He's gonna have to think about this for the rest of his life. That he rejected Amir, and as a result our son killed himself." Sabrina sobbed so hard it doubled her over.

Brooklyn locked eyes with her sister.

"For what it's worth, I'm sorry." She was speaking to her mother, too, though she doubted the words brought her any comfort.

She turned to leave. As she neared the gate, she heard her mother's voice behind her.

"All this family ever tried to do was love you. But the only person you've ever loved is yourself!"

Stacey could see the hurt on Brooklyn's face as she climbed into the car.

Brooklyn stared straight ahead and spoke flatly.

"I need to go to the church to see my father."

Stacey glanced back toward the house and hesitated. Brooklyn's mother and sister had retreated inside, and she shook her head.

"You sure that's a good idea?" Stacey asked gently. "They might be looking for you after that money came up missing."

She shrugged. "Fuck it. Let them lock me up. I have nothing

to lose at this point." She looked at Stacey. "I just want to see my father."

Stacey started the car and followed her directions to the church. She could sense Brooklyn's nervousness and tried to offer her some consolation.

"You said that your father told you to come home. That he forgives you. For your mother, it might take time. But at least you still have your pops."

Brooklyn prayed that was true. She tried to speculate about which church members might be there and imagined a packed house of nosy congregants trying to get the inside scoop on the pastor's family scandal. She wasn't surprised when they arrived at the church and saw that the parking lot was full of cars.

"You sure about this, Brooklyn?" Stacey asked again. "I would offer to go inside with you, but I'm afraid the place might burn down."

Brooklyn tried to muster a grin at the half-hearted joke. But she couldn't do it. She shook her head. "I got this."

She got out of the car and began walking toward the church.

"Brooklyn!"

She turned toward the familiar voice and saw her friend Erica. Both girls rushed in each other's direction, embracing feet away from the church.

Brooklyn cried.

"I'm so sorry, B." Erica stroked her friend's back. "Don't blame yourself."

Brooklyn pulled back, frowning slightly. "You know what happened?"

Erica nodded. She looked around, cautiously, then pulled Brooklyn by the hand to a corner of the block obscured by trees.

"After your parents threw Amir out, he went to Jordan's apartment. They called me, hoping that I could get in touch with you somehow. Amir was upset and he wanted to confront you."

Brooklyn cringed a little but tried not to show it. She didn't want Erica to censor herself to protect Brooklyn's feelings.

"I never knew that Amir was gay. When him and Jordan called me, they assumed I knew—that you had told me because we're so close. Jordan was worried that you might tell *everybody*. I swore that you never told me about it, and Amir explained what happened last night at your house. That your father beat him up and threw him out. He wanted me to call your house so he could talk to you. I tried a few times, but I think somebody must've taken the phone off the hook. I kept getting a busy signal all night."

Brooklyn imagined herself lying in bed devising a plan while her brother tried desperately to contact her. She assumed that her father had prevented calls from coming through, blinded by his rage.

Erica continued. "Last night around ten o'clock, Jordan and Amir called me again. Amir wanted to try and convince you to take it back. He wanted you to tell your father that you didn't mean what you said, that you were lying. It seemed like he wanted to put it all back together again before the church and the family fell apart for good. He sounded really upset. So, I agreed to call you this morning before school."

Erica got emotional at the thought of Amir's voice on the phone the evening prior. He had always been laid-back and easygoing. But the man she had spoken to last night was barely holding himself together. He had sounded hopeless.

"When we hung up, I stayed up half the night waiting for you to call. It was around eight o'clock in the morning, and your mother was frantic. She said you ran away the night before. They were looking all over for you."

Brooklyn was grateful that Hope had filled in some of the blanks for her. There were things that Erica didn't know. By the time Erica called Brooklyn's house that morning, Amir had already been there. Like Brooklyn, he probably hadn't slept all night. When the sun rose, Amir had gone back home. Had been rejected a second time. Instead of going after him, her family had wasted valuable time searching for Brooklyn.

She thought back to what she had been doing during the time that Amir had taken his life. At noon she was just waking up on Stacey's sofa, and the first thing her eyes had rested on was the shoebox full of stolen cash.

"Jordan said that Amir didn't come back. So, Jordan went down to the church to see what was going on. Your father was there, and he was furious when he saw Jordan. He fired him, told him to get his paycheck and leave. He didn't say why, but Jordan already knew what was up. He said there was a big board of trustees meeting going on. A lot of them were calling for your father's resignation. Including my aunt." Erica shrugged. "I'm not sure what her problem is. Normally, she's your father's biggest cheerleader. But not this time. We all assumed that she heard about the relationship between Amir and Jordan. The church and homosexuality and all of that."

Brooklyn's mind raced. She realized that Mrs. Hutchinson's outrage was probably more about the money Brooklyn stole—money Erica knew nothing about—than about Amir's sexuality. She glanced at the church, aware that she was probably the trustee board's most wanted. She looked at Stacey's car and understood her questioning Brooklyn's decision to come here.

"I kept trying to look for you. You didn't come to school. Nobody knew where you were. I got home at 2:30 and saw all the police and everything with the block roped off. I didn't know what happened until I got upstairs and Jordan called me. He was crying."

Brooklyn closed her eyes, aware finally of all the lives she had impacted by her actions.

"He said that Amir never came back to his apartment. Jordan got worried. He went out to look for him. When he came outside of his building, he found out what happened. Amir had jumped off the roof. The cops said he left a note up there. Addressed to your father."

Brooklyn cried and Erica held her.

"This isn't your fault," Erica said, though she wasn't sure she believed that. "Don't blame yourself."

Brooklyn leaned against one of the trees and took a deep breath to steady herself.

"I knew he wasn't strong like me," she said. "He never was. And I tried to force him to be. I kept encouraging him to come out of the closet and be himself. Then when I got in trouble, I dragged him out for my own selfish reasons. Now he's dead."

She thought about the note he left and wondered what was written in it. She wished she had called Erica sooner, that she had called Jordan and gotten to Amir in time to save him from himself.

Brooklyn looked toward the church and saw her father solemnly exiting the front doors. He walked through the parking lot toward his car parked in his reserved space.

Brooklyn looked at Erica. "I gotta go. I'll call you later tonight."

Erica nodded and watched as Brooklyn rushed off in her father's direction.

"Daddy," she called out to him.

Elias turned in her direction. His eyes settled on her, and she saw how emotionally drained he was. She ran to him, stopping short when she reached his side. She wasn't sure whether he would embrace her or if he was still as repulsed by her as he had been the last time they were together.

"Brooklyn. Come here."

She went to him then, fell into his arms, and cried.

"I'm so sorry, Daddy. This is my fault."

Elias held her, his back rigid and straight, his expression blank. He pulled away and looked down at her.

"Thank you for coming back. Your mother is hurt. She said some things I wish you hadn't heard. But I'm glad you listened to me and came back here. We need you right now."

Brooklyn wasn't so sure about that.

"I said some things, too," Elias said. He stepped back and held her face in his hands. "Horrible things to you and to your brother. I'm sorry."

He let her go.

"I hit him, threw him out of my house. I rejected him when he tried to come back and talk to me. And as a result of my actions, he took his own life. This ain't your fault, Brooklyn. I'm the father. I failed both of you."

She had never heard her father sound more beaten, and it crushed her. She hated herself for it. The man she had grown up admiring was never so tormented. She looked at him and knew that he would never be that man again. The old Elias James was gone. In his place stood a man who had been humbled, reduced, and defeated.

"Daddy, I'm sorry."

He shook his head. "You did what we taught you to do. I thought about what you said. You watched me playing with God's word all these years. Using it to my advantage. Your brother, too. I taught you how to be the person you are."

"No, you didn't."

"I don't deserve to pastor this church. From the sounds of it, I'm about to lose it. They want me to step down. My son was gay, and he took his own life. My daughter lied, stole, and murdered her unborn child. What kind of pastor can't control his own family?"

"I'll give back the money," she said, desperately.

Elias shrugged his shoulders and looked at her. "That won't fix this. I lost Amir. I'll blame myself forever. But I can still save you. Save what's left of this family. Come home now, Brooklyn. Your mother will come around."

She shook her head. "I love you. But I can't go back there. Not after all of this." She choked back a sob. "I don't want you to lose everything you worked so hard for. If Mommy leaves you, the church will vote you out. If I come back, they'll never stop whispering about me. You'll have to step down. I can't live with that." She looked at him. "I'm all grown up now. It's time for me to go."

He stared at her, tempted to protest. But deep down he knew that there would be no returning to normalcy for them. Amir was gone. Brooklyn, as they knew her, was gone, too. What remained was a fractured family and a church congregation that was questioning its leadership. As much as he hated to admit it, Brooklyn was right. Her return would mean the end of their life as they knew it.

She hugged him tightly. "I'm sorry I let you down. I'm sorry that Amir is gone. I never meant for this to happen."

"Brooklyn—"

"Tell Hope that I love her."

Brooklyn pulled away before she could change her mind. She rushed back in the direction of Stacey's car and quickly climbed inside. She looked through the windshield and saw her father still standing where she had left him. Their eyes met, and she looked away as she fought back the tears.

"Let's go," she said to Stacey. "Get me out of here please."

Stacey started the car and pulled away slowly.

Elias watched his daughter driving away until the car turned the corner. It would be the last time he ever saw her face.

Erica became Brooklyn's lifeline, connecting her to what remained of her family in the wake of Amir's suicide. Through Erica, Brooklyn learned that Amir's funeral was being held on Friday morning and that her parents had released a statement to the congregation that Brooklyn had been sent away to deal with the emotional toll of losing her brother so tragically. Brooklyn imagined that her mother had written that carefully crafted statement and that she was the one controlling the narrative surrounding the tattered fragments of their family. Jordan had been replaced by a new drummer, and the church seemed prepared to move on gingerly in the wake of the scandal.

Erica made no mention of her cousin, Mrs. Hutchinson, or the money Brooklyn had stolen from the church and from Zo. Brooklyn didn't bring it up either, hopeful that the disappearance of that shoebox would become a mere footnote in the tragic chapter unfolding in all their lives.

Stacey and the crew dealt tenderly with Brooklyn following the news of Amir's death. Brooklyn stayed holed up in her room most of the time, only emerging to use the bathroom or to try and force herself to eat something. She was riddled with guilt and shame, and sickened by the loss of Amir.

Hassan knocked on the door to her room that Thursday afternoon. When he entered, he was holding a black suit. He held it up, smiling.

"What you think?"

She stared back at him, cluelessly. She shrugged her shoulders, annoyed. She was in no mood for his guessing games.

"I got a suit so I can go with you to the funeral tomorrow." He hung it on the doorframe and sat down at the foot of her bed. "Stacey told us what happened with your brother. I'm sorry to hear about it. I've been trying to give you your space and everything. I know it's hard to deal with. Stacey's having a hard time watching you going through it, too. She said it reminds her of when she lost Buster."

Brooklyn sat up in the bed, her guilt compounded by that news. She had been so consumed by her own grief that she hadn't realized how seeing her moping around might affect her host. Stacey had been kind to her but distant for the past few days.

"She told me that you want to go to your brother's funeral tomorrow. But she don't have it in her to go with you. The cemetery, seeing people crying, shit gives her flashbacks."

Brooklyn nodded.

"So, I'm gonna take you. I got me a suit." He pointed at it proudly. "And I'll be here in the morning to pick you up."

Brooklyn sighed. "Okay. Thank you."

"You can talk to me, you know? If you need a shoulder to lean on, mine are pretty strong."

She forced a smile.

"I gave you my number before. But you didn't use it." He handed her a piece of paper. "Here it is again. Don't make the same mistake twice."

Brooklyn felt a chill run down her spine. Amir had said those very words to her once. Weeks ago when they had been sitting together on that sun-soaked afternoon in the church sanctuary. He had been warning her about her relationship with Zo.

"Don't make the same mistake twice."

She wondered if it was a sign. She wasn't sure. But as Hassan left that day, she felt a little bit stronger.

She waited until the hustle and bustle of Stacey's illicit business waned down. Then Brooklyn emerged from her self-imposed dungeon and joined her in the living room.

Stacey was counting money with a lit blunt hanging from her lips. She looked at Brooklyn and nodded.

Brooklyn sat down across from her.

"I want to thank you for being so nice to me. You didn't have to open your door to me. You definitely didn't have to go with me to Staten Island. I know I laid a lot on you. I want you to know that I'm gonna get out of here soon. Soon as I get my paperwork together, I'll be out of your way."

"And where you going?" Stacey asked the question sarcastically. "You think the money you have is gonna last you for long?"

"I was stupid to spend money like that the other day," Brooklyn admitted. "I was high off adrenaline." She closed her eyes in an effort to block out the fact that Amir was being scraped off the sidewalk while she was on a shopping spree on her first day of so-called freedom. "I'm gonna be smarter from now on."

Stacey nodded. "When that money runs out, how are you gonna survive? You need to take a course or something. Get you some marketable skills. I'm not trying to come down on you. But you gotta grow up now, Brooklyn. You're on your own for real now. Ain't no turning back. You gotta strategize and spend the next few days figuring out what you want to do with your life. Who do you want to be and how are you gonna make that happen?"

Brooklyn realized how silly she had been to think that she could figure it out as she went. She never really had a plan. The only thing she had figured out was that she wanted out. Now that she had gotten what she wanted, she felt like a confused little girl.

"I couldn't put my finger on what it was," Stacey said. "But I knew there was something I liked about you. The other day when I took you home, it hit me. You remind me of myself. Me and Roscoe grew up hard. I met Buster and he changed my life. Put me in the game, put my brother on. He saved my life. When I lost him, I had no fuckin' clue what I was gonna do next. Everybody expected me to fold. But I'm not built like that. And I don't think you are, either."

Stacey tapped her blunt out.

"I'm not," Brooklyn said. "I'm gonna survive this."

Stacey nodded.

"I'm sorry I've been so depressing. I know you didn't ask for all of this." Brooklyn wished she could snap out of it. But she was mentally, physically, and emotionally exhausted.

"What happened with your brother would drive some people crazy. You're going through a very deep and painful loss. Just take it one day at a time. You'll come out on the other side stronger than before."

Brooklyn felt like she might cry. She thanked Stacey again, went back to her dungeon, and thought about what she'd been told.

She awoke the morning of the funeral, put on a black dress she'd bought the day that Amir died, and considered the irony. She hadn't known then that this would be her attire for such a somber occasion. She had imagined herself wearing it to a club for the first time. Instead, she stood staring at her reflection in the mirror wondering if it was too short, too tight, too inappropriate. She told herself that it didn't matter. She had no one left to impress.

Hassan waited for her downstairs in his black Toyota Camry. She put on a pair of dark sunglasses as she emerged from Stacey's building and slid into the passenger seat.

She looked at Hassan and thought he looked handsome in a suit.

"Thank you for coming with me today," she said. "I know this ain't part of your job."

Hassan shrugged. "It's no problem. You ready?"

Brooklyn nodded. Together, they drove to the church in Staten Island for the funeral service.

When they arrived, Brooklyn suddenly found herself overcome with emotion. She sat in the car in the church parking lot and watched as mourners poured in. With her hand on the car's door handle, she sat perched and ready to step out. But her legs wouldn't move. Her heart raced, and she felt sweat pooling on her forehead.

Hassan looked at her, concerned. "Are you okay?"

She shook her head. "I can't go in there."

He waited.

She rolled her window down and reclined her seat. She closed her eyes and shook her head again.

"He's already dead. What am I going in there for? Not to pay my respects to him. He can't hear me anymore, can't see my face or know that I'm sorry."

Hassan reached for her hand and held it comfortingly.

"My mother hates me," she said. "My father seems like a huge piece of him died, too. My little sister—she's probably better off without me. All these years she's had to play mediator, getting between me and my parents, trying to keep the peace. It's my fault she's so mature for her age."

"You're beating yourself up," Hassan said. "That's not what your brother would want you to do."

She huffed. "My friend Erica said that he was trying to get in touch with me before he did it. He was mad at me, and he wanted to confront me. I never gave him the chance. I left too soon. I ran away from home like a coward and hid out in Harlem. Started over like nothing ever happened. Meanwhile, my brother was back here dying inside."

She wiped her eyes with a tissue and stared at the hearse parked outside of the church. She shook her head again. "I can't go in there," she repeated. "But I want to stay here until it's over. I need to be close to him." She looked at Hassan. "Okay?"

He nodded without hesitation. "Of course. Whatever you want to do."

They sat together in the car outside as the funeral service went on inside. The sound of the church organ drifted through the stained glass windows and out to the parking lot where Brooklyn sat with her eyes pressed closed. She thought about all the times she and her siblings had heard those chords on the organ—all the times they tapped their feet, pounded tambourines, and clapped their hands to the beat of Jordan's drum. The realization that she would never see those days again caused her tears to fall more rapidly. She never thought she would long for the chance to sit beside her brother in the front pew of the church and snicker at their inside jokes. But she would have given just about anything to do that now.

She thought about Hope, left to mourn her siblings alone. Brooklyn wondered if they would ever see each other again if enough time could pass to heal these kinds of wounds. She thought about her mother and rolled her eyes. Sabrina's rejection had not been unexpected for Brooklyn. She had always sensed her mother's quiet disapproval of her. Even as a child, she had always been too loud, too flashy, too outspoken for her mother's liking. Those things had delighted her father by contrast, and

Brooklyn had loved him for it. She knew that now he was second-guessing his parenting style. Having lost her and Amir to the very sins he had spent so many years preaching about had sent him over the edge emotionally. Brooklyn knew that she had broken her father's heart. That was enough to grieve all by itself.

Hassan touched her hand again, gently.

"Hey. What's on your mind?"

She smiled, weakly. "I'm just thinking," she said. "About everything. What I should have done differently." She looked down at her hands. "When Amir killed himself, I wonder what he was thinking."

Hassan shook his head. "Don't do that to yourself."

"No. That's part of my process. I keep trying to imagine what was going through his mind as he walked across that roof and looked over the edge. Was he thinking of me? Thinking I betrayed him and the whole world would turn their back on him if they knew the truth? Why didn't he wait a few days and give me time to come back around?" She glanced at the church, helplessly. "Even now, that shit sounds selfish. I'm wondering what he thought about *me*, why he didn't wait for *me*. My family said I always make everything about me. Maybe they're right. I'm a horrible person."

Hassan shook his head. "Nah. Everybody makes mistakes they wish they could take back. Even me."

Brooklyn looked at him.

"My brother Dawan," Hassan said. "When he got locked up, I was supposed to be with him that night. I was young then. Sixteen, seventeen. I was new to the game. Just getting my feet wet. His name was already ringing bells uptown. On his strength, I was starting to make a name for myself, too. He told me he had to make a drop-off in the Bronx, asked me to go with him. I said 'yeah' and we planned to meet up at my Mom's crib. That night, I ran into a shorty I knew from around the way. We went and got something to eat, went back to her crib and all that. Her mother was out of town or whatever. Next thing you know, it's nine o'clock and I fucked around and missed the meetup with my brother. He waited for me for about an hour, couldn't get in contact with me, so he went and did the shit on his own. His whole timeline was off, and he was by himself. He got pulled over before he could make the drop. Now he's doing ten years up north and I'm out here trying to make it up to him, to my family, and to prove to myself that I'm worthy of being Dawan's little brother."

Hassan looked at her and rolled his eyes. "We all make mistakes. Don't beat yourself up for yours. We all have choices. My brother chose to be in this game. Yours chose a way out. That's not on us."

Brooklyn thought about that. She sat in silence until the church doors swung open and the funeral attendees started pouring out. The crowd gathered in front of the church and stood talking together, many of them still crying.

Brooklyn watched from the parking lot across the street. She saw so many people she knew, including family who had come in from out of town. She wondered what they were saying in their private moments about the scandal that had rocked their world. She knew that she would never be welcome there again. This was a part of her life she would be leaving behind for good after today.

There was a commotion at the church doors, and Brooklyn watched as her mother was escorted out. She was wailing loudly with women from the church's nurse ministry on either side of her. Deacons and their wives followed her out, bracing themselves in case she fainted. Sabrina was inconsolable. They helped her to the waiting limousine parked behind the hearse. Brooklyn marveled at her. Still so beautiful despite the ugly occasion. Sabrina wore a black hat with a black veil that covered her face. Her black dress had a dainty bow at the neck and her hands were adorned in sheer lace gloves. She clutched a handkerchief in her hand and a Fendi bag on her arm, and even in her grief she looked elegant and poised.

Hope emerged next. She was alone, which seemed especially

poignant to Brooklyn. While all of the attention was focused on their grieving mother, Hope walked stoically in solitude toward the limousine. She was dressed in a dark gray dress and wore her hair pulled back from her face. She looked so sad, so heartbroken. Brooklyn fought the urge to call out to her, knowing that her presence wasn't welcome at this point.

The pallbearers walked out with Amir's bronze-colored casket held high. They walked solemnly toward the hearse as several of the mourners wept openly. At the church doors, Brooklyn saw her father's silhouette.

Elias stood and watched as his son's remains were loaded into the hearse. He had preached many funerals over the years. Due to the drug war that had plagued the city, many of those funerals had been for young men like Amir. When he had overseen those services, the expected sadness had always been deepened by the tragic loss of a life so young and full of hope. He had consoled countless parents during those times, counseled their families in the months after their loved ones were laid to rest. Never in all those years had he imagined a time when he would be in their shoes. Now, he was the grieving parent, his was the family in need of grief counseling. The death of his son, the guilt of his own actions, and the awareness that the eyes of the church and the greater Staten Island community were squarely on him made Elias weak in the knees.

He walked slowly toward the limousine where his wailing wife and despondent daughter waited for him. He had no idea that Brooklyn was watching his every step from behind the tinted windows of Hassan's car.

Brooklyn noticed the hunch in her father's shoulders, usually so tall and square. She saw him walking with his head hung low and remembered his confidence, swagger, and electric smile. That part of him was gone for good, she knew. She dabbed at her eyes as she watched him disappear into the car and the driver shut the door behind him.

They followed the funeral procession at a safe distance. Hassan was careful to leave at least a few cars between them and the other cars so that no one would sense Brooklyn's presence there. She had made it clear to him that she didn't want to add to her family's pain. She just wanted to see her brother laid to rest, pay her respects, and try to start anew.

They arrived at the cemetery on Victory Boulevard, and Hassan parked across the street near Silver Lake Park. Brooklyn watched as the funeral procession meandered through the cemetery to a plot near a large oak tree.

The pallbearers and the assistant pastor emerged from their cars and set the casket up on the lowering device. The mourners began to emerge from their cars and gathered around the open grave.

Brooklyn clutched her hands to her face and watched. She couldn't hear what the preacher was saying. But she imagined that he was speaking of Amir's goodness, his love for his family, and his desire to please God. She hoped they all remembered the way his smile lit up a room and how his calm, soothing voice made it seem like everything would be alright no matter what. She watched her family hold on to each other with Sabrina and Hope flanking Elias and gripping him tightly as Amir was lowered to his final resting place.

Hassan didn't speak. He watched in silence as Brooklyn stared sadly at the scene of her brother's funeral. She was grateful for his patience as she watched each person slowly drift away until only her father remained standing at Amir's grave site.

She wanted so badly to run to him then and beg his forgiveness. Part of her wanted to jump into that grave with Amir. After all, she had no idea how she could ever move forward with the weight of this guilt on her shoulders. She held her hand against the window and watched as her father's shoulders quaked as he cried.

Finally, Elias walked slowly back to the waiting limousine and climbed inside. It drove away just as slowly, maneuvering through the cemetery exit and back in the direction of Promised Land. Brooklyn knew that the repast was being held there. Erica had told her all the details. She hated the thought of her family having to put on their well-rehearsed poker faces and host a gathering of genuine mourners and nosy parishioners alike.

She looked at Hassan.

"I'm going to go over there now and pay my respects," she said.

Hassan nodded. "You want me to come with you?"

She shook her head. "No. I want to go alone."

He watched her climb out and wait for passing cars before trotting across the street. She walked through the cemetery gates and headed up the walkway to her brother's grave.

She approached the scene slowly, crying openly.

"Amir . . . I'm so sorry. I can't believe this." She dabbed at her eyes, futilely. "Why did you do this? We could have fixed it. I would have told you that I was wrong, and we could have fixed it." She gestured with her hands as she spoke. "I know you trusted me. You told me the truth and I used it against you. I never meant to hurt you. But you didn't stick up for me. I felt like you were taking their side and I wanted you to feel what it was like . . . but, Amir, I never meant for you to hurt yourself."

She wept loudly then; her heart shattered in a thousand pieces.

"What do you think he'd say back to you?"

The deep voice behind her startled her so badly that her whole body shook. Brooklyn spun around and faced Jordan standing so close to her that she wondered how she hadn't noticed him sooner.

She stared at him with her mouth agape and pondered the question he had just asked her. She studied his face and found his expression impossible to read. She couldn't tell if he was asking the question as a challenge or as an earnest inquiry about the man they both loved.

"I think . . . he would probably tell me that he hates me," she cried. "That I fucked up his life and left him no choice but to throw himself off a fucking building and kill himself!" She covered her face with her hands, hiding herself from the shame.

Jordan watched her, assuming that she expected to be consoled. But he offered her no consolation.

"He would never say that to you," Jordan said, flatly. He stared down at the open grave. "Amir was full of nothing but pure love. He was a good man with a kind heart. He would have told you that he was looking for you. Calling you. Not because he was mad at you. But because he was afraid. He thought your family was all he had. He would have told you the things that he told me. How he felt tormented for years by his feelings. Growing up as the only son made him feel like he was living under a microscope. He wanted to please your father. Live up to the expectations that were placed on him from the moment he was born."

Brooklyn wiped her tears and thought about the things Amir had said to her in the quiet of his bedroom. She could tell that Jordan had loved her brother, and that the two of them had shared all their secrets with each other.

"Before he died, Erica told me he was with you. What did he say?" Brooklyn asked. "What was he thinking?"

Jordan's eyes washed over her. "He was worried about you. Even with everything he was dealing with, he was still thinking about you. He talked about your father a lot. How he wanted to explain to him in his own words what he was feeling—how me and him felt about each other. But he wanted you to go there together. He still thought he could depend on you to give him courage."

Jordan shook his head at the thought and looked at the ground again. "When he went to your house that day, he said he was gonna try to talk to your parents. But he never came back."

Brooklyn stared at him. It was clear that his heart was as broken as her own. "Jordan, I owe you an apology. I'm sorry for everything. You didn't deserve this. Losing your job—"

"That job at the church was nothing," Jordan said. "Losing Amir. That's what hurts."

He looked at Brooklyn again. "He's the only person I ever truly loved. I loved him so much that I understood him completely. I could tell that he was desperate for your father's approval. It's hard enough being gay out here. But being a pastor's son made it worse for him. That's why I stuck around. If not for him, I would have left a long time ago. Whenever I tried to get him to talk about leaving, he changed the subject."

Brooklyn frowned. She hadn't known that. "You wanted to leave?"

"I suggested it all the time. But Amir wasn't ready, and I loved him enough to be patient. Enough to see that being exposed and having your father find out would kill him. I knew he trusted me. That was something I didn't take lightly. Maybe you didn't know how hard it is to trust somebody when you've been lying to the world your whole life. But Amir trusted you with the truth. That's what broke his heart."

Brooklyn waited for him to say more but there was nothing. Jordan stared at her in silence as a cold breeze rustled through the trees above them. For reasons she couldn't explain, she suddenly felt uneasy.

"Y'all okay?"

Brooklyn turned and saw Hassan approaching. She smiled, nodded, and reached for his hand, grateful for his presence.

Hassan nodded at Jordan. "How ya doing?"

Jordan nodded back, looked at Brooklyn one last time, then walked away without another word.

Brooklyn and Hassan stood watching him as he exited the cemetery and walked north on Victory Boulevard.

"Who was that?" Hassan asked.

"That was Jordan. Amir's . . ." She struggled to find the right terminology.

Hassan nodded. "I get it." He spared her the trouble. "I was watching from the car, and I couldn't tell if y'all were having a friendly conversation or not."

Brooklyn shook her head. "Me either."

She looked down at her brother's grave, pulled a note from her pocket that she had written to him that morning, and dropped it down on top of the casket.

She sniffled, wiped her nose, and turned to Hassan.

"I'm ready to go now."

They walked back to his car, peeled off toward the bridge, and left that chapter of Brooklyn's life behind.

Chapter Eight

Baltimore

Brooklyn was ready to leave New York City for good. But Stacey's words kept repeating in her head. She needed a plan. On the way back to Harlem, she got her first real lesson on the game from Hassan.

"I know that you stepped in for your brother and all that. But how did you get to the point where you make enough money to support yourself and your family?" she asked. "What type of stuff did she have you doing at first?"

"Stacey gets money here in the city. But she makes most of her money flipping birds out of state."

Brooklyn frowned. "What does '*flipping birds*' mean?"

Hassan smirked. "Damn. Zo really had you out here clueless, huh?" He shook his head. "A bird is a kilo of coke. They cost a lot in the five boroughs. But if you take it out of state, you can get a lot more for it. Stacey has money all up and down I-95. I started making those kinds of trips for her at first. Then it got hot for me down there and I had to come home."

She thought about that. "Where's '*down there*'?"

"Baltimore, DC, Virginia, North Carolina."

Brooklyn's eyes widened. Now she had her plan. All she had to do was set it in motion.

She waited for the right time to talk to Stacey about it. She found the opportunity two days after Amir's funeral. Brooklyn found her in the kitchen cooking breakfast. It was the first time Brooklyn had seen her cook anything in the days since she had been there. Typically, she ordered food from local restaurants and ate sandwiches from the deli down the block just like her brother and his friends. In many ways, Stacey seemed like one of the guys. The only clue of her femininity was her undeniable curves that couldn't be camouflaged by the loose-fitting clothes she typically wore.

"I have a plan," Brooklyn said as she walked into the kitchen. "I want to talk to you about it before the guys get here."

Stacey waited.

"I want to take the money I have and put it in the game."

Stacey looked simultaneously surprised and amused.

Brooklyn continued. "I have about ten thousand dollars. Hass told me that's not enough for a bird. But I can put it in the pot with your money, and you can send me out of town to flip it."

Stacey leaned against the counter with her arms folded across her chest. Brooklyn spoke so matter-of-factly that it made her chuckle.

"What's a flip, Brooklyn? What's a bird? What you know about that?"

"Not much," she admitted. "But I know that you can take that money I have in the room and buy some drugs with it. Then you can send me down South with those drugs and make us a nice little profit. Right?"

Stacey nodded. "Yeah. I could do that."

"Let's do it then."

Over breakfast, they ironed out their plan. Brooklyn knew that she had more than $10,000 left. But she told Stacey that she had a little less than she actually had, just to give herself a cushion. She thought of it like taking a gamble, and she wasn't willing to bet it all. Still, she couldn't deny the feeling of excitement she got as Stacey explained what was expected of her.

She would bring duffel bags of cocaine to different locations, meeting up with Stacey's people along the way. She would travel alone in order to draw less suspicion. Stacey seemed to think that Brooklyn's youthfulness would be an asset, making her seem like a harmless student on her way home for the holidays. It was winter, which would also serve them well. She could hide large packages of drugs in the pockets of big coats, use the hoods to shield her face, Plus, lazy cops made fewer foot patrols in winter months. It hadn't taken much coaxing for Stacey to see that the plan was kind of genius.

Brooklyn would make a few trial runs first. Just as she had done for Alonzo in the beginning. The difference was that Stacey let Brooklyn know up front what she was facing in the event that she got caught. Major time behind bars, even for a first offender.

"I'm not gonna send you out there blind like Zo did. It's your life, your freedom you're putting on the line. You should know what comes along with that. Now that you've been told, act like you know. Be safe out there."

Stacey would give her smaller quantities at first, then she'd increase Brooklyn's load over time. In exchange, Stacey would multiply Brooklyn's investment with the promise that she could pull out at any time.

"This is real simple," Stacey said. "A key costs twenty thousand right about now. If you got ten thousand, I'll match that ten and we can do a clean flip. You take the work down there and make it happen. Bring the money back and we'll split it fifty-fifty."

"How much do I sell it for down there?" Brooklyn asked.

"Thirty," Stacey said.

Brooklyn liked the sound of that. She could make a $5,000 profit in just a day or two.

"Don't go down there making side deals with niggas," Stacey warned. "That's a trap. You don't know who's who down there. Lots of Feds and shit all over the place. You meet with who I tell you to meet with and you'll be alright. You go down there doing some dumb shit and get caught, and you're on your own." She locked eyes with Brooklyn. "If you ever get caught, don't you mention my name. They ask you who you work for, you tell them you're self-employed. Because I didn't ask you to do this. This is your plan. Remember that."

Brooklyn nodded.

"Otherwise, I'll have your head sliced in half, from one of those pretty little dimples to the other. Because as nice as I am, as kind, I'm also not the one to fuck with, Brooklyn."

She stared at Brooklyn for long, meaningful moments before she spoke again. "I like you a lot. You remind me of myself. But this is business. It ain't personal." Stacey had to bear in mind that a girl who would snitch on her own brother might be capable of doing the same to her.

"I understand," Brooklyn said. "I don't want no problems. I just want to get money."

She took her first trip that Tuesday afternoon. Stacey gave her a ticket for a Greyhound bus to Baltimore and had Roscoe drop her off at the Port Authority in Times Square. Brooklyn wore a John Jay College sweatshirt, a baggy pair of sweatpants, and a pair of Air Max. Her duffel bag was packed with neatly folded clothes for her trip, along with a wad of Bounce dryer sheets to cover the scent of the drugs tucked beneath those clothes. She had only been given one kilo for this first trip. Stacey told her that New York City was only second to Miami in terms of their reputation for cocaine quality. So, the price of importing such a high-quality product was higher for her Baltimore clientele.

Brooklyn's job was to go down to Maryland and check into a hotel in the area. She would only be in town for one day, then she'd make the trip back home with the cash. If it all went well, she would be in and out. Brooklyn didn't allow herself to imagine what would happen if it went badly.

She stood around Port Authority waiting for her bus. She was trying not to appear too nervous. She wondered now whether Zo had been smart not to tell her about the risks involved. Now that she knew that she could be sent to prison for more than a decade, she was paranoid about getting caught. Her eyes darted around the bus station nervously, searching for people who might be cleverly disguised undercover officers like Stacey had warned her about. She coaxed herself to relax and rushed aboard as soon as the bus arrived.

She found a seat near the window and tucked her bag beneath her seat. Stacey told her to never allow the bag to leave her sight. Even if she had to go to the bathroom. That bag was supposed to be her appendage for as long as she was on the move. She rested her feet on top of the bag for good measure.

She had a pocket full of snacks for the journey. Instead of getting off the bus at rest stops along the way, she would travel the whole way surviving on Snickers bars and Doritos. Less movement equaled less risk, according to Stacey. Brooklyn intended to follow Stacey's advice to the letter. Brooklyn was fine with sitting still for the three-hour trip. All she wanted to do was put some distance between herself and her old life.

She pulled herself closer to the window as the bus rumbled along the highway. She felt her pulse quicken as they crossed over into New Jersey. Her plan to break free of her family's chains had finally succeeded.

She only wished Amir was free, too. She wished he hadn't given up so soon, that he had found the courage within himself to withstand the storm. She thought about what Jordan had said to her at Amir's grave site.

"*Amir trusted you with the truth. That's what broke his heart.*"

She still wasn't sure what to make of those words. She couldn't tell if Jordan blamed her for her brother's death or absolved her of it. Still pondering the thought, she drifted off to sleep with her head leaning against the window as the bus journeyed further south.

She woke up as the sun set over Baltimore Harbor. It was love at first sight.

She sat up in her seat and stared out the window at the dawn of a new day in a new city and what she hoped was a new chapter in her life. Sitting up taller in her seat, she felt proud of herself for making it this far. She silently congratulated herself.

I knew you could do it. You got this.

She was nothing like her mother after all. She assured herself of that. Sabrina would never have been bold enough, courageous enough to do what Brooklyn was doing. As she looked at her vague reflection in the bus window, she stared back at her own steely gaze and knew that she was going to make it after all.

She was all on her own now with nothing to lose. No safety net or soft place to land. Just her own resilience and will to survive. She had to have her own back from now on, she reasoned. And tonight would be her first test.

Stacey had given her clear instructions. Once she got off the bus at the Baltimore Greyhound terminal, she took a taxi to the Days Inn at Hopkins Plaza.

A young Black girl with a perfect bone-straight doobie wrap greeted her at the front desk. The brown-skinned beauty greeted Brooklyn warmly, smiling wide as she stepped forward.

"Good morning! How can I help you today?"

Brooklyn smiled back at her, praying that this went as smoothly as Stacey promised her it would. "Good morning. I have a reservation. The name is Stacey Cash."

It was an alias, of course. Brooklyn had been crashing in her spare bedroom long enough to know that Stacey's last name was actually Anderson. "Cash" was a not-so-subtle password for the system Stacey had established for trips like this one.

Brooklyn and the girl locked eyes for what seemed like endless moments. The girl seemed surprised. Her smile slowly faded away. Brooklyn began to worry that something was wrong.

"ID please?" The girl looked at Brooklyn meaningfully.

Brooklyn frowned. Then she remembered the most important part of this interaction. "Yes!" She dug into the front pocket of her duffel bag and handed the attendant a small envelope.

"Okay. Thank youuuu," the girl sang. She took the envelope

with the tip, slid it quickly underneath the front desk, and smiled again.

"Thank you," she said, sweetly. She looked around to make sure no one was listening. She whispered, "I'm sorry. This is the first time I've seen a female doing this. Stacey usually sends big, scary-looking men down here. You're not what I was expecting."

Brooklyn relaxed a little. "Okay. Yeah. It's cool."

"Rooms 210 and 410." The attendant slid the room keys across the desk and gestured toward the elevators that would take Brooklyn upstairs.

"Thank you."

"My name is Dawn. Let me know if I can help you with anything while you're here."

Brooklyn nodded.

"I like your New York accent," Dawn said. "Soon as you started talking, I got distracted. That accent is so dope." She giggled like a little girl. She was obsessed with all things related to New York City. She had never been there but imagined it to be an exciting and fast-paced town where only the strong survived.

Brooklyn thanked her, wondering why this girl was gushing over her so much. She hadn't ventured outside of New York City much, and therefore had never realized how pronounced her speech pattern was. She made a mental note to keep that in mind. Her inflection would be a dead giveaway that she was an out-of-towner. She nodded.

"I'll let you know if I need anything."

Brooklyn went to room 410 first and decided that this would be her room for the night. It wasn't much. But to her, it felt like paradise. She knew this was where she belonged. Not in Baltimore, but in this life. She believed that she had wandered into her own Promised Land and it excited her beyond description. It wasn't just the money or the potential to increase what she already had. It was the fact that she hadn't chosen the safest route. What she was doing took guts. It took heart.

She called Stacey to let her know that she had arrived safely.

"Good," Stacey said. "So far so good. Now call that number I gave you and ask for Chance. He's gonna come meet you there at the hotel."

"Okay."

"Chance is good people. You can trust him. But don't let your guard down. Stay on point. You're alone in a new city. Keep your eyes open. Let me know when it's all done."

Brooklyn hung up and did as she was told. She dialed the phone number Stacey had given her and a guy picked up on the third ring.

"Can I speak to Chance?"

His voice was deep and throaty. "This is Chance."

"My name is Brooklyn. Stacey told me to call you to let you know I'm here."

Chance knew the drill by now. He didn't need to ask where "here" was since Stacey's people always met him at the Days Inn. This was the first time Stacey had ever sent a girl, though. He couldn't wait to meet her.

"What's the room number? And what you look like? I bet you're cute."

Brooklyn felt sweat pooling on her forehead and wiped it. It suddenly occurred to her that she was nervous. She tried to remember everything Stacey had told her.

"*Don't say too much over the phone. Keep it short and sweet.*" Stacey had said.

"Room 210." Brooklyn hung up.

She paced the floor, breathing deeply, and willing herself to calm down. As brave as she had felt just moments ago, she now felt just as nervous. But she reminded herself that she was not a quitter, that this would be an easy flip if she could just see it through to the end. She assured herself that nothing was amiss, and she had everything under control.

She picked up her backpack and the key for room 210 and

left. She took the elevator down two floors and entered the second "dummy" room that would be used to conduct the sale. She pulled the kilo out of her backpack and placed it on the dresser. Looking at her reflection in the mirror, she spoke out loud.

"Don't be scared," she told herself. "They'll know if you're scared."

While she waited, watching *Jeopardy* and *Wheel of Fortune* on the TV, she tried to ignore her stomach rumbling. The snacks she'd eaten on the bus ride down had been her only sustenance for the day.

She sat on the bed staring at the cocaine on the dresser. It had been an hour since she hung up the phone on Chance. Brooklyn began to worry that she had fucked up somehow. She thought about what Dawn had said at the front desk when she checked in. Stacey had never sent a girl to do this job before. Brooklyn's mind raced with varying scenarios. Chance could be setting her up. She knew that she was taking a big risk. All of this was insane. Stealing from Zo and the church, now making drug deals in Baltimore with strange men and no backup. She was risking her life. But she couldn't back out now.

The knock on the door startled her a bit. She walked to the peephole and saw three big Black men standing outside the door. She opened it and welcomed them in.

Brooklyn shut the door to the room and stood with her trembling hands shoved down in the pockets of her sweatpants.

Chance looked around while his friends spread out, opening up the closets, checking the bathroom and shower for any signs of a setup.

Chance smiled. "No offense. Just making sure you're here by yourself."

Brooklyn drank him in. He wore a ski cap and a North Face jacket, a pair of Iceberg jeans and a matching sweater. She nodded, her mouth too dry to speak. She prayed that she looked more confident than she felt right now.

"This is it?" He pointed to the dresser.

"Yeah. Test it out."

He laughed. "Nah. That's what Booker's here for." He patted one of his boys on the arm.

The tall, thin guy walked over to the dresser and opened the bag. He stuck a finger inside and scooped some of the powder out, sniffing it into his nostril in one motion. He sniffed a few more times, shook his head, waited.

He looked at Brooklyn. Finally, he nodded.

"New York, New York!" A broad smile crept across his face. He looked at Chance. "We can break that down and make a hundred. Easy!"

Chance shushed him.

Brooklyn relaxed a bit. Stacey had given her a crash course on flipping birds. So she knew that Booker was suggesting that they break the kilo down into smaller quantities and more than triple the price they paid for it. She looked at Chance, expectantly.

"You only got the one key?"

"You got the money?" she asked.

"Wouldn't be here if I didn't." He shrugged a bit. "I can't do thirty-three, though. Let's do a flat thirty."

"I can't do that." Her heart rate sped up. Stacey had warned her that Chance might try this.

"Why not?" Chance had a slight smirk on his face.

"Because I'm not stupid. Price is thirty-three. I know I can get thirty-five for that out here. Stacey's working with you as it is. To sell it to you for thirty flat, you'd have to take more than one key."

"You said you only had one."

"That's all you asked for. If you want to negotiate the price, call Stacey. Talk to her." Brooklyn nodded toward the phone at the bedside.

He stared at her in silence for a few moments, then he gestured to the shortest guy in his crew. The man stepped forward and handed her a large manila envelope.

Brooklyn sat down on the bed and started counting the money. There was $30,000 exactly. She glared at him, annoyed.

"I told you—"

"Calm down, pretty girl. I'm just fucking with you." He handed her a stack of hundred-dollar bills.

Brooklyn counted them and nodded when she realized it was the extra $3,000.

Chance smiled at her. "I had to try and see if I could get a little discount. That's what y'all do in New York, right? Go down to Chinatown and Delancey Street and negotiate with the store owners?"

Brooklyn nodded. "Yes. But this ain't Chinatown. And Stacey don't play about her money." She stood up and gestured for them to leave.

Chance didn't budge. There was something about this little cutey that amused him. He looked at his guys. "Y'all go start breaking that up." He stopped Booker as he walked toward the door. "Don't overdo it, nigga!"

Booker grinned and nodded. Then both of the guys left.

Chance looked at Brooklyn when they were alone. "You mind if I sit and have a drink with you real quick?"

He took his hat off and she got her first real look at his face. He was handsome with lips that looked kissable.

She thought about it. Stacey might not approve. She looked Chance up and down. He was cute. Tall, muscular, chocolate-hued. She figured it couldn't hurt. She nodded.

He pulled a pint of Hennessy out of his inside coat pocket and sat down in one of the chairs at the desk.

"I want to know more," he said, gesturing at her. "Beautiful girl from New York named Brooklyn. Selling cocaine in a town all by herself. What's your story, baby girl?"

She shrugged. "My story is no different from yours. I'm just out here trying to make a dollar out of fifteen cents."

He looked her in the eyes, probingly.

"How old are you?" he asked.

"Grown."

He nodded his head. "Okay. If you're so grown, why you got me in here drinking alone?" He held out his pint of cognac, offering her a sip.

She shook her head. "I'm not a big drinker," she said. "I like to keep my mind clear. Stay focused."

"I understand."

"What do you understand about me?"

He shrugged. "I think you're scared."

She hated how true that was, but she kept her poker face on.

"Probably been on your own your whole life. Young girl out here playing a grown man's game. Yeah. You're scared." He searched her for signs that his guesses were correct, but she stared back at him deadpanned.

"What you running from?" he asked.

She looked at him, seriously. "Myself."

"You're far from home. You think Stacey's gonna protect you?"

She shook her head. "I'm gonna protect me."

He smiled. "I like that. I like *you*, Brooklyn. You got me wanting to know more." Chance rose to leave. "How long are you in town?" he asked her.

She smiled back at him, enjoying their banter. "I'm already gone."

"Okay. Well, let me take you out next time you're in town," he said. "We'll get the business part out of the way first. Then you can let me show you around a little before you start running again."

She smiled. "Sounds good, Chance."

She walked him to the door and waved at him before shutting and locking it behind him.

Brooklyn remained in the spare room for a few minutes, then snuck down to the lobby to make sure that the coast was clear.

Seeing no signs of Chance or his friends, she went to the front desk and waited for the attendant to come back. Within seconds, Dawn was back with that same bright smile as before.

"Hey! Can I help you with anything?"

Brooklyn rubbed her stomach for emphasis. "Where's a good place to eat around here? I'm starving."

"Oh! Well, there's a bunch of good restaurants nearby. You like seafood?"

"Yup!" Brooklyn's mouth was already watering.

Dawn rattled off a list of steak and seafood spots that were close by.

Brooklyn thanked her. She slid a $50 bill across the counter. "I need to order something for delivery. I'm waiting for an important phone call in my room, and I don't want to miss it."

Dawn was already nodding, tucking the crisp $50 into the pocket of her blazer. "Yes! What you want, girl? I got you. I'll bring it right to your room. No problem!"

Brooklyn smiled. "Perfect! Let me get a fried catfish sandwich and some fries."

Dawn jotted it down quickly. "Which floor should I bring it to?" Dawn asked, discreetly.

"Fourth."

Dawn nodded and watched with fascination as Brooklyn sashayed over to the elevators and went back to her original room. She wasn't expecting any call. But she knew that walking around an unfamiliar city with $33,000 in cash and no weapons was a dumb move. She needed to sit tight until morning, get back to New York without interruption, and prove to Stacey that she was capable of handling this responsibility and more.

She called Stacey to tell her how everything had gone. She didn't leave out any details, including the fact that Chance had attempted to see if she would sell him the work for less.

Stacey huffed. "He was testing you. Trying to see if he can sense a weakness in the chain. He tries the same tricks all men use with females in the game. He'll see if he can outsmart you. And if he can't, he'll try to charm you. You played it right. Good job. I'll see you tomorrow."

Brooklyn smiled, hung up the phone, and settled in for the night.

Within thirty minutes, Dawn had knocked on the door with a bag of Baltimore's finest cuisine. Brooklyn thanked her and latched the locks on the room door. She took a shower and sat on the bed feasting on the best fish sandwich she had ever eaten. Stacey had told her to sample Baltimore's unparalleled seafood and Brooklyn had only half believed her rave reviews. But now she knew how right she was.

After she ate, she counted the money again for good measure. She wondered how much money Stacey and her crew made on a weekly basis. She felt a mixture of adrenaline and nervousness at the thought of it all. The possibilities were endless. On this flip alone, they had each made an easy $6,500 profit. This was a small transaction compared to Stacey's usual deals. So, Brooklyn couldn't imagine what the crew was bringing in consistently.

She kept thinking about Chance, wondering what his story was. She sensed that he was trouble, and she had to admit that she was drawn to guys like that.

She slept like a baby that first night in Maryland. She had never been so far away from home alone before. Or whatever "home" had meant prior to this night. It was like breathing new air that was ripe with possibility. When she woke up the next morning, she felt rejuvenated. Her bus back to New York was scheduled for noon. She repacked her bag, careful to put the cash in a stack between layers of clothing just as she had watched Stacey do with the cocaine. Although she wasn't bringing any drugs back with her this time, she wanted to get in the habit of being careful. She wanted to play the game smart.

She looked around the room twice to make sure that she didn't leave anything behind. Then she grabbed both room keys and headed down to the front desk. Dawn wasn't there. There was a short white girl with dark hair and glasses at the desk that morning. Brooklyn wasn't sure what to do. She didn't want to assume that the girl was in on Stacey's system. Brooklyn slid her sunglasses on her face, set the room keys down on the counter while the brunette was checking in a new guest. Distracted by the task at hand, the woman didn't notice Brooklyn slip smoothly out the door and into a taxi headed back to the bus station.

The ride home seemed much quicker. She was back in New York by three o'clock and Hassan was parked on Eighth Avenue waiting for her, just as Stacey promised he would be.

She climbed into the passenger seat, strapped on her seat belt, and tucked the duffel bag at her feet.

Hassan fist-bumped her. "Nice job, rookie! How do you feel?"

Brooklyn tried to find the words to explain it. The only emotion she could compare it to was the one she felt the day she'd lost her virginity. She felt like she had passed a milestone in her journey to womanhood—on her own terms.

"I feel good," she said, simply. "I'm ready to do it again."

Hassan laughed. "Slow down. You gotta take time to celebrate before you get back to work." He pointed to the back seat where a bunch of gift boxes adorned in ribbons and wrapping paper decorated with balloons were piled. "You're coming to a party tonight. Time to shake things up."

Brooklyn frowned and looked down at her clothes. "A party? I'm fresh off a bus from Baltimore! I'm not going to a party tonight."

"Stacey said you are. She's not at her place and you don't have a key to it. So, you have no choice but to go wherever I take you. I'm kidnapping you for the night."

Brooklyn looked at him skeptically.

"Just kidding. Tonight's Carla's birthday. That's Roscoe's girl. He's having a birthday party for her and the whole crew is over there. Stacey, too. She wants you to come and meet everybody. She figures if you're gonna be sticking around, you might as well get to know your peoples."

Brooklyn sighed. She looked down at the black turtleneck and jeans she had on and shrugged. "Next time let me know it's a special occasion so I can be prepared. I don't like surprises."

"Tell that to Stacey. It's nothing big, just a little get-together."

He drove to West 149th Street and parked his car. They climbed out with Brooklyn hoisting the duffel bag of cash onto her shoulder while Hassan grabbed the pile of presents from the back seat and carried them like a tower to a brownstone at the end of the block.

As they got out of the car and approached the house, Brooklyn could already hear the music bumping from the speakers.

Brooklyn looked up at the impressive home. "Who lives here?"

"Roscoe and Carla."

Brooklyn frowned. "Roscoe lives *here*? Then why is Stacey living in the heart of the hood?"

Hassan shrugged. "Because she chooses to. That's where she feels comfortable. Trust me, if she wanted to, she could own this whole block. Quiet as it's kept, she owns a lot of real estate. Stacey just likes to play the shadows. Roscoe's a typical Harlem nigga. WILD!"

Brooklyn laughed.

Before he could ring the bell, the door swung open, and Roscoe stood greeting them with a huge smile on his face.

"Finally! Everybody's waiting on you. Where the weed at?" Roscoe held his hands out, expectantly.

Brooklyn laughed as Hassan shook his head and led the way into the house. He pulled a baggie of weed out of his pocket and handed it to Roscoe.

The house was decorated for the festivities. Purple and gold balloons and streamers hung from the ceiling. A large banner with the words HAPPY BIRTHDAY hung across the wall. The music was almost drowned out by the laughter coming from the kitchen. Roscoe led the way in there.

The eat-in kitchen wasn't very large. So, it seemed full despite the fact that only a handful of people were in the room. All of them turned to the doorway as Roscoe entered with Hassan and Brooklyn in tow.

"Finally!" Wally echoed his friend's sentiments.

Brooklyn followed him, smiling at everyone as she entered. "Hey, everybody."

"Wassup, BK?" Wally said, waving.

"My bad, Brooklyn," Roscoe said, laughing. "I was so glad the weed walked in the door that I forgot to say hi to the people!"

Hassan laughed. He looked at Stacey standing near the refrigerator flanked by two other women. "What's up, y'all? This is Brooklyn."

The two women stared back at her, appraisingly.

Hassan broke the ice.

"Brooklyn, this is Carla—the birthday girl." He gestured toward a girl with a shoulder-length doobie wrap. She wore a skin-tight black catsuit, Gucci heels, and was dripping in jewelry. Her body was shaped like an hourglass and Brooklyn suddenly felt underdressed.

"Happy birthday!" Brooklyn said.

Carla's expression was uninviting. She looked Brooklyn up and down and nodded. "Thank you."

Wally and Roscoe busied themselves crushing and rolling up the weed Hassan had brought.

Hassan continued making introductions. "This is Missy. She's Wally's wifey."

Missy fluttered her fingers in Brooklyn's direction and grinned. The pale blue minidress she wore hugged her curvy frame. The plunging neckline was accented by a thick gold and diamond rope chain. Her curly hair was piled high in a ponytail, and her diamond hoop earrings gleamed in the light.

Brooklyn shifted her weight, self-consciously. Prior to her arrival, she had felt confident and excited to meet everyone. Now she felt like a country girl in the big city. She wished she had some expensive jewelry, some designer clothes, or had at least brought a gift for the birthday girl. She stood there, uneasily, at Hassan's side.

"Hi, Missy. Nice to meet you."

"Same here, Brooklyn. Heard a lot about you."

Brooklyn glanced at Stacey and wondered what she had told them. Stacey winked and walked over to her.

"Hey, partner! This is Carla's birthday party. But it's your welcome home party, too. Come in the living room."

Stacey linked her arm through Brooklyn's and led her into the large living room a few feet away.

"Don't be scared." Stacey nodded toward the women in the kitchen. "They like to bark but they don't bite."

She took the duffel bag out of Brooklyn's hand and set it on the large oak table near the wall. She looked inside the bag and smiled.

"You already got your half separated from mine. I like that. You're organized, forward-thinking, resourceful!"

Brooklyn laughed, enjoying being lavished with praise for the first time in a long time.

Stacey reached into the bag and handed Brooklyn her cut. "You got a nice little chunk of change now. What you gonna do with it?"

"I want to put it back in the mix. Let's do it again, partner."

Stacey smiled. "Okay. We're gonna step it up a notch at a time. Baby steps. Soon, you'll have enough to start copping your own keys, making your own flip. Just follow my lead."

Brooklyn intended to do just that.

She followed Stacey back into the kitchen where the party was in full swing.

Carla turned to Stacey as she entered. "Thanks again for the case of Moet!"

"You're welcome. That's your gift from me and Brooklyn. She's working with me now. So, y'all make sure Brooklyn feels at home."

Carla and Missy both looked at Brooklyn, seemingly unsure.

Missy was the first to break the ice.

"I made some food for everybody. Help yourself to a plate." She gestured toward a bunch of food steaming in aluminum pans.

"Missy's the master chef of the crew. She throws down in the kitchen. So, don't be shy." Stacey nodded at Brooklyn.

Brooklyn thanked them and walked over to the counter where the plates and cutlery were stacked. She scooped some stewed chicken, rice and peas, and cabbage onto her plate. Everything looked and smelled delicious.

Carla picked up a bottle of the champagne Stacey had given her and held it aloft.

"Come on, ladies. Let's eat and drink in the living room while the men turn the kitchen into a smokehouse." She nodded toward Roscoe, who was already sparking a blunt and inhaling.

Brooklyn, Missy, and Stacey brought their plates of food along and followed Carla into the living room. She set the champagne down on the coffee table, turned the music down a few notches, and sat on the sofa.

The other ladies followed suit, taking seats throughout the room, and balancing their plates on their laps. They wasted no time digging in, each of them complimenting Missy on how delicious the food was. She beamed proudly and watched them all devouring her hard work.

"Carla's my girl," she explained. "So, I had to make sure she had the best of everything for her birthday. Roscoe was talking about getting a caterer. But I told him not to worry about it. I know what she likes."

Carla nodded. "Sure do!"

Brooklyn could understand why. The stewed chicken was the best she'd ever had. "How long have you been friends?" she asked.

Carla and Missy locked eyes, each of them doing the math mentally.

"About eight years?" Missy tilted her head as she pondered it.

Carla nodded. "Yeah. I met Missy at a party. Roscoe and Wally were posted up in VIP, gold chains and leather jackets. I was there with Roscoe—we've been together since high school—and Wally was fresh off a breakup. He saw Missy in the crowd and told us that was his future wife. We laughed at him. But he went out there and talked to her, danced with her. The next thing we knew, she was in the VIP section with us. The rest was history."

Missy nodded. "Me and Carla hit it off right away. Now she's my best friend."

"All they do is shop and gossip," Stacey teased. "Of course, they hit it off."

Brooklyn laughed along with the rest of them.

"Wifey gotta stay icy!" Carla proclaimed. "We hit up the stores on Fifth Avenue yesterday. Gucci, Louis, Versace, baby!"

While Carla and Missy bragged about the designer clothes and shoes they purchased, Brooklyn thought about her shopping spree on 125th Street with Hassan. She wondered if he had laughed to himself when she loaded up on accessible brands while the women he usually hung around were dripping in luxury. She felt like a fish out of water among these two, who were clearly used to the finer things in life. She silently reassured herself that these girls were older and more experienced than she was.

"How old are you today?" she asked Carla.

"Twenty-five." Carla popped the bottle of champagne and all the ladies cheered. She began pouring it into purple plastic champagne flutes Stacey had picked up from Party City. She stopped when she got to Brooklyn. "You don't look twenty-one," she said, skeptically.

Brooklyn shrugged. "Age ain't nothing but a number, like Aaliyah said."

Carla laughed and poured her a full glass. She took her seat again and looked at Brooklyn.

"What's your story? How did you and Stacey meet?"

"Fate," Stacey answered for her. "Brooklyn came across my path through an old client of mine. She fell on hard times and needed a friend. She found one in me."

Stacey held her glass up in toast and Brooklyn reciprocated.

Carla and Missy exchanged covert glances.

Carla cleared her throat. "You seem kinda young to be in the game."

Brooklyn sipped her champagne. "I'm mature for my age."

"Hm!" Carla huffed. "I don't care how mature you are. Ain't no way I'd be out there risking my freedom on a Greyhound."

Missy and Carla both laughed.

Brooklyn felt defensive. "That's the same thing Wally and Roscoe are doing, right?" She looked at Stacey for clarity. "Don't they hop on Greyhounds or drive down I-95 and risk everything?"

Carla stopped laughing and looked at Brooklyn seriously. "That's because they're men. They're supposed to be the risk-takers and the go-getters."

"What do you do?"

Brooklyn hadn't meant for the question to sound offensive. She had asked it in all sincerity. But the second the words were spoken, she saw the look of outrage on the faces of both ladies.

Stacey appeared amused.

Carla scooted forward in her seat. "I've been with Roscoe since high school. I was with him when he had nothing. So, I don't have to do anything except hold him down. I'm sorry you don't have a man who loves you like that." She sipped her champagne.

Stacey rolled her eyes. She loved her sister-in-law, but she was the definition of a trophy wife. She barely cooked, constantly spent money, and her full-time job was looking good.

Missy fanned her hand at Brooklyn. "You sound like Stacey. Some of us like being taken care of. Why should I work when

Wally makes enough money for me to stay home and make sure everything's straight?" She shrugged. "Since I was in high school, I always attracted the 'get money' niggas. I knew I was gonna wind up with a man who would have the means to take care of me and hold our family down. I found that with Wally and I'm content."

"What I like about Brooklyn is she's a fighter. She might not look like it. When I met her, I thought she looked like a kid, all wide-eyed and innocent. But she showed me a few times how tough she is. She's not waiting for Prince Charming. Bitch jumped on her own horse, grabbed her own sword! I respect that about her." Stacey looked at Carla and Missy. "No offense to y'all."

Carla sat back, knowing better than to challenge Stacey. Not only did she respect her, but she knew that Roscoe never sided with her against his sister.

"I'm thinking about starting a business someday," Missy said, a bit defensively. "But me and Wally are thinking about settling down, starting a family." Her face lit up at the thought of that. "So, I might have to wait a while before I do that."

Stacey changed the subject. "I got a little secret. I think Hass has a crush on somebody." She looked at Brooklyn and grinned. "He was spraying on cologne and checking his breath and everything before he went to pick you up today."

Brooklyn blushed a little. "He's been flirting with me for a while now. But you know I've had a lot on my mind."

Stacey nodded. "Well, for the record, he's a good dude. Hass has a good work ethic and a lot of heart. But he's too smart for this game. Just like you."

Brooklyn took another sip.

"I could see you two building something dope together. You're both young, ambitious. Both hustlers. My advice is give him a chance. Might be a good look." Stacey shrugged.

"I think y'all would be a cute couple," Missy said, smiling at the thought. "I've only known him a few years. When I met Wally, he was working with Hass's brother Dawan. They're like complete opposites."

Carla agreed. "Dawan was bold and ruthless. Sometimes he used to act without thinking. Hass is different. He's strategic."

Brooklyn liked what she was hearing. She glanced toward the kitchen and made a mental note to compliment him on his cologne before the night was over.

"Just keep in mind," Stacey said. "Hass is like a brother to me. Like I said, he's a good guy. So, don't break his heart."

Stacey's expression was serious. Brooklyn took it as a threat.

"I'm glad to meet you finally," Missy said. "For the past week or two, I keep hearing your name. Stacey and Hass must really care about you if they brought you to meet us. 'Cause we're like a big family."

Carla raised her glass in the air. "That's right. So, welcome to the family, Brooklyn!"

They all toasted, Carla turned the volume up on the radio, and they downed the rest of the bottle together.

The party lasted a few hours. The men eventually joined them, and they played a game of Spades. Brooklyn was unfamiliar with the card game, and the other ladies didn't pass up the opportunity to tease her about it.

"Your name is Brooklyn—and you can't play Spades?" Carla seemed disgusted.

Stacey looked at her, pityingly. "Sit next to me, bitch. I'll teach you."

Missy shuffled the deck and shook her head. "She'll teach you how to cheat!"

Everybody laughed and Brooklyn paid careful attention as the game got underway. By the end of the night, she had the hang of it. She was also quite drunk.

She wasn't alone. Carla passed out on the sofa by the end of the night. Stacey crashed in a room upstairs. Wally helped a belligerent Missy to the door with great effort.

Hassan turned and looked at Brooklyn.

"You want to stay here with them?" He shrugged and pointed at the scene around them. "Or you want to come to my crib. I won't try nothing funny. You can sleep on the couch."

Brooklyn glanced around the room at Missy tumbling toward the door while Wally yelled out "Good night!" Carla was sprawled out across the sofa and Roscoe was stumbling around in the kitchen trying to roll a late-night blunt.

"I'll go with you," Brooklyn said. "You live far?"

He shook his head. "Not at all."

On the ride to Hassan's apartment, she couldn't stop talking about the party.

"I like your friends," she said. "They know how to have a good time."

Hassan nodded. "I told you."

"I need to step my wardrobe up, though. They had Versace and Gucci on while I'm wearing a dress from some average store in the mall. I gotta do better."

He laughed. "Don't change up on me now. The way you are is just fine." He glanced at her from head to toe and nodded. "You walked in there with some Air Max on and shut it down. You don't need all that extra shit. You're naturally gorgeous."

She beamed. "Thank you, Hass." She leaned over and planted a drunken, wet kiss on his cheek.

He grinned. "Don't thank me yet. You kiss me like that again, and I'm not gonna be responsible for my behavior."

She waited until they stopped at a red light. She unhooked her seat belt, got on her knees in the passenger seat, and grabbed him by the face. She pulled him close and planted a long kiss on his lips.

A car horn blared behind them. She let go and sat back down.

Hassan drove on, licking his lips as he peeked at her. "Okay," he said. "It's on."

Chapter Nine

Tainted Love

Brooklyn awoke naked the next morning, realizing that she had underestimated the effects of alcohol. It was her first time drinking and she was clearly unprepared for how it would feel the morning after.

She wasn't sure where she was at first. The room she was in was unfamiliar. The bed, too. Then it slowly started coming back to her in flashes.

It seemed like Hassan knew her body in advance. He had touched her tenderly in places, ravaged her in others. He had held her gently and choked her roughly, taking her to paradise in a wide range of positions. She remembered staring at his body as he slept, memorizing the muscles in his arms and the moles on his skin. The sex had drained her, but she still couldn't sleep. She was filled with an unfamiliar feeling that she couldn't name. There was something mysterious about Hassan that excited her. Something about his arms that made her feel safe, protected. There was a look in his eyes that let her know that he understood her. She felt drawn to him in a way that she couldn't explain.

She turned over and reached for Hassan but found that he was already out of bed. She sat up and looked around the sun-drenched room, clutching the sheets against her naked body. She could hear music coming from another room and wondered what time it was. She looked around for a clock and spotted one on the dresser. It was 10:51 in the morning.

Brooklyn got out of bed and headed into the adjoining

bathroom. Again, she recalled the previous night in fragments. Stumbling from Hassan's car to the modest building at the corner of a quiet, tree-lined block. Walking to his apartment on the first floor, kissing and tugging at him as they tumbled through the door together. She beamed at the memory.

She turned on the shower and looked around for a washcloth. She marveled at how neat he was, staring at all of the men's body wash and shaving cream stacked neatly in the cabinet beneath the sink.

"What you looking for?"

Hassan's voice startled her, and she jumped.

"You scared the shit out of me!"

He smiled. "Shit in the toilet," he teased.

She sucked her teeth. "I'm looking for a washcloth."

He handed her a fresh one and a towel that he had brought from the linen closet.

"Thank you," she said.

"You need some help washing up, sleepyhead?" He admired her naked body as she stood by the sink.

"I need a toothbrush."

He chuckled. "There's an extra one in the medicine cabinet."

"Oh. You keep extras for the girls who spend the night?"

"Something like that."

She swatted the towel at him, playfully.

"After you finish, come downstairs. I made you breakfast."

She smiled and her dimples shone. "Really?"

He rolled his eyes. "Don't be corny about it."

"That's so sweet! I can get used to this type of treatment."

Hassan shook his head. "I only do this the first time I hit it. After that, you're on your own."

"I guess you don't want to hit it again," she teased.

He held his hands up in surrender. "Breakfast it is!"

She laughed. He left the bathroom and she climbed into the shower.

As she bathed, she thought about the way her life was going. She realized that she had landed herself in a whole new family. Stacey and Hassan, and Wally, Roscoe, and their girlfriends were her village now. They were all she had.

The idea of calling home came to her from time to time. She couldn't bring herself to dial the number or to even think about the family she had left behind. She convinced herself that they were all better off without her.

She considered calling Erica. Once her best friend, Brooklyn wondered if they had anything in common anymore. Erica was the sweet soprano with the bright future ahead of her. Brooklyn was the prodigal daughter.

She decided to focus on her current life instead of the old one. She got dressed in a Tommy Hilfiger sweater and jeans she had packed in her duffel bag for her trip to Maryland. She combed her hair and did her best to tame the flyaways. Then she walked down the long hallway and found Hassan in the kitchen.

"Smells good."

"It is good," he promised. He passed her a plate of eggs, toast, and bacon, and they both sat down at the small kitchen table.

"So, this is your bachelor pad, huh?"

He nodded. "This is my hideaway. I come here to get away from the bullshit. I don't usually have company over here. Stacey's apartment is headquarters. Roscoe's house is the gathering place. Wally stays at Missy's place out in Queens most of the time. He's out of town a lot, though. So, mostly it's just me in here doing my own thing."

Brooklyn looked around as she chewed her food. "It's pretty neat for a man."

He chuckled. "My moms would love to hear you say that. She takes pride in that type of shit."

Brooklyn pointed at her plate with her fork. "This really is good, Hass! You can really cook."

"See? I'm not just good for sex."

She smiled, remembering. "You have a lot of talents." She finished her eggs and sat back. "Stacey speaks highly of you. She said that we'd make a good couple."

His eyes widened. "Is that why you took advantage of me last night? Because Stacey told you to?"

Brooklyn chuckled. "First of all, nobody was taken advantage of. And, no. That's not why. She just mentioned that she thought we had a lot in common. She said you're too smart to be in this game."

"She said that?"

"Yup."

"Wow. That's a big compliment coming from Stacey." He drank some of his grape juice. "I never saw myself doing this," he admitted. "This was my brother's lane. When crack hit the block, niggas made a lot of money really fast. It got us out of the projects. He bought my mother her first car, made sure we had what we needed. Then he got knocked. I was finishing high school. Moms had trouble keeping up with the bills. So, I went to Stacey and asked her if I could take Dawan's place. She told me no at first."

Brooklyn was surprised by that.

"Said I wasn't ready. But I went back so many times that she started sending me out of town like she has you doing now." He looked at her, impressed. "But I didn't come to her with my own money like you did. I had to work my way up. Took me a while. But I'm doing alright for myself now."

"How much longer you planning on doing this?" she asked.

"Hard to say." He wasn't sure when he would stop. The game had become so ingrained in him at that point that he wasn't sure if he could ever completely leave it behind.

"What would you do if you weren't hustling?" Brooklyn asked.

He exhaled deeply. "Real estate."

Brooklyn folded her arms across her chest. Now she was the one impressed. "Really? You would sell real estate?"

He shook his head. "Buy it, mostly. Like strip malls, office buildings, mansions, and that type of thing."

Brooklyn clapped her hands playfully. "I saw how good you look in a suit. So I can imagine you getting all dapper and being a boss!"

He popped his imaginary collar. "Exactly. How about you? What you gonna do when you meet your goal with Stacey?"

She thought about it. "Maybe open up a hair salon and barbershop all in one. Upscale and fancy, but also cozy and relaxing." Brooklyn could picture it the more she spoke about it. "I would paint the ceilings, serve wine and beer, and the whole nine yards."

"Sounds dope. I can rent you a spot in one of my strip malls."

They clinked glasses.

"I'm gonna give you a ride back to Stacey's," he said. "I have some business to handle with Wally today."

Brooklyn nodded.

He paused before standing up. "I think Stacey's right about us making a good couple. What you think?"

She smirked, pausing before she answered. "I think so, too."

They got into Hassan's car and had only driven a few blocks before he pulled into the driveway of a yellow house with white shingles. Brooklyn looked at him, confused.

"This ain't Stacey's building."

Hassan nodded. "I know. I need to make a quick stop." He got out of the car before Brooklyn could reply.

Frowning, she got out and followed him to the door. He rang the bell and winked at her.

"Don't be nervous. Mom's gonna love you."

"Your MOTHER?" Brooklyn swatted him on the arm. "Why didn't you tell me that's who we came to see?"

"Relax!"

Brooklyn could hear loud music playing from a radio inside

the house. She raised her eyebrows at Hassan as the sound of a woman's loud voice drew closer to the door.

"What you doing ringing the bell, Hass? You lost your keys again? I ain't gonna keep giving you keys if you—"

The door swung open and a petite older woman with a pixie haircut like Toni Braxton stood staring at the two of them through the screen door with her mouth agape.

Hassan chuckled. "I didn't lose my key, Ma. I just didn't want to walk in unannounced without letting you know I have company."

She looked Brooklyn up and down, curiously. "Who is this?"

"This is Brooklyn." He put his arm around her shoulder.

Brooklyn noticed how young his mother looked. Clearly, Hassan's mother was making the same observation about her.

"How old is she?" Skepticism was written all over her face.

"Ma! Let us in."

She unlatched the lock on the screen door and stepped aside as they entered. Brooklyn's heart pounded nervously in her chest, and she forced a smile. Up close, Hassan's mother looked even younger. She wore a white T-shirt, a pair of denim shorts, and some gold doorknocker earrings. She stood with one hand on her hip batting her eyelashes at Brooklyn.

"Nice to meet you, young lady. I don't mean to be rude. I'm just trying to understand what my son is up to."

Hassan kissed his mother's cheek and smiled at her.

"You always think I'm up to something."

"That's 'cause you are." She turned to Brooklyn, sizing her up once again. "Brooklyn," she said. "That's your name?"

"Yes."

"That's where you're from?"

Brooklyn nodded. It was true, she reasoned. That was where she had been born. It seemed smart to withhold the story of her Staten Island ties. At least for now.

"How old are you?"

"I'm eighteen," Brooklyn lied.

"Mm-hmm." Hassan's mother rolled her eyes as if she didn't believe it. But she didn't press the issue. "My name is Candy. Come in here and make yourself at home." She led the way into her living room.

Brooklyn followed her, looking around as they walked. She was impressed by how well decorated the place was. On the outside, the house hadn't looked like much. But inside it was plush and well furnished. A large curio in the hallway was full of crystal figurines and framed photos of the family. The living room was decorated in jewel tones with large plants all around.

Candy walked over to the stereo system and turned the volume down.

"Come on! Sit down." She gestured with her hands impatiently.

Brooklyn and Hassan sat down on the couch. Candy sat in a leather recliner facing them.

"We can't stay long," Hassan said. "I gotta make a run with Wally today, but he's still hung over from last night."

"What happened last night?" Candy asked.

"Roscoe had a little get together for Carla's birthday."

Candy's eyes widened. "Why didn't you tell me? I would have went with you! Was Tawana there?"

"No," Hassan said, shaking his head at his mother. "It wasn't a big party. Just a handful of us *young folks* having a good time."

Candy sucked her teeth. "I'm only sixteen years older than you, boo. Mama's still young enough to hang!"

Hassan laughed at her, and Brooklyn watched them, smiling. She could tell that he enjoyed his mother's youthfulness and that the two of them had an easy, almost sibling-like relationship. Nothing at all like the one she once had with her own mother.

"Tawana is Wally's mother. When her and my mother get together, there's usually a lot of drama."

"There's usually a lot of FUN!" Candy corrected him. She turned her attention to Brooklyn. "So, are you my son's girlfriend now? Is that why he brought you over here to meet me?"

Brooklyn chuckled and looked at Hassan. "Yeah. I guess so." She saw a school picture of him framed on a nearby wall and gestured toward it. "What was Hassan like as a kid?" she asked.

Hassan groaned.

Candy laughed. "He was a handful! Always curious about everything, following his older brother around. He's the middle child, so he's sneaky. He liked to dig around in closets and drawers and find stuff he had no business finding. Like weed and money and shit like that."

Brooklyn laughed. "Okay. So, he's nosy."

"What's your story?" Candy asked, bluntly. "Who's your family?"

"My family and I don't get along. I left home the minute I got the chance.

"Why?" Candy pressed. "Where do you live now?"

"With me," Hassan answered for her. "That's why I brought her to meet you. Brooklyn's with me now. You'll be seeing her a lot."

"Mm." Candy looked Brooklyn up and down. "What part of Brooklyn are you from?"

Brooklyn stammered a little. "Um . . . I'm not really from Brooklyn. I was born there. But I grew up in Staten Island."

Candy clapped her hands, dramatically. "I knew it. You don't act like girls from Brooklyn. You're not tough enough. No offense. Girls out there have more grit. You seem like you came from a small town. I've never been to Staten Island before. But from what I hear, you might as well be from Arkansas."

Brooklyn laughed. "It's not that small. But you're not that wrong either."

"I know that's right." Candy huffed. "You're living with my son now, huh? What happened with your family?"

Brooklyn didn't want to answer. But she didn't want to be rude. So, she gave Candy an abbreviated version of the story.

"My family is churchgoing and strict. They were going to kick me out. So, I left before they had the chance."

"Your young ass ran away from your churchgoing family to be with my son?"

"Ma!" Hassan covered his face with his hand.

Brooklyn nodded. "Not just to be with Hassan," she corrected. "I had to get out of there anyway."

"So, you were out there cutting school and acting grown?"

Brooklyn admitted that she was.

"So, they were right about keeping a close eye on you. They just wanted to keep you from getting yourself in trouble."

"Ma," Hassan said again. "Leave it alone. I just wanted you to meet her. I didn't bring her over her for questioning."

"It's okay," Brooklyn said, smiling. "I like people who speak their mind. That's why I had to leave home. I couldn't be myself there. But I'm not a bad person, Miss Candy. You'll see."

Candy nodded. "Well, it's clear that my son likes you."

Brooklyn was comforted by that. "I like him, too."

Candy didn't respond right away. She eyed both of them carefully before a slow grin spread across her face.

"Okay, Miss Brooklyn. If you're cool with Hass, you're cool with me."

Their conversation was interrupted when a younger girl walked in and rushed toward Hassan. He held his hands up in front of his face, defensively, as she rained down blows on him. She wasn't hitting him hard, but the frenzy sent Brooklyn sliding to the other side of the sofa.

"Yo! What's your problem?"

"Where's my twenty dollars?"

Brooklyn looked at Candy, confused. Candy laughed.

"This is my daughter Laray. They play like this all the time."

Brooklyn smiled and watched the siblings play fight. Hassan pulled Laray onto his lap and started tickling her, mercilessly.

"Stop, Hass!" she protested.

"Nah, you started it!" He mushed her hard and sent her tumbling to the floor.

She kicked him and snatched his wallet from the pocket of his hoodie.

"Chill, Ray!"

She ignored him, rifled through the bills in his wallet and pulled out a crisp fifty. She tossed the wallet back in his lap and smirked.

"You bet me that I wouldn't pass that history test and I did! So, now I'm taking the twenty dollars you owe me, plus interest."

"What kind of interest rate are you charging?" Hassan tucked his wallet away quickly. "You took fifty."

Laray looked at Brooklyn and waved.

"Hi. You're with him?" she asked.

"Yes. I'm Brooklyn. Nice to meet you."

Laray smiled. She looked at her brother. "She's cute. What's she doing with you?"

"Stay out of grown folks' business, KID," Hassan teased her.

"Still smarter than you," Laray shot back.

"You're lucky I got somewhere to go. I'm gonna come back later and take back all the clothes I bought you. You can use your fifty to buy new ones." Hassan pretended to be mad, but Brooklyn could tell he was joking.

"Before you go," Candy said. "Let me get some money for the light bill."

Hassan groaned a little. "Ma, I just gave you money."

"I spent it on the cable bill. Come on now! Stop acting all stingy and shit."

Hassan sighed heavily, pulled his wallet back out, and tossed it to his mother.

She caught it in midair. She opened it up, pulled out a handful of bills and tossed it back to him.

"Stop acting like I ask you for money all the time."

"You don't?" he asked, rhetorically.

She chuckled. "No! And if I did, I earned it. Being your mother wasn't cheap. Feeding and clothing you was hard." She tucked the money under an ashtray on the table beside her. "Anyway, thank you."

Hassan looked at Brooklyn, his expression blank. "Let's get ready to go."

Brooklyn nodded.

Candy rose from her chair and smiled at them. "Okay, Miss Brooklyn. Take care of my baby. I'll stop by later this week and take you out to lunch. Just me and you." She shot a glance at Hassan.

He smiled and shook his head, helplessly.

"Okay," Brooklyn agreed. "Thank you."

They rose to leave. Laray took a step closer to Brooklyn.

"I like your outfit," she said.

Brooklyn smiled at her. "Thank you. We should go shopping one day."

Laray smiled back. "Cool."

As they left the house, Hassan held the door for Brooklyn. Once in the car, they talked about the encounter while he drove to Stacey's apartment.

"They're so nice!" Brooklyn said. "Your mother seems like a lot of fun."

He nodded. "Too much sometimes. She's ride or die for real."

Brooklyn couldn't imagine. She looked down at her hands.

"You should have experienced my family. They're the complete opposite of yours. My mother is so uptight and fake. My father put all these unrealistic expectations on us and made it impossible for us to be real with him. I wish I could have been myself around my family like you are. Your mother knows everything about you, and she has your back. Your sister and brother depend on you. In mine, it was every man for himself."

He glanced at her. "Your parents were probably hard on you. I think they wanted the best for you, though." He turned his eyes back to the road ahead. "Giving a kid too much freedom and responsibility ain't always the answer. I used to wish my moms would be more like yours. Not the fake part. But the parenting part. We had to figure a lot of shit out on our own. My mother was always partying. Revolving door of boyfriends. The one she has now is a loser just like the rest of them." He shook his head. "You should try to fix everything with your family."

Brooklyn stared out the passenger window. "That will never happen." She shrugged. "And I'm cool with that. I'm sure that to you my family doesn't sound so bad. But, trust me, it's not all it's cracked up to be."

Hassan didn't respond immediately. They drove in silence for a while with the radio playing in the background. When he got his words together, he spoke at last.

"I know you gave up on your family and all that. But I like you because you're different. You didn't grow up running the streets and all that. Your father was hard on you. That's what good fathers do. They keep their daughters from getting smutted out. And they teach their sons how to be men. I think he had good intentions. He just went about it the wrong way."

"Honestly, I adored him until he turned on me. All these years, I looked up to him. Even though I knew he wasn't perfect. I thought he loved me unconditionally. But I was wrong. Good fathers don't despise their daughters and throw their sons out in the street."

Hassan decided to let it go. It was clear that Brooklyn's mind was made up and she had no intention of reconciling with her family.

They got to Stacey's apartment and Brooklyn climbed out of the car.

"I'm gonna go get Wally and make this run. You want me to pick you up afterward?"

Brooklyn thought about it. She had gotten comfortable at Stacey's place. But she didn't want to overstay her welcome. "Yeah," she said. "I'll pack a bag."

He nodded. "Cool. See you in a little while."

Brooklyn liked him. She could tell he was nothing like Alonzo. Hassan listened to her. He asked her questions that made her think. He challenged her without pushing too hard. As she knocked on Stacey's apartment door, she realized that her advice had been solid. Hassan was a good guy, and they could make a great team.

Stacey opened the door and Brooklyn entered the apartment.

"Welcome back," Stacey said, smiling. "I see you and Hass hit it off. That's a good look." She sat down on the couch. "You got the chance to meet Carla and Missy. So, what's it gonna be? You joining the hustlers' wives club or you still on your grind?"

Brooklyn laughed and plopped down across from Stacey. "I like Hassan. But I'm still focused. How soon can I get back on the road?"

"Next week!" Stacey clapped her hands excitedly. "Let's get this money!"

Chapter Ten

New Levels

Time seemed to pass in the blink of an eye.

Now that she was fully immersed in Hassan's world, his friends and family had adopted her as one of their own. When she wasn't wrapped up in his arms or helping him count money and strategize, she spent the bulk of her time with his mother and sister, and even accompanied Hassan on a visit to a prison in upstate New York to meet his incarcerated brother. Dawan looked like an older, rougher version of Hassan and had seemed happy to finally meet the new lady in his brother's life. The visit had gone by so quickly that Brooklyn hardly realized hours had elapsed.

Stacey, Carla, and Missy became her only friend circle, sharing a sisterhood centered around their individual relationships with Wally, Roscoe, and Hassan. Brooklyn was on cloud nine. The sadness that had shrouded her so relentlessly had finally begun to wane. Hassan watched as the bond between Brooklyn and his sister Laray deepened over time. It wasn't lost on him that Laray was about the same age as Brooklyn's sister Hope. He watched the love and care Brooklyn showed Laray and knew that it was a reflection of how deeply she missed her own family.

When she wasn't helping Candy and Laray cook meals or shopping and lunching with Missy and Stacey, Brooklyn was working her way through the 1,000 hours of course study required to obtain her cosmetology license in New York City. The license would allow her to legally operate a salon within the city limits. She enrolled in a school in downtown Brooklyn and began working toward a new goal.

She made new friends in the borough she was named after. People from all walks of life studying for careers in the same field. Most were girls with ambitions of making a name for themselves in a competitive industry. There were a few men, too, who she bonded with over fashion, hair, and makeup styling. They taught her to take chances with her wardrobe, encouraging her to buy coveted pieces that they wished they could afford to buy for themselves. They never asked where Brooklyn got her money from. They assumed she was from a wealthy family with all her talk of piano lessons and professional dance, as well as her poise. They just accepted her, and she did the same in return. Without realizing it, Brooklyn had dazzled her way into the center of a whole new circle of friends. All of their outings to bars, parties, and shopping sprees revolved around her. She could feel her dreams becoming a reality, and life felt fuller than it had before.

She got a tattoo on her wrist to commemorate Amir. She chose a Gothic cross with Amir's initials in the middle. Each time she looked at it, she smiled, imagining him by her side where he belonged.

It took months. But Brooklyn finally amassed the 1,000 hours of training required to obtain her cosmetology license. Now all she needed was to find the ideal location and she could start her own business. She started pressing Hassan to help her search. She was disappointed to discover that he wasn't as enthusiastic about the idea as he had once been.

"My mother thinks we're moving too fast," he said flatly the next time she brought it up.

Brooklyn frowned. "Really?" She had always been given the impression that Candy appreciated her drive. Whenever she brought up the subject of owning her own business, Candy had applauded her.

"She's scared that I'm jumping out the game too soon," Hassan explained. "Giving you too much say over my decisions."

Brooklyn thought about that. She had to admit that she had cemented herself as Hassan's confidante. She chided herself for not anticipating how envied that would make her.

"I'm not trying to persuade you to do anything bad, though. If anything, I'm working hard to give you a way out of this life. So, you don't have to look over your shoulder all the time. As a mother, she should be happy about that."

Hassan agreed. "I think she's a little jealous, honestly. She used to be the one I went to for advice. The first person I blessed whenever I got a windfall of cash. You're the first girl I've been with in a long time. Definitely the first I've lived with and shared my space with. She's probably just trying to get used to being in second place."

Brooklyn forced a smile and pretended not to notice when he quickly changed the subject. They celebrated her achievement with a bottle of tequila and the wildest sex she had ever experienced in her young life.

Brooklyn didn't forget that conversation. She wondered what was going on with Hassan's mother and what her true motivations were for questioning the trust he had placed in Brooklyn. She didn't bring the subject up again, but Brooklyn kept the thought of Candy's disapproval in the back of her mind as the weeks wore on.

She rarely reached out to Erica anymore. Once her best friend in the world, Erica was now a faint memory that snuck back into Brooklyn's thoughts from time to time. An old song they liked to sing would come on the radio or a movie they had watched together, and Brooklyn would be reminded of the friendship she had left behind.

She found herself immersed in a whole different world from the one she once imagined for herself. As a little girl, she had always pictured her future vividly. She saw herself as a boss, managing a group of people in a business capacity. She reminisced sometimes about the days she had spent walking around lower Manhattan people-watching as a teenager. She had envied the wealth, access, and luxury those people enjoyed. Now she was enjoying those things for herself, thanks to the hard work she was putting in and the determination she had to succeed.

Nearly a year had passed since she made that first trip to Baltimore on a Greyhound bus. Since then, she had made the trips more times than she could count, each time loaded down with more and more work for Stacey's southern clientele. In addition to Chance, Brooklyn had encountered several other hustlers who got their cocaine from Stacey's Harlem connection. She traveled throughout the area known as the DMV—DC, Maryland, and Virginia—with her luggage loaded down with narcotics. There, she met up with her contacts, made her sales, and carefully maneuvered around the town until it was time to head home.

The length of her visits in each town varied. Most of her contacts bought kilos that they broke down into smaller quantities in order to maximize their profits. Those sales were typically quick and easy. Brooklyn would be in and out of town within twenty-four hours in most cases. Other hustlers preferred to buy the product prepackaged for sale. Instead of paying in full for the entire package up front, they spent a few days selling $20 to $50 bundles until they made enough to pay Stacey her portion. Those transactions required a longer stay in town before the money was made and their business was done.

Stacey was wise enough to know that sending Brooklyn alone on trips like that was too risky. She sent Wally and Roscoe on those longer assignments, and limited Brooklyn's stop in each town to a maximum of three days.

Brooklyn met a new friend during one of her trips to Baltimore. She had gone down to meet Chance, as she had countless times before. By then she had made enough money to rent good rooms at ritzier hotels in the area and used the rooms Stacey secured at the Days Inn only to conduct her business. Brooklyn had gotten familiar with the town. She knew where all the best restaurants were, where the good hair and nail salons were located, and which areas to avoid after dark.

Brooklyn had time to kill one Saturday while she was in Baltimore and she asked Dawn, the front desk clerk at the Days Inn, for a reference.

"Every time I see you, your hair looks so good! Where do you go?"

Dawn was incredibly flattered and thanked her profusely for the compliment.

"I go to Miss Molly's over on East Chesapeake Avenue in Towson."

Brooklyn resisted the strong urge she felt to laugh. "Miss Molly's" and "East Chesapeake" sounded like the countriest things she had ever heard. She smiled at the girl and thanked her.

"Who should I ask for when I get there? Who's the best stylist?"

Dawn seemed tickled by every word Brooklyn uttered in her New York accent.

"Ask for Angel."

Brooklyn took her advice and caught a taxi to the next town over. Miss Molly's salon was located in a tidy little strip mall just off the highway. Everything was so much neater and more polished on this side of town. There was no litter on the streets, little graffiti on the walls, and the atmosphere felt far more suburban. Baltimore even seemed gritty by comparison. The pink and black sign above the door had Miss Molly's name written in flowy script.

Money was no object, so she tipped her driver generously and went inside.

As she entered, Brooklyn looked around. The space was well lit and open. Several hairstyling stations were scattered across the room. But only one was occupied. A pretty woman with shoulder-length hair and a bright smile greeted Brooklyn.

"Hello. Welcome to Miss Molly's!" She had a client in her chair who was getting a relaxer. The client smiled at Brooklyn, too.

"Thank you," Brooklyn said. "Are you Molly?"

The stylist chuckled. "No," she said. "Molly is the owner. I'm just one of the stylists. My name is Angel."

Brooklyn's eyes widened. "Good! You're just the person I'm looking for!"

They hit it off right away. Angel was two years older than Brooklyn but was far less experienced. They made small talk while Angel finished up her client. Then they chatted in depth while Angel styled Brooklyn's hair in flat twists.

"You grew up here—in Maryland?" Brooklyn asked. She thought she detected the hint of a southern twang.

"Yes. In Baltimore. My whole family's from here. But now my parents moved to Silver Spring." Angel angled Brooklyn's head to the side and parted her hair with the tail of a comb. "Baltimore changed a lot over the years. It's not as safe as it used to be. Soon as they retired, my parents got up out of here."

"Silver Spring is a lot nicer."

"Yes! It's quieter. They worked their whole lives. My sister lives close to them—in Tacoma Park—and she has twins. So, my parents go over there and spoil them every chance they get." Angel giggled. "What about you? Born and raised in New York City?"

"Yup."

"Sounds so exciting! I always imagined what it would be like to live there. Do you know anybody famous?"

Brooklyn laughed. "No. Don't believe everything you see on TV."

"What brings you to town?" Angel asked.

"I'm visiting family."

"How nice!"

Brooklyn quickly moved on to avoid further questioning. "You said you grew up in Baltimore, so you must know where the best clubs are out there."

"Uh-uh, girl. You don't want to go to any of the clubs out in Baltimore. Two college kids just died a few weeks ago hanging out at a spot out there. Five other people got shot, too, but they survived. Thank God. You should be careful if you decide to hang out there. I know New Yorkers are tough. But nobody's bullet-proof."

"I hear you," Brooklyn said. "But I like a little adventure. So, where do I find it?"

Angel laughed. "Okay! Umm . . . there's Club Trilogy. The Gallery."

"Okay! I'll check them out."

"What type of adventure are you looking for?" Angel asked.

"I want to spread my wings a little. Explore, you know? Find out what the party scene is like outside of New York."

"I hear you. I guess no matter where you live, it's good to explore a little."

"That's all I'm trying to do."

Brooklyn looked around at the handful of women in the salon having their hair done by other stylists. They all seemed like regulars, engaged in deep conversations about their relationships, kids, and other personal details. It all sounded pretty mundane to Brooklyn. She thought about what it would be like at the salon she planned to open someday. It would certainly be far more upbeat, and the conversations would be a lot more interesting.

"What do you do for fun?" Brooklyn asked.

"Hang out with my man." Angel smiled as she said it. "His name is Josiah."

"Aww shit!" Brooklyn teased her. "You sound like you're in love."

"We've been together for almost two years. Met him at a seafood restaurant called Phillips. Has your family taken you to eat there yet?"

"No. Not yet. I haven't been in town too long."

"Well, you have to go! The crab cakes are legendary. Baltimore

Harbor has the best seafood in the world. Make sure you take advantage of it while you're here."

Angel spun her around in the chair to inspect her work. "What do you think?"

Brooklyn turned her head from side to side examining her work. "Nice!"

"I know the stylists in New York are a lot better. I see all the music videos and pictures in the magazines. That's where all the stylists down here get our inspiration from."

Brooklyn smiled. "You did great!" She took the handheld mirror Angel offered her and used it to check out the back. "I love it."

"I'm so glad! I won't lie to you. I was nervous. I'm always a little edgy when I work on a new client. But I definitely wanted to impress you. I've always wanted to go to New York. Everybody from there seems so cool and everything."

Brooklyn was immediately drawn to the warmth that radiated from Angel. She was a constantly smiling beauty with flawless cinnamon-hued skin and deep-brown doe-shaped eyes. She wore her own hair in a sleek ponytail and wore minimal jewelry. Despite her outward beauty, it was her welcoming energy that Brooklyn found most appealing.

Brooklyn followed Angel to the front desk and paid her bill. She handed her a fifty-dollar bill as a tip and waved her hand modestly as Angel thanked her exuberantly.

"Oh, my goodness! This is too much!"

"You earned it," Brooklyn insisted. "Let me get your number," she said. "I'll call you later on and see if you feel like tagging along with me to Club Trilogy tonight. When's the last time you went out and shook what your mama gave ya?"

Angel laughed. "Um . . . I don't know. Yeah! Okay." She wrote her home phone number down for Brooklyn and the number to the salon beneath it. "That sounds like a plan."

Brooklyn got to the club before Angel that night. She had been bored in her hotel room. Her money was locked securely in the safe. Her bus back to New York was leaving the following afternoon and her bags were already packed. She felt restless, so she had gotten dressed early, slipping into a pair of tight jeans and a black top with spaghetti straps. She did her makeup and opted for minimal jewelry. She was, after all, a woman on her own in a rough city. She put on a pair of Gucci stiletto boots, grabbed her winter white-wool trench coat and headed out.

It only took her driver about twenty minutes to arrive at the club on Eutaw Street. The wind howled around her as she trotted toward the venue. Brooklyn pulled her coat tighter around her and ignored the catcalls of the men outside as she rushed through the nightclub's heavy doors.

She found a packed house of people crowded around the bar and moving on the dance floor. The music was loud, and the deejay was spinning a mix of hip hop and R&B. Brooklyn checked her coat and headed straight to the bar. She had to wait a while before she got the bartender's attention. When she did, he came over smiling at her cleavage rather than looking her in the eye.

"Let me get a rum and coke please." She watched and waited as he made the drink and brought it back to her. She handed him a twenty and told him to keep the change. She knew from her occasional nights out with Carla and Missy that tipping the bartender well ensured better service.

She turned her back to the bar and sipped her drink through the tiny straw as she eyed the crowd. It was a lot different from the party scene in New York City. When she went out with her friends to parties in the city, she could always expect eclectic crowds of people dressed in varying styles, bold hairdos, and flashy jewelry. The club scene in New York was about posturing, sitting in VIP, popping bottles of expensive champagne, designer labels everywhere. In Baltimore, the scene was much grittier. The partygoers weren't particularly interesting according to Brooklyn's standards. The women weren't dressed provocatively, no towering heels or expensive bags. And all the guys looked gritty, as if they had just walked in from off the block. Baggy jeans, oversized T-shirts, sneakers, and unsmiling faces were the uniform that all the men present seemed to wear. Everyone appeared to be posing, standing around looking bored.

She took her drink and headed to the dance floor. An Aaliyah song was playing and Brooklyn winded her hips to the beat and sang along. She smiled, swept up in the music. She didn't need a dance partner, didn't need any friends or any man to help her be happy. She was high off life.

She twirled around and caught sight of a pair of women dancing together nearby. They were whispering to each other and eyeing Brooklyn jealously. She laughed and kept dancing. She wasn't going to give them the benefit of interrupting her good time.

The song ended and the deejay mixed in the next hit. She kept dancing, now purposely hoping to piss off the two haters watching her every move. She danced until she finished her drink, and the deejay played a song she didn't like. She headed to the bar in search of a refill. As expected, the bartender came right over and gave her another one. She slid him another $20 but he slid it back across the bar to her.

"The guy right there said he's got you covered."

Brooklyn turned and saw a tall, brown-skinned man with a Baltimore Orioles fitted cap standing at the end of the bar. He lifted his glass in her direction and nodded. She smiled and raised her glass in gratitude. She walked over to where he stood.

He was slightly taller than six feet, stocky, and cute. He smiled as she approached.

"Thank you," she said, gesturing at the glass in her hand. "I thought guys only sent drinks to girls in movies."

He laughed, revealing his perfect teeth. "You walked in here looking like a movie star. So, it's only right."

She blushed a little.

"My name is Chris."

"I'm Brooklyn," she said. "Nice to meet you."

He smiled. "I'm not surprised. The second you walked in, I could tell you're not from around here," he said. "Hearing you speak was a dead giveaway."

"Seems like every time I open my mouth around here, people automatically know where I'm from. I never thought New Yorkers sound so different from everybody else."

"That's a good thing," he said. "Makes you stand out even more. Not that you need any help in that area. Like I said, I noticed you the second you walked in the door." He took a sip of his cognac. "What you doing in town?"

"Visiting," she said. "Thought I would come out and see what the nightlife is like."

"By yourself?" He seemed surprised. "That's bold for a woman in a town like B'more."

"You're here by yourself," she observed.

"No, I'm not." He nodded toward four guys dressed in baggy streetwear and sneakers looming large around the perimeter of the dance floor. They looked rough and rugged, none of them smiling. "My crew is in here." He looked at her. "Where's your crew?"

"Right here."

"You don't look so tough," he teased.

"Looks can be deceiving."

"It looks like you're a pretty, single lady from out of town searching for some trouble to get into. Am I right about that?"

She smirked. "Thank you. And yes. You hit the nail on the head." A couple left the bar and Brooklyn scampered onto a stool. She crossed her legs and took a sip of her drink.

"What kind of trouble you looking for?" he asked.

"I'm trying to see what my options are."

His grin widened.

"Hey, Brooklyn!" They were interrupted by Angel. "I just got here." She smiled at the guy next to her. "I see you're making friends already."

Brooklyn set her drink down on the bar and lifted her hands

toward Angel for a hug. "Hey, girl. I just got here, too." She looked at Chris. "This is my best friend, Angel. She's thirsty, too." She smiled.

Chris knew he was being hustled but he didn't mind. He waved the bartender over and asked Angel what she was drinking.

Shocked, Angel looked at Brooklyn, beaming. "Whatever she's having!"

"Rum and coke," Brooklyn confirmed.

The bartender walked off to make the drink and Angel turned to Chris and thanked him.

"Thank your homegirl. She got me looking like the man in front of my boys over there."

Angel looked in the direction of Chris's friends and spotted her own friends seated nearby. "Oh! Brooklyn, I invited my friends to meet me here tonight. Is that okay?"

"Of course!" Brooklyn turned to see who Angel's friends were and her eyes settled on the two haters in the corner who had been whispering about Brooklyn when she hit the dance floor. "Those are your friends?"

Angel waved at them. "Yes. They were shocked that I was coming out to a club tonight since I never go out. They wanted to meet the person who coaxed me out of my shell." She giggled, innocently.

Brooklyn looked at Angel's friends and nodded. "Oh, this will be fun."

The bartender brought Angel's drink and Brooklyn turned to Chris. "Thanks again for the drinks. Take my number." She rattled off a fake number with a 212 area code and walked away with Angel.

They headed over to the banquette where her friends were seated. Angel hugged them both and blew them kisses.

"Hey! I'm so glad you both could make it! Brooklyn, these are my friends Kia and Renee."

Brooklyn greeted both women warmly. Kia was a chocolate

big-boned sister with a short haircut. Renee was tall and slim with a long face and a warm smile.

"Nice to meet you, ladies. I'm Brooklyn."

"Oh! I hear that New York accent," Kia said.

Brooklyn had barely said anything but shrugged it off. She sat down, set her drink down, and smiled.

Kia and Renee looked her up and down.

"I love those boots," Renee said. "How much did they cost?"

Angel squirmed a little, aware that her friends were acting weird.

Brooklyn shrugged. "I'm not sure. Thank you. I like your sweater."

"Those are the *new* Gucci boots," Renee added. "I'm a shop-aholic and you must be, too."

Brooklyn resisted the urge to roll her eyes.

Angel laughed. "Sorry, Brooklyn. I should warn you that Renee is the model of the group. She knows everything about fashion."

Brooklyn glanced at Renee's wardrobe and assumed that the bar for models was lower here than in New York.

"What do you do for a living?" Kia asked.

Brooklyn took another long sip of her drink. She looked at Kia. "I'm an entrepreneur."

"I thought you were a dancer." Kia said. "Soon as you came in here you hit the dance floor."

Brooklyn looked at her, meaningfully. "Is *that* why you were staring so hard?"

Kia seemed rattled by Brooklyn's directness. She was used to exchanging subtler jabs in her friend groups.

Angel frowned at her friends, wondering why they were interrogating her new friend so extensively.

"Brooklyn got us free drinks," Angel pointed out, holding hers up for good measure. "That never happens when we go out. I think we can learn a thing or two from her."

Kia and Renee forced fake smiles.

"What do you do for a living?" Brooklyn asked them.

"I'm in real estate," Kia answered.

Brooklyn nodded. She looked at Renee.

"I keep telling these two that the way to a man's heart is through his stomach," Renee said. "They're working all those long hours doing hair and selling homes. Meanwhile, their men are at home hungry!" She laughed. "I make sure my man eats like a king every night. And we've been together seven years."

She stared at Renee. "Do you work?"

"Yes! I work at looking good and keeping my king happy!"

Brooklyn looked away, embarrassed for her. She sounded like First Lady Sabrina James.

"So, Kia," Brooklyn said. "If I wanted to rent an apartment in this area, could you help me?"

Kia nodded. "I sure can. We can find you something really nice." She dug in her purse and handed Brooklyn her business card.

Brooklyn thanked her.

Angel squealed. "Good! You're thinking about staying."

Brooklyn grinned. "Maybe."

She spent about an hour entertaining Angel's friends by her presence. Then she walked over to the bartender and asked him to summon a taxi to take her back to the Sheraton. She collected her coat from coat check and went back to the table where Angel and her friends were huddled. As she approached, she could tell that they were whispering about her again. Angel's body language and facial expression seemed defensive. Renee and Kia were leaning in close to her trying to make sure they weren't overheard. They didn't see her approaching until it was too late. Then they all smiled at her like nothing was going on.

"Hm!" Brooklyn smiled, too. "Okay, ladies. It was really nice to meet y'all. Angel, I'll give you a call."

Angel hugged her goodbye. "Sorry about them," she whispered.

"Don't worry about it." Brooklyn winked at her and walked away.

The minute she was out the door, Renee felt relieved to speak freely. She turned to Angel and shook her head.

"I don't like this Brooklyn bitch."

Brooklyn was back in New York the following afternoon. Hassan met her at Port Authority with flowers.

"What's the occasion?" she asked, kissing him gratefully.

"Just 'cause I missed you. That's all."

She sniffed them. "Thank you. I'm glad to hear that because I missed you, too."

She had done a lot of thinking on this trip back to New York. She had ideas and wanted to know what Hassan would have to say. She decided to test the waters.

"I had an idea."

"Uh-oh," he teased.

"For real!"

"Okay. Let me hear it."

"What if I move down to Maryland. Like part time."

Hassan frowned. "What if *you* move down to Maryland? That's how it is with us now?"

She shook her head. "I didn't mean it like that. I meant that we could open a hair salon down there for way cheaper than we can here. That could be our exit plan. We set up a spot down there and hire some dope-ass stylists. Funnel all this money we're getting through there. When we make enough to stop, we can move down there for good."

He thought about it. "I used to go down there making runs for Stacey all the time. Then I had a close call with a cop one time. He tried to search my bag and I ran. Damn near got caught but thank God I made it out of there. After that, Stacey put me on time out. But that was a while ago. The coast might be clear by now."

Brooklyn had learned from Stacey that there was a bigger risk of getting pulled over while driving. Plus, license plates from northern states attracted attention down South. So, they avoided driving dirty. Instead, they used the buses and railways to make their trips.

"We'll talk to Stacey about it," Hassan promised. "Wally's having his housewarming in a couple of weeks. That might be a good time to check out the scenery down there. See what the possibilities are."

Wally and Missy had spread their wings, moving part of the crew's operation down to Richmond, Virginia. Wally's mother Tawana had just bought a home there. It seemed like a world away from New York City. But when Wally had gone down to help with the move, he came back excited. He told Stacey that he wanted to set up shop permanently in the small town, expanding to an underserved community of drug addicts looking for some quality product. He packed his bag and grabbed up two of their youngest, hungriest street soldiers who were desperate to get money. Now, Wally was splitting his time between New York and Virginia, and the crew was making more money than ever before.

That's what Brooklyn was trying to do. She had gotten a copy of her birth certificate and Social Security card, and she and Hassan had researched all the necessary steps to opening a business. She thought Maryland could be the perfect place to do it, allowing her to enjoy the best of both worlds. For a while at least, she would juggle life as a legitimate business owner and as a hustler.

In January of 1997, Hassan and Brooklyn drove down to Virginia and spent a week visiting Wally and his family. Candy and Laray drove down as well, and they all enjoyed a few fun-filled days making memories. When they weren't out handling their business in the streets, Hassan and Wally spent time sitting around the fire pit in the yard smoking spliffs and sipping beer. Brooklyn and Missy sat together on the porch swing watching Laray beating Candy and Tawana at a game of cornhole. Brooklyn giggled as she watched Candy protesting and Tawana threatening to whoop Laray's "young ass."

Missy wasn't amused.

"This is the most boring place on the planet," she said, pouting. "Wally done lost his mind if he thinks I'm staying down here for good."

Brooklyn frowned. "It's not that bad. I mean . . . it's not Harlem, but it ain't the worst place to live. Look at all this land. In New York, all we have is concrete and noise."

"You have FUN. It's a party 24-7 at home. Down here, the most exciting thing to do is go fishing. I hate it, Brooklyn."

Brooklyn patted Missy's leg, reassuringly. "You'll change your mind. You can start a family here."

Missy sucked her teeth. "You sound like Wally. He would love that. Leave me down here on the plantation barefoot and pregnant while he's running up and down I-95 having all the fun."

Brooklyn thought Missy was bugging. She was charmed by the provincial southern life. After all the drama and pain she had endured, the stillness and serenity of suburbia was a welcome change of pace. She thought about Amir a lot during that trip, imagining him sitting beside her on the screened-in wraparound porch laughing at their own private jokes. With her eyes pressed shut, she could see his beautiful face smiling at her and hear his voice as clear as a bell. "*I still love you, B.*"

She began to make peace with what happened. She would never fully forgive herself for the role she played in her brother's suicide. But she comforted herself with the assurance that he would want her to keep moving forward.

"Amir would have liked you," she told Hassan the night before they returned to New York. "I wish you got the chance to meet him."

Hassan interlaced his fingers with hers. "What do you think he'd like about me?"

"The way you love me. How you protect me and look out for me. And he'd like the fact that you're serious about your footwear. He was into shit like that."

Hassan laughed. "Okay." He pinched her nose, playfully. "I like the way your eyes light up when you talk about him. Makes me feel like I knew him, too."

She rested her head on his shoulder tenderly.

"You ready to go home tomorrow?" he asked. "It seems like getting out of the city brings out the best in you. I like seeing you smile." He stroked her right dimple for emphasis.

She nodded. "I'm ready to go back. But let's make a little detour on the way home."

Early the next morning, they bid farewell to Wally and Missy before they made the drive back to New York. Candy and Laray decided to extend their trip by another day. Everyone stood on the front porch waving at them as they drove away.

They stopped in Baltimore for some of the town's world-famous seafood on the drive back to New York. Then Brooklyn let him know why she had really brought him there.

"I want you to meet my friend Angel."

Hassan frowned. "Your friend? When did you make a friend named Angel?"

Brooklyn sucked her teeth. "What's with all the questions?"

"I'm just saying it's not smart to be making friends outside of the circle. People seem like they have good intentions sometimes but—"

"Angel's not in the game. She's a chick who does hair. Just trust me." Brooklyn handed him the address to Angel's house. She had called ahead and set up this meeting. All she needed was for Hassan to go along with the program.

He stared at the paper reluctantly. Finally, he looked at her and shook his head. "You're lucky I love you."

They drove through the rougher parts of Baltimore and merged onto a highway. As they continued on, the homes looked increasingly expensive. Well-manicured lawns with expensive cars parked in the driveways. She looked at him, questioningly.

"Where are we?"

"This is the nicer part of Baltimore," he said. "It's not *all* cracked out."

He drove her to a large townhouse on Saint Paul Street in Mount Vernon, an upscale section of Baltimore where the wealthy dwelled. He got out of the car and opened her door for her. She stepped out and he followed her up the stairs to a large black oak door.

"She owns this house?" he asked, unsure why he was whispering.

"I think so," she whispered back, smiling. She rang the doorbell, still looking at the property in amazement.

"You sure she's not in the game?" Hassan asked.

Angel opened the door and invited them in excitedly.

"Welcome, y'all!" She hugged Brooklyn. Looking at Hassan, she smiled wide. "You must be Hass. Brooklyn told me all about you. Come in!"

Brooklyn stepped inside wide-eyed and looked down the long foyer that led to the interior of the home. She stared at Angel in amazement.

"You live here?"

"Yeah. This is my family's house. My parents bought it in the fifties." Angel led the way and Brooklyn and Hassan followed closely behind.

The wood-floored foyer led to a carpeted spiral staircase that led to the upper level.

"Josiah's in the kitchen. Make yourselves at home and I'll take you in there."

They took their coats off, and Angel hung them in a large walk-in closet.

Angel led them down a hallway that led to a spacious living

room filled with big statues, expensive furniture, and large ornate lamps. Nearby was a kitchen with cherry wood cabinets and a large stainless-steel refrigerator.

They stepped inside and Brooklyn laid eyes on Angel's beloved Josiah.

He was tall, dark, and extremely handsome. Brooklyn felt guilty for noticing but it was impossible not to.

"This is Josiah. Josiah, this is my friend Brooklyn and her man Hassan. They're on their way back to New York, so they can't stay long."

Josiah shook hands with Hassan and Brooklyn. "Nice to meet you both."

Hassan looked him over, thinking Josiah seemed corny. "Nice pants. Where can I find those?"

Brooklyn pinched Hassan discreetly as she tried hard to suppress a laugh.

"Macy's," Josiah said, innocently, glancing down at his Dockers.

"The shoes, too?" Hassan teased.

Brooklyn cleared her throat. "This HOUSE!" She could hardly believe her eyes. "Damn, girl. I came here to offer you a business proposition. But now I see that you don't need it."

Angel laughed and opened the refrigerator. "Want something to drink?"

Brooklyn nodded. "Yes."

Angel pulled out a few bottles of water and some lemonade, setting them all down on the island at the center of the kitchen. She retrieved glasses from the cabinet and put some ice in each glass and poured their drinks.

"What kind of proposition?" Angel asked. "I thought you just wanted Josiah and Hassan to meet."

Brooklyn looked guilty. "That was true. I knew we were passing through your town, so I thought it would be good for them to meet. But I've also been trying to sell Hass on the idea of opening up a business down here. Maybe settling down here eventually."

Angel lit up at the sound of that. "Sounds amazing!"

"I was thinking of opening a hair salon and I was gonna offer you the position as the lead stylist. But if you're living like this, you don't need my help."

Angel laughed. "My parents are both doctors. My sister is a lawyer for one of the top firms in the country. I'm the family fuckup, out here being creative instead of professional like the rest of them." She said it sarcastically, but it was truly how she felt in her family.

Brooklyn grinned, feeling much more at ease. Maybe Angel was more like her than she thought.

"I don't own this house. My parents let me live here so that they don't have to sell it."

"Okay," Brooklyn said. "So, they won't finance your dream. But what if you had an investor?"

Josiah chimed in, directing his question at Hassan. "What is it you two do exactly? You're investors or developers or what?"

Brooklyn looked at Hassan. "We're whatever you need us to be."

Hassan nodded and began talking business with Josiah. "Let me break it down for you."

While the men talked, Angel turned to Brooklyn.

"Come on. Let me show you upstairs."

They passed by a large dining room, a guest bathroom, and a laundry room. As they climbed the spiral staircase, Brooklyn stared at the elaborate chandelier. Upstairs she found three oversized bedrooms, each with arched doorways, curved walls, and floor-to-ceiling windows.

She looked at Angel in amazement. "It's just you and Josiah living here?" She imagined living somewhere this lavish with Hassan.

"My family stays here when they're in town. My sisters and my nephews mostly. But the majority of the time it's just the two of us here."

"What are your neighbors like?" she asked.

Angel shrugged. "Rich. They mind their business, and I like that. Everybody gets along."

Brooklyn looked around, impressed. "I didn't expect you to live in a place like this."

"What were you expecting?"

"Not THIS, bitch!"

They both laughed.

"Well, now that you know where I am, you can feel free to stay here whenever you're in town. We can sit up all night drinking wine and having girl talk about those two downstairs."

"I'm gonna take you up on that offer," Brooklyn assured her. "Trust me!"

They went back downstairs and spent some time getting to know Angel and Josiah. They learned that Josiah was a chef with a job at a fancy restaurant overlooking the harbor.

"I just started working there," he said, modestly. "But I like it so far."

He made them lunch before they got back on the road. Brooklyn and Hassan promised to return soon, then climbed back into his car for the rest of their journey.

"I like them," Hassan said. "Josiah seems kinda corny. But Angel's cool."

Brooklyn laughed. "I'll tell you what's *not* corny. That house!"

Hassan nodded. "Don't worry. I'll get you one just like it someday."

Brooklyn smiled. She was already plotting on how to get it for herself.

The time away from the grind left them both feeling refreshed. They watched the sunset over the inner harbor and sang duets to the songs on the radio all the way home.

Chapter Eleven

Double Take

Brooklyn and Angel became best friends for real after that. When she was in town, Brooklyn continued to check into a hotel suite as she'd always done. But she spent most of her time with Angel. They spent afternoons together shopping, trying out different restaurants and nightspots. After conducting her meetings with Chance and other local hustlers, Brooklyn locked her contraband in her hotel room and darted off to hang out with Angel.

Sometimes Josiah was there, other times he would be off catering a private event, working nonstop to make a name for himself in the culinary world.

Hassan was making a name for himself, too. Now that Wally was gone, he and Roscoe were working harder than ever. There were weeks when he and Brooklyn barely saw each other. But the money was rolling in, so neither one of them complained.

Brooklyn still thought about her old life sometimes. She knew that Erica was in college now. Brooklyn called her from various cities, always careful not to call from somewhere that could be easily traced. They never talked about it, but Brooklyn wasn't sure if Erica knew that Brooklyn had stolen Alonzo's money all those years ago. Alonzo was out of jail now and back on the streets of Staten Island. Still, Brooklyn could never be sure that Erica was fully on her side. So, when she called it was always from pay phones or at rest stops along the way to Baltimore.

Erica always sounded happy to hear from her. She had done all the things Brooklyn had missed out on, things they had planned on doing together. Going to prom, graduating high school, and enrolling in college. She was studying nursing at the College of Staten Island. And, though it was all part of the plan Erica had made for herself, Brooklyn couldn't help feeling sorry for her friend, stuck in a place as claustrophobic as their hometown.

Brooklyn's calls to her old friend decreased significantly over time. Brooklyn's life was so much bigger and busier now that she hardly recalled her old one. Before long, she couldn't remember the last time she had spoken to Erica.

One afternoon, Hassan was out making a run and Brooklyn had the apartment all to herself. She had rented a stack of DVDs from Blockbuster and was just getting started on the first one. She got an alert on her pager and saw the same phone number with a 718 area code that had been paging her for days. She blocked her number and called right away, hitting the pause button on the remote.

"Hello?"

Brooklyn squealed, recognizing Erica's voice right away. "Hey, E! What's going on?"

Erica was pleased that her friend sounded happy to hear from her.

"I miss you," Brooklyn said.

"I miss you, too. Staten Island ain't the same without Brooklyn."

They laughed at that.

"How've you been?" Brooklyn asked. "I know it's been a while since I called. Things have been busy around here. What's going on back in Shaolin?" She giggled at Staten Island's popular nickname and the fact that thanks to the Wu-Tang Clan, the borough was suddenly on the map.

"Your father had a stroke."

Brooklyn's heart stopped. "What?"

"He's okay," Erica said, quickly. "It happened a few days ago. I've been paging you, but you didn't hit me back."

Brooklyn thought about all the times she had ignored the unknown number and cursed under her breath.

Erica went on. "Your mother woke up on Monday morning and found him in distress. She called 911 and they got him to the hospital. He's paralyzed on his left side. Speech is affected, that type of thing. But he's in stable condition now. He had preached really hard the day before. Had the whole church catching the Holy Ghost. I guess it took a lot out of him."

Brooklyn shut her eyes and wondered how things could possibly get worse.

"Where is he now?" she asked.

"At St. Vincent's Hospital. Your mother asked a few members of the choir to go there today and sing for him at his bedside. I just got back. He looks good considering everything he's been through. They said his condition is improving. Hard to understand what he's saying. But your Mom said that can get better. The whole church is praying for him."

Brooklyn opened her eyes and let out a deep sigh. "How's my mother and sister holding up?"

"Hope is strong," Erica said. "She was at your father's side, giving him water, wiping his mouth, waiting on him hand and foot. Your mother is handling her duties as First Lady. She enrolled in theology school. I don't know if I told you that the last time we spoke."

Brooklyn rolled her eyes and said, "No."

"She's one of the associate ministers at the church now. So, she's basically stepping up and taking your father's place until he's better."

"*How convenient!*" Brooklyn thought. She imagined her father crippled and unable to orate the way he loved to do each Sunday. Unable to control his own body, trapped inside of himself. She thought about her mother in a position of real power and authority within the church, just as she had always wanted. It all made Brooklyn feel sick to her stomach.

"I can't visit him in the hospital," she said, more to herself than to Erica. "My mother is probably posted at his bedside like a guard dog." She shook her head. "I miss him, though. I know part of the reason he had that stroke is because of everything he went through with Amir. And with me."

"He's gonna be okay," Erica promised. "God is in control. He watches over his flock. And your father is a good man."

Brooklyn tried not to let the news dampen her mood as they hung up. She closed her eyes and whispered a prayer for her father. She wasn't sure if God heard her prayers anymore. Not after all the destructive things she had done in her lifetime. But if there was a chance that He was listening, she prayed hard for her father's recovery.

When Hassan got home, she told him the news. He offered to go with her back to Staten Island.

"We can sneak up to his room in the middle of the night when your mother's not there," he suggested.

"No. I think seeing me might upset him even more. Seeing my face again after everything . . . I'll wait until more time has passed."

"You sure?" He wanted to remind her that too much time elapsing had cost her the chance to talk to her brother one last time. But he didn't want to upset her. "It can't hurt to try."

She shook her head and turned her attention back to her studies. "Not right now."

He left it alone after that. Brooklyn seemed determined to leave that part of her life in the past for now.

They had enough on their plate as it was. Stacey was warning them that the game was changing, and not for the better. It was getting harder to move their product in a market that had become oversaturated with ambitious hustlers. Prices were lower than they used to be, and the money wasn't coming in like it used to. In the beginning, Brooklyn made tens of thousands of dollars in a matter of hours. As the nineties drew to a close, she was lucky if she managed to make that amount in a week.

She began spending more time with Angel down in Maryland. Instead of leaving town within twenty-four hours, she hung around for days at a time. She spent afternoons in Angel's salon having her hair styled while they talked.

"What do you really do?" Angel asked one afternoon. She asked it gently and didn't fill the silence that followed. She waited patiently for Brooklyn to decide whether to answer honestly.

Brooklyn knew she could trust Angel. She wasn't part of the same world, didn't have the same trauma. Angel was one of the few people in Brooklyn's world who didn't envy her. Carla and Missy envied her guts and drive. Angel's friends Kia and Renee hated on her confidence and style. Angel wasn't interested in competing with Brooklyn. They were both following their dreams, enjoying their romantic relationships, and bonding over their similarities and differences alike.

"What do you think I do?" Brooklyn asked.

"I'm not sure. But I know you don't really have family down here like you said. All this time we've been hanging out, you've never introduced me to any of them. You always check into hotels when you visit instead of staying with your 'family.' At first, I thought you might be super private. Maybe you just wanted your own space. But whenever you stay at my house, you seem to be comfortable around me. So, that doesn't add up. Then there's Hassan."

Brooklyn chuckled a bit.

"He's everything you described. Smart, good-looking, outgoing. But the second I met him, I could sense a little danger in him. Maybe '*danger*' isn't the right word . . . but definitely an edginess. Just like you."

"I could answer your question," Brooklyn said. "But you should ask yourself if you really want to know the answer. We have fun together. I like the fact that you don't let your stuck-up friends stop you from rocking with me. But I'm scared that if I tell you the whole truth, you might see me a little differently. You have legitimate money and a loving family. But I don't. So, maybe that's the best answer I can give you."

Angel was content with that. "To tell you the truth, it doesn't matter. You're my friend no matter what you do for a living."

Brooklyn was relieved to hear that.

"Unless it's sex trafficking, bitch. You ain't sex trafficking, are you?"

Brooklyn laughed so hard that her sides hurt.

"OH MY GOD, ANGEL! You're crazy! *HELL NO*!"

"Just checking!"

Brooklyn began to confide in Angel the way she once did with Erica. She told Angel about her growing frustration with Hassan. He was pressuring her to settle down, to stop getting illegal money, to start a family. What he wasn't in such a rush to do was open the salon Brooklyn had dreamed of. She shared with Angel that she believed Hassan was heeding his mother's warnings about Brooklyn. She was convinced there was a concerted effort to get her to stifle her ambition.

For Brooklyn and Hassan, the prospect of starting a new business seemed like an unreachable goal. Her cosmetology license had expired, and Hassan had never been proactive about opening a salon anyway. Their whole operation was starting to show signs of weakness.

So it was around the world, apparently. Brooklyn watched the Twin Towers fall on September 11, 2001, and cried. She had walked those same streets, had met her first love in lower Manhattan where thousands were now perishing live on national TV.

The attack on the Pentagon had the DMV area on high alert also. The entire country seemed to be in a state of shock, grief, and fear.

Brooklyn called home that September. Or as close to home as she was willing to reach. She dialed Erica's number and listened as her friend once again urged her to come home.

"You've been gone a long time, Brooklyn. This is a time when everybody's realizing how precious life is. And family. Why don't you call your parents? Or at least call Hope. She's all grown up now and going to NYU."

"I'll call them," Brooklyn promised.

She knew it wasn't true. So much had changed in the years since she ran away. Her father's health had deteriorated significantly. He was paralyzed on his left side, unable to walk or perform most tasks unaided. Her mother was the pastor of Promised Land now, overseeing the kingdom she had toiled to build at her husband's side throughout the years. Mrs. Hutchinson and all the faithful parishioners were still in attendance each week, tithing faithfully, and playing their assigned roles.

In the aftermath of his stroke, Elias had finally found it within himself to forgive Jordan. His son's lover and the best drummer the church had ever employed was back behind the drums each week playing for the Lord. The way Erica described it, Brooklyn imagined everything returning back to normal now that the stain of her sins had finally disappeared.

"Jordan and Hope started a scholarship in Amir's name," Erica told her. "They presented it to the committee a few weeks ago and we've been praying about it. We weren't sure if they would approve it since Amir . . . the church has their feelings about . . ."

"Suicide. Homosexuality. I know," Brooklyn said. "I get it."

"Well, they approved it. So, this year we'll select the first recipient of the Amir Paul James scholarship." Erica smiled as she said it. "You should be there when we present it, Brooklyn. Amir would have loved that."

Brooklyn sighed. "I don't want you to think that I don't care, E. I love my family. I miss them. Even my mother, believe it or not. I miss Hope. I miss you. And I would give anything to sit and talk to my father again. But he can't talk to me, Erica. That's the reality. Hope wouldn't know what to say to me. The life she's living is so different from the one I'm in. If I walked into that church, every head would turn in my direction. Every mouth would whisper '*There she is. That's the one nobody talks about.*' I wish it was different. But I'm okay with the fact that my family is better off without me."

"What about you, Brooklyn? Who do you have out there to love on you and pray for you?"

"I pray for myself."

"I pray for you, too," Erica said. "All the time."

"I appreciate you for that. And for keeping me updated about my family. Maybe you can give Hope a message for me."

"Yes! Of course."

"Tell her that I'm sorry. I miss her. And that I'm proud of her. All those years I was worried about her turning out like our mother. But she's so much smarter than all of us."

Erica knew what Brooklyn meant. Hope had done what her siblings failed to do. She pleased and honored her parents without getting lost in the dogma of religion. She was leading the youth of the church in a revival of sorts, encouraging them to lead Sunday service, to use the church as the venue for plays and spoken word nights, and advocating to give them more of a say in the church's policies. Thanks in large part to Hope's efforts, Promised Land was packed with young people from all over the borough who were hungry for the Word of God.

"Hope is shaking things up in there," Erica said. "I'll be sure to tell her what you said."

Brooklyn thanked her.

"I have some news," Erica teased.

"What?"

"I'm pregnant!"

"Congratulations!" Brooklyn said. "That's so amazing! I know you and Shawn have been trying for a long time."

"As soon as we stopped trying, it happened. I'm so excited!"

"So am I! I hope it's a girl."

Erica laughed. "Usually, it's your best friend who hosts the baby shower."

Brooklyn's smile faded. "I'll be there in spirit," she promised.

Brooklyn traveled down to Baltimore again a few weeks later. Angel insisted that she stop by her place the moment she got to town. Brooklyn did just that and the moment she reached the door, Angel swung it open, excitedly.

"Guess what?"

Brooklyn prayed that she wasn't pregnant, too. She was starting to feel like the last woman alive who wasn't desperate to procreate.

"Josiah proposed!" Angel flashed the large ring on her left hand and danced around.

"AAAAAAHH!" Brooklyn jumped up and down and hugged her friend tightly. They rushed inside. "Tell me everything! When did it happen?"

"Last night! He cooked dinner here and when he brought out the dessert, the ring was inside the ice cream."

Brooklyn laughed. "That's so romantic. And *so* Josiah."

"We're having a little celebration next weekend. Nothing too big or fancy since we're all still reeling from 9/11. Just a dinner party at my house. Can you and Hassan make it?"

"I'll be there. But I'm not sure if Hass can make it. You know how busy he is."

Angel nodded.

"I'll ask him. Either way, *I'll* be there."

Angel hugged her. "I'm so excited. You have to be one of my bridesmaids. Will you?"

Brooklyn pretended to be thrilled at the idea. "Yes, girl. You know I will. As long as you don't put me in one of those ugly ass puffy dresses."

Angel laughed. "I promise."

It didn't take much to convince Hassan to make another trip to Maryland for Angel and Josiah's engagement party. Truth be told, there wasn't much he wouldn't do for Brooklyn. She was the light of his life. They lay in bed at night making love and making plans for their future together. Her melodic, sweet voice lulled him to sleep. Her smooth, buttery skin, pressed against his, roused him from his dreams each morning. Brooklyn's infectious laughter had become his favorite song. He admired and respected her resilience and drive. She was cunning and calculating, constantly maneuvering. In those ways, she reminded him of himself.

They stayed in the penthouse suite of the hotel. Hassan sat in a chair by the window sipping some Hennessy while he waited for Brooklyn to finish getting ready.

"You look good," he said, stepping into the room. He admired her legs in the short black dress she wore. "I like your hair like that." He walked over and kissed the back of her neck. "Makes me want to bend you over and hit it from the back."

"Put your dick away," she said, laughing. "We're late."

"It's not my fault this time. I've been ready."

She grabbed her earrings and her purse and slid her feet into her red Jimmy Choos.

They took her car, but Hassan drove. He had bought a new Mercedes for her the year prior. He slid the seat back and laughed.

"I forgot you drove to the pharmacy earlier. I don't understand how women drive all close to the wheel like that. My mother does the same thing. Why do you need to be that close for?"

She laughed and buckled her seat belt. "I need to see the road. You might as well be driving from the back seat!" She gestured at the angle he had reclined to. She got comfortable as they drove to Angel's house.

"Do me a favor, Hass. Please be nice to Angel's friends. Especially Renee. She likes to make slick comments. I try to ignore her. Please do the same. Don't say anything that you know is gonna set her off."

Hassan made an innocent face. "I don't know what you're talking about."

"Last time you saw her, you asked if she meant to do her hair like that." Brooklyn laughed. "I don't like her, either. But this is

Angel's engagement party and it's her night. I don't want us to be the ones to spoil it."

Hassan nodded. "I got you."

"Be nice to Josiah, too."

"I'm nice to him all the time."

"You pick on him on the low. Asking him what's the name of his sneakers or where you can find pants like that."

Hassan laughed. "Okay. So, I won't talk to him then. Because we don't have nothing in common. He don't watch sports. What you want me to ask him about? His job?"

"Yeah. What's wrong with that?"

"He's a fuckin' cook."

"He's a chef," she corrected. "At a very fancy restaurant now."

Hassan rolled his eyes. "I'll ask him about that then."

They were fifteen minutes late when they got there, something Renee was quick to point out when they sat down at the table.

"Thank you for joining us!" she sang.

Brooklyn shot her a warning look that Renee promptly ignored.

"We got started without you. Josiah was just telling us how he'll be paying off Angel's ring until their kids are in college."

Hassan groaned. Already, Renee was on his nerves. She was so pretentious, always counting other people's money, mentally tallying up the cost of their outfits, sizing them up to decide how much respect to give them. Of all of Brooklyn's friends, he liked Renee the least.

Renee's husband Franklin sat by her side looking annoyed by her as usual. He quickly tried to shift the subject.

"Good to see you guys. Brooklyn and Hassan, how are things with your family back in New York? Is everybody safe and accounted for? Ground Zero looks like a war zone."

Brooklyn nodded. "Yes, thank you for asking. Everyone is okay."

"Do you have a big family?" Renee asked. "You don't talk about them too much."

Brooklyn scooped some pasta onto her plate. "I check in on them," she said. "Like I said, everybody's fine."

Josiah cleared his throat. "We want to thank all of you for coming tonight. Me and Angel are so excited to have something positive to celebrate. And we're happy you're here with us."

They all clinked glasses and congratulated the newly engaged couple.

"Josiah, this food is delicious. As always." Brooklyn smiled at him.

"Thank you," he said, proudly. "I tried something new this time. I'm getting more adventurous in the kitchen."

"That's good," Kia said. "Try new things! We'll be your guinea pigs."

Brooklyn agreed. "I wish I could cook like this. I try sometimes."

"Me too," Angel said. "I fail every time."

Josiah laughed. "It's not that bad. But we agreed that after we're married I'll do the cooking and she'll take care of the cleaning."

Brooklyn and Angel laughed.

"I know it's early," Kia said. "But have you started discussing wedding dates yet?"

Josiah shook his head quickly. "Too soon."

Hassan laughed involuntarily and Josiah and Franklin joined in.

Brooklyn, Angel, and Kia exchanged glances.

Renee defended the men.

"They act like they're in no rush to set a date, but men love being married. Having a wife is a sign of a good man." She rubbed Franklin's hand, sweetly. She set her sights on Hassan. "You two have been together a while. You ever think about popping the question?"

Hassan stared at her, grateful that she couldn't read his mind. He thought she was one of the most miserable bitches he had ever met. "Nah."

Brooklyn tried not to laugh. She knew that Hassan didn't mean it. They had discussed marriage several times. It was clear that he was fed up with Renee's constant jabs.

"Marriage isn't for everybody," Josiah said. "Me and Angel want to have kids. And her parents expect her to be married before she starts a family. So, this is the next step for us. But that doesn't mean it's the right thing for everybody."

Hassan nodded. "Exactly."

Kia agreed. "I started going to church to try to find me a man. So far, no luck. But I got my eye on the guy who drives the church van. He's cute."

Brooklyn laughed. "Stay away from the church men," she warned. "They're the biggest womanizers."

"You don't strike me as the churchgoing type," Renee quipped.

Brooklyn's eyes darted in her direction, and she smiled at Renee, sinisterly. "Yes, lord. I'll quote the Bible to a heathen in a heartbeat! Which church do you go to? The House of Judas?"

Josiah nearly spit out his wine. He coughed as Angel patted his back.

Hassan glanced at Brooklyn. He wasn't sure what Brooklyn had just said to Renee. But, judging from the look on her face, she had just told her to fuck off in the name of Jesus.

"Oh, wow," Renee said, clutching at her chest, dramatically.

"Yeah, wow." Brooklyn glared at her.

Renee opened her mouth to say something slick, but Josiah cut her off.

"I can tell this bachelorette party is going to be one for the history books."

Laughter erupted around the table again.

Hassan nodded. "Have y'all seen Brooklyn when she's drunk? Y'all are about to go to jail!"

Renee looked at him, smiling. "Have you ever been to jail, Hassan?"

The question was so rude, unexpected, and unwarranted that all conversation ceased. The thickness of it hung in the silence between them. It had been this way since the moment Brooklyn stepped on the scene. While she and Angel bonded, Renee seemed to grow increasingly threatened by their friendship. Brooklyn had always been aware of it. Renee was envious of her wardrobe, her car, and seemingly Brooklyn's entire being. She took every opportunity to make digs about the questionable way Brooklyn and Hassan made money. But Brooklyn had prayed that tonight would be different.

Franklin looked at his wife. "What's wrong with you?" he asked.

Renee feigned innocence. "What did I say?" She frowned. "It's just a question." She looked at Brooklyn. "I could ask you, too. It's an innocent question."

Brooklyn stared back at her for a moment. Then she looked at Angel and Josiah, apologetically.

"We're gonna go."

Josiah shook his head. "Don't do that."

Brooklyn shook her head. "No. This is your night." She pointed at Renee without looking at her. "She's your friend. And you deserve to enjoy yourself. I'll call you guys tomorrow."

Hassan was already at the door.

Renee was apologizing under her breath, still pretending not to understand what she had done to ruin the mood.

"Let me walk you out," Angel said, rising from her seat at the table. "But before you go, Brooklyn, let me say something. You're my friend. I love you and I want to celebrate this next chapter of my life with *all* of my friends." She glared at Renee, thoroughly pissed. "It's not about how long I've known you or how much history we have. I love you for who you are and how you support me as my friend. Thank you for coming tonight."

She walked over to Brooklyn and hugged her tightly. Josiah gave Hassan a handshake and they walked them out.

At the door, Angel apologized again.

"You shouldn't be sorry," Brooklyn said. "You didn't do anything wrong. Renee's a hater. She can't help it."

In the car, Hassan shrugged it off. "Franklin gotta have a side chick, right?"

Brooklyn nodded as they pulled out of the circular driveway.

"I like the way Angel came to your defense," he said. "Renee likes to fuck with you because she's territorial. She wants Angel to be her friend only. Tonight, Angel stood up for you. That was dope."

Brooklyn smiled, comforted by that. She tried to remember the last time anyone stood up for her. The fact that she came up empty filled her eyes with tears.

Chapter Twelve

Whirlwind

Brooklyn wasn't sure what it was about that dinner conversation that shifted things for her. Not just with Angel and her friends, but with her adopted family in Harlem.

She began to pay more attention to the gulf between her and the ladies. Missy and Wally would be welcoming a baby later that summer. Unbeknownst to Brooklyn, Carla decided to throw an early baby shower of sorts while Missy was in New York visiting her mother.

Brooklyn was shocked to learn that she hadn't been invited. None of them had even mentioned it until after it was over.

They were all gathered at a barbecue in Candy's backyard when she heard them discussing it.

"Missy looked gorgeous!" Candy exclaimed. She fawned over Missy as they passed the newly developed pictures around. "That lavender was so pretty against your skin tone. I think you should wear that same color to your real shower."

Brooklyn listened to the ladies chatter on about the charcuterie tray, the champagne tower, and the ice sculpture and frowned.

"Why wasn't I invited?" Brooklyn asked.

Missy sipped her lemonade.

Candy held her hands up, defensively. "I got the invite at the last minute."

Brooklyn looked at Carla. She smiled back at her, guiltily.

"Girl, I didn't want to bother you. I knew you were busy with Stacey and everything. I didn't think you had time."

Brooklyn chewed her food and knew that Carla was full of shit. She listened as Missy launched into a story about the perils of her last prenatal appointment.

Brooklyn slowly began to withdraw then. She reluctantly started to accept that holding the keys to Hassan's heart had ostracized her from people closest to him. Maybe it was her ambition that intimidated them. All she knew for sure was that she had fewer allies than she once believed. It hurt because they had become her family in the years since she had abandoned her own.

Once again, Brooklyn felt like an outsider. It reminded her of the feeling she had standing in her family home while it seemed like her whole family gathered around her in condemnation. She began questioning whether she ever truly fit in with Missy and Carla. She knew that they had never really seen her as one of them. Brooklyn was getting money with the fellas instead of posturing and posing with the girls. She felt the same thing happening again with Angel's friends. Despite the years she had spent in their midst, Renee took every opportunity to remind Brooklyn that she wasn't one of them. She didn't have a prestigious career or a dream home. She was a gate-crasher to them, an impostor.

She began to question all of her relationships then, asking herself if she was disposable to everyone. Brooklyn went into survival mode.

She had been hustling since she was seventeen. Now she had more money to her name than most of her peers. Drugs were a lucrative business. But there was no denying that it was a volatile one, too. Some years had been better than others and lately the competition was tough. Chance and the other Baltimore hustlers weren't buying as much as they used to, and Stacey had been forced to accept less than she once demanded for her product. The profit margins were much slimmer than before. Brooklyn began to quietly reevaluate everything.

Through the years, she had built an especially close bond with Stacey. As Roscoe's older sister and the leader of their crew, she offered a wise and informed perspective to all of them about the things they were witnessing and the situations they found themselves navigating. While Missy and Carla were in relationships with hustlers, Stacey didn't date the boys in the hood. In fact, Brooklyn had never known her to be romantically involved with anyone. Stacey was someone they all relied on to keep them on track.

She often broke it down for Brooklyn.

"Don't think this life will last forever. Ask yourself how many retired hustlers you know. I hear you and Hass talking about starting that beauty salon barbershop thing. And I think that's dope. I wish y'all the best. But I want you to be realistic. Hass is probably never gonna stop hustling. I doubt that you will either. Even if you make the most successful business imaginable. The life he's living is an addiction. There's a thrill we get when we go out there in those streets. When we pick up and drop off drugs and count money until the wee hours of the morning. This shit is a thrill. How do you work a regular job after this? I watched niggas try to leave the game countless times! No matter how many times we get arrested, robbed, or come close to getting killed, we keep going back to it. We're all addicted."

Brooklyn heard the truth in Stacey's words but prayed that she was the exception to the rule. She needed to believe that this life wasn't a trap.

When she asked Hassan about it, he assured her that Stacey didn't know what she was talking about.

"Everybody's not the same," he insisted. "I'm not planning on doing this shit forever. As soon as we find the right spot, we're setting up shop and never looking back."

Brooklyn tried to believe him. But there was a voice inside of her reminding her that she was her own hero. She didn't need to wait for Hassan to decide that the time was right. She was ready for a change of scenery now.

On her next trip to Baltimore, she met with Chance as usual. He was alone this time.

Their interactions were far more relaxed now than they once were. Chance always complimented Brooklyn, flirting with her the same way Hassan had done in the beginning of their courtship. Unlike Hassan, Chance had no loyalty to anybody for long. Through the years, Brooklyn saw so many of his crew members come and go that she had lost count. Often, she encountered those same workers in Baltimore's streets, and they all had the same complaints about Chance. He cut corners, paid little, and only looked out for himself.

To Brooklyn, those weren't necessarily negative traits. In their line of business, survival was the common goal. Chance was a survivor. So was she.

He took her for breakfast at a restaurant his aunt owned. He had no crew with him when he arrived to pick her up at the hotel just after 9 A.M.

His black Pathfinder was clean and smelled like vanilla. Brooklyn greeted him as she climbed inside.

"Good morning. I see you're an early bird like me!"

"Good morning. The early bird gets the worm." He drove off to the restaurant.

"Where are we going?" she asked.

"My aunt owns a spot out in my hood. She cooks better than anybody I know, including my mama. So I think you'll enjoy it."

"Okay! Don't let your mama hear you say that."

"She would whoop my ass!"

They both laughed.

They discussed music and celebrity gossip during the short drive. When they arrived at the restaurant, he held the door for her as she stepped inside. The place was bright and airy, and the scent of the delicious food made Brooklyn's mouth water instantly.

"What's up, Chance?" A woman yelled out from the kitchen.

"Hey, Auntie!" He walked over and gave her a kiss. Then he returned to Brooklyn's side. "Come on. Let's sit down." He led her to a table in the back, explaining that it was his favorite. "When I sit here, I can see who's coming."

She sat down and perused the menu. "Everything smells so good. I want all of it."

"You can't go wrong. No matter what you order."

When the waitress came, he ordered chicken and waffles while Brooklyn got the shrimp and grits. They brought out biscuits for them to nibble on while they waited, and Brooklyn gobbled hers, hungrily.

"Damn." Chance laughed. "Your man ain't feeding you good enough."

She wiped the crumbs from her shirt and giggled.

"Speaking of eating, we both know the money is slowing up out here in these streets."

Brooklyn nodded. "I used to make these trips to see you at least twice a month. Lately, I hardly see you."

"That's because Stacey is being hardheaded. Much as I look forward to seeing your fine ass strutting through Baltimore, lately I'm working with niggas from other places with better prices."

"Not better product though," Brooklyn assured him. "Stacey's shit is better than whatever you're getting elsewhere. I'll bet you that."

He nodded. "True. And that's the tragedy of the situation. She could do more business with me if she'd drop her price. Her stubbornness is stopping *you* from eating right."

"Stacey dropped her price already."

"She could drop it more and you know it. Niggas from New York come down here all the time. Y'all ain't the only ones coming into town on Greyhound, setting up shop in Virginia and all that. This work is easy to get to."

Chance leaned in. "I told Stacey that I'm done fucking with her. I need her to cut that price by three thousand."

"She's not gonna do that."

"So, I gotta pass. You can take that work you brought down here and bring it back to Harlem."

He took a bite of his biscuit and chewed.

Brooklyn's heart sank. She had four kilos of cocaine with her and had been counting on her cut of the money. She hadn't told Hassan yet, but she'd found the ideal location for a beauty salon in Towson, Maryland, and had gone to meet the property owner. They hit it off instantly and within minutes had settled on a price to rent the place. In order to finalize everything, she needed to leave a sizeable deposit, buy equipment and furniture, and hire employees. Now was not the time to slow things down.

"Nothing against you," he said. "This ain't personal. I told Stacey the same thing."

She watched Chance finish his breakfast. Brooklyn knew that what Chance had just said was completely factual. The game was different now. Their competitors had better prices. Stacey was about to lose a very lucrative stream of income if she lost Chance and his crew. The wheels in her head were turning, thinking of how she could convince him to change his mind.

"Okay," she said. "We'll do twenty-eight."

She decided to deduct the difference from her own cut this time so that she could reel Chance back in. She had made up her mind that she was moving down to Maryland for good, with or without Hassan. Having Chance back onboard on a consistent basis would be beneficial for all of them. Stacey's money wasn't coming in the way that it used to. She was playing hardball with Chance unnecessarily. Brooklyn was convinced that she could get her to see the bigger picture.

"I'll work it out with Stacey when I get back to New York."

Chance sat back and smiled. "Then it's a deal."

When she finished her dealings with Chance, she went to see Angel and get her hair done. She hadn't seen much of her since the engagement party. She wanted to gauge the temperature between them. To her relief, they hugged and gushed over each other as if nothing had ever happened.

"I missed you! How long are you staying?"

"I'm leaving in the morning," Brooklyn admitted.

Angel groaned. "How long have you been here?"

"Just a couple of days."

Angel frowned. "Why didn't you call me?" She folded her arms across her chest.

"Don't act like that. I was only here to handle business. I have good news!"

"What news?"

"I found a property in Towson and I'm gonna open that salon I've been talking about. I'm gonna lease for now. Then I'll see if Kia can help me establish a legitimate line of credit and I can buy a place and really do it right."

Angel was so excited that she was jumping up and down already.

"So, you and Hassan are moving down here?"

Brooklyn laughed. "Well, I'm not sure about Hass. I still have to convince him. But yes. I'm ready to leave New York for good."

Angel hugged her tightly and linked her arm through Brooklyn's as she led her to the sink to begin her shampoo.

"This makes me so happy, Brooklyn. You can start all over again down here. These chicks will buy anything you're selling."

Brooklyn laughed. "Not all of them. Kia and Renee would probably stand outside with pitchforks and picket signs."

Angel sighed as she reclined the seat, rinsed Brooklyn's hair, and began massaging the shampoo in gently.

"I'm sorry about them. I know we talked about this, and you said it's not my fault. But I hate that you had to go through that. Josiah and I let them all have it after you left. They come off real bitchy. But they're just fascinated by you. The jewelry, the clothes, the cars. They want to know how you got it on your own when they had to inherit it or work their asses off to get it. They ask all those invasive questions because they wish they could be like you."

"They should be careful what they wish for," Brooklyn said. "I don't talk about how I grew up. Not because I'm ashamed of it. I didn't have it rough like people assume. I had two God-fearing parents, a house with a picket fence, piano lessons, and structure. I know Renee—maybe Kia too—assumes that I'm ghetto because of who I date or the way I live my life. People make assumptions."

Angel listened closely since Brooklyn rarely shared details of her past.

"I left that life behind by choice," she continued. "I wasn't forced to be out here on my own. So, when Renee talks her shit about me, I laugh on the inside. She thinks she has me all figured out. But I chose not to be stuck in a life like hers. Nothing about who she is or what she has appeals to me."

"I think Renee has issues," Angel said. "Don't pay her no mind."

"I won't."

"Now that you're moving down here, you can help me plan this wedding!"

Brooklyn groaned. "I don't know about all that. I'll be there smiling in all the pictures and everything. But I'm not the fairy-tale type. I wouldn't be good at planning something like that."

"You don't want to get married someday?" Angel asked, curiously.

"Never found the thought appealing," Brooklyn said. "I guess I didn't have good examples growing up."

"I get it. I'm excited about it, though. I want to fill that house up with babies."

She toweled Brooklyn's hair and led her to her workstation.

Brooklyn saw the joy on Angel's face at just the thought of it and knew then that she was losing her friend. Soon their brunches and lunches would be canceled in favor of playdates and kids' parties where Brooklyn would be the odd woman out.

She smiled back at Angel. "I bet you are."

Brooklyn took the long way home the next day. She had driven down this time and she was glad she did. It gave her the chance to take in the scenery and think about how she would put the next phase of her plan in motion. First, she would talk to Stacey. Convincing her to lower the price a little in exchange for Chance's consistent business seemed like the best solution for all of them. Wally was already doing well down in Virginia. Brooklyn would set up shop in Maryland. With Roscoe and the rest of their crew in New York, they would have a stronger hold on the game as a conglomerate. Hassan would have a choice. He could stay in New York and heed his mama's warnings, or he could follow his heart, which always led back to Brooklyn.

By the time Brooklyn got to Harlem, it was nearly 10 P.M. She went to Stacey's apartment and knocked on the door. She waited but got no answer. She lifted her hand to knock again but paused when she heard the locks unlatching. Stacey opened the door, looked at her, and walked away without speaking.

Frowning, Brooklyn stepped inside. She looked around the apartment and saw the usual faces. Roscoe walked out of the kitchen with a Heineken in his hand. Hassan stood near the window. He waved at Brooklyn as she entered.

"Hey."

"Wassup?" Stacey sat down on the couch and continued crushing up some weed.

The TV was on, but no one seemed focused on it. Brooklyn could instantly sense some tension.

"I just got back." She set the bag down on the coffee table and sat across from Stacey in her usual spot.

"I see." Stacey packed a Backwoods full of weed and proceeded to roll it up.

Brooklyn glanced at Hassan. He had a serious expression on his face.

Roscoe picked up the bag and started counting it. Brooklyn

watched him. She watched Stacey, too, as she sparked her blunt and inhaled. She sat back and looked at Brooklyn.

"How'd it go?"

Brooklyn's mind raced. She could tell that something was off. This wasn't Stacey's usual energy with her. She hadn't smiled at her once.

"It went alright. Hit a little traffic on the way back, but nothing serious."

Stacey smirked. "Okay."

"What's going on?" Brooklyn asked, tired of the guessing game.

"You tell me." Stacey flicked the residue into the ashtray. "What do I know?"

"All here," Roscoe said, done counting the money. He looked at Stacey and nodded. He put the bag back on the table, picked up his beer, and sat down nearby.

Brooklyn had been working with them for so long that having the money counted in front of her felt disrespectful. She had never come up short in all the years she'd been part of the team.

"How much did you charge him?" Stacey asked, locking eyes with Brooklyn.

Brooklyn hesitated. "Roscoe just told you it's all there."

"That's not what I asked you."

Brooklyn knew she had fucked up. She just couldn't figure out how Stacey found out before she had the chance to tell her herself. Brooklyn thought about lying. Somehow that seemed like a bad move.

"I don't understand what you're mad about. Every dollar is in there. What did I do wrong?"

"You're dancing around the question and I'm about to start losing my patience." Stacey pointed at her as she spoke. "You think I don't have eyes and ears everywhere I have my money? Did you think I wouldn't hear that you're down there cutting deals with niggas when I told you not to do that shit?"

"Stacey, I don't know what Chance told you—"

"Chance didn't tell me shit! Why would he? He got your stupid ass in his pocket already. You cut a side deal with that mutha-fucka and he's down there bragging to all the other niggas about how much he's getting it for. If you were smart, you'd know that fool can't keep his mouth shut." Stacey set her blunt down. "Now, I'm gonna ask you again. What price did you give him?"

Brooklyn sighed. "Twenty-eight, Stacey. But I didn't short you. I took the difference out of my cut."

"You don't make the decisions, bitch. I do. I set the price on these niggas and my word is bond. When I give them a number, that's the fuck it!"

"So, forget it. I'll tell him you said no."

"I ALREADY SAID NO! I told him what it cost. I sent you down there to get it. And you let him play your stupid ass!"

Brooklyn stood up, her hands spread wide, backtracking desperately.

"I'm sorry. Damn! I'm the one who took the hit, though. What are you so mad about?"

Stacey looked at Roscoe and Hassan, incredulously.

"What the fuck am I mad about?" Stacey pounded her fist into her hand for emphasis. "I got other niggas down there charging the right price. The price I told them to charge. And Chance is making it known that he's getting the same shit from me for less. How do you think that looks?"

Brooklyn looked at Hassan for some help. He shook his head.

The scene felt like déjà vu. For a moment, she wasn't sure if she was looking at Hassan or Amir.

"Fine. I'm sorry, Stacey. It won't happen again."

"Nope! It sure won't because I'm not fucking with you no more. Not on some business shit anyway. You *and* Chance can kiss my ass." Stacey pulled Brooklyn's portion of the money out of the duffel bag and set it on the table. "This was your last trip on my behalf."

Brooklyn frowned. "Don't put me in the same category as him, Stacey. Fuck the money. I've been like family to you for a long time now. I made a mistake. I apologize. But don't cut me off the first time I step out of line. This shit ain't that deep."

"It is, though. I can't trust you. I probably should've seen that shit coming considering how you came to me in the first place."

Brooklyn stood speechlessly letting her words sink in.

"That wasn't the same," Brooklyn said.

"Maybe not. But I still took a gamble trusting you. For a while, it seemed like a smart move. Now I'm second-guessing it, and that's not good. When I have to doubt somebody's loyalty, I'd rather not fuck with them at all. So, our little business arrangement is done."

Brooklyn shook her head. "I came to you when I was at my lowest and now you want to throw that shit back in my face?"

"I opened my door to you, put you on the team, and I told you that rule number one is to do what the fuck I say!"

"You're not my mother."

Stacey laughed, tempted to point out that Brooklyn hadn't listened to her either. The words were on the tip of her tongue.

"Grow up, little girl."

"Was I a little girl when you put me on that bus to Baltimore?"

"Yup!" Stacey said. "And I told you that Chance would test you. All you had to do was call me. I would've told you not to let him hustle you."

"He didn't hustle me. The price you're charging is too high."

"That's not your choice to make," Stacey reminded her.

"But I'm the one making the trips back and forth," Brooklyn said. "I see things you can't see from Harlem. We're losing customers. The money is slowing up. I made a decision for both of us. I thought we were partners."

Stacey laughed. "Partners! I said that shit as a joke. How are we *partners*, Brooklyn? I put you on. I gave you a shot. But you can't be walking around thinking me and you are on the same level. *You* don't have the connect. I do. You're a runner. And runners don't set the price." Stacey pointed at her head, signaling for Brooklyn to use her brain. "Go sit on the sidelines now."

Brooklyn was visibly fuming.

"Let's go home," Hassan said, stepping forward. "Y'all are emotional right now."

"Don't come at me with that *emotional* shit, Hass! You know she's dead wrong." Stacey looked at him like he was crazy.

"She fucked up. But she gets it now. She's sorry."

"She got me looking like I don't have control over my crew. Got us looking weak out there when all she had to do was follow instructions."

Brooklyn stepped toward her. "Stacey, you don't know everything! I respect you, and I know you've been doing this a long time. But the game is changing."

Stacey looked at Roscoe and Hassan in amazement. "You hear this shit?"

Roscoe shook his head in dismay. Brooklyn was only making things worse.

Stacey locked eyes with Brooklyn. "You know the game better than me?"

"I'm not saying that. But I know the price we're charging is too high. Everybody down there is complaining. Not just Chance. If we made it lower, we could move more work. I have a plan! I'm gonna go down to Maryland full time."

"Good for you. Hass told me about the friends you made down there. I think that's a good look. Move down there and start over. You made enough money."

"I'm not stopping now."

"You're not working for me anymore. Period."

"Stacey, you're bugging!"

"Since you know so much, go do your own thing. Build your own team."

Stacey shrugged, lit her blunt again, and exhaled the smoke

in her direction. Brooklyn felt dismissed. The feeling was all too familiar.

"Wow." Brooklyn felt like she was free-falling. "That's it? First time I make a mistake, you want to cut me off? Seems like you've been waiting for your chance to do this."

"You should listen to your man and go. We had a good run, Brooklyn. You made some money, made some friends. I'm only cutting you off on the business end. As long as you're good with Hass, you're still good with me."

"Now I see why you're by yourself," Brooklyn said, spitefully. "I looked up to you like a big sister, an aunt or something. I thought we were family. But you're heartless. You're a cold, miserable bitch."

Stacey stood up and took a step in Brooklyn's direction. "Word?"

Hassan grabbed Brooklyn by the arm. She pulled away, roughly, glaring at Stacey.

"You sit in here calling the shots like you're the queen. Ordering everybody around like you're so fuckin' smart! We're not your little minions."

"You should go home before I lose my patience." Stacey pointed in Brooklyn's face.

"Let's go," Hassan said again.

Brooklyn couldn't control the rage bubbling up inside of her. "You know what? FUCK YOU, STACEY!"

"Fuck you, too!"

"You've been dead inside ever since your man got killed. That's why you're by yourself."

Stacey smirked at her. "At least I never snitched on my brother."

Brooklyn charged at Stacey with all her might. Hassan caught her midair and held her back. Roscoe blocked his sister from Brooklyn's wild kicks and swings in Stacey's direction.

"Take her home, Hass," Roscoe pleaded.

Brooklyn followed Hass out, not bothering to say goodbye as

she left. When they got in the car, neither of them spoke at first. Hassan wasn't sure what to say. He knew that tonight had been a turning point for all of them. Even if Brooklyn and Stacey might be able to patch things up later on, things had been said to ensure that their relationship would never be the same.

Brooklyn was too upset to utter a word.

Hassan cleared his throat at a red light and broke the silence. "What happened in Baltimore? How'd you let that nigga talk you into lowering the price?"

Brooklyn closed her eyes, regretting the decision now. "Stacey's charging more than everybody down there."

"That's her business."

"This is our business, Hass! We're the ones out here getting our hands dirty while she's up in that apartment calling all the shots."

Hassan shook his head as the light turned green and kept driving. "That's just how it is, Brooklyn. You knew that from jump. So, why do this now? Why start questioning her decisions after all this time?"

"Who is she? God?"

"She's not God, but she's smart. She's been doing this a long time. A lot longer than you."

Brooklyn sighed.

"And she's been good to you. I think you owed her a phone call at least before you made that deal with Chance's bitch ass."

Brooklyn shook her head. "Call her for what? If we're partners—"

"That's where you went wrong. You took that shit too seriously. Ya'll were never partners, Brooklyn. Stacey's the one taking the most risk. Everything starts and ends with her. She thought you understood that. All of us did. She called you '*partner*' because she respected your hustle. You're not like Carla and Missy. You weren't afraid to get your hands dirty. She was showing you love as a female in the game. She says you remind her of herself sometimes. But don't get it twisted. That's *her* work we're moving."

Brooklyn rolled her eyes. She was done talking about it. "Fuck it. Whatever."

They got back to their apartment and Brooklyn could tell that Hassan was upset with her. Typically, when she returned from her trips out of town, he showered her with affection and attention. This time, instead of pulling her into his arms and asking how her trip went, he sat on the leather sofa in the living room with his head in his hands.

Brooklyn stood watching him for a while, wondering what he was thinking.

He looked at her, seriously. "You shouldn't have lowered the price for Chance. And you definitely shouldn't have said those things to Stacey."

Brooklyn hadn't expected that. "Did you hear what she said to me? About my brother?"

Hassan didn't respond.

"So, she gets to call me disloyal and a snitch, but I can't defend myself?"

"That's what you were doing?"

"Yes!" She huffed. "Somebody had to defend me! You stood there playing peacemaker the whole time."

"Wow." Hassan shook his head. "Okay."

"It doesn't matter," she said. "Stacey doesn't have to fuck with me anymore. We can still stick to our plan."

"What plan?" he asked, confused. "I heard you telling Stacey about some move to Maryland. When were you gonna tell me about that?"

"Tonight! I thought I was going to tell Stacey about the deal I made with Chance, and she would see the light. The shit just makes sense, so it never occurred to me that she would say no. Then I was gonna tell you that I found a spot in Towson where we can open a business. I spoke to the guy who owns it, and all we have to do is put a deposit down and start setting up."

He listened as she outlined the details. The money and time needed to get the necessary licenses, buy equipment, hire stylists, and find a place to live in the area. Brooklyn laid it all out for him, not even flinching as she rattled off numbers in the six-figure range. He had always thought Brooklyn was so smart. But hearing her now, she sounded like a kid playing with Monopoly money like it was the real thing.

"That's not happening now," he said when she was done. "Maybe someday down the line."

Brooklyn frowned. "Why not?"

"Because my money's tied up right now. I told you my mother found a house in Westchester she likes. I'm gonna help her make that happen. Better schools for Laray and all that."

Brooklyn vaguely recalled him mentioning something about that months ago. She had been half listening at the time.

"The money I have is going toward that. It'll be a while before I have enough to do this business thing." He sighed.

"Then let me put my money with yours from now on. Instead of working with Stacey, I can work with you. She doesn't have to know—"

"We don't operate like that."

"So, you just do what Stacey tells you to do, like a little kid?"

He shook his head. "I think you see this as a 'crew' and Stacey is the head of it. But that's not how we see it. It's a family. Stacey's the matriarch. We trust her because she earned it. Ever since I met you, it seems like you've been desperate to prove how 'grown-up' you are. Establishing your independence and whatnot. That's been your whole story. So grown that you didn't want to listen to your parents. Now, you're too grown to listen to Stacey. You don't see a pattern?"

She sucked her teeth. "No, Dr. Phil. Why don't you help me out."

Hassan got up and walked to the kitchen. He pulled a bottle of water from the fridge, took a long swig, and came back to the living room.

He looked at Brooklyn long and hard. As beautiful as she was, as unique and unpredictable, he had seen more than a few warning signs throughout their relationship. Red flags that he had excused or ignored before that were now starting to concern him. She seemed to have no sense of what it meant to be part of a family. In the years since her father's stroke, she had barely mentioned it. He wondered if her ability to cut ties with those she claimed to love was something he should watch out for.

"I'm going out," he said. "I'll be back."

Brooklyn watched him leave, feeling more frustrated and misunderstood than she had in years. Chance and his big mouth! She was convinced that things would have gone differently if she had been able to explain the deal to Stacey before it got back to her through the streets.

Stacey's icy demeanor and cold rejection of her stung deeply. She had called Brooklyn a snitch, conjured up memories of what happened with Amir, and had questioned her loyalty.

"*Go sit on the sidelines*," Stacey had said.

Brooklyn scoffed now as the words echoed in her mind. She would never be relegated to sitting on the sidelines with the likes of Carla and Missy. She was not about to be demoted, not in Stacey's life or Hassan's.

It all seemed so clear to her now. Stacey had been right all those years ago when she warned Brooklyn that she and Hassan were chasing a dream. He was married to the streets and to the hustle. Not just the streets in the sense of the drug game. But he was specifically addicted to the streets of New York. No matter how much money he and the crew made or how much power they attained, Hassan wasn't going to leave his family behind. Candy would always have more influence over her son than she did. Brooklyn hadn't minded it at first. But now she realized that

Hassan's mother wasn't the only woman who held more power over him than she did. Stacey had power, too.

She hated the feeling of being an outcast. Stacey and Hassan had both demonstrated to her that night that she wasn't truly one of them. The stain of Amir's blood, Alonzo's incarceration, and her theft of the church's money had always clouded Stacey's view of her. Her ambition and drive made Hassan and his mother question the advice Brooklyn gave him about his plans for the future. Her desire to steer her own life rather than be subject to the whims of a man put her at odds with Carla and Stacey. With her old life in Staten Island little more than a distant memory, Brooklyn realized more than ever that it was time for her to get out of there. It was now or never.

She ran into her bedroom, grabbed her suitcase from the back of the closet, and began packing desperately. She pulled clothes from their hangers roughly, sending them clanging to the floor. She grabbed the tampon box from the back of her closet with her hidden cash and tucked it into a large duffel bag along with all of her jewelry, designer bags, and shoes.

She thought about Hassan and how he would feel when he found out what she had done. She assumed he would feel betrayed, probably curse the day he met her. She imagined that he would tell his mother that she had been right all along, that he never should have trusted Brooklyn in the first place.

She thought about Stacey, too, and realized that she had her to thank for this. Stacey had always reminded her that she was too smart to be just a hustler's wife. And now Brooklyn had finally gotten the message. She didn't need a man to rescue her. She would save her damn self.

She knew that Hassan could come back at any minute. Racing against time, she started making trips to her car loaded down with everything she could carry. She took Hassan's expensive watches, his thick gold chains, and diamond stud earrings. She grabbed a kilo of cocaine and tucked it all into her pink Nike backpack. With her heart racing, she locked the door to the apartment, loaded the trunk of her car with the remaining bags, set her pink backpack on the passenger seat, and rushed around to the driver's seat. As she pulled the door open, she saw headlights approaching and squinted in the direction of the car screeching to a halt behind her.

Hassan jumped out of the passenger seat of Roscoe's car and started rushing toward her. Brooklyn leapt behind the wheel and stuck the key in the ignition. She pulled the door closed behind her, but Hassan was there to block it. He stuck his arm inside and grabbed her arm.

"What are you doing?"

She floored the gas, but the car was still in park. Hearing the engine revving, Hassan grabbed her roughly by her sweater and tugged her out of the car. Brooklyn tumbled to the pavement cursing wildly.

"Get the fuck off of me!"

"What's wrong with you?" Hassan demanded as she fought him. Brooklyn was clawing at his face, scratching and slapping him. He grabbed her arms and held them, frowning. "What's your problem?"

Brooklyn kept fighting, scared now that she had been caught red-handed. "I'm leaving. That's it. Get off of me!"

Roscoe took out his cellphone as he watched the melee. He dialed his sister's number.

"You should come over to Hass's crib. Brooklyn's wilding out." He hung up and walked over to the fracas.

"You're leaving?" Hassan asked Brooklyn.

"Yes. I'm out. Stacey don't want to do business with me, you don't want to move or open a business or do anything! So, I'm leaving. It's as simple as that. All this snatching me out of the car, and grabbing on me for what? I don't want to do this anymore, Hass!"

She saw the hurt on his face for a quick moment. Then he nodded, let her go, and stepped back. "Okay. So, leave."

Roscoe shook his head, peering at the pink backpack on the passenger seat. It was unzipped and some of its contents were visible. Suddenly, he understood why Brooklyn was making such a scene. He opened the door and pulled out the bag.

"Nah. She can't leave with this." He held up the kilo of cocaine.

Brooklyn's heart dropped. Hassan's mouth fell open and he looked at her, shocked.

"You can't be serious."

"That's *my* shit!" she lied.

Roscoe dug into the bag and pulled out Hassan's jewelry, his watch. "This yours, too?" he asked Brooklyn sarcastically.

She looked at Hassan, her eyes pleading. "How do you think I feel, Hass? You took Stacey's side over mine. You heard that shit she said to me about my brother. You know how much that hurt me. Talking about 'patterns' like I haven't been fighting my whole life to survive! I asked you to come with me. Let's get the fuck out of here and start over. And you walked out!"

Hassan saw red. "You're trying to blame this shit on me? You ain't never been shit! You stole from a nigga when he was at his lowest, took your Pops' money, too, and never looked back. You're mad at Stacey for telling you the truth. YOU'RE the reason your brother killed himself."

Brooklyn threw a punch at him and missed. Hassan grabbed her again, this time securing her in a reverse bear hug as she kicked and bucked her body desperately trying to break free.

"I should fuck you up!" He spoke the words directly into her ear. "You wanna leave? GO! But you trying to steal from me?"

A yellow taxi approached, and Stacey got out. She approached the scene wearing a black hooded sweat suit and a scowl.

"What's the fuckin' problem?"

Roscoe walked over to her, shaking his head at all the drama.

"We pulled up and Brooklyn was leaving. Hass tried to talk to her, and she got all agitated. While they were going back and forth, I peeped this in the passenger seat." He held up the pink backpack and held it open while Stacey peered inside.

"This bitch done lost her mind." Stacey stormed over to where Hassan was still struggling to hold on to Brooklyn. "Let her go!" Stacey yelled.

Hassan pushed Brooklyn away and she tumbled to the ground. Scrambling back to her feet, she rushed toward the car, but Stacey blocked her. Stacey reached inside and took the keys out of the ignition. She turned and faced Brooklyn.

"It's not bad enough that you're running again? You had to steal from this man?"

"Give me my keys, Stacey."

"These ain't your keys. Hass bought you this car, didn't he?" Stacey reached inside the car and popped the trunk. She looked at Roscoe. "Take all that shit out."

Roscoe began unloading the trunk. Brooklyn stood with her chest heaving.

Stacey locked eyes with her. "You're the type of bitch that don't listen. What did I tell you when you started fucking with Hass? I told you he's a good dude and I warned you not to break his heart. And what did you do? You tried to run off on him? Tried to steal from him?" She shook her head in disbelief. She pointed her hand like a gun and pressed it to the side of Brooklyn's head. "I should blow your fuckin' brains out!"

"This ain't none of your business, Stacey. Back up!"

Stacey had heard enough. She scooped Brooklyn up like a wrestler and tossed her hard onto the trunk of the car. She punched Brooklyn in the face, grabbed a fistful of her hair, and pulled her onto the ground.

"Hass can't hit you. But I *can*, bitch! Get up!"

Brooklyn scrambled to her feet and looked around. She saw Hassan standing on the sidewalk watching her with a pained expression on his face. Roscoe finished unloading the trunk and lined all the items up inside the gate.

Breathless, Brooklyn looked at Stacey. "I just want to go. Y'all ain't fucking with me no more. Fine. Let me get in my car and you'll never see me again."

Stacey grinned at her. She felt sorry for Brooklyn. She knew the young lady thought she had it all figured out. The qualities she once admired about her now gave her cause for concern. She saw how ruthless and selfish Brooklyn's survival instinct caused her to be.

"You can go," Stacey said, nodding. "Take the clothes on your back, the money in your pocket, and get the fuck out of here."

Brooklyn looked at Hassan in disbelief. She looked at Stacey again.

"That's not right, Stacey. I've been putting in work! Even before all that, I had my own money when I came to you. I'm not leaving with nothing!"

Stacey stepped closer to her. "You might not leave here at all if you keep talking shit!"

Hassan walked over with Brooklyn's Fendi bag in his hand. He handed it to her and took the car keys out of Stacey's hand. He slid the key to his apartment off the ring and stuck it in his pocket. Then he handed the remaining keys to Brooklyn.

"Take the car." He tugged Stacey by her hand. "She can have it. Let her go."

Hassan turned around and walked back into the house. Roscoe hoisted Brooklyn's duffel bag onto his shoulder, wheeled her suitcase, and followed his friend inside.

Brooklyn watched, tempted to fight for at least the contents of the duffel bag. That's where the bulk of her money was, along with her jewelry and items she could easily sell for cash. But the look on Stacey's face stopped her. She could tell that one false move would give Stacey all the permission she needed to whoop her ass.

Stacey got in her face so closely that Brooklyn could smell her breath.

"If I ever see you again, I'll leave your body right where I find you."

She pushed past Brooklyn roughly and followed the men inside.

Brooklyn began to cry. Frustrated and lost, she got into her car and drove away slowly. Reality set in. She had no drugs, nothing but the money in her purse. She stopped three blocks away and counted it. $4,800. That's all she had to her name.

She laid her head back against the headrest and exhaled. She was back at square one. Any hopes she had for starting over as a business owner in Maryland were gone. She banged the wheel in frustration and wept.

An hour later, she put the car in drive again. She merged into traffic and dialed Angel's number as she drove. Angel picked up on the second ring.

"Hey, girl. What you doing calling so late?"

Brooklyn spoke between sobs. "I fucked up, Angel. I need help. I don't have anywhere else to go."

Chapter Thirteen

Castaway

The drive to Maryland this time felt different than all the others. She remembered the first time she'd made the trip. She had been a bundle of nerves with her backpack stuffed full of contraband riding the bus down I-95. Back then she had plans to be a contender in the game just like Alonzo and Stacey. It had worked for a while. But there was no denying the fact that those days were over now.

She needed a friend right now. She was broke and alone. She had burned every bridge except one. She couldn't return to Staten Island, would never be welcome in Harlem again. Her only hope was to fall at Angel's feet and beg for mercy.

She got to her friend's sprawling home just before dawn. Angel was waiting for her with open arms.

"I canceled all my appointments for the day," Angel said. "Clients are mad, but they'll get over it. I could tell by how you sounded on the phone that you don't need to be by yourself right now."

Brooklyn looked as weary as she felt. She followed Angel into her living room and slumped down on the sofa looking defeated.

"What happened?" Angel asked. She sat across from her on the chaise, concerned. She had never seen Brooklyn so broken.

"Me and Hass broke up. He threw me out with nothing but my purse and my car." Brooklyn began to cry.

"What? Why would he do that?" She thought back to the

times she'd met Hassan and couldn't imagine what would make him treat Brooklyn like that. "He loves you."

Brooklyn couldn't deny that. Even as she spun a convenient tale for her friend, she knew that what she said was true. Hassan had loved her. Just not enough to live up to her expectations.

"It's complicated," Brooklyn said. "Part of it has to do with a business deal that went wrong. The team was mad at me, basically. And instead of siding with me, he sided with the team." Brooklyn wiped her eyes with the tissues Angel gave her. "The bottom line is I lost everything. Everything I spent years working hard to build, everything I own. I can't reach out to my family, and I made the mistake of having no friends besides the ones I made with Hass."

Angel's heart broke for her. "You have me." She sat beside Brooklyn and hugged her. "Don't worry. It's gonna be okay."

Brooklyn wanted to believe it. She had the tough lessons life had taught her in her arsenal. She prayed they'd be enough to help her make it on her own.

Brooklyn was cloaked in a thick fog of sadness and despair. Angel was an incredible comfort to her, alternating between giving her the space she needed to grieve and doing everything she could to lift her friend's spirits up. Nothing seemed to work. Brooklyn had no desire to hang out with Angel and her friends and didn't protest when she left to go to work or fulfill her social obligations. In fact, Brooklyn looked forward to the time alone. She stayed holed up in one of the spacious guest rooms at Angel's house watching music videos, talk shows, and Judge Judy between naps.

Angel's fiancé Josiah had all but moved in as their wedding date approached. Now that Brooklyn was their houseguest, he spent most of his time upstairs in their bedroom while Angel and Brooklyn hung around downstairs. The arrangement was working out fine, but Brooklyn was concerned about overstaying her welcome.

"I'm depressed," she admitted to Angel one night as they stood around the island in the kitchen snacking on leftovers from the dinner Josiah had prepared. "I don't need a doctor to diagnose me. I know that's what I'm going through."

Angel was no psychologist, but she agreed.

"My life has been one big battle," Brooklyn said. "Since I was a kid, I've been fighting nonstop. And I'm tired."

Angel thought about that. "You told me that you grew up in a house with a picket fence and piano lessons. Was it abusive? Why were you fighting as a kid?"

Brooklyn stared off into space, recalling the first time she had to fight. "My uncle touched me. He told me it was my fault. He said that I was to blame because I was inviting his attention. I told my mother, and she chose not to believe me. I told my father, and he chose to ignore me. So, I fought back the only way I could. I started doing whatever it took to make myself happy because no one else was going to."

Angel had tears in her eyes. "Brooklyn, I'm so sorry."

"Every time I think I found my path, it turns out that I'm on the wrong track. I just want to live a normal life for once." Brooklyn shrugged. "So, I made up my mind. I'm gonna get my cosmetology license again and work my way up to owning a salon one day."

She painted on a convincing smile and tried to sound optimistic. But the very thought of starting back at square one made her feel nauseous. She had already been on the brink of her dreams. To have that stolen away felt like an incredible injustice.

Still, she knew that she couldn't leach off her friend forever. "If you let me crash here for another thirty days, I'll find a job, get my own apartment, and put the pieces of my life back together again."

Angel set down the flatbread she was eating and walked around to Brooklyn. She hugged her tightly. "I know you will. I have faith in you. But don't be in a rush to leave. You can stay here as long as you want."

Brooklyn thanked her and sipped her water. "What are Kia and Renee saying?" she asked. "I'm sure they were thrilled to hear about my fall from grace."

Angel rolled her eyes. "I didn't tell them all the details. All I said was that you and Hassan broke up and that you're staying with me until you figure things out. That's all they need to know."

Brooklyn sighed. "Thank you."

"That's what friends are for."

Josiah walked in wearing a T-shirt, sweatpants, and bare feet. He looked at the women and paused. "Am I interrupting a Hallmark moment?"

Both women laughed.

"No, silly. We were just tearing up this flatbread and talking about men." Angel walked over and kissed him. "I'm going to take a shower. Got an early day tomorrow." She looked at Brooklyn and waved. "Good night, girl."

"Good night." Brooklyn broke off another piece of flatbread and looked at Josiah. "This is delicious!"

He smiled and walked to the refrigerator. "That's simple to make. I'll show you how next time I do it." He took out a bottle of lemonade and reached in the cabinet for a glass.

"Hopefully, I won't be here much longer," Brooklyn said. "I'm looking for an apartment of my own. I doubt I can afford anything around here. But I should be able to find something affordable closer to the hood." She chuckled, though she hated the thought of lowering her standards. "I'm looking for a job, too. So, let me know if any of those fancy restaurants you work at are hiring. I can wait tables or something. Angel said that I should get my bartending license since I'm good with people."

Josiah sat down at the table with his lemonade. He had a million questions about Brooklyn. She was the only friend Angel had whose story he didn't know in its entirety.

"That's good," he said. "I'll let you know if I come across any openings."

"Thanks."

"Can I ask you a question?"

Brooklyn looked at him. "Sure."

"How did you end up here?"

She was confused, unsure how to answer the question. "Hassan got mad at me—"

"No," he said. "I mean how did you end up at this point in your life? With a man like Hassan, in a world like the one you operate in?"

"You wouldn't understand," she said.

He chuckled. "You'd be surprised."

"How so?" She chewed as she listened.

"I grew up in Baltimore. All my cousins and two of my brothers hustle. Or at least they did. Now, they're all locked up serving double-digit sentences. I'm the youngest in the family. So, to me the choice was obvious. I knew for a fact that I didn't want to wind up where they did."

Brooklyn nodded. "Smart man." She shrugged. "I got involved in this life by accident. I was looking for some fun and excitement. For somebody to pay attention to me. I found all of that in this guy. And he was in this life. Soon I was, too. Once you get in it, it's kind of hard to get out. Part of me wants to live a normal life like Angel, find a normal guy like you, and live happily ever after. The other part of me thinks that shit sounds boring as hell."

Josiah laughed. "I like your honesty." He stood up and pushed his chair in.

She smiled. "I'll figure it out eventually," she said.

He nodded as he left the kitchen. "I know you will."

Brooklyn's job search proved to be fruitless. One interview after another ended in disappointment. She was told countless times that she was unqualified for every job she applied for. Angel and Josiah suggested that she might be setting her sights too high.

"You might have to start at the bottom, Brooklyn. Take something entry level and work your way up," Angel said.

"Maybe you can take a course or two," Josiah suggested. "Get some clerical skills like typing and bookkeeping. That'll help you become more marketable."

To Brooklyn, it all sounded like bullshit. Her money was dwindling, and she was desperate. She felt like the third wheel when Angel and Josiah curled up together on the sofa to watch movies. She felt like a failure whenever she heard Angel speaking about her busy schedule and her dinners and brunches with her equally successful friends. She longed for a sense of belonging and felt a tug of envy when Angel went to Silver Spring to visit her family for the weekend in early February. Brooklyn wanted some happiness of her own.

She drowned her sorrows in a bottle of Alizé that Friday night. It was rare for her to have Angel's house all to herself and she relished in it. She turned the radio up to full volume and sang "No More Drama" along with Mary J. Blige at the top of her lungs.

She laid across the chaise with her legs dangling over the arm and cried.

Josiah cleared his throat as he walked in.

Brooklyn jumped up, embarrassed. She wiped her eyes and rushed to grab the remote control for the stereo system. She turned the volume down and looked at Josiah apologetically.

"I'm sorry. I thought you were—"

"I was supposed to be in Bethesda catering a wedding this weekend. Bad news is the bride called it off. The good news is I get to keep the deposit."

Brooklyn laughed. "Okay." She began gathering her things to return to her room now that Josiah was home.

"You're good," he said. "Don't let me interrupt your pity party."

Brooklyn was tipsy, so it took her a moment to realize what he said. She looked at him and frowned. "Heeey! That's not nice."

He sat down on the couch. "That's what it is. You've been moping around feeling sorry for yourself for weeks. I thought you were gangsta. Snap out of it!"

Brooklyn was surprised by his bluntness. She sat back down on the chaise and shrugged.

"I don't like the person I'm becoming," she said, honestly.

"What kind of person is that?"

"Regular," she said. "Ordinary. Average." She chuckled. "You ever feel like that?"

He nodded. "Every single day."

"How can you stand it?"

He walked to the bar and poured himself a glass of whiskey. He returned to his seat and held it up in a toast.

Brooklyn held her glass up, too.

"I think about the alternative," he said. "The risk of a fast life doesn't outweigh the reward to me. It would be nice to drive a Porsche, shop without worrying about the price, and travel whenever and wherever I wanted. But I'm not at home in the streets. This right here is where I belong."

She stared back at him wondering if she had ever felt like that. Or if she ever would.

"Have you reached out to your family?" he asked.

She shook her head. "Army of one."

He smiled. "Okay, soldier."

She listened to the music playing in the background as Mary sang now about destiny. Brooklyn took another sip of her drink. "I don't know where I belong," she admitted. "Still trying to figure that out."

"Where do you feel at peace?" Josiah asked. He took a swig of his whiskey.

She swished the liquid around in her glass and pondered that. "In chaos," she said. "That's how it seems sometimes."

He stared at her.

She shrugged. "It's when everything is going nuts around me that I feel at peace. That's crazy, right?"

She stared back at him.

"I don't think it's crazy," he said. "I think I understand where you're coming from."

She nodded.

"You didn't find enough chaos with Hassan?"

"For the most part, yeah. But then things got too routine. Too predictable. I tried to shake things up. I wanted us to go legit. I had a property all picked out in Towson. I was ready to finalize the lease and everything, open up a hair salon and barbershop. For the first time in my life, I'd have something real to call my own. But when I suggested it to him, he gave me excuses. His mother and his friends made him doubt me. It started feeling like . . ."

"Like rejection?" Josiah offered.

Brooklyn nodded. Tears flooded her eyes. She hated that feeling.

He handed her a tissue.

"I know what that's like."

He didn't really. But he did the best he could to offer her some consolation. He told her a story about the countless times he applied for coveted jobs after he finished culinary school, only to be rejected by prospective employers. He expressed how that rejection had forced him to question his own talent, his own worth.

"I read something once that said, 'Rejection teaches us where we stand.' I try to keep that in mind when things don't go my way."

Brooklyn appreciated Josiah's kindness.

"Angel is lucky to have you," she said. She sipped her drink, thinking that she was lucky in a lot of ways. She had her family, a dream home, a loving fiancé, and the life Brooklyn wished she could be living. She downed the rest of her drink and tried not to think about it.

"So, tell me about this bride calling off the wedding you were supposed to cater."

Josiah laughed. "Yo! From what I heard, the bride changed her mind."

Brooklyn laughed, too. "Good for her!"

She finished off the bottle of Alizé while they talked. Before they knew it, it was nearly one in the morning.

"It's late," Josiah noted. "I'm about to call it a night." He stood up and began tidying up the living room.

Brooklyn agreed, stumbling slowly up the stairs to the extra bedroom. "Good night, Josiah,"

"Good night." He took her empty bottle and their two glasses into the kitchen.

Brooklyn went to her room, took a long shower, and climbed into the bed naked.

She lay awake in the darkness for a while, rubbing her hands across her body, trying to remember the last time she had felt any pleasure.

Brooklyn wasn't sure what washed over her, what drove her to do what she did that night. Maybe it was the music, the liquor she drank, or the feelings of frustration and jealousy at war inside of her. Maybe it was the need to feel something other than the sting of rejection she felt from Hassan, from Stacey, and from her family. Whatever it was sent her walking naked down the hallway toward Angel's bedroom. She entered and stood quietly in the doorway with Josiah staring back at her.

He was speechless seeing her there and froze. Brooklyn walked toward him slowly, letting him see all of her, and pressed herself against him.

"What are you doing, Brooklyn?"

"This." She kissed him softly on his lips and touched his arms.

Josiah grabbed her hands and held her back from him. "No."

She thought he sounded unconvincing. She leaned into him again, brushing her lips against his face. He exhaled slowly.

"Brooklyn, this isn't right."

"I don't care," she whispered, breathlessly.

She kissed him again. This time he didn't protest. He let go of her hands and she wrapped herself around him. She reached for his pants, freeing him, and they crossed a line there was no coming back from.

Angel's scream roused Brooklyn from a very peaceful sleep. Confused and still drunk, she opened her eyes and stared at the wall, disoriented.

"JOSIAH! WHAT THE FUCK DID YOU DO?"

Brooklyn heard Angel's voice before she saw her. It took her a few moments to recall where she was. This was Angel's room, and she was in Angel's bed with Angel's man.

Brooklyn jumped up and turned around. Josiah was already on his feet, standing naked with his hands up as Angel advanced toward him.

"I was . . . Angel . . . listen . . ." Josiah was stammering.

Brooklyn pulled the sheet off the bed and wrapped it around her own naked body. She cursed under her breath, aware now that they had been busted.

"You fucked her?" Angel was in Josiah's face, her finger pressed against his forehead. She had cut short her trip to visit her family once she learned that Josiah's weekend gig had been canceled. She hoped to surprise him with her early arrival. Now she was the one surprised, disgusted, and hurt by what she had come home to.

"We were drinking . . ." Josiah struggled to explain. "It got late . . . I don't know what happened."

Angel slapped him so hard that Brooklyn took off running. She ran down the hall toward the spare bedroom with Angel hot on her heels.

"You fucking BITCH! I let you in my home. Took you in when everyone else turned their backs on you. And this is what you do to me?"

Brooklyn got in a defensive stance and turned around to face her former friend.

"Angel, I swear this wasn't planned. I never meant to do that. I was drinking last night, feeling sorry for myself."

"That's all you ever do," Angel said. "Always the fucking victim. I want you out of here!" Angel went to the closet and started pulling Brooklyn's clothes out. She tossed them in piles over the stairway banister. Brooklyn's wardrobe cascaded down to the foyer below as she watched in horror. "GET THE FUCK OUT!"

Brooklyn got dressed in a hurry while Angel stormed around the house cursing loudly at the two people she had trusted most. Brooklyn had been here before, packing in a hurry, being rejected, having to come up with a new plan. She felt sick, likely from the liquor in her system, and fought the urge to vomit.

Angel was back.

"I'm calling the cops. I'm telling them about the drugs you sell and the lives you fuck up."

"Angel, I'm leaving. I fucked up. But I didn't mean to do this."

"GET OUT OF MY HOUSE, YOU DIRTY BITCH!" She was right in Brooklyn's face when she screamed it. Brooklyn wanted to fight back, to lash out. But she knew that Angel had every right to hate her. Brooklyn was beginning to hate herself. She grabbed her things and hurried out of the room. She ran down the stairs and stopped in the foyer to gather her scattered belongings. She could hear Angel upstairs still yelling and screaming at Josiah. She could hear Josiah pleading, insisting that he was sorry, and that Brooklyn had been the aggressor. She shook her head, aware that Angel would probably forgive Josiah. But she would certainly never forgive Brooklyn.

She left Angel's home, piled her things into her car, and drove around for a while. For the first time in her life, she had no backup plan. No emergency parachute to open in case of an emergency. Brooklyn knew that she was about to fall flat on her face.

Chapter Fourteen

No Place like Home

Brooklyn was all out of maneuvers. She had a couple thousand dollars to her name and no lifelines left. She drove to a Walmart parking lot, reclined the driver's seat, and slept in her car.

She woke up and realized how dire her situation was. She was homeless, jobless, and friendless. Angel had accused her of being a perpetual victim. Brooklyn thought about it now and saw the ugly truth. Her parents, Amir, Alonzo, Hassan, Stacey—she had felt slighted, hurt, and unsupported by all of them. But she had missed their other commonality. All of them had done their best to make her happy. When they failed, she had lashed out with all her might.

With no source of income and no place to stay any longer, she grabbed some fast food for breakfast and checked into a cheap motel just to have a chance to take a shower and have a good, long cry.

The room was no frills. Just a bed and a TV. She felt dirty, both physically and emotionally. She felt like hell. What she had done to Angel was a new low, even for her.

She had been able to rationalize it every other time she lashed out. With her parents it had been their hypocrisy, with Amir it was his refusal to defend her. She had stolen from Alonzo and from her father because they had hurt her. She had felt abandoned by Stacey and rejected by Hassan, and she had been able to live with her actions against them for those reasons.

But Angel was different. The girl had done nothing but love Brooklyn, had welcomed and defended her. She hadn't asked for a penny during the time Brooklyn stayed with her. She had been a friend in every sense of the word. And Brooklyn had betrayed her in the worst way. She was disappointed and disgusted with herself. She knew that it had little to do with the alcohol or the depression she had been enduring since leaving New York for good. She remembered the details of the night prior and felt ashamed. She could still see the helpless, wide-eyed look in Josiah's eyes when she'd unzipped his pants—could still hear his moans as she took him into the warmth and wetness of her mouth and sucked him deeply. She had mounted him afterward, fully aware that he was Angel's man and that what they were doing was wrong. As she sat in the cheap motel room that day, she faced herself for the first time and admitted that everything that had happened to her was her own fault.

She took a steamy shower, slipped on a T-shirt and some leggings, and picked up the phone. She needed to hear a familiar voice.

Erica answered the unknown number suspiciously. "Who's this?"

"It's Brooklyn."

"Girl . . . what kind of area code is this?" Erica eyed her caller ID again. "Where are you?"

"In Maryland," Brooklyn said.

"How did you end up there?"

Brooklyn thought back to their last conversation. A lot had changed since then.

"I needed a change of pace." It was the best excuse she could think of. "How's mommyhood?" Brooklyn tried to sound upbeat as she asked.

"It's great. My son Luke is walking and talking now, getting into everything."

Brooklyn marveled at how much time had passed. She had never even met Erica's child. She felt guilty knowing that she hadn't given much attention to their friendship through the years.

"Is this the number where I can reach you?" Erica was already writing it down. "It's been so long since the last time I heard from you. I had a pager number. But no one uses those anymore. And whenever you called me, your number came up private. I almost didn't answer this call since I didn't recognize the number."

"I'm calling from a hotel room," Brooklyn explained. "I have to add minutes to my cellphone. I'll do it later on."

"Everyone's been trying to find you for months," Erica said. "They kept asking me if I knew how to contact you. But I didn't."

Brooklyn's heart sank. "Everyone like who?"

"Your family."

Brooklyn closed her eyes. "Why are they trying to contact me? What happened?"

"You should sit down."

Brooklyn sat on the bed, sweating. "I am."

"Brooklyn, after your father's stroke, he was doing okay for a while. But a few weeks ago, he had some complications. He passed away."

Brooklyn was speechless. She sat with the phone in her hand and a stream of tears cascading down her face.

"Brooklyn, I'm so sorry."

Erica spared her the details. Elias's funeral had been abuzz with whispers about his missing daughter. The James children had grown up at Promised Land and were part of the fabric of the congregation. Her absence at Amir's funeral years ago had been explained as an inability to cope with the loss of her brother. But there was no palatable reason for her absence from her father's homegoing service. First Lady Sabrina James had seen to it that her husband was laid to rest in grand style. Pastors and preachers from across the country attended the service along with local politicians, nationally recognized civil rights activists, and past and present members of the congregation. All of them wondered where Brooklyn was. Sabrina did her best to make excuses without telling a boldface lie. She told them her daughter was traveling abroad and unable to make it back to the States in time. Only the church's inner circle knew the truth. Brooklyn hadn't been seen or heard from in years.

"Oh, my God," Brooklyn managed. Life was dealing her one crippling blow after another.

Brooklyn didn't know where to begin. "I . . . I've been going through a lot. I meant to call you. Things have been so crazy." Brooklyn shook her head. "I can't believe this. How's my sister?"

"Hope is okay. She's been helping your mother keep the church going," Erica said.

"I haven't spoken to my family in years. What kind of shit is that, Erica? I'm a terrible person."

Erica wasn't sure what to say. She didn't think Brooklyn was terrible. But she did think she had allowed way too much time to pass.

"Everything that's happening to me . . . I deserve it." Brooklyn cried openly. She was so weary from years of battling, running, scheming, hiding. She laid her head back against the wall and wept.

"What's happening, Brooklyn? What's going on with you?" Erica didn't know much about Brooklyn's movements over the years. But it was obvious that it hadn't been an easy road for her.

"I have ruined every single relationship that ever mattered to me. First with Amir. I'm the reason he's dead. I've been carrying the weight of that around with me for so long. Losing Amir broke my father. The last time I saw him, I hardly recognized him. He was a shell of the man he used to be, even before the stroke. So, I can only imagine how he declined even more in the years since then." She sniffled. "I feel like I drove him to an early grave."

Erica listened sympathetically. "You've been gone a long time. We were kids when you left here. A lot has changed. I know you had a lot to run from back then. But things are different now."

Brooklyn opened her eyes and stared at the wall. "I'll be honest with you, Erica. I'm fucked up. I don't have any money. I have no place to go. I've ruined every relationship I had. So, hearing this . . ." She shook her head. "I just feel like giving up."

"Don't talk like that," Erica said. "God is telling you to come home."

Brooklyn thought about it, doubtfully. She was out of options and that didn't sound like a good one either.

"It's been long enough. Come back and resolve things with them." She asked Brooklyn to hold on while she comforted her crying toddler. Within moments, Erica was back on the line. "Sorry about that. Anyway, it was Hope who came to me asking if I knew how to get in contact with you. She said that your father had a will, and that he left money behind for your whole family, including you. I'm not sure how they handled it since they couldn't find you. But she told Jordan and me that your father hadn't cut you out. He was still praying that you would come back home. It's not too late. You should come back and connect with your family."

Brooklyn felt the clouds parting. "A will?"

"Yeah," Erica said. "I don't know how much it is. But Hope and her husband have been helping First Lady James handle all the paperwork and stuff since Pastor died."

Brooklyn's mind was reeling. "Hope . . . husband?"

Erica chuckled. "Hope got married last year. His name is Eddie and they're so perfect for each other. He's a professor at Wagner College and they're happy."

Brooklyn tried to imagine Hope all grown up and married. She imagined the church in the absence of her father. It all sounded completely opposite of the home she had left behind.

She nodded. "I think you're right, Erica. It's probably time for me to come back. It's been long enough."

"Yes!" Erica agreed. "God's timing is perfect. Trust Him and come home."

Brooklyn hadn't been back to Staten Island since the nineties. As she steered her car through the once familiar streets on that Sunday morning in February, those days seemed like a lifetime ago. She saw places she used to frequent all the time and smiled as the memories flooded back. Going with her father and her siblings to Brother's Pizza in Port Richmond, shopping at the mall with Erica, cutting school and making a beeline for the ferry terminal. She remembered the excitement of those things and wished she could rewind time. There were things she would have done differently and things that she wished she could relive in order to bask in the beauty of those moments. Like sitting with Amir and talking about the future. She would give anything to go back to times like that with him.

She glanced at the dashboard clock as she drove. It was 12:31 P.M., which meant that Sunday service would still be going on. She had rehearsed her opening lines during the trip back home, practicing what she would say to her mother and sister when they were face-to-face again. None of what she'd rehearsed seemed adequate enough. So, as she pulled her car into the packed parking lot of Promised Land Church, she prayed.

"God, give me the right words to say. And open their hearts. Let forgiveness and love light the way."

It was freezing in New York City the day she came home. Every radio station she turned to had announcements about the impending snowstorm, which was expected to dump several inches of snow across the city. Brooklyn wasn't worried about the cold weather or the storm looming. She didn't care that she wasn't dressed to impress, that her hair and nails weren't done, or that she wasn't wearing makeup. Those things had been of major importance to her—and to her mother especially—in the old days. But Brooklyn was returning as the prodigal daughter. She didn't give a damn about her appearance. What she wanted was redemption.

She stepped inside the church, and felt her pulse quicken. The sound of the organ was so nostalgic that she smiled. She hadn't expected to feel the sense of warmth, lightness, and familiarity that washed over her. An usher handed her a program, then paused as she recognized Brooklyn's familiar face.

"Brooklyn?" Miss Nancy stared at her through narrowed eyes. "Is that you?"

Brooklyn nodded, tears welling up in her eyes, and took the program. Miss Nancy pulled Brooklyn into her arms and hugged her tightly.

"We've been missing you, Brooklyn. Your father was missing you. Welcome home."

Brooklyn sobbed as she held on to Miss Nancy. All the years of pain, angst, and turmoil poured forth and she wept openly at the back of the sanctuary.

One by one, the congregants began to turn around in the direction of all the noise. The guest preacher at the pulpit paused a moment. Several congregants stood up, offering comforting words as they watched the scene unfolding in the rear.

"Amen," someone called out. "Let Him heal you."

"Yes," came another voice. "Touch her Lord!"

The organist played softly, and someone began to sing "It Is Well with My Soul." Someone appeared at Brooklyn's side with a church fan. Brooklyn would have once considered this entire spectacle laughable. She would have noted how orchestrated it all was, down to the soloist singing the perfect song at the ideal moment. But Brooklyn wasn't amused this time. She was at the lowest point in her life.

Miss Nancy rubbed her back and began leading Brooklyn slowly down the aisle at the center of the church.

First Lady Sabrina James stood up in the pulpit. She looked down the aisle and laid eyes on her daughter for the first time in years.

Brooklyn was weak and struggled to walk down the aisle. She was crying so hard that her body shook from the sobs. The whole congregation was on its feet praying, singing, watching Brooklyn as she slowly made her way to the altar with the help of the church ladies.

Sabrina spread her arms wide as her daughter got closer. Silent tears fell from her eyes, and she tilted her head skyward. Sabrina began to pray loudly.

"Thank you, Father! THANK YOU! You are a promise-keeping God. You're the redeemer! There is nothing too hard for GOD!"

Shouts of "Amen!" and "Hallelujah" resonated around the sanctuary. Sabrina stepped down from the pulpit and met her daughter as she was led to the foot of the altar.

"This is my daughter," Sabrina said as she laid her hands gently on the top of Brooklyn's head and looked around at the congregants. "But she's God's child first."

"AMEN!" Miss Nancy said firmly.

"Brooklyn was consorting with PIGS! She was eating the pigs' food and adopting their habits. She had forgotten that she was royalty, and she was lying with PIGS!" Sabrina shook her head from side to side as the "my God" and "Amen" chorus of the congregation continued. "But God watches over his flock. He never took his eyes off her. Through His grace, she came to her senses and realized who she is and WHOSE she is! He brought her home, and today is a reason for celebration! This child of mine was dead and now she is alive. She was lost and now she's found!"

Sabrina pulled Brooklyn into her arms and held her tightly. Brooklyn hugged her back and held on to her, crying. "I'm sorry, Ma. I'm so sorry."

"You are forgiven," Sabrina said to her again and again. "It's okay, Brooklyn. You're forgiven." She held on to her daughter as the deaconesses came forth with holy water. Sabrina blessed her daughter with it, making the sign of the cross on her forehead. She wiped Brooklyn's tears and rocked her as they embraced. "Welcome home."

The guest minister took the mic and led the congregation in a prayer. Sabrina led Brooklyn tenderly over to the front pew of the church. They sat together holding hands while the service went on. Brooklyn listened to the sermon, rapt. The preacher seemed to be speaking directly to her as he delivered a sermon on God's boundless, limitless, unconditional love. She dabbed at her eyes intermittently, moved by the powerful reassurance she felt hearing the same scriptures she had heard countless times throughout her upbringing. Those scriptures took on new meaning now as they resonated in her spirit.

As the congregation stood for the benediction, Brooklyn watched her mother walk to the altar to help lead the prayer. Sabrina stood alongside the guest preacher and all of the associate ministers as the congregation stood to their feet. As they bowed their heads to pray, Brooklyn felt a soft hand slip into hers, giving it a light squeeze. She looked to her right and saw her sister Hope standing beside her. Hope gave her sister a soft smile. Brooklyn smiled back and squeezed Hope's hand tighter.

When the service concluded, Sabrina stood at the back of the sanctuary saying goodbye to each person as they exited the sanctuary. The trustees headed to their office to handle their business. Brooklyn and Hope stood near the altar receiving an outpouring of love from the deacons and church elders.

"Brooklyn, we've been praying for you."

"I asked God to bring you home safely. I knew He would answer my prayer."

"Your father never stopped talking about you. Until the very end, he was always praying for you."

Brooklyn took it all in, nodding, smiling, thanking them for their prayers. Little by little, the number of people in the sanctuary waned. With the crowd surrounding Brooklyn thinner now, Erica and Jordan approached. Brooklyn smiled at them, marveling at how they had all changed over time. Jordan looked much more mature, more confident than he had the last time she'd seen him. He wore a well-fitted dark blue suit and a gray shirt and glasses as he strode over.

Erica, too, had changed. She had gained a little weight, but it looked good on her. She wore a long-sleeved blue dress and had her son in tow. She didn't hesitate to rush right in and wrap Brooklyn up in her arms.

"You came! I'm so proud of you."

Brooklyn hugged her back. "Thank you."

They pulled away and Brooklyn locked eyes with Jordan. She smiled at him.

"Hey."

"Hey." He had a slight grin on his face, but his expression was otherwise hard to read. He seemed just as surprised as everyone else to see her there.

The five of them were alone now in the sanctuary. Brooklyn looked at her sister, marveling at how beautiful she was. "I heard you got married," Brooklyn said. "Congratulations."

Hope nodded and flashed her ring. "Thank you."

With the last of the congregants gone, Sabrina joined the group. She looked at her older daughter and sighed.

"God is good." She nodded. "I'm glad you're safe."

Instinctively, Erica and Jordan retreated to a nearby pew to allow the family some space. They were reuniting after nearly a decade of estrangement. Erica perched her son Luke on her lap and pretended not to listen.

Brooklyn looked at her mother. "I made so many mistakes," she said. "Too many to count. I've spent years running from God and from you. You were right about what you said. I was hanging around with pigs when I should have been living in the palace. I can't go back and change what I did. But I want you to know that I'm sorry."

Sabrina clutched her hands together in front of her. She hadn't laid eyes on her child in so long that she took the time now to admire the details of her face. She could tell by the way Brooklyn was dressed and by the absence of any makeup or jewelry that she was down on her luck.

"We lost your father," Sabrina said.

Brooklyn nodded. "I just found out. If I had known, I would have been here."

"God has forgiven you, Brooklyn."

Sabrina wondered where her child had been for so many years, how she had survived. Even as Brooklyn stood in front of her now, she knew that her daughter might never tell the whole truth about her life so far. Sabrina had never really known Brooklyn like she thought she did.

"What made you come back now?" she asked.

Brooklyn answered honestly. "I lost everything. Everyone. I called Erica because she was the only person I had left to call. She told me that Daddy was gone. So, I got in my car and came right away."

Sabrina nodded. "You've kept in touch with Erica through the years. That's the only way we knew you were even alive. Every now and then, she'd tell us that she spoke to you and that you seemed to be managing alright. She told us that she spoke to you a few years ago. Right around the time that your father had his stroke."

Brooklyn nodded.

Sabrina glowered. "Why didn't you come home then?"

Brooklyn opened her mouth but wasn't sure how to respond. It took her a moment to get her words together. "I . . . thought that seeing me would only make it worse. I thought it would upset him."

"What upset your father was losing his family. That's what killed him." Sabrina's tone was even, flat. "Amir died. You left. He was never the same. He got over the money you stole. Paid Mrs. Hutchinson back out of his own pocket. But he never got over Amir's suicide."

Sabrina walked to the front pew and picked up the Bible. She held it up in front of her daughters.

"This is what your father stood for. Eli wasn't perfect. He sinned just like we all do. But he did his best to raise his family in the fear and admonition of God and the laws written in this book. An abomination. That's what this book calls the life Amir was living. That's what your father was thinking when he tried to beat the truth out of him. Eli's reaction to the truth was unfortunate. He judged him because he believed that God would do the same. His reaction was violent and impulsive. He never forgave himself for what happened. It ate him alive. Hope and I tried to help. We kept thinking you would walk through these doors one day and your father would understand that there was still a family left to salvage. But that didn't happen. Did it?"

Brooklyn didn't respond. Didn't know how to.

Hope sighed.

Sabrina continued. "When your father suffered the stroke, I used every tool in my arsenal to help him recover. Nothing helped. Erica told us that she spoke to you while your father was still in the hospital. Said she urged you to come home then. You didn't, though. You kept on doing whatever you were doing out there. Living your life while your father was losing his."

"Mom," Hope said, gently.

Sabrina looked at her and smiled. "It's okay, baby. We're gonna tell the truth today." She looked at Brooklyn again. "You didn't come home then, while your father still had a little fight left in him. You waited until now. Why? Because you found out that he's gone and there might be some money here waiting for you?"

Brooklyn stared back at her, convicted. Though she was overcome with guilt and shame, she had to admit to herself that the inheritance had put her on the road to New York City that morning.

"I didn't come home all this time because I didn't know if you would even want to see me," Brooklyn said. She looked at Hope, too. "Coming back here today was hard for me because I had no idea what I was walking into. For all I knew, you could have shamed me in front of the whole church and kicked me out. I had no clue if you would welcome me or push me away."

Hope rubbed her sister's back, comfortingly as they stood before their mother.

"The Bible says ALL have sinned and fall short of the glory of God." Sabrina clutched the leather-bound book to her chest for emphasis. "You're not the only one whose hands are dirty in this family. I've made my mistakes, too. I should have been a better mother to all of you. I lost Amir. You ran away. But Hope stayed. When you ignored your father and his illness, she cared for him. When you betrayed your brother, your sister stayed and helped us survive that tragedy as a family. She stayed on the battlefield here at Promised Land and ensured that Jordan was welcomed back into the fold. She started a scholarship in your brother's name to help ensure that no other member of this church is ever ostracized or rejected because of their sexuality. She helped him forgive your father. Before he died, Eli was able to understand the love between Amir and Jordan, and that happened because Hope stayed." Sabrina pointed at everyone present. "Jordan stayed. Erica stayed. I stayed. But you ran."

Brooklyn couldn't hold her head high anymore. She stared down at the floor, ashamed.

"And you only came back when you smelled money." Sabrina tucked a finger underneath Brooklyn's chin and lifted it. Eye to eye, she spoke to her daughter. "God has forgiven you. But I can tell you this. You won't get a single penny of the money your father left behind. So, if that's what brought you back home after all these years, you might as well turn yourself around, walk back out that door, and go back where you came from."

Brooklyn felt her lower lip quivering and felt like a child again. She stared into her mother's eyes while her own welled up with tears.

"You keep saying that God forgave me. Have you?"

Sabrina didn't respond.

Brooklyn blinked away the tears. "So, all of that was just for the audience, huh? All that blessing me and praying over me was for show?"

Sabrina stepped back, looked Brooklyn up and down, shook her head, and walked away.

Brooklyn stood at the front of the sanctuary with Hope by her side. She felt like a fool. Her mother's dramatic display in front of the congregation had been one big performance. Brooklyn had to hand it to her. Sabrina had been so convincing that she had fooled her, too. For a brief while, she had felt her mother's love, forgiveness, and warmth. Then Sabrina had cruelly snatched it all away.

Hope looked at her. "She's taking Daddy's death really hard. It may not seem like it now, but she's glad you're back. I am, too." Hope smiled at Brooklyn, sympathetically, and hugged her. "Come home with me. We'll take this one step at a time."

Chapter Fifteen

Reaping

Brooklyn was in such a daze as she climbed back into her car and followed the caravan to Hope's house that she barely noticed how cold it was outside. Her body shivered as she drove, and minutes passed before it occurred to her to turn on the heat in the car. She arrived at the house on Slosson Avenue and marveled at how well Hope had clearly done for herself. She parked in the driveway behind her sister.

Jordan and Erica had followed them in Jordan's car. As Brooklyn climbed out of her car, she couldn't help thinking that the only person missing from the equation was Amir. If he were alive, she imagined, he would be getting out of Jordan's passenger seat, and the picture would be complete. She walked into the house behind Hope while Jordan and Erica parked.

Brooklyn stared at the large wedding portrait hanging in the foyer of her sister's home.

"How's married life?" Brooklyn asked. She slid out of her coat and Hope hung it in a hook on the wall.

"I picked a good one," Hope said. "So, I can't complain."

A dog came running toward them, barking. Brooklyn jumped, instinctively, but caught herself when she realized it was a little Yorkie.

"This is Scrappy. He's a little hyper, but he means well."

Hope scooped the dog up and led Brooklyn into the living room where her husband was sitting on the couch with a beer watching ESPN.

"This is Eddie," Hope said as she entered.

Brooklyn smiled at him. Eddie was tall and athletic looking. He stood up with a beer in his hand and extended his free hand to her.

"Nice to meet you."

"Eddie," Brooklyn managed as she shook his hand. "Nice to meet you, too." She looked at Hope and smiled. "Firm handshake!"

Hope chuckled as she set Scrappy down on the floor and sprinkled some doggie treats for him. "Eddie, this is my sister Brooklyn."

Eddie was visibly shocked. He gasped a little and looked at Brooklyn.

"OH! Okay. Wow!"

Brooklyn imagined what he had heard about her—the bad seed of the family. She felt a little embarrassed. "Sorry I missed the wedding."

Eddie wasn't sure if she was serious or joking. He nodded, uneasily.

Jordan and Erica walked in, and he seemed grateful for the interruption.

"Hey, y'all. How was church?"

Jordan found the question ironic and chuckled a bit. "Eventful."

Erica's son, Luke, rushed toward Eddie and threw his arms around his legs. Eddie scooped the child up in the air playfully.

"Hey, little man!"

Hope slid out of her shoes and invited everyone to sit down.

"Make yourself at home, Brooklyn. This is our usual routine after church on Sundays. We come back over here and unwind while I cook dinner. You can help me tonight if you want."

Brooklyn nodded.

"I already ordered food," Eddie said. "We both have to work on Valentine's Day. So, I figured I'd get started early. I got food from your favorite spot, so you don't have to cook tonight."

Hope smiled, sat on his lap, and gave him a long kiss on his lips. "Thank you!"

"That's sweet," Brooklyn said.

She sat down and watched the lovebirds snuggling up beside each other on the couch. "I'm glad to see you so happy." She shook her head. "I thought for sure that you would marry one of the junior deacons at the church or an associate minister or something." Brooklyn had been certain that Hope was destined to follow her mother's blueprint to the letter. But Eddie seemed so normal. She stared at the beer in his hand, longing for one.

Hope laughed. "Eddie believes in God, but he's not the church-going type."

Eddie agreed. "I go with her to the big events. Easter Sunday, Christmas, and church anniversary."

Brooklyn approved. "How'd you meet?"

"I introduced them," Jordan said. He was seated across from Brooklyn in a recliner. "I taught a music class at Wagner College for a semester. Soon as I met Eddie, I knew he'd be a good match for Hope."

Brooklyn studied Jordan's face as he spoke. There was a sadness in his eyes that she recognized.

"I love kids," Eddie explained. "Jordan brought little Luke here to school with him one day."

"I needed a babysitter," Erica explained. "Jordan is Luke's godfather."

"Of course!" Brooklyn said, smiling.

"I had to work late one night, so Jordan picked him up from daycare and took him to class with him that day."

She smiled at Luke as he crawled around on the floor playing with the dog.

"Luke wouldn't cooperate," Jordan said. "He wouldn't sit still, kept making noise. So, Eddie stepped in and the next thing I knew, Luke was sitting with Eddie in a corner of the classroom coloring. I don't even know where Eddie found crayons that day!"

Eddie laughed. "Me either! Probably in one of the art classes. All I know is me and Luke became best friends after that. Jordan told me I should meet Hope. That was how it started."

Erica watched Brooklyn's face as Hope and Eddie regaled her with the story of their romance. She could tell that Brooklyn was happy for her sister, but also that she felt bad that she had missed out on so much of her life. Brooklyn proudly showed off her tattoo on her left wrist of the cross bearing Amir's initials.

"I take him with me everywhere I go," she said.

"Brooklyn, where have you been?"

Hope's voice was sweet and held no malice as she asked it. She stared at her sister, whom she had always admired and resented in equal measure, and wondered what life had been like for her.

"Everywhere," Brooklyn said. "And nowhere at the same time. After Amir's funeral, I vowed not to come back here. I lived in Harlem for a few years. Then in Maryland for a while." She spared them the sordid details. "I made a lot of friends, then I managed to turn all of them into enemies. I got depressed, started drinking too much, feeling sorry for myself. Made some stupid decisions. I came home looking for . . . I don't know what I was looking for."

Jordan did. Erica had told him all about her conversation with Brooklyn on the phone the day prior. He smirked, cynically, as he listened to her.

"How have you been surviving?" he asked.

Brooklyn looked at Erica and wondered again how much she knew about the circumstances surrounding her departure. She decided that it didn't matter anymore. This was rock bottom.

"Back in high school, I was messing around with Alonzo. He was giving me money to go uptown and buy drugs for him. When I ran away, I went to the people I'd met uptown, sought shelter with them. I fell in love."

Jordan recalled seeing the man with Brooklyn at Amir's gravesite on the day of his funeral. He imagined that was who Brooklyn was referring to.

"We were a team for a while. But I didn't want to hustle forever. I got my license in cosmetology, and I was gonna start a business. But instead of staying focused, I got distracted by the life. The adrenaline rush, the money, the power. Before I knew it, my license had expired, and I was just a hustler without a plan. So, I panicked. I made a move that got me kicked out of my adopted family. Then I tried to find refuge in a friend. But I ended up doing to her the same thing I do to everybody else. I let her down. I did what felt good to me, what helped me numb the pain, and I didn't think about how it would affect her. So, she threw me out. I've been sleeping in my car, at motels. Just trying to survive."

Hope was crying silently while Eddie rubbed her leg, comfortingly.

"Mom was right," Brooklyn said. "I don't deserve a penny of Daddy's money. Not after everything I did. But I'm down to nothing. I have no place else to go. So, I came home."

"You did the right thing," Hope said.

Erica nodded in agreement.

Jordan and Eddie locked eyes. Both sat quietly.

"What's your plan now?" Erica asked. "Now that you're back."

"I don't have one," Brooklyn admitted. "Not a good one, anyway. Tonight, I'm going to check into a hotel and get a good night's sleep. Tomorrow, who knows?"

"You don't have to stay in a hotel. You can stay with me," Erica offered. My apartment is small, but my couch is comfortable."

"Don't be silly," Eddie said. "You can stay here. We have plenty of room."

Brooklyn shook her head. "I appreciate the offer. But I'm not down to my last dollar yet. I have enough to afford a room for the night. That's all I can focus on for now. I just want to get through tonight. It's been a rough and emotional day. I found out my father is dead, got rejected by my mother again, and now I'm reuniting with you guys for the first time since we were kids. I just want one night to sit in a bathtub, close my eyes, and think. Tomorrow, I'll wake up and try again."

Jordan sat forward in his seat. "I became really close to your father before he passed."

Brooklyn was surprised to hear that. "How did that happen?"

"Hope." Jordan smiled at her. "After Amir's funeral, she came to check on me every day for a whole year. She prayed with me, told me what was going on with your family, asked me to tell her stories about Amir."

Hope smiled, recalling those days. "We became family then. To me, it was like Amir never left. He wasn't with us physically. But when we got together and talked about him, it felt like he was with us in spirit. Like he pulled up a seat and joined us in those moments."

"I was lonely," Jordan said. "Hope had no idea that she was my only friend at that time. There was nobody else I could talk to about what I was going through. Nobody knew I was gay. I was only myself when I was with Amir. Hope came around and got me through the hardest days of my life. Then your father had a stroke, and I got the chance to return the favor."

"I cried on Jordan's shoulder so many times I think I left a dent in it," Hope said.

"One night, after visiting hours were over, Hope snuck me into your father's hospital room, and we talked. Pastor wasn't thrilled to see me at first. But he listened. Maybe he had no choice. But he listened to me talking about Amir and what he meant to me. I told him how much Amir loved him and how desperate he was to please him. And I apologized. I told Pastor how sorry I was for what happened, sorry that he lost his son. He cried. I did, too. He couldn't really talk, but I understood him when he told me that he was sorry, too."

Brooklyn nodded.

"It's never too late for forgiveness. It's not the easiest thing to do. But it's the right thing. I think Mom will come around," Hope said.

"She has to. I need that money. Daddy wanted me to have it. It's not her choice to make." Brooklyn could still hear her mother's flat, emotionless tone as she spoke to her in the church sanctuary that afternoon. "I'll take her to court if I have to."

Jordan's squinted slightly. "How? I thought you were down to nothing. Lawyers cost money."

Brooklyn sucked her teeth. "I don't think it'll go that far. You know what my mother's like. For real! Not that fake persona she puts on for the congregation. The *real* her. She's all about image and public perception. The last thing she wants is for me to make noise."

Hope stared at her sister in disbelief. Brooklyn hadn't changed at all.

"So, you really just came back for the money? Not to try to reconcile with us?"

Brooklyn nodded. "I came back for both." She looked at Erica. "When I spoke to you yesterday, I thought about what you said. God was calling me home. And then I walked in that church today and the dam broke. All the tears I that poured out of me were the burdens I've been carrying since the day I left here. I know that it was all for show. But those words my mother spoke over me in that church today were prophetic. I had no business lying down with pigs when I belonged in a palace. Daddy knew where I belonged. And even though I broke his heart, he made sure that I would be taken care of if I ever remembered who I was and came home."

Jordan stared at Brooklyn, tempted to give her a standing ovation for such a rousing performance. He had never been more disturbed by a human being in his life.

Erica was speechless, too. Moments ago, Brooklyn had sounded regretful and ashamed. Now she sounded more defiant than ever. In her eyes, Erica swore she saw dollar signs.

Erica glanced at Hope, suddenly regretful that she had mentioned the inheritance to Brooklyn in the first place. Erica wondered if Brooklyn would have returned home if she hadn't mentioned the money. Erica could see the crestfallen expression on Hope's face and knew that she was crushed.

Eddie rubbed his wife's leg, lovingly. Everything she had said about Brooklyn made sense now. He knew about the circumstances surrounding Brooklyn's departure. He also knew Hope had been praying for her sister for years—that she had felt guilty about inheriting Brooklyn's portion of their father's trust. Sabrina had given Brooklyn's share to Hope a week after the will was read. Sabrina had sat Hope down and insisted that she take Brooklyn's share, reminding Hope that she alone had weathered the family's storms. Eddie knew how Hope had struggled with that decision, ultimately accepting the money when it seemed unlikely that Brooklyn would ever return.

Eddie also knew his wife well enough to discern that she had brought her into their home with the intention of giving Brooklyn her share. Now he prayed that she was smart enough to change her mind.

"I just want my share of the money, and I'll go," Brooklyn said, summarily.

Eddie cleared his throat. "Well, Brooklyn, I think you and your mother have some things to talk about."

Brooklyn nodded. She looked at Hope. "Will you help me?"

Jordan chuckled and shook his head. "That's a lot to ask of her, Brooklyn. Hope has been getting in the middle of your issues with your parents since she was a kid."

Brooklyn sat forward in her seat, tempted to tell Jordan to mind his business. Out of respect for her brother's memory, she kept her voice down.

"So, are *you* gonna help me? Sounds like you got really close to the family since I've been gone. Maybe she'll listen to you."

Jordan's face contorted at that.

"The bottom line is I need help!" Brooklyn held her empty hands out, demonstratively. "If you have some better advice on how I should move forward, let's hear it."

"Brooklyn, it's your first day back. You said it yourself. It's been a rough day. Emotional. I think you should take tonight and think. We can meet tomorrow. I'll go with you and we'll talk to your mom." Erica spoke to her in the same tone of voice she used with her toddler son.

Brooklyn nodded. Erica was right. Tomorrow was another day.

"Let's eat this food I ordered," Eddie suggested. He looked at Hope.

She stood up and led the way to the kitchen.

Jordan and Erica didn't stay long after dinner was over. The conversation had gotten awkward after Brooklyn revealed her intentions. While they ate, Eddie told stories about Hope's accomplishments through the years. He bragged about all the children she worked with in her career as a social worker and how instrumental she had been in her father's care prior to his death. Brooklyn listened, giving all the proper responses, and congratulating her sister on a job well done. But it seemed lost on her that Eddie was describing all the things Brooklyn had opted not to do.

Erica strapped Luke into his car seat and got into the passenger seat of Jordan's car. He drove away from Hope's house slowly, still shaken by the reappearance of Brooklyn Melody James.

Jordan looked at Erica, sidelong. "I told you she only came back for the money."

Erica shook her head sadly. "I was rooting for her. I heard her on the phone yesterday and she sounded so lost. She seemed like she was ready to give up on life. You saw her at church earlier. Same thing. She looked like a broken doll."

He nodded. "But that didn't last long. Soon as she realized Mrs. James wasn't gonna hand over the money, she turned right back into the Brooklyn we all know."

Erica stared ahead, disappointed. "That wasn't the Brooklyn I thought I knew. She was my best friend. I thought she was fun and unpredictable. Not heartless."

"Did you know she stole that money from your cousin?" Jordan asked.

Erica shook her head. "Not really. When she ran, Zo told me that she did him dirty. But he didn't go into specifics. I think he charged it to the game—said he had no business messing around with her young behind anyway."

"Probably made it easier for him to swallow since Pastor James paid the money back out of his own pocket." He recalled Sabrina telling Brooklyn as much at the church earlier.

"I feel so dumb," Erica said. "I thought she changed."

"I didn't," Jordan admitted. "Every time you told me you spoke to her throughout the years, the story was the same. She was too selfish, too cold-hearted to come back. But the minute you told her about the money, she reappeared. Should have used that bait to get her back here a long time ago."

Erica turned the radio up a notch as the announcer warned about the storm that was brewing. "They're saying this snowstorm is gonna be massive. I need to stop at Pathmark for some Pull-Ups and milk. Do you mind?"

Jordan shook his head. "Get everything you need before I drop you off at home. Sounds like nobody's gonna want to be out in that storm tomorrow."

He drove to the supermarket on Forest Avenue and pulled up to the front. "Go in and get what you need. I'll sit here in the car with Luke and wait for you."

Erica nodded. She pulled her hood up over her head and opened the door. She trotted inside, bracing herself against the brutal February wind.

Jordan watched her go inside. He turned around and smiled at Luke sitting peacefully in his car seat. "You good, little man?"

"Yeah!" Luke answered.

Jordan turned back around and caught sight of Erica's cellphone perched on top of the cupholder. He picked it up, scrolled through the recent calls, and stopped when he spotted it. Grinning, he grabbed a pen from the glove compartment, jotted the number down on the back of his hand, and put the phone back.

Erica came back to the car within minutes. She stuck the bags in the trunk and rushed into the car, blowing into her cold hands to warm them.

"WHEW! It's freezing out there." She shook her head. "Thank you, Jordan. I have everything I need now."

He nodded. "Me too."

Brooklyn left Hope's house at close to eight o'clock that night. She stood with her sister in the foyer of her home as she slipped her coat on and braced for the winter blast outside.

"Hope, I want you to know that I can never repay you for what you did. You were the baby of this family and you wound up having to bear all the responsibility. You defended me when no one else did. You stayed here and honored our parents. It's probably unfair for me to ask for your help again. But I need your help with Mom. She'll listen to you."

Hope sighed. "Brooklyn, I'm tired. I am. I just want to get some sleep. Tomorrow we can talk about it."

Brooklyn wasn't satisfied with that answer. But she decided not to push it. "Thank you. I wrote my phone number down and stuck it on your refrigerator. Call me when you wake up tomorrow."

She hugged her sister tightly.

Hope watched from her front window as Brooklyn rushed to her car and drove away. Eddie came up behind her and wrapped her in his arms.

"So, that's the infamous Brooklyn, huh?"

Hope nodded. "That's her."

Brooklyn drove to the newly opened Hilton Hotel on South Avenue. She marveled at how much the borough had changed since she left. This strip of road had once been surrounded by a swamp but was now bustling with office buildings and a fancy hotel. She paid cash at the desk and checked into a standard room.

Once she sank into the steamy water in the oversized bathtub, she felt the tension in her body begin to ease. She closed her eyes and pictured her mother's face.

The years had been kind to Sabrina. She still looked as beautiful as Brooklyn remembered. She recalled the temporary comfort she found in her mother's arms that morning as she cried, how her mother had rocked her and assured her that it was okay. Brooklyn hadn't realized how much she had been longing for her mother's love.

Her thoughts drifted to Hope and how well her life had turned out. Brooklyn was happy for her, happy that she had gotten the chance to meet her brother-in-law. And it had been good to see Erica and Jordan again, too. But as the water in the tub grew tepid, Brooklyn knew this wouldn't be a long visit. She wasn't back in Staten Island to stay. All she wanted to do was get her portion of the inheritance and start her life over again somewhere new.

She stepped out of the tub and dried off. She went to the bed and began to put on her pajamas. Then she heard her cellphone beep.

Brooklyn walked to the dresser and picked it up. It was a text message from a local number.

Brooklyn, this is Hope. I know it's late but I didn't want to say this in front of everybody else. You deserve that money. Daddy wanted you to have it and that's how it should be.

Brooklyn read the message and smiled. Another text followed.

Mom will never give it to you without a fight. I want to help you. But I'm tired of fighting. I need peace in my life.

Brooklyn's smile faded. "Fuck!" she muttered. Then another text message appeared.

Let me give you a check for your share of the inheritance. Mom will make sure that I get it back.

Brooklyn began texting back immediately.

Are you sure?

She waited again. Her heart pounded at the thought of getting out of this godforsaken town as soon as possible. Another text from Hope arrived.

I'm sure.

Brooklyn typed back feverishly.

Thank you so much, Hope!

Brooklyn set the phone down and held her hands in the air in praise.

Big snowstorm coming tomorrow. Can you come get the check tonight?

Brooklyn couldn't believe her luck. With that money in hand, she could be on the road by morning. She replied.

Yes. No problem.

She started getting dressed. Moments later, the phone dinged again.

I'm about to take Scrappy for a walk. Eddie's asleep. Want to meet at Clove Lake Park?

Brooklyn had her car keys in hand already.

Yes. I'll call you when I'm close by.

Brooklyn grabbed her purse and rushed out the door.

Walking through the lobby, she felt like herself again. When she had arrived back in Staten Island, she felt hopeless and desperate. Now, thanks to her sister, she would be able to start all over again. On the right foot this time. Once she had her shit together, she would slowly begin the process of rebuilding her relationship with her mother and sister. Someday, she would make her father proud. The first step was for her to get back on track.

She drove to Clove Lake Park feeling optimistic. The forecasters were hyping the impending storm so much that Brooklyn understood Hope's suggestion to meet tonight. Tomorrow they might be snowed in. The storm was supposed to arrive midmorning on Monday. By then, Brooklyn planned to be holed up in her hotel room ordering room service while she plotted her next move.

She got to the park and dialed Hope's number. After a few rings, she got an automated voice message.

She parked her car on Victory Boulevard near the basketball courts. This side of the park was well lit, and the adjacent streets were busy with pedestrian and vehicle traffic. Brooklyn dialed Hope again and got the same message. She looked around, anxiously. After a moment, she put the car in drive and thought she should head to Hope's house.

Just then the phone pinged again.

Sorry. Bad reception in the park. I'm on the corner of Slosson Avenue and Martling. Are you close?

Brooklyn typed her response.

Yes. Right around the corner. Coming now.

Brooklyn drove the few short blocks to the other side of the park. She looked at the armory with large military tanks parked on the lawn. She had always found that sight an odd one in the borough. It was a military museum and a symbol of the borough's patriotism. Brooklyn looked around as she parked her car, talking to herself.

"Hope you're one brave bitch walking your dog over here by yourself."

Brooklyn looked around and saw no other cars. It was close to 11:00 and freezing. She glanced around eagerly for her sister. Another text came.

You here? Scrappy's taking a dump. Walk up the pathway near the corner. I'm right here.

Brooklyn looked around. She pulled her scarf around her face to block out the cold and got out of the car.

The pathway Hope was referring to was right near Brooklyn's parking spot. She began walking, peering ahead for her sister.

"It's freezing!" Brooklyn talked to herself as she walked into the park. She spoke aloud, certain that no one was around to hear her. It was the middle of the night on the coldest night of the year. She shoved her hands into the pocket of her North Face coat and tucked her chin into its collar.

"Hope, where you at?" she called out. She continued up the pathway for several feet. "Hope!"

Brooklyn stopped walking, listening for the sound of Scrappy barking or Hope calling back to her. She heard nothing. Suddenly, she felt an uneasy feeling in the pit of her stomach and realized this was a bad idea. She looked around, anxiously, for any sign of her sister.

"HOPE!" she called out again.

Silence. Brooklyn turned, scared now, and decided to run back to her car. She took a step then felt a heavy thud against the back of her head.

The force of the blow sent her barreling forward. With her hands out in front of her, she tried to brace her fall. But another blow followed, harder than the one before. She lay on the ground face down and dazed. She opened her mouth to scream, but her attacker was on her. With her vision blurry and a ringing in her ears, she felt her body being flipped over.

Dazed, Brooklyn was face to face with her killer.

Jordan! She thought. *Oh shit!*

The look in his eyes was crazed. He wrapped his hands around her throat and began to squeeze. Brooklyn gasped for air. The pressure on her throat increased.

She felt herself slipping in and out of consciousness. The pressure on her neck made it hard to breathe or even move.

Brooklyn began to fight back. She clawed at Jordan's hands to no avail. Desperately, she tried to pry them away. She could feel her nails digging into the gloves he wore, felt several of her nails breaking in the process. She kicked, bucked, flailed, and tried to scream. But Jordan was unrelenting.

He straddled her, groaning ferally as he dug his hands deeper into the flesh around her throat.

Brooklyn began to feel an unwelcome sense of weightlessness. She stared into Jordan's vacant eyes and felt herself dying.

It was so quiet as he killed her that she found it ironic. Her life had been full of noise, full of drama and tumult. But the end came silently, without an audience, so unexpectedly.

Brooklyn's body went limp.

For minutes afterward, Jordan continued to press his fingers into the hollows of her throat. He squeezed the life out of her remorselessly. In his mind, he imagined Amir's face the last time he saw him. Amir had been so afraid, betrayed by the sister he loved and trusted. Jordan imagined Hope's face that afternoon as she realized that her long lost sister had come back for her share of the money and not for the relationships she had ruined years ago. Jordan imagined Erica's face as she expressed regret over mentioning the money to Brooklyn in the first place. He imagined Pastor James twisted up from his stroke and still hopeful that his prodigal daughter would return. Brooklyn had left a trail of broken hearts in her wake. Jordan squeezed harder, believing that he was ridding the world of a plague.

Jordan straddled Brooklyn's remains for a while after she was dead. Her eyes bulged, her mouth gaped open, and it was clear that all life was gone. Still, Jordan stared down at her, transfixed.

Finally, he stood up, looming over her lifeless body as the brutal winter wind blew around them.

Slowly, methodically, he peeled the winter coat and boots from her body. He roughly tugged off each article of her clothing and set it aside in a bundle. He gripped her lifeless arms, dragged her body through the overgrowth, and dumped it callously along the edge of a bank. He looked around and started cleaning up the scene. He grabbed the pile of clothes, glancing around to ensure that no one else was in the park. Satisfied that he had removed all evidence of the crime, he began to walk away. But Jordan paused when his eyes settled on one remaining piece. One of her socks was caught in the bare and frozen branch of some brush at the bank's edge. He snatched it, roughly stuck it in his coat pocket, and glanced around once again. He took one last look at the body lying cold and alone in the wooded overgrowth and walked off in the same direction from which he came.

My spirit floats above my body now, disposed of like garbage in such a cold and barren place. As Jordan's silhouette fades into the frigid night, it finally sinks in that this is it. I played a deadly game. And I lost.

Chapter Sixteen

Stormy Weather

Tuesday, February 11, 2003

The forecasts proved to be accurate. New York City slowed to a crawl as the sanitation department dispatched salt spreaders and plows across the five boroughs. Staten Island was hit with close to a foot of snow, and most schools in the borough were closed during the city's cleanup.

Detectives Lee and Ramos were relieved that constant news coverage of the storm this week had provided the public with some momentary distractions and that the frenzy of inquiries about the Clove Lake Park case had lessened.

They arrived at the precinct on Tuesday morning and were pleased to find several reports from the Clove Lake Park case. With breakfast and coffee spread out in front of them, they sat together in their office, poring over the details of the reports, each of them frantically reading, eating, and silently flipping through the pages.

Finally, Lee tossed his trash away, set his coffee aside, and sat back with the reports laid out on the desk in front of him.

"No DNA underneath her fingernails, only fibers from a pair of brown gloves. No drugs in her system. Toxicology reports are all negative."

Ramos nodded as he continued reading. "She had petechial hemorrhaging."

He had seen that in a prior case. It had been a domestic violence call and police arrived to find that a woman had been strangled with a belt from behind by her abusive husband. That case had been early in Ramos's career, so he remembered it well. He would never forget the tiny, popped blood vessels in the eyes and across the face of a victim who had been asphyxiated.

"Medical examiner says that manual pressure—the killer's fingers pressed against the throat—was the method used to kill her. No semen, no blood, hair, or saliva from the perp. Only the victim's. She had bruises on her cheek, blows to the head, scratches on her stomach."

Lee nodded. "Like Tony said. It's consistent with her being dragged down the trail to her resting place."

"He was right about the murder happening on the main trail, too. Check out the CSU report. They found the victim's urine in that area where the blood and footprint were found. She died there, released her bodily fluid, and then got dragged to the wooded area."

"Sounds like the killer is a man," Lee said. "I can't imagine too many women who would have enough strength or time to do all of this."

Lee huffed. "My wife has a black belt in jiujitsu and she would disagree with you. I don't want to rule anybody out yet," he said. "It's too early to make assumptions."

He stared at the wall, deep in thought. "Is it a stranger, random predator? Or someone she knew and trusted?" He picked up a photo of the deceased from the file on his desk and looked at it long and hard. "What happened to you?"

Staten Island Advance

February 12, 2003

An unidentified woman whose body was found in an isolated area of Clove Lake Park was the victim of strangulation, according to the results of an autopsy that were released Tuesday.

The medical examiner determined the manner of death to be homicide. No signs of sexual assault were found during the autopsy. Police said the victim was discovered in Clove Lake Park just after 7 A.M. Monday. Shortly after, police found a second crime scene nearby with blood matching the victim's.

Neighbors told Eyewitness News that police have increased their presence in the neighborhood in the wake of the crime. According to police sources, it is believed the woman was slain by her assailant on the southeast side of the park and was dragged to the location where the body was dumped prior to daybreak. Defensive wounds on the body suggest the victim put up a fight before she was ultimately killed.

So far, police have not been able to identify the victim, but they describe her as a five foot seven Black woman with a tattoo of a cross on her left wrist. No suspects have been named.

Police are asking anyone with information to contact them.

Ramos plopped the newspaper down on his desk.

Allison, a precinct clerk, knocked on the office door.

"There's a woman here who wants to talk to you about the Clove Lake case."

The detectives exchanged glances and leapt to their feet. They followed Allison to the lobby area of the precinct. A flurry of activity was going on as they neared the front desk.

"That's her," Allison said, discreetly. "In the brown coat."

A slim caramel-skinned woman wearing a tan knitted hat and a brown wool coat stood with her hands clasped together in front of her, gripping a pair of gloves. A crossbody bag draped across her and she had a serene expression on her face. She watched them all closely as they approached.

Allison made the introductions, speaking gently and discreetly.

"Detectives Ramos and Lee are assigned to the case. This is Hope James-Kirkwood. She heard the news about the discovery in the park, and she thinks it might have something to do with her sister."

"Nice to meet you," Hope said, shaking hands with the detectives.

"Thank you for coming in," Detective Lee said. "Let's go back here and talk."

He led the way to his office a short distance down the hall. Once inside, he gestured toward a seat and smiled at her.

"What made you come in today?"

Hope sat in the chair and tried to calm her nerves. Her voice shook a bit as she spoke.

"I read the story in the paper about the body you found in the park on Monday morning. I haven't heard from my sister in a few days. She left town years ago and we didn't keep in touch. But our father died this year. My sister surprised us all and came back to town a few days ago. It wasn't a pleasant surprise."

Hope looked at the detectives trying to gauge their reaction to what she had said so far. Detective Ramos stared back at her blankly. Lee nodded, urging her to go on.

She cleared her throat. "Not everybody was thrilled to see her."

"Why not?" Detective Ramos asked.

"Old stuff," she answered quickly. "Hurt feelings, that type of thing."

"We need you to be more specific," Detective Ramos said. "Was she on drugs?"

Detective Lee shot a piercing look in his partner's direction.

"No. We grew up in the church. Our father was a pastor. Brooklyn was rebellious. She left the family behind years ago and didn't look back. Until now. My father left us an inheritance. She came back looking for her share. My mother was upset and there was a confrontation. Brooklyn left and said that she was going to meet my mother and me the next day. But that was on Monday morning, and she never showed up. I haven't heard from her since. I tried calling the cellphone number she gave me, but it goes straight to voicemail."

Detective Lee nodded. "Okay. It's possible that she was upset by the argument and left town. Where has she been living for the past few years?"

"Maryland, I believe. The number she gave me has a 410 area code." Hope watched as Detective Ramos walked to the desk and rifled through a file. "The article in the paper said something about a tattoo," she said. "My sister had one like it. It had my brother's initials in the center."

The detectives locked eyes. They hadn't released that detail to the public, but it was true.

"What were the initials?" Lee asked.

"AJ," Hope said.

Her heart sank as she noted the change in the detectives' demeanor. Ramos's eyes widened. Lee looked at his partner intently.

She could sense the shift in energy, and she knew in her gut that her worst fears were about to be confirmed.

Ramos retrieved a picture from the file and looked at Hope. The woman was so petite and seemed so fragile. He prayed that she didn't fall apart.

"We have a photo of the deceased," he said. "I'll warn you that it's a graphic autopsy photo. Is there someone you want to call to be here with you?"

She pressed her lips together tightly and shook her head.

"You sure?" he asked.

"Yes. Please let me see it."

He set it down face up on the desk in front of her. He watched as Hope leaned in and stared at it for long silent moments. When she looked up at him again, her eyes were full of tears. She wiped them away quietly with the tissue Detective Lee offered her and nodded.

"That's her."

They gave her a few moments to gather herself as she cried silently.

"I'm so sorry for your loss." Detective Lee set the photo aside and touched her gently on the arm. "I can imagine how hard this must be for you."

"She was strangled?" Hope was nearly breathless as she asked the question.

"Yes. The autopsy came back with that result."

She let out a sob, then closed her eyes and hung her head in disbelief.

Ramos pulled up a chair and sat close to her.

"I don't mean to add to your pain. But I gotta be honest with you. We haven't had any similar crimes in the area recently. Your sister wasn't sexually assaulted. She had some jewelry on, so we don't know if robbery is a likely motive. This doesn't seem random. Strangulation is personal. It's not a quick and easy thing. This appears to be a targeted killing by someone she knew. Somebody who was angry with her. Do you have any idea who could possibly be that mad at your sister?"

Hope's eyes darted in Detective Ramos's direction.

"Mad enough to kill her?" She huffed a little at the irony of such a question. "I wouldn't even know where to begin."

Ashley Williams

Tracy Brown is the *Essence* bestselling author of *Boss*; *White Lines III: All Falls Down*; *White Lines II: Sunny*; *Aftermath*; *Snapped*; *Twisted*; *White Lines*; *Criminal Minded*; *Black*; and *Dime Piece.* She passed away two days after turning in this final, arguably her best, book.